Bendy Elephant

Steph Daniels

authorHOUSE®

AuthorHouse™ UK Ltd.
500 Avebury Boulevard
Central Milton Keynes, MK9 2BE
www.authorhouse.co.uk
Phone: 08001974150

This book is a work of fiction. People, places, events, and situations are the product of the author's imagination. Any resemblance to actual persons, living or dead, or historical events, is purely coincidental.

First published by AuthorHouse 1/4/2010

ISBN: 978-1-4389-8541-1 (sc)

Library of Congress Control Number: 2009904602

This book is printed on acid-free paper.

This book is dedicated to the memory of my father Clement Daniels. Also to my mother Dorothy Rose, for her unconditional love, to my sister Brenda - the ties that bind - and to all my teachers, known and unknown.

10% of this book's sales will be donated to Help for Heroes.

BELLING
SHENROTH
Adair
Jamari
St Giles
Hamilton
QUEENVILLE
Tomsdale
Chessletown
JUXON
Carlton
Parrish
Gilbey
USHQUEL
Kavari Quay
SEa
KARTERLI

MAP OF JUXON

Prologue

"The Wiggins have arrived. We're here, at last." Ma looks at Papa as they hug in our new lounge.

"*Mmmm,* I'll say YES to that. Prestige Street. In Scholar's Close. Parrish's best neighbourhood. How's that for a post code! Couldn't be any better now, could it?" I watch as Papa says this, his grin widening as he caresses Ma's ever increasing belly.

My younger sisters Sapphira and Ellie dart in and out of the room, exploring our new home. I hover around my parents even though I seem to be invisible to them.

"Benedict will be born here, synergising my promotion and the launch of your second boutique. Another son! So many blessings." Papa says, caressing and kissing Ma.

"Mmmm" Ma says between kisses. "Three beautiful children and another on the way. My beloved, distinguished husband, the first Juxonese to be appointed Headmaster at Montgomery High School, the only English-medium high school in Parrish. About time the British recognised your worth!"

"Ha! What about you? First '*Allure*', now '*Poise*'. Two boutiques. *Both* on the *main* street in the city! Both runaway successes! Angelina, my angel, our children will *never* want for anything! Whatever we never had, they will have in abundance! I promise you that."

Why does Grandma Meertel's constant proverb suddenly enter my ten and a half year old brain – 'too much of a good thing is *bad*.' Hmmm.

Leaving Parrish

Chapter One

The clanging of the phone goads my fourteen year old body from the depths of sleep. The ringing and ringing in the lounge and its echo in the kitchen goes on and on. I squeeze one eye open. Left eye up against the pillow. Wrong eye. Open right eye. Squint at my digital bedside clock. 06:23! On a Saturday morning! My heart starts to pound and a ball of flames starts burning in my guts. Who's dead or injured? Where's Ma and Papa? Is it Ellie making sure we're fetching her soon?

"What? Never! Oh my God! Oh *my God*! Frederick! *Frederick*! The President's been murdered! President Jameson Welter. Assassinated. Oh! My! God!"

My mother's shouting from the lounge makes my heart thump right up to my throat. Keeps on thumping there. I sprint to the lounge, grabbing a T-shirt as I go and beating my father by a whisker. Ma has switched on the television. BBC News 24.

"....... President Jameson Welter's death at ten o'clock last night. Whilst most Juxonese are still in shock, there are reports of early signs of unrest in Queenville, the capital of Juxon, a previous colony of Great Britain, situated close to Indonesia. The growing tension between the Conservative Cartons and the Liberal Frees has been escalating since the election three months ago. The Cartons are accusing the Frees of assassinating the Conservative President. President Jameson Welter has been in office for less than three months. He leaves behind his wife Ermilinia and five young children.

The Frees have consistently accused the Cartons of rigging the election that brought President Welter to power. Since their independence from Great Britain more than sixty years ago, the Cartons have been in office only three times, but totalling less than eleven months.

The Cartons remain mistrustful of the Frees' continuing connections with the British. This is aggravated by the chronic tension between the two sides regarding land ownership. Put simply, the Cartons are demanding that the land 'stolen' from them last century during British rule be returned to them as the rightful owners. The Frees deny the Cartons' right of ownership and argue that they have papers to prove legal ownership.

Speaking to people on the street this morning, the angry Cartons vow to take every inch of land back ***and*** *avenge their president's death. They say they have military support from neighbouring Shenroth in the north where many Cartons supporters have lived in exile for decades....."*

Behind the reporter the camera shows a horde of shouting people; men, women and children, smashing car windows and shop windows, and looting from the sports shop. Others are laughingly running from the few on-duty police with their stolen electrical fans, microwave ovens, raincoats, anything and everything. My mouth dries; I can feel my rough pre-breakfast tongue sticking to my palate. I struggle to swallow. Phew! My heart is thumping and booming under my T-shirt like when Mark next door plays his heavy metal music ultra-loud. I've seen scenes like these before, but this is *Queenville,* my capital, not some far away place! I *know* that street! We had lunch at The Gravy Boat! This is near! This is here! Bad, very bad indeed!

"Papa, what's going on?" I ask my great supporter. He merely puts his fingers to his lips whilst nodding to whoever on his mobile phone, his grey eyes glued to the screen, the furrows in his forehead deepening into giant ridges. Normally cool and collected, leaving passionate outbursts to my flamboyant mother, I watch sweat dribbling from his forehead down to his black and grey stubbled cheeks. His usually neat hair is all awry from his fingers constantly raking through it. He cannot sit still; tut-tutting, shaking his left leg, juggling the telephone and the remote control, changing channels so often and so quickly they become a blur. I stare at the vein in his neck, pulsing like mad. I've *never* seen him like this before, *ever*. His panic is making *me* panic. I don't like it one bit.

My heart starts to thump even harder and faster, right against my chest wall. I feel sweaty, panicky, weak. I plop down on the sofa next to Sapphira, my twelve year old sister – when did she appear? I feel a deep sense of doom as my father settles on the BBC News 24 again.

"...the unrest is spreading. It is moving southwards and our reporters in both Tomsdale and Chessletown speak of mounting tension, people gathering in the streets of the town centres and throwing stones at the few on-duty police and passing motorists. The main roads from Queenville to Chessletown to the Ushquel border are rapidly becoming congested, due to rising panic. Traffic is moving at snail's pace as frantic families are starting to flee from the unrest.

While the shadow cabinet, the Frees, are urging calm and an urgent invitation for dialogue with the Cartons, the Minister for Safety and Security, Mr Deekan Deekain, broadcast a statement on Radio QV, the local radio station, urging Cartons supporters to even the score from being the underdog for decades. He said "Everything and anything you do is legitimate if it avenges the untimely death of our beloved President Jameson Welter and rectifies the humiliation generations of Cartons have suffered at the hands of the Frees!"

Riot police are struggling to maintain order and stop people from looting and killing. I believe the army is being called to assist. The hospitals and clinics in Queenville have started to fill up with injured people...."

I notice our sleepy three year old brother Benedict curled up on the sofa, little red Mercedes Benz sports car clutched in his hand. He *has to* know everything, asking questions even when half asleep. Jolene, our housekeeper, is standing at the door, twisting her pinafore as she does when she is upset.

My heart stops.

"*Ellie!* What about Ellie?" My little sister.

"Right! Everybody. It is now two minutes past six thirty. We leave for the airport to Singapore at seven o'clock sharp. Hand luggage only! The bare essentials. We have everything at our home there, so please go and pack now! We'll leave from Carton airport and pick up Ellie and Grandma Meertel on the way." Papa's deep bass rings out between receiving phone calls, phoning and changing television channels.

"I *knew* she shouldn't have slept over at Grandma Meertel's last night! She *should* have been *here,* celebrating your wedding anniversary *as a family*! I just knew it! You should have listened to me___"

Ma interrupts my seething retaliation. "Stop 'shoulding' Luther! Grandma Meertel is family as well! The decision was made yesterday and we cannot undo it now. Ellie is there and we are here. We will pick both of them up on our way to the airport. You know it's only twenty minutes to Carton."

Above this noise, my father is asking Jolene, where we can take her and her husband, our gardener, Jacob.

"We stay right here, Dr Frederick! We look after the house until you return."

"Jolene, it may not be safe! President Welter has been killed. You've just seen the pictures on television. Big trouble. I want to lock up the house. Completely."

"Dr Frederick, we stay in our place. This is home. Now, let me get some breakfast ready before you go and ___"

"Frederick. *Frederick*! Carlita is at Carton airport. Says there is mayhem there. Absolute panic. Planes are being delayed. Or being diverted. The planes that are there are fully booked. The foreigners have first priority, so, *marties* out first. Parrish airport is less busy. Less *marties* here."

"Angelina, we cannot go to Parrish airport. We *have* to collect Ellie!"

My sister Sapphira, the 'all-wise one' pipes up. "Why can't Papa and Luther go to Carton to pick up Ellie while Ma, Benedict and I go to Parrish airport and get the tickets and everything? Surely ___"

"NO! NO! *No*! We can't split up the family even more! *We stay together!* We all go to Carton to fetch Ellie. More planes will come, won't they, Papa?" I ask tentatively.

"Yes, son, we hope ___"

"Frederick! I've just spoken to Chandler, Chiya and Kiaran. They are returning to Parrish. They cannot even get into Carton airport. Those who had rushed to the airport at ten o'clock last night when the news broke, are only leaving now ___"

"Why didn't *you* know? Why didn't anyone phone us last night? Why ___"

My father's deep bass interrupts me. "OK! First things first. Pack. Breakfast. Pick up Ellie. Return here to Parrish airport ___"

"Frederick! That was Keith. Parrish airport is closed as well."

∞

Right now, I really don't care which airport is open and which is not. I'm much more concerned about having *all* our family together again. *Ellie*! We *have* to get Ellie. I watch my father and mother as they look at each other. Silently; a painful kind of silence. Papa looks at me and takes a deep breath. Then Ma's on the phone again.

"OK! It is now twenty minutes to seven. We leave for Ushquel, to Aunty Kathy's in Stonehouse, at seven thirty sharp. It will take less than fifteen minutes to wash, dress and pack your bags. Bring your bags to the kitchen so that Jacob can stow them into the Land Rover. Breakfast is at a quarter to seven sharp! Any questions, your mother and I will answer in the car on our way to Aunty Kathy's. Angelina, have you managed to speak with your sister or anybody at Stonehouse yet?"

"No. I've left a message on their answer machine and I've texted her and Brian. I don't know where they are so early on a Saturday morning. I'll ring every half hour. I'd hate to just pitch up there, even though we are family."

"Why do we have to go? Can't we just say we're sowee?" Benedict asks Papa.

"It is far, *far* deeper than that, Benedict." Papa gives him a slight smile as he tickles his chin.

Papa continues. "Right, all of you, use your overnight bags and pack. What do you suggest, Angel? Two changes of clothing plus a set of Sunday clothes and an extra pair of shoes? Yes? Right. That's your quota. And remember to pack toiletries, hairbrush, pyjamas, a hand towel, books and your games. The zip *has* to close. Sapphira, do you understand?"

"Jolene, we're now heading for Ushquel and Mrs Angelina's sister in Stonehouse. We can drop you and Jacob off on the way to the border. Please pack Benedict's bag before you pack your own. Add a few extras for him. Fill his bag to cover the odd accident. Thank you for organising the quick breakfast. I'll go and tell Jacob what else needs to be packed in the car."

Papa and Ma organise and interrupt each other and everyone else in between phone calls, moving from room to room, giving orders to Jolene, answering Benedict's 'Why? Why, Why?', making a list.

"And Sapphira, please pack a bag for Ellie as well. You know what she likes."

Jolene is bumping about, spilling Papa's coffee into his saucer, letting the milk boil over, saying "Oh my God! Oh my God!" over and over again.

Ma looks at her, says "Jolene! Enough now!" then rushes out to her and Papa's bedroom. Papa takes Jolene by her shoulders and says quietly and firmly: "Jolene, calm down now. Take a few deep breaths and concentrate on what needs to be done. First pack Benedict's bag, then yours. You know the things that need to be packed. Help Jacob. He is already preparing the Land Rover for a long journey. He knows what to do. We will be leaving in less than an hour's time. Seven thirty sharp!"

Jolene, still twirling her pinafore and looking confused and bewildered by all the orders coming from everyone including myself, starts shaking her head vigorously, tears running down her cheeks, wiping her nose with her apron.

"Dr Frederick! I am going *nowhere*! *This* is where I'm going to stay. This is my home! And Jacob's! We stay here! Who will clean and keep the house tidy until you return? No Sir! We will protect the house. *And that's that!*"

I look at Papa. Nobody argues with Jolene when she says '*and that's that!*' so emphatically. He and I look at each other while Sapphira continues to hover around.

"Papa, if Jolene and Jacob can stay, why can't I?"

"Sapphira, a very short answer to your question. History has shown that, in order to bring about total submission through fear in the masses, the perpetrators will get rid of the educated class. That's why we had the killing fields in Vietnam before you were born. They don't want people to think; they want absolute unquestioning submission to their demands. The Frees' colonial education system has always been a key issue. Added to this now is the Cartons revenging our Carton President's death. Double trouble. Can you see? As the first Juxonese Head Master of Montgomery High School, with a British based education, can you see the dangers I, as well as you as my family face if we remain here? They see me as having a massive influence over all the students that have passed through my school. In Vietnam everyone wearing spectacles was considered educated and an intellectual and destined for the worst jobs or death. Now *pack*!"

∞

I rush to my room. Stand still. Look around. I have to leave all of this? A sob escapes. Papa is a main target for killing, just so that others can't listen to his good advice?! Wow! 07:30! I think we should leave by 07:00! How could they want to kill *him*? What will *I* do? Would I have to be man of the house? Please, please, *please*, let us all come back here soon. Why can't the UN come and talk with both sides and stop the killing? Why do they have to target all Papa's friends? Please, please, *please*, let *us all come back here soon*.

I glance at the pictures on my walls as I stuff clothes into the bag. My heroes. Pop idol Twining living in California. Sidney Gilbert, international soccer star, goalkeeper for Arsenal in London. Tommy Thomas, 2008 Olympian, silver medallist marathon man. That must be sooo amazing! To stand on the podium waving your medal in your hand, for all the world to see. *Everybody* witnessing your great achievement! All that hard work and effort being acknowledged. Of course I have what it takes to practise, practise, practise, until I too become a top professional.

What would I do with all that money I earn? Ma would certainly love it! She would probably open a few more boutiques. Invest it wisely. Why would I want to live *soooo* far away from home? Who cooks and cleans for them? Who do they talk to? Papa and Ma and all the others will be here and I will be over there – hmmm, I'd rather stay here, thanks.

I suppose I *could* use some of their determination, some of their focus. That is what Papa would like of me, instead of my constant socialising. Hey! I'm a handsome young man; the girls like me. I am *practising* my social skills. I know Papa and Ma would like me to work harder and achieve something, to have a dream like Sapphira. I just dream and dream and dream. And I get *sooo* irritated when people tell me what to do—I *like* dreaming. Maybe one day one of my endless dreams will become a massive success, then everybody will be ashamed of having pestered and nagged me so much!

Morning Harry Potter! Craving a family. Despite everything he has, he hasn't got a family. I pull Harry Potter off the wall. Fair exchange: he wants a family and I, we, need his magic.

As I button up my black Levi jeans, I see my computer. Oh *No*! My Wii! My fourteenth birthday present. Three months old. Oh *No*! Which games do I take with? What's the point! Nobody has a Wii in Ushquel! And the Wii can't fit into my bag. Damn! And I will *have to* share a computer with Sapphira *and* my ten-year-old twin cousins. *Three* other people. That means less than three hours a day!

I take out my Sunday clothes and see my new pair of trousers, specially tailored for my *Onashi* celebration. Ooooh! My *Onashi*! I'm supposed to become a man in two weeks' time. What *now*? Stuff that into my holdall with a new white shirt.

What is going to happen to my *Onashi* celebration? Will we be back in two weeks' time? I race to my parent's bedroom. I stop dead when I hear them talking about me.

Papa is saying, "Luther was thoroughly annoyed about Ellie's absence at our anniversary celebration last night. Now he has got himself into such a panic about us having to divert to pick her up."

"Frederick, you know he is a real 'family around me' lad. This is going to be a huge learning curve for him, more so than anybody else. Bad timing for him – adolescence *and* an uprising – two crises. Will he sink or will he swim? Whatever happens, it will make a man out of him."

Wow! What is this 'sink or swim' thing? In my haste to ask, I forget to knock yet again and open the door. This time, no rebuke. Papa is standing on his side of the bed, looking at Ma and a huge heap of clothing on her side. Ma's boutiques sell designer clothes, so she has the pick of the bunch, 'a size 16 walking advert of a true woman' - she calls this unrestricted broadcasting. 'If you can't flaunt it, you can't sell it!' Ma's bright floral silk gown covers her 'sculpted body' as she calls it; hours of gym work with a personal trainer to maintain her look of elegance. Ma is tall and 'voluptuous' according to my school friend's father. I remember the playground conversation: "How do you spell that?" asked a school friend.

"*Spell* it? You *eye* it. And you want to *feel* it. *Not spell it*!!"

She has a kind of loose-limbed walk and I too have begun to notice men eyeing her as she 'flaunts around' as Papa smilingly remarks. Why is he not jealous like my friends say their fathers are? Is he so certain of their love? I'd like to be like that as well. This 'size 16 walking advert' normally takes at least an hour to decide on her 'mixes and matches' for the day. She has been 'advertising' big floral prints lately and her heap of clothes looks like a wild exotic garden. Tears are brimming in her honey eyes.

"Angelina, Angel, we *agreed*! Two changes of clothing and a Sunday set plus an extra pair of shoes. There is no space for all of these! There are foam mattresses, blankets and boxes of food. And, and, *and*! And there are seven of us now! There is no space for all these clothes! The car can only take so much! Come on now! Be sensible. We are not going away forever – surely you can bear it for a few weeks? And we can buy clothes in Ushquel; you normally do so anyway! Let us be an example to the kids. Time is rushing on – it's nearly a quarter to seven – breakfast is in less than three minutes!"

Papa looks at her, pauses, and then asks whether she had brought the tills' cash home last night and does she still have to pay her workers. Between sniffs and choosing then discarding a number of dresses, she answers angrily that her head manager Koney will be here any minute to collect six weeks' wages for all the staff. She takes a few deep breaths whilst looking at Papa just looking at her, then starts talking in a quieter voice.

"It's in that brown envelope over there. How fortunate that we are between nannies for Benedict. Fortunate too that we had a 'special Friday' yesterday, so lots of cash. Enough to give Jolene and Jacob two months' pay so that they can look after the house properly. I hope they pay *your* salary into the bank; something to come home to. And Frederick, have you taken the US Dollars from the safe? We may need that in Stonehouse.

OK! I'm packing as we had decided. After all, as you keep saying, we're *only* going to Ushquel where we have been *countless* times. I shall reward myself with a slinky little outfit before we return; now *that's a promise*!"

∞

I go to my room to fetch my bag. My digital wristwatch, a recent birthday present, shows 06:45. Breakfast time. I am packed. My iPod, battery charger, phone charger - what else do I need? I pick up a small mirror. This one's far too small. I need one that magnifies by ten. Oh well! I'll buy one in Stonehouse. I look deeply into my warm honey eyes. Tiger eyes, Papa calls them. Funny how all the oldest three children inherited Ma's honey coloured eyes. My little tigers, Papa used to call us, until Benedict was born. Deep grey eyes like Papa's. My soul child, that's what Papa calls Benedict.

Let me see what has the best effect here: narrowing my eyes, or half closing, fully opening; I think *all* dazzle the girls, especially when I end with a slow, huge wink. A tiny smile? Practise, practise, practise, and *more* practise.

Hmmm, moustache looks and *feels* more prominent, at least two extra hairs since yesterday morning. Fuzz on cheeks getting thicker; well, when the light shines on it? Nothing much really. Will I need to shave soon? Will Ma buy me a rechargeable shaver? What kind of aftershave shall I use? I wonder if Ma has a few samples tucked away somewhere. Must ask her later. No acne. Well, two small spots. I remember our conversation about this only last week.

"Ma, why don't I have acne? I don't want a mess like Kelo – please God *no*! I just want one or two small spots anywhere but on my nose to show the girls I am growing all over. Abel says it is our way of *externalising* our growing manhood."

I can't tell Ma that Kelo must be huge in his pants.... Then again, Abel is no way bigger than me down there and yet he has more spots.

"Is it because I have low testosterone levels, like Sapphira says? What does *she* know! She reads about law all the time, not about boys or their changing physiology."

Ma giggled before saying: "My mother used to tell my brothers it was because they were growing so much, their testosterone never had time to settle under their skin. But Luther, you really don't need acne as yet another sign of your transformation? We can all see your face and body changing. What about having a *knowing* within? So much better, don't you think? I suppose with women it's easier – when we wear sexy underwear, we don't need to broadcast the fact by having it showing now, do we? To me that would be rather vulgar, badly dressed. No, it's that *inner* knowing that makes us walk around with an enigmatic smile and a sensual strut. Can you see the difference? It's about a *knowing* within you. So, what will you use?"

I look at myself. Gosh, I'm only fourteen, and I'm nearly as tall as Papa! Nearly six foot tall at fourteen, and Ma says I'm soon to have another growth spurt. Six foot at fourteen! *Awesome*! Awesomely awesome! Soon I can look Papa in the eye. Who needs pimples when you are so tall? Bang goes that useless theory; I already stand out in a crowd, surely I do?

But I'm sooo clumsy! Was Papa or any other man as clumsy as me? My feet are way too big for my body; Ma says she is buying only open-toed sandals for me this summer. And look at my hands; they are like spades! And my brain! Why is my brain taking its time catching up? I really, truly, don't like being so clumsy! Or so irritable! Ma says I can win Olympic Gold for irritability.

I don't want to be like this, but they *don't realise* that *I do know* things and they *won't listen* to me! If only they would *listen* to me! *And* Sapphira keeps poking fun at me all the time. She's my younger sister, for goodness sake! Twelve years old, not forty-twelve! She is just like Ma: quick as a flash with an answer. Papa is becoming really fed up with our arguing. But she should *listen* to *me*! I am the first born, *I am the eldest. I am going to be a man*! Why can't she be like the other girls? Especially Kelsy-Anne. Now *that* is the one I *really, really, really* fancy.

Except she is in Sapphira's class; and I can't bear to be the butt of her sarcasm. Then again, on the other hand, the girls in my class are sooo pushy, pushing their breasts up to me when they come to ask a stupid question. *I* want to be in charge, doing the hunting. Although, I guess, a little bait helps! It certainly helps being the Head Master's eldest son! And that I have the most gorgeous eyes in the whole school, not to mention the coolest haircut, thanks to Ma's hairdresser friend. God! Life was just getting a whole heap better and *now this*!

"Luther! *Luther!* Breakfast!" I rush towards the kitchen-diner. At fourteen years I can eat anything at any time. Everybody's already there. Jolene, still snivelling, is packing sandwiches, bottles of juice and packets of biscuits, serviettes and apples and oranges into our picnic basket. I eat some of the prepared snacks that were going to be party food tonight. No anniversary celebration for my parents' friends tonight! All this food going to waste! Jolene and Jacob will be feasting for days to come. I might as well stock up on all these luxuries. Nobody has even mentioned the party.

∞

"Sapphira, why is your bag not packed? Jacob has everybody's bag, except yours. Please pack your bag as soon as you've finished your breakfast." Papa finishes his scrambled egg on toast and coffee, leaves the room, only to return seconds later, glaring at Sapphira.

"You haven't even started packing yet. Why?"

"I had to pack Ellie's bag as well! How long are we going for?" She asks.

"Sapphira, I don't know. At this moment, nobody knows much about anything. We will go for as long as we need to stay away, for as long as this unrest takes to settle. You have two minutes to pack, so start!"

"A few days, a week, a few months, how long?" Sapphira is a very persistent future lawyer.

"Sapphira! I've just told you I *don't know*! It has nothing to do with your packing. We are leaving in less than thirty minutes!"

"Well, how long did the last two uprisings last?"

"The last one lasted for about ten days, the one previous to that, before you were born, lasted about six months. Neither had presidents killed."

"So, that is an average of ninety five days! I can't *possibly* be expected to take *one* book with me to last for ninety five days! I need my CDs, my player, batteries, all these things. I cannot *possibly* exist without them!"

"Why did you ask for an MP3 player?" I ask her. "The whole reason for having an MP3 player is so that you can put all your CDs onto one small gadget. It is so much more transportable! Why haven't you transferred your music? Why ask for something and then not use it? What's the point?"

"Because I have other things to do as well, you know. Have you seen the number of books I still have to read? When *you* begin to read as much as *I* do, you will see that the time needed to transfer music is of much lesser importance!"

"Yes! And now, when you need to have your MP3, it's empty. Useless. Very, *very* clever! Very forward thinking! You've just lost the case, *lawyer* Wiggins!"

"Luther! Sapphira! *Enough*! Time is running out and you two are bickering. Leave Sapphira alone so that she can pack. We are leaving at seven thirty!"

∞

My watch shows 07:18. We have phoned Ellie a dozen times, at least, and she tells us each time she is ready and waiting. Papa, Ma and I are bumping into each other as we flit around each room, triple checking that everything is turned off, switched off, all windows have their security screens secured, everything covered and tidy.

Jolene, who has been with us since before I was born, is standing at the kitchen table, wringing her hands, sobbing and sobbing, wiping her tears and her runny nose with her pinafore. Every time I go to the kitchen, she touches my arm and says "Luther, Oh Luther, what is happening, what to do, what to do indeed?"

Sapphira is sitting on the sofa in the darkened room, staring at where the television used to be. Just sitting. Ma calls her to check if the girls' room is in order.

"Ma, three of you have already checked everything at least a thousand times. All I will be doing is bumping into you and increasing tension. I think it is wiser to remove myself to the Land Rover and settle in there."

∞

Papa is calling us to gather in the lounge. I hold back my tears as I leave my room, backwards. All my worldly possessions are neatly stacked in my room. The neatest my room has ever been for months. Will I ever see them again? Will someone come and steal them or destroy everything? When we return, will I need an upgrade on my computer? What am I going to do without my Wii? I'm going to be sooo bored.

We gather in the lounge. "Where's Benedict?" we all ask simultaneously. "Jolene, where's Benedict?"

"Mrs Angel, I thought he was with the family."

"Oh God! Not again! Not *now*! Has someone left the gate open? Jacob? Quick! Luther, run outside and find your brother."

I run across the neatly mown lawn, look to my left and right, to all the beautifully maintained houses in Prestige Street, Scholar's Close. Funny I should only notice its beauty now; the morning sun opening the roses and border flowers, releasing their fragrance to the morning air. The usual array of vehicles is missing though, as is the early morning greeting of friends. Maybe it is too early for a Saturday morning? Our new gunmetal Land Rover is standing in the driveway, packed and ready. Ma's red Mercedes Benz Sports stowed in the double garage. Ma's Mercedes! My God! We have to *leave that* behind as well? What to do, what to do, indeed! Four houses to my left, Benedict is peddling his tricycle towards his friend's house. He is reluctant to return home. I tuck him, screaming and kicking, under one arm and grab hold of his tricycle and run home.

Ma speaks to all of us. "From now onwards, it is *all* of our responsibility to make *absolutely sure* Benedict is with one of us at all times – understood? I don't want avoidable crises. Can we promise?" All heads nod. "And Benedict – we have told you repeatedly to tell us when you leave the house. Everybody else has to do so, you included."

"Maybe I should tell you where I'm going, yes?"

"Yes Benedict, *always* tells us."

Papa clears his throat. Starts to speak, but no sound comes. I have a flashback of assembly one morning last year. Papa was standing on the stage with a notepad in his hand. He did the same then, cleared his throat, started to speak but no sound coming. When eventually he could speak, it was to tell us that Duncan, in year ten, his brother Hugo in year nine, a younger sister called Shelly and their parents had all died in a car accident over the weekend. A truly *bad* idea to think such lethal thoughts now.

Papa starts speaking again.

"Let us hold hands in prayer. Benedict, please close your eyes. Benedict! Thank you. Dear God. We are so grateful that we are leaving as a family and that we have this home to return to. Keep our love strong no matter what we see or do. We don't know what awaits us. May we all have the courage to face the hardships that come our way. May we be compassionate. May we retain our integrity at all times. We remain grateful for your Divine protection. Let only love guide us all now, let love keep us together and let us continue to be grateful for all that we have and for all that we are given. Keep ourselves, our loved ones and our home safe until we return. Thank you again and again. Amen."

∞

We are all in the Land Rover, waiting for Papa to lock the front door. Ma is sniffing. Occasionally a sob breaks through. The sky blue paint on the walls is one week old; Jolene hung the new curtains two days ago. Jacob mowed the lawn yesterday. Benedict was born in this house.

"Ma, your Mercedes Sports. In the garage ...."

"Yes, Luther. What is much more important to me right now, is fetching Ellie and getting out of Juxon. New Mercedes Benz sports cars, designer clothes, organic food, vintage wines, boutiques seem like nothing now, compared to *all of us* reaching safety."

I nod my head whole-heartedly.

As he locks the door, my father leans his head against the door, his hand on the handle. His whole body shakes. Takes a few deep breaths.

The shuddering stops. Why's he reacting like this? We're on our way, probably for a few weeks, then back here again. What does he know? What's he not telling me, us? A few more shudders, this time with a deep sigh. I too am shaking now. Only because he is shaking. He removes the key from the door, looks at it, looks at the door, the front of the house, another huge sigh, puts the key in his pocket. Stays facing the door. Puts both hands over his heart in our deepest greeting. *Kelsho; my heart greets your heart; my god welcomes your god.* Stands a while like this, shaking occasionally, taking huge slow breaths. Turns towards Jolene and Jacob, says *Kelsho* to them. Comes towards the car. Great tears are falling down his cheeks. Only now do I allow my tears to fall as well.

∞

We wave and wave to Jacob and Jolene until we turn the corner. I've known Jolene and Jacob all my life. Jolene, my second mother, nursing me when I am ill, giving me extra helpings of dessert when Ma clearly said no. Always there. Doing whatever I ask of her, practising my charm on her. My family is breaking up. I don't like this one bit. Not at all.

Chapter Two

While Papa is driving, Ma is phoning everyone on her phone list, reporting to the car in general where all her various friends and associates are. I am fascinated by the lengths people are going to. I ask why Uncle Barry and his family have gone to England? And why were we going to Singapore? We only returned from our home there a few weeks ago. "We've seen the news of riots on television many times before, in London, Mumbai, Sydney, Athens, America - those people didn't fly out of their country or even a city, so why are people doing it here, Papa?"

"Those were riots, civil unrests that have happened here as well - many times before. *This* is something totally different. This is a simmering volcano that has blown its top and the scalding lava is now touching all of us. The volcano is the Cartons' grievance against marginalisation by the *marties* eons ago. They see the historical colonial exchanges as inequitable and unfair. For instance, taking vast expanses of the best land and giving a trivial amount in exchange. Then these *marties* dig themselves so deeply into the country, through commerce and development, that they begin calling it their own.

It happens all over the world. When the indigenous people protest at all this unfairness, the *marties* call in support from their motherland, as well as all the other countries that would feel huge financial pain if they were to lose the battle against the original people of the land. So, uprisings are quashed and more and more petty rules are applied to keep the indigenous people submissive, until, like now, the volcano of frustration erupts.

Here, in Juxon, the British colonials favoured the Liberal Frees over the Conservative Cartons, mainly because the latter were vehemently against the changes the British brought here. Also the *marties'* poor rapport; they just did not follow or respect the age-old rules of interaction and interface. Changes such as education and health care, but especially trade. Another clear case of 'divide and rule', so favoured in politics. As Grandma Meertel never tires of telling you, she is a Carton, not a *marty*-mate like all collaborators with foreigners are labelled. She will always be a staunch fighter for their rights to maintain the traditional Juxonese life.

As you also know, we and our friends and colleagues in Parrish are more concerned with educating everyone and offering everyone an opportunity to reach their highest potential. Maybe, after this, the new Democratic Party may gain recognition and more credibility. Who knows." He shrugs and sighs.

Sapphira chips in, "Why do we always have to say Grandma Meertel instead of just Grandma? We call Ma's ma Grandma, not Grandma.... Ma, what your ma's name?" Papa answers. "When my mother eventually decided to go to school at aged twelve or thereabouts, the British could not say her name, so they changed it to Myrtle. They did that to many children, changing their given name to a British one, so that it was easier on their tongue. Even Rolihlahla's name was changed to Nelson Mandela when he started school. Amazing, isn't it? I believe they were still doing so in the 1980's.

Anyway, when your grandmother left school she reclaimed her original name. When your mother was expecting Luther she told all of us that she will be called Grandma Meertel the day her first grandchild is born. And so it is."

Ma asks Papa, "Do you think your mother will come with us? After all, your brother and sisters have *all* gone there and pleaded with her to leave and they *all* left *without* her. Such a staunch Carton supporter; it might feel like treason for her to be taken elsewhere by her children."

I am half listening whilst sorting out the seating arrangements in my head. I will squeeze between Ma and Papa in the front and Grandma Meertel can sit with the girls at the back with Benedict on someone's lap. However, now is definitely *not* the time to disturb Papa with my seating plan.

"So, Papa, given that you are such a high profile target for the Cartons, why did you not plan such a flight as well?" Sapphira, our future lawyer, asks.

"Because I feel that this is our country and what we do now will leave a legacy for the future generations. I do not want my children to grow up in a country alien to their culture, where they forget their customs and who they really are, forever aliens and cursed by their adopted country. We are Juxonese and we will be here to support our country through thick and thin."

"Yet we were going to Singapore, and now we are on our way to Ushquel. If this unrest is going to continue for *years*, then won't we adopt Ushqueli ways too and forget our culture?" I ask tentatively.

Ma interrupts her phone conversation to say vehemently "Your father and I will see that *never* happens!"

"But Ma! If we can do so in Ushquel, surely we can maintain our culture *anywhere*?" I persist.

"Yes Luther, but I hope that our stay in Ushquel will be much shorter *and* it will be quicker to return home. There will also be so many more of us Juxonese there than in say England or Australia. Much more supportive. Returning from abroad will cost a lot more and take longer, I'm sure."

Papa's mobile phone rings. "Ah, Royce" he says with a broad smile. In Papa's last year at Queenville University there were two serious civil unrests. During the most serious uprising he met Royce, a rookie journalist from England. Same age as Papa. They became bosom pals, regularly exchanging news and information. Visiting occasionally. Papa puts his phone on 'speaker mode' and we all listen.

"Royce! Greetings! You're not in Juxon *already*, are you?"

"Hello there. Love to everyone. No, I'm on my way there. I am just swapping planes here in Dubai and then the long haul eastwards to you. As soon as I heard the news yesterday evening, I left for the airport! I'll be in Queenville by tomorrow morning. You need to leave ASAP! I'm getting reports this is going to be hell. Where are you now?"

"We are on our way to pick up my mother and young Ellie in Carton, then we'll be heading for Angelina's sister's place in Stonehouse in Ushquel. Maybe we'll see you there?"

"Not if I can help it. Does your sister-in-law have Skype so that we can communicate there?"

"Luther and Angelina are nodding, so yes. Safe journey, my friend. Text or call me when you arrive on Juxonese soil."

∞

I check my watch; it shows 07:40. We have turned onto the Carton road. Half way to Ellie. The traffic is slowing down to a snail's pace. We are less than ten minutes from Carton. Soon Ellie will be in the car and I can breathe a huge sigh of relief. I told *everyone* she should have returned home, like all her classmates, from the farming museum visit in Carton! Now look at the mess we're getting ourselves into. But, who listens to a fourteen year old boy! I do have brains, you know! Soon I will have my *Onashi* ceremony and be a man, then they will *have* to heed what I say! She is my best sister!

"Luther! Will you please stop fidgeting like that! I'm phoning to find out where our friends and family are. Please! We'll be with Ellie as soon as we can."

"But Ma, I told____"

"Hush!" She cuts me off before I can say more.

It is now 07:51 and we have not moved an inch. All three lanes are at a standstill. Bumper to bumper. We should have been there by now. Three truckloads of soldiers pass by on the hard shoulder of the motorway, sirens wailing all the while.

Damn!

We are still half way to Carton. Motorists ahead of us are beginning to turn their cars around. What the hell is happening now? Oh God! Please allow us to pick up Ellie and Grandma Meertel if she wants to come and then let us head safely for Ushquel, please, please, *please*!

Papa gets out of the car and speaks to someone who is waiting his turn to turn his car around.

Returns to the car after a few minutes. Just sits. Staring ahead. Taking slow deep breaths like he is always telling us to do to calm down.

Ma takes off her huge designer sunglasses, looks at his increasing grey pallor.

"What? Frederick. What now! Speak to me!" She shakes his arm. "*Frederick*!"

After another deep breath, ending in a stifled sob, he says: "The road to Carton is closed. Incoming traffic only. No leaving. The Carton supporters are gathering there, in full swing. Anybody leaving is considered a Free and therefore attacked. Army awaiting reinforcement ..." he breaks off with a sob.

"*See!* I *told you* she should have returned with her class! See! Now look___" My anxiety about Ellie makes it hard to hold my tongue and Ma interrupts quickly.

"Luther! Enough! *Stop*! Let's look at the situation now, instead of what it should have been."

I can't! I jump out of the car, run into the field nearby. I collapse into a heap, crying tears of frustration, anger, fear, sadness, and rage. I, a 'soon to be man', am utterly unable right now to deal with all these shocks and obstructions to what I want to happen. Head down, I scream and scream and *scream* into the earth.

Until emptiness.

∞

Eventually I feel Papa standing next to me, not touching. He hands me his handkerchief and squats down next to me. Sits a while.

"Sometimes I wish I could do that; get it all out of my system. Tiger, sometimes we make decisions that we believe to be absolutely right at the time and we ignore other's intuitive feelings, like we did with you. This has taught me to listen, *really* listen. Your gut feeling was so strong about having Ellie return with her classmates, wasn't it? I thought it was because you wanted her at home to celebrate our wedding anniversary, but this was more than your usual tendency to play shepherd and keep the family together, wasn't it? I'm sorry - truly sorry. We should have listened to you."

After a long pause, during which I remain unable to speak, Papa speaks again.

"Let's return to the car and discuss what needs to be done. Your mother has spoken to Ellie, and you know our little sunshine, she is happy to stay with her grandmother. It is us who are feeling the pain. So, come, let's discuss this in the car. Hand up?"

I take his hand to stand up, and then his arms are around me, giving me a crushing bear hug before linking his arm into mine to walk back to the car. Although calmer now, I remain shattered by the turn of events.

"OK you ladies, what have you discussed so far?"

Ma has Benedict on her lap. She is sobbing into his little shoulder. He is stroking her cheek.

Sapphira says with less of her usual arrogance. "When we spoke with Ellie, she was quite scared about us leaving her behind. Then the line went dead and when we reconnected, she was calmer. Grandma Meertel must have been talking with her. Grandma Meertel said they will have fun together, and as a lifelong Carton supporter, *of course* they will be safe, even protected! She would never even think of leaving Carton. So yes, Ellie will not be with us, but she is safe in Carton."

"Thanks Sapphira. Angel. Angelina! Decision."

"Oh God! I don't want to *have* to choose. If we go into Carton, we cannot leave. They will *surely* kill you and me and then the children. So, despite your mother being such a staunch Carton supporter, we cannot even consider going into Carton to fetch Ellie. She *will* be safe there! I *have* to believe this! Oh Frederick, our daughter, our sunshine!"

"Luther?"

"Why can't she walk to us? It will only take about twenty minutes. We've done it before! She can come to us. I can go to meet her halfway!"

"Stay in the car! Close the door! Now!"

Only Papa's deep breaths breaking into the silence.

"Tiger, it is *not possible*. She *cannot* walk here, or be brought here. The soldiers have orders to shoot anyone or anything moving out of Carton. The motorist told me they just shot a dog for trotting this way."

Silence in the car, broken by Ma's sobs, then Benedict's smothered voice: "Ellie, I want to play with Ellie. Maybe we should fetch Ellie, yes Papa?"

"Maybe we should call her again and tell her our plans. We don't seem to have much choice here."

When it is my turn to talk, I say "Ellie, *I promise you,* I will make *absolutely sure* we will ring you *twice* a day *and* bring presents from Stonehouse. You make a list."

∞

Papa answers his phone for the 'nth time. "Dr Jenson is at the border. They are closing the border for now; don't know when it will open again. Ushqueli military have arrived to man the border so that people don't slip through unofficial openings. Apparently drivers from Tomsdale are joining with those from Carton and Parrish and creating a dense bottleneck at Gilbey, where we would have crossed into Ushquel. His advice is to go to Hamilton as speedily as possible and get accommodation there. The official report is that the Ushqueli government is keeping the border closed until the local emergency aid agencies have set up a refugee camp inside their border."

How long does it take to build a camp? People waiting in the hot sun. Sitting ducks to any Cartons supporters on the rampage. Dear God! This nightmare is getting worse. We need some help here, *please*!

∞

My watch shows 08:08. All that emotion and drama and it has been less than forty minutes since we left home.... We are now on our way to Hamilton in the west of the country.

Silence and deep, dark emotions hang like a rain-laden black cloud in the Wiggins Land Rover. A thought blazes through my mind. Amazing! In the field, in those moments of screaming, of absolute emotion, my voice started to break! At *last*.

∞

Benedict is whingeing non-stop. Papa first looks at Ma, her eyes covered by sunglasses, then stops the car and turns to us, "Luther, Sapphira, one of you please take Benedict outside so that he can play around for a few minutes. Sapphira! *Now*! Take turns!"

Ma's head flops against the headrest. Dark glasses hiding her eyes, releasing sobs every now and again to Papa's deep sighs. He finds her hand, covers it. I sit in our air- conditioned car, observing my parents and wondering what if something horrific happens to them, what if we never ever see Ellie again?

I shudder as ice grips my heart. I start talking before my mind goes into freefall. "So, Papa, what's in Hamilton? Have you been there? Would we then have to cross the border into Belling? Why have we never been to Hamilton before? Do you know *anybody* there?"

Papa looks at Ma, finds no response, takes a deep breath before speaking. "Hamilton is our smallest town. It's a garrison town, created around the military base there after a civil war in Belling before I was born, to prevent Belling people escaping into Juxon. It's rather cut off from the rest of Juxon, a sleepy little place. Many years ago the mayor had a rather ostentatious civic centre built there. This building was recently converted into a conference centre. That's its importance for Juxon. Many 'out of town' meetings and workshops take place there. Don't worry, Hamilton will, no doubt, have all the necessary conveniences we are used to."

He looks again at Ma. "Angel, could you ring Rose and David and find out what's the situation between Tomsdale and Hamilton? Are others fleeing east as well? Or are some heading towards Hamilton?"

Ma does not respond; it's as if she hasn't heard. Papa puts his hand over hers again, then caresses her arm, her thigh. There is a long silence before he says "Angelina, Angel. My heart is shredded into painful splinters, just like yours. This madness is going to test our love. Please, *please*, let us support each other. We *have* to keep trusting, hoping and believing we shall all be together again soon."

The lump in my throat gets bigger and bigger and threatens to burst. *Please* Ma, Papa's begging. I silently pray. I am missing Ellie already. She is such fun, always full of giggles and so funny! I stare out the smoke-tinted window, seeing nothing. When I look to the front again, Ma has her hand on Papa's leg. Papa holds her hand, squeezes it for a moment before returning his hand to the wheel.

I breathe a huge sigh of relief and look out of my window again.

∞

In the now lighter silence of the car, I remember the times Papa and Ma would hear a 'special' song. At one time, Ma's special was '*Come away with me*' by Nora Jones. Ma once said that if Benedict had been a girl he would have been called Nora Joy, now he is Benedict Jones. Looking at each other with that special look I could never fathom, they would start dancing. Not dancing, more a kind of smooching. Percy Sledge's '*When a man loves a woman*' is one of Papa's favourites. He would come into the kitchen where Ma was helping Jolene prepare supper and we kids were doing our homework, and he would turn up the volume of the radio in the kitchen.

"What now?" Ma would ask with a knowing smile. Papa would take the spoon or whatever out of Ma's hands and, holding her ever so tightly, they would dance slowly around the place. It always felt so deliciously electric. I would stare at them with a silly grin on my face. After a while one of them would suddenly become aware of us and say "Come on little tigers, join in the Wiggins family dance" and we would all hug together, moving around the kitchen table, Jolene clapping her hands to the music. At night I would again hear Ma's throaty gurgle in bed. Was she reliving the dancing, or what?

Will we ever be able to do these things again?

Chapter Three

Ma resumes her phoning. According to her sources, the road from Tomsdale to Hamilton is relatively empty. Papa says to pray that it remains so, at least until after we arrive and have settled into our accommodation.

I check my watch: 09:23.

After a few minutes the nine thirty news update on Radio Queenville, Radio QV starts.

"This is Radio QV. Here is the news read by Gregory Gaston.

Gangs of Carton supporters are having running battles with Free supporters in the Queenville suburbs. There are also reports of widespread looting in the shopping malls of the capital. Businessmen estimate damage has already run into thousands of Kutek[1].

The capital remains the worst affected. Reports of increasing unrest are coming in from Chessletown

---

1 *The Juxonese currency*

and Tomsdale. Rioters are targeting the cars heading towards the Ushqueli border. The military is being deployed to all major towns to assist the police in keeping order and preventing further looting and fighting. Many arrests have been made.

The Vice President, Harrie Pitenshi, has ordered troops to shoot any person found looting, attacking others or destroying property. The Shadow Cabinet Minister for Law and Order, Kathleen Hindley, has appealed for calm on both sides and has asked Vice President Harrie Pitenshi for an emergency meeting.

Here ends the news bulletin."

Sapphira asks Papa why people have to fight; could they not discuss issues around the table, like we do?

"Ah, well, look at the two of you; constantly squabbling over such minute issues, some of which have occurred in the 'long ago' past – gone and forgotten, although, apparently, not for one of you. Bringing up old grievances time and time again. Each wanting to score a point. Each one thinking he or she is done by, losing out, or better, smarter, more deserving than the other. Am I right?" Papa pauses and looks at us in the rear-view mirror, then adds, "It's the same here – issues that have not been buried, forgiven or forgotten keep on surfacing, becoming more and more contentious and vicious, until lives are uselessly lost."

Ma interrupts. "Yes, all that, and more. See these farmlands on the right here? We're in one of the richest valleys on earth. *Everything* grows here – you don't need green fingers! The soil is enriched by the rivers that flow from the hills and mountains both sides of the valley. This Carton valley has always fed the Juxonese and those beyond its borders for many centuries. The farmers would take their produce to Carton, the original capital of Juxon. The hills between Tomsdale and Hamilton were excellent grazing land, producing fat cattle."

Papa takes up the story. Even Benedict is listening now. "Your history teachers will have told you that Kavari Quay, where we are heading for lunch, is the place where hundreds of years ago, the *marties,* the foreigners, first set foot in Juxon and changed our Juxonese way of life forever. From their ships that docked there, they brought their culture, their ways of doing things, their laws and their values. This divided us Juxonese into the Liberal Frees and the Conservative Cartons.

They plundered the land that had been farmed for generations by land-loving people whom they labelled Conservative Cartons. They educated the willing traders and called them Liberal Frees. Before their arrival, we had no such distinctions; we were all Juxonese, either farmer or trader, living symbiotically and, for most of the time, peacefully."

After a pause, Papa continues. "In addition to all these things, they brought biomedicine and Christianity to Juxon. They also came to this tiny seashore and took all our gold from the southern hills, which we are passing right now on your left. Many families' farms were plundered by hungry mobs of fortune hunters, *marties* coming from all across the globe and accepting the British as their authority. There were constant fights until the *marties* either killed the farmers or drove them off their land."

Papa pauses to let the magnitude of these historical events sink in. He continues.

"In gratitude for the gold and their subsequent wealth, but more likely to salve their conscience, the now prosperous and thriving British established Parrish as the university town, offering higher education to every Juxonese. According to Grandma Meertel, they put their dividing knife between the conservative agriculturists and the more liberal thinking traders. The pain of that division, of brother fighting against brother, is the legacy we are left with. Not because of religion like some other countries; neither due to race, but due to one set of people wanting to hold onto their trust in the land and another set of people ready to embrace new ideas.

Grandma Meertel has always been a fighting Conservative Carton. She was forever telling us, and now you, stories of how the *marties* and the traders came into the lush green valley,

Juxonese agricultural land, and looted her great-great-grandparents' farm, the largest and most prosperous farm called Carton.

According to her stories, they killed most of our family and then, not having any skills of the land, rented the stolen farms back to them at extortionately high rates. Grandma Meertel still lives in the very house her family was forced to build after one such uprising. All of her children were born in that house.

None of your grandmother's family attended school; it was unheard of - unthinkable! They refused to do so, seeing education as one of the *marties'* wily ways to become more entrenched in Juxon. My own view is that they were far too busy on the land, everyone helping to scrape out their hand-to-mouth existence, and thus had neither time nor money to be educated.

However, your grandmother later decided to go to school in order to beat the traders and *marties* at their own game! She had this dream at the age of twelve, so she started school then. She told her parents that it was the lack of education that kept the Conservative Cartons forever subservient to the Liberal Frees and the *marties*. As you know, she eventually became a teacher and taught both the children and the adults in this valley. Two of the boys she taught became Conservative Carton presidents, if only for a very brief period.

Did you know that Grandma Meertel taught the assassinated President Jameson Welter in primary school? He was about five years ahead of me. He was just fifty-four years old when he was killed. So young. She stopped teaching full time once we children started coming along."

Remembering this history and the stories we were told, I can see why Grandma Meertel was never going to leave Carton. She has been a fighter all her life and survived all previous uprisings. Papa and Ma are not active members for either party. I know they both vote for the Liberal Frees because they are liberal thinkers and told Sapphira and myself so. But they have become more and more interested in the grassroots Democratic Party.

I wonder if Grandma Meertel knows this? Is this why any political discussion stops abruptly or the subject is quickly changed whenever Grandma Meertel is present in our family? The Liberal Frees were educated and Grandma Meertel's Conservative Cartons remained the labourers, the poorly paid. Although times have changed considerably now and we *all* have access to education, the majority of the uneducated remain Conservative Cartons and their leaders defiant and angry, according to my parents.

"My mother and her cronies only see black and white. There is no grey!" My father often complains of his mother's views and attitude towards life.

Ma has all kinds of people working for her: *marties*, conservatives, liberals. She says she doesn't care what their political views are, so long as they are eager to work and to learn and do not judge others. Papa and Ma have a mixture of Liberal Frees and Cartons friends, even family. It's more about politics now than absolute divide. Both Ma's brothers are married to Liberal Frees. We heard that they and two of Papa's sisters and their families went abroad this morning. Who knows, maybe we will see some cousins and family in Hamilton? At least we know we have family somewhere 'out there' if we need to leave Juxon.

∞

Into the silence my father says, "I remember when I was ten years old; there was terrible unrest then. My parents sent me to stay with my grandmother and my two eldest sisters were sent to Ushquel to my Aunt Kathleen. I stayed there for about six months before returning home. Ten years later, when I was twenty and studying in Queenville, I looked after my cousins when the fighting became exceptionally violent around Parrish and Carton. It seems that history is repeating itself."

∞

Benedict wakes from a nap just as we pull into Kavari Quay at 11:42. "Ellie. I want Ellie. Papa, where's Ellie? Ma, where's Ellie? Maybe I should see Ellie NOW!" He opens all our raw wounds again.

I put him on my shoulders and run towards the sea. We'd visited here only a few weeks ago – how can situations change *soooo* dramatically and so quickly? "Let's go to the sea! See the sea? Do you remember the sandcastles we built?"

He giggles and I put him down on the sand so he can run on the beach. "Maybe I should build another sand castle."

∞

We are drawn to the cacophony of sounds at the quayside. My parents and Sapphira are heading that way and I race towards them, piggybacking Benedict.

Two ferry boats are tied alongside each other, listing dangerously, almost dipping into the water then swaying swiftly towards the opposite side. As we near the boats, we hear the captain speaking over a loudhailer: "Last boat for the day sails at noon. Next available boat tomorrow at eight o'clock."

Instant bedlam! A stampede! A surge of bodies clothed in multi-colours move into simultaneous action, *all* wanting to board the boats. *Immediately*! Both boats list in every direction as more people jump down, tossing screaming small children into willing arms, hurling bundles and filled-to-bursting black bags onto passengers who start instant shouting matches as even more bundles are being hurled. The boats seem dangerously unsteady. Makes me queasy just looking at it. I sit down.

I listen to the screaming above the screaming. The crew are overwhelmed by the sudden stampeding influx. Even as the captain is shouting *"only one bag per passenger! Only ONE bag per passenger!"* people continue to toss in bag after bag. Around these dangerously moving ferries, young boys in tiny boats are rowing perilously close, selling and shouting their wares in shrill voices, *laughing* and making a game out of it. *Awesomely awesome*! They're going to die! I can't watch, yet can't *not* watch.

Ma is shouting, "Look at that little boy in the red boat. He's standing on one leg and his boat is at a ninety degree angle! Oh my *God*! Frederick! Oh my goodness! He's going to drown! Get crushed! *Do something*! No! Not you Frederick, him! *Tell him* to move away!"

"Angel, he can't hear me! He's probably done it dozens of times before! He is as sure footed as a mountain goat. Don't look! Look at the woman's dresses – very floral, very 'today', do you see?"

"Yes, yes. Karen Millen and the other one is Stella McCartney, for sure. Oh, look, Frederick! He's in the water! Right between the two boats.

That big boy is going to be crushed! Oh, my GOODNESS!"

"Papa, *listen*! The captain is saying the price has just *doubled* and it is as if people are deaf! They must be *really* desperate! Where are these boats going anyway?" I ask as we watch the rapidly overfilling boats with bated breath.

Sapphira shouts in the mayhem "Who wants to bet that at least two people will fall into the water?"

"Sapphira! That twisted dark humour of yours will get you into trouble one day. No such betting! Pray they will all be safe."

"There's no adrenaline in that; it's *utterly* boring. Why do people have to have *all* these belongings when they don't even know where they're going? What use are clothes to them? How are they going to carry it on the other side? Both Belling and Karterli are poor countries – they should know – Juxon is filled with their migrant workers. Where's Benedict?"

"Your father has him."

I listen to the people shouting from the quayside. "Text me when you get there." "Text me what it's like." "Book a room for my family" "I'm taking the next boat out." How do they know whether they'll get a seat on the boat? It's exciting and scary. Too much 'not knowing'; too many people taking too many chances. Thank goodness we're off to Hamilton – I know Juxon and, therefore, know what to expect. I look at Ma and Papa's faces. They are filled with excitement, the fear of the unknown like a great adventure to them. Adrenaline pumping, Ma is holding Papa's arm and jumping up and down and Papa is laughing his head off at some of the people's antics.

Please don't change your minds and say we're going on these boats, *please!* Remember Ellie. *Please* Captain; say the overfull boats are departing now! Blow your horn! Take the ropes off the quayside! Go, go, *go*! Ma and Papa might change their minds! My iPod is in the car and there won't be time to fetch it!

The captain duly blasts his horn and I am weak with gratitude. In the blur of movement of people running alongside the quay shouting last minute messages and instructions, tossing packets of biscuits and other foodstuffs to passengers, the only constant is the clear blue sky and a slight breeze dissipating midmorning heat. I look at my parents who are looking at each other with a look of regret, as if they would have relished that sea trip to wherever.

∞

"It's about a two and a half hour drive to Hamilton, so, what shall we do? A half hour lunch here and tea in Hamilton?" Papa asks. "I'd like to get there way before sunset."

As we walk past the stalls towards the cafés, we pass people inspecting the jettisoned possessions and belongings, glancing around furtively before claiming some as their own. Others are looking on, faces twisted in disgust at what these people are doing. Microwave ovens, carry cots, toys, coats, clothing, a long mirror, a small television, books and magazines. Cars too stand abandoned in a haphazard way along the narrow road, keys still in the ignition.

Sapphira asks what will happen to all this stuff. Ma looks at the things and says "Oh, the local people will probably come sniffling through it when it is dark and disapproving eyes are absent. They will most likely take what they want and sell the other stuff. Who knows? You know the old saying: one man's loss is another man's gain."

∞

We eat our sandwiches on the nearly deserted beach. Benedict starts to play with his little red car; a gift from the salesman when Ma bought her red Mercedes Sports three months ago. Another three year old boy comes up to him. We watch as they size each other up. Both have little red cars in their hands; the other boy's car is a Volvo. Instant friendship! They talk together, gesticulate, laugh. I can't hear what they are saying. His parents come and talk to Papa and Ma. They are from Chessletown. The father tells Papa and Ma they had attempted to cross into Ushquel from Chessletown as well as from Parrish; both times they were too late. They did not want to wait in the heat, with the few shops at the border having already run out of vital foodstuffs. Now they too are on their way to Hamilton. They hope they are in time this time round. Their son Simon, who is playing with Benedict, is their only child. The mother is pregnant with her second baby. The father introduces himself as George Brunson and his wife as Amanda. He is a primary school teacher, in Chessletown. Soon afterwards they call Simon, as they want to reach Hamilton early. We all say our goodbyes and hope that we will see and support each other in Hamilton.

∞

While we all enjoy a double helping of ice cream at our favourite café, Ma continues to phone people and report their whereabouts and difficulties in getting to where they want to go.

I like sitting here. We had spent many days on the beach here and I know the cafés that sell the best ice cream. I ask my father why we can't stay here. "We know Kavari Quay. Leonard in the café says no rioting ever happens here and I remember Grandma Meertel telling us that Belling people used to flee here during their civil wars or unrests for that very reason. Can we not use Hamilton as a last resort? I really don't understand why we *have to* go to Hamilton. No one Ma has spoken to so far is going there. No family, no friends. *And* we are *nearer* to Carton and Ellie and *much* nearer to home."

Papa is reading a text message from someone. After a long pause he says, "Funny you should be asking that question this very minute. Royce has excellent, reliable sources, always accurate. He has literally just texted me *during* flight, as you were asking that question. He says: *if not in Ushquel yet, go to Hamilton ASAP. Every other town a target.* I trust his information. If Royce says every town is a target then Kavari Quay is a target as well. There's always a first time.

So! This is my thinking. Yes, no one is going to Hamilton, so we will have better choices in accommodation. It is also a garrison town, so the military are already there, which is safer, already protected. City dwellers would rather go to Ushquel because it has a better standard of living, so Hamilton will be less crowded, I hope. So, based on sound, trusted intelligence, we are heading to Hamilton before everyone else. Let me first go to the bank and withdraw some more cash, just in case."

∞

Papa sits down heavily when he and Benedict return from the ATM. "Banks closed. No more money from the hole in the wall. Can't get any money out."

"How *dare* they do that!"

"I remember the banks closing for a few days before, when severe disorder erupted a few years ago, remember, Angel? Hopefully, like then, this is merely a temporary precaution. Don't worry. We do have sufficient money to see us through a week or two."

"Well! How very fortunate we had a Friday 'Special Day' yesterday and I was too late to bank the day's taking from both boutiques. Luckily I don't have to worry about staff finances for a while; all the money we have now is ours. Thank goodness, too, for the American Dollars. I think we should hold onto those until our Kutek are exhausted. Keep an eye on the Black Market, as usual."

After a while Ma continues, "Tonight we will have a family meeting. Set some ground rules. Each one will be responsible for a wad of money. Frederick, I sincerely hope that when we return to normality, we will find that the British have been paying your salary faithfully into your account."

∞

Ma drives on the last leg of our journey. A blessed relief from Ma's constant phoning. Her phone is recharging. Papa had bought us each a chocolate toffee bar at Kavari Quay. Ma worries about our teeth rotting with so much sugar. "Angelina, it is a *treat*. Let them enjoy it. I bet you none of their teeth will fall out tonight or tomorrow morning." We giggle at Papa while chewing contentedly.

Reality returns when Papa switches on the radio to listen to the two o'clock news. This time we listen to the BBC World Service.

"In Queenville, Chessletown and Tomsdale, running battles continue between Carton protesters, the military and looters. The military have been given orders to shoot looters and aggressors. Hospitals are reporting a rapid rise in casualties and are begging for blood donors.

There are scenes of increasing panic at the Juxon – Ushquel border. More and more people are arriving despite border crossings being halted since eight this morning. The Ushqueli military are now guarding border crossings and plugging all the unofficial entry points. Reports of heavy-handedness and shots being fired have not been officially verified. The Juxonese waiting at the border fear the militants will come to the border and kill them off like sitting ducks. At Gilbey, the Juxonese border crossing nearest to Parrish, the few shops have run out of water, petrol and food supplies. Panic is visibly rising.

A mother has given birth to a premature baby in the overheated back seat of her family car. A midwife waiting at the border with her family attended her.

The Ushqueli government spokesperson is defending their closing of the border with Juxon. They say the Ushqueli Red Cross Society, together with other NGOs[2], are preparing a huge camp some distance away from the border and need the time to collect, set up and install the family tents, water, sanitation and other relief supplies.

Other news...."

These news slots bring me back to reality with a jolt. That knot starts burning in my guts again. I sigh. It doesn't go away. Sapphira is reading a story to Benedict – I have already read his Book of the Alphabet three times this morning. He refuses to listen to the other books because he says he wants to read by himself before he is four years old. I switch on my iPod. I listen to our star, Twining, but her upbeat drumming makes my heart beat even faster. I am sweaty, panicky. I switch off the music and keep the earphones in my ears, locking out life, reality and everything else.

∞

2 Non-Government Organisations

I am scared! I am really, *really* scared. What am I specifically scared of? Don't know - everything unknown. As we travel parallel to the sea, I am reminded of my parent's conversation about me this morning: "*....will he sink or will he swim? ...*"

Sink or swim? I'm sinking! I'm sinking!

I turn towards Sapphira. She's so cool and collected, as if she is the only one who knows the solution. Is she worried about events? How can I show fear – she will maul me with her acid tongue. She hates not being the eldest, even though she thinks she is *so* clever, so focused on her future as the world's best lawyer and ultimate manager of the universe.

Papa once whispered to me that I could be or do anything I want, because we are *all capable* of achieving whatever we wish for in life. It's just, well, she already knows what she wants to do and I really don't know what I want to do. Dream, I suppose. Socialise. Help others. Not be scared. Swim, rather than sink. Not even contemplate sinking.

How do I keep swimming against all these things? What would Harry Potter do? What does our goal keeper Sidney Gilbert do in Arsenal in London? What does our 2008 Olympian Tommy Thomas do? Tommy Thomas had said during an interview a few months ago that he had the goal of the Olympic gold medal to keep him going. Don't know what Sidney Gilbert does to swim – probably practise, practise, practise. And Harry

Potter? What keeps him going? Seeing those pictures of his parents loving him?

It takes me a long while before deciding that I am going to be *all three* of them and swim through this. I am going to be A MAN. My goal that will keep me going is to keep my family together.

Papa said not to think of what should have happened because it has already happened. To think of what to do now that it has already happened. OK! So, Ellie is not with us. How can I keep the family together? I promise to think of ideas, ask for help from who ever, so that we *always stay together*! Swim, swim, swim.

"Papa, can we ring Ellie?" I ask.

"Maybe I should speak with Ellie, Papa." Benedict pipes up.

We have a quick chat with her. Benedict and Ellie sing *doh, rey me* from The Sound of Music, after which we all shout 'Bye Bye' to her.

It works! This swimming works! Yes! More practice later. My cells are singing, jumping out of my skin. I am becoming a man. I am ready. I look around for the change that has just occurred, but everything seems just the same.

Chapter Four

We leave the sea behind. I look at my watch. 14:52 on a Saturday afternoon. At this moment in Parrish I would be finishing my second last *Onashi* preparation class. I just *love* the way our mentors sit and have quiet moments of thinking before coming up with an idea. These appear to be deliberate moments of silence before anybody deigns to talk.

It is all so *measured* and thought out. Not like at home, where Ma is sooo explosive! And she is *never ever* stuck for an analysis or an opinion. And, wow, what a fast thinker she is! Personally, I think Ma would sweep most of the men there off the floor with her quick thinking and accurate assessment of things. Razor, *razor* sharp! Best not to let her near some of those men.

This week would have been all about our relationships with girls and women. Well, sex, actually. How could they kill President Welter just as I was about to learn something sooo important?

Unfair! Not having had the session on sex, will Papa have the time to tell me about it? Else, how will I know the true facts? Can I eventually get married not knowing this vital information? I won't have my *Onashi* group to ask anymore.

Only Edward could brag about being with a girl. Ma would kill me! Not before the legal age of eighteen, Ma said; four more years – I will have forgotten everything by then. On the one hand adults say we have to practise, practise, practise, practise so that we can perfect our skills, but on this sex thing they demand we wait four years. Even as a non-lawyer, this doesn't make any sense to me!

All the way, Edward said! Awesomely awesome! One out of eight of us. Did he know what to do? Do these things come naturally? Was the girl older than him? Someone we know? Would she do it for others? Is it true – did he really do it?

Five haven't even kissed a girl yet. At least I did that with Caroline. Hmmm! That was *sooo* pleasant. All tingly, an instant fire spreading from lips to toes, making me harder than I've ever been. If that's what kissing does, what does the rest do?!

I was all set to touch her breasts the next time. This evening! *Oh my goodness*! I am missing touching breasts for the first time. Really bad timing from the Frees in killing President Jameson Welter – how could they *do this to me*! I left her note in my jeans pocket. Jolene will read it. Damn, damn,

damn! *"I love tall men. You're the tallest. So I must like you a lot. I can still feel your lips on mine. Can't wait until Saturday evening. I'll be waiting outside Fraser's. Caroline xxx."*

My first love letter. Hope she has mine with her, wherever she is. I bet they flew to London.

Swim, swim, swim.

"Ma, do you know where Dr John went to?"

"John Neville? They're on their way to his brother in Singapore. Caroline? Weren't you going to meet Caroline after your *Onashi* prep class this evening?" Ma looks in the rear view mirror at me. Fortunately I am wearing one of her freebie designer sunglasses that hide most of my face and its burning blush. "Poor boy! Your date! Isn't life cruel?"

Swim.

Change subject. Fast.

"Papa, what's going to happen about my *Onashi* ceremony?"

"That is two weeks from now, Tiger. We don't know what will happen. Keep an open mind. It may have to be delayed, or we could find other boys in the same situation and have the ceremony in Hamilton. Wherever it is, it will be special, believe me."

"But Papa, does this mean I can't be a man now? That I will never be a man because there will be no *Onashi* ceremony for me? Can one be a man without that special ceremony? Can people be married without a special ceremony? Can one be a professor without that special degree?"

"Relax, Tiger! Other countries do not have *Onashi* ceremonies and they become men. It's ___"

Sapphira interrupts Papa. "Why do boys have to have the *Onashi* celebration? Why do girls not have anything like that?"

Ma gives a little laugh. "When I was a young girl, we *had* a coming of age ceremony. It was called *Clevelli*. We were talking about this very issue at the boutique on Friday. A group of us were thinking of organising a *Clevelli* for you girls. At around age ten to twelve because girls mature earlier than boys. We would also have six sessions like the boys do and discuss more or less the same things except of course that it would be from a girl's perspective. Modernise the sessions the way the *Onashi* has been modernised. What do you think would be an appropriate symbol to give to girls? The boys always had the special necklace whilst we were given trousseau. What do you think Saph?"

"I have always liked Papa's single stone in his necklace. Maybe we too can have a special necklace. Maybe a bangle, in case we want to wear a necklace to suit our dress for that day. What did you choose, Luther?"

"I have a single Tiger's eye stone. Have you brought it with you, Ma?"

"Oh *yes*. Papa remembered it and I will keep it safe until your *Onashi* ceremony. If we can get a few girls together in Hamilton, we can set your *Clevelli* in motion as well, Sapphira. Start thinking about your bangle. We will see what Hamilton can produce."

∞

I check my watch for the thousandth time: it shows 15:30. According to the satnav navigator, we are about twenty minutes from Hamilton. Papa wakes from his catnap and switches the radio on.

"This is Radio QV and here is the news read by Gregory Gaston.

Despite an increasing police presence, many shops in Queenville have been ransacked and looted. For a short time the police were powerless against a screaming mob of about two hundred men, women and children rampaging through the city centre, beating up everyone in their way and emptying the shops of all its wares. Army reinforcements have now secured the city centre.

The Conservative Cartons are blaming the Frees for assassinating the Carton President, and the Frees are blaming the Cartons for starting and escalating the violence.

Cartons supporters have commandeered buses from the Queenville depot and have driven to Chessletown and Tomsdale with the Frees supporters in hot pursuit. Now, similar carnage is being reported in these two towns. Troops have been sent to quell the violence. Troops are also on their way to Carton, Parrish, Kavari Quay and Hamilton, to prevent any further outbreaks of violence and looting. The police and army have been ordered to shoot all looters and rioters on sight.

World leaders have been sending messages of condolence and appeals for calm. The United Nations has asked for a meeting with both parties.

Each party continues to blame the other for continuing violence. People are frantically attempting to escape to Ushquel. The Ushquel border remains closed whilst the Ushqueli workers prepare a refugee camp to accommodate the thousands of Juxonese fleeing there. The roads to Karterli in the south and Shenroth in the north are relatively quiet while the road from Tomsdale to Hamilton is becoming increasingly congested......."

With every news bulletin it seems the situation is getting worse and worse. Now we won't have such an easy time in Hamilton because Tomsdale people are fleeing there. What do I do with this burning knot in my guts! How do I swim?

"What now, Papa?" Sapphira asks.

"Take a deep breath, and then another and then another."

I do so as well, turning to my side of the window so that Sapphira does not see me doing this. Feel heaps better. Without even asking, I am swimming again - excellent.

Still I am little concerned. Are we ever going to get home again? I turn to look at Sapphira. Her head is turned towards the farmlands where people are harvesting carrots and onions. Who on earth is going to be able to afford these vegetables when the banks have closed? Don't these people or the farmers know that there is an uprising?

Would the rebels do what Grandma Meertel told us happened in former uprisings and simply help themselves to any available food? Would they eat carrots even if they don't like them? Will I *have* to eat green beans and cauliflower now that we have a limited amount of money? Can I get them past my mouth or will I be sick? How do I swim through this? Breathing is not going to help! I will *definitely* need something else.

Because of my ponderings I have only just noticed that we have slowed down considerably. Ma is not moving out of second gear. We are *still moving,* though. I check my watch. It is 16:07 and nobody has checked the news, thank God! It's only getting worse.

Benedict has woken from a catnap and wants his Alphabet story read again. My turn. By the time I get to 'Z is for zebra' we have come to a halt. On my side of the car, the kerbside, there are people walking now, walking *away* from Hamilton! What do they know that we don't?

I do my breathing exercise again to cool my knotted guts. Then I notice the people are carrying lots of produce and chickens, and leading goats and sheep. Market day! Not escaping. Phew! What a relief that is.

I love walking through markets. Parrish does not have a particularly large one but Carton has a huge, varied market and I love the hustle and bustle of markets. Good! I shall be visiting Hamilton market for sure!

I see many stationary cars on the roadside. "Overheating" Papa says when I ask.

"Over-packing more likely," Ma comments, tapping the steering wheel with her deep purple nails. "Look Benedict. See the chickens all fluttering about in the car there! Could they not have left these chickens for the domestic staff like we did? Do they think they will starve? Hamilton is part of Juxon, not some distant part of Belling!"

"Well, they could sell the chickens or keep them for food later. You know how prices soar in times of crisis! Remember the boat fares this morning, the prices after the Tsunami in 2004, or 9/11 in 2001? You too upped your prices. I remember a negligee went from 60 Kutek to 105 Kutek in 2001."

"Frederick! How is it you remember the price of a negligee?! Anyway, I was merely protecting my business. And I felt men might appreciate their womenfolk more – paying higher prices would demonstrate more appreciation, love and so on. This is a *local* crisis, not some *one off* event. We should *all* be helping each other!"

During a pause Sapphira observes, "Ma, if you were in the fruit and veg business and had shops in Hamilton as well, would you charge the same price as in Parrish?"

"No, I would charge local rates, so that people will continue to buy from me. Once it becomes difficult for the farmers and traders to transport their wares, they will increase their prices and I would then *have to* do the same. The rarer a commodity becomes, the more it costs. That's normal."

"So, Ma, how long will our money last?" I ask.

"Well, given that you're going through another growth spurt and need to eat every other hour, it is going to be tricky."

"I will eat only three meals a day then!"

Papa laughs out loud. "Luther, if it is a choice between you eating every two to three hours or you being moody and having such erratic behaviour, then I will do my utmost to have you eating every two hours until this phase passes."

"It's not my fault. I can't help it!"

Sapphira comments loftily, "It's merely your hormones. Well, actually it's not entirely ___"

"Shut up Sapphira! You know nothing!" How *dare* she dare to comment on something she will *never* know anything about?

Ma turns around and thunders out. "*Stop* it, Sapphira! *Both* of you stop this at once! Sapphira, you too are going through changes now, so please, stop goading each other. The last thing we need is constant bickering. There's enough turmoil in Juxon. Let there be harmony in our household, *please*."

∞

We have come to a complete standstill. We all get out of the air-conditioned Land Rover into the temperate afternoon sunshine to stretch our legs and check the road ahead and behind us. Papa stops frequently to greet other drivers, asking where they came from, recognising a few familiar faces from Parrish.

I say hello to a few students from my school. We had never before bothered to speak with each other, now we're saying hello like old friends. Funny that. Different circumstances.

I wonder if, when we return, we will go back to not noticing each other again in school? Or will this crisis start new and lasting friendships? Do we have anything in common apart from fleeing to third rate Hamilton instead of Ushquel, or even better, Asia or Europe?

My digital watch is showing the time to be 17:27 and we're on the outskirts of Hamilton town. We have been inching our way forward. Benedict has had two major temper tantrums and I have been walking around with him for the third time now. Once inside the car I begin to smell the stale sweat on my shirt. With all the rush and panic this morning, I didn't have enough time to wash or 'groom' as Ma says.

When did I start to have smelly sweat? Is this a man's thing? Papa never smells of sweat, but then Ma has all these promotional samples for Papa to test. I hope he has brought some with him, or maybe Hamilton will have some? Ma will know when we get there.

Of course we listen to the BBC World Service. Again, a repetition of previous repetitions. I shut off until I hear them talking about Parrish.

" .... no reaction from the international community. There are as yet unconfirmed reports that the library of Parrish University's Literature Wing has been fire bombed this afternoon. Fortunately, it being Saturday, very few students and staff were in the building. However, the staff and students that were in the library suffered severe burns and injuries.

Parrish General Hospital is appealing for urgent blood donors. A report just handed to me says that Parrish Cathedral is at this moment being targeted by an angry mob that have allegedly travelled on stolen buses from Queenville... "

It goes on and on. It was not as bad as this even twelve hours ago – is it even possible that a situation can deteriorate so rapidly? I begin to feel a kind of detachment. This is not Juxon; these are not Juxonese. It *can't* be! We are taught from our first year at school to *respect everyone*.

Ma lets out a groan. "We are being abandoned by the very people we have helped to achieve their great wealth. They have trampled on our sweaty backs to take what they wanted. And now, having gotten what they wanted, and moulded us to what they see as right and proper, they abandon us to our death!"

"At least they haven't said anything about Hamilton, which I am taking as a good sign." Papa tells us. "Tomsdale to Hamilton has the highest and most hills. It will take them much longer. Even if they have vehicles and *even if* they have militants in all the towns, people will flee to the hills. You'd have to be very desperate and determined to reach the tops. The local people know the hideaways, so they will be relatively safe for a while, anyway."

"Yes, but Papa, if you say every village may have their own militants, then they *too* will know all the hideouts, won't they? And one crazy man can wreak a lot of havoc. He can scare the whole village" Sapphira reasons.

Damn! Why didn't I think of that! I just accept what Papa and people say without thinking about it any further. I *must* start thinking things through more. Listen to that logic of Sapphira's. How do I develop that kind of questioning mind? She is always angry and questioning. Can I be questioning *without* having to be angry?

It's not that Papa and I are slower thinkers; we just have to reason things out in our mind first before we say something. Ma and Sapphira are complete opposites: they say what they think, even if sometimes it is quite outrageous and radical. But they seem to have many more hits than misses. If I do what they do, I seem to always have more misses than hits! Am I just wired differently? Is this a man thing or a lawyer thing? I bet Ma could be one of the best lawyers going; she uses her superstore of tactics to pick holes and scrutinise every small detail deeper than microscopically until she reaches the nucleus of the matter. 'Squirm like a worm until truth comes out!' is one of her famous sayings.

"Sure, Sapphy. I am merely looking at it from the positive side."

Yes! I agree with that. I look at things from a positive side. That's me.

"But Papa, shouldn't we look at it from the realistic side?" she persists.

Ma turns her head to us. "Sapphira, whatever side we look at, the *reality is there*. At the moment, *everybody* is cautious because we really don't know specifically who the enemy is because there are many informers. Money makes people talk. People will sell their grandmother for a song. Others choose to accuse others above being killed themselves. One never knows what drives some people to betray others, truly or falsely. So we *have* to be careful. This means keeping a *very* low profile, not showing any wealth or intelligence, dressing down and starting to think like everyone else. To look and think like Cartons or Frees pretending to be Cartons. We all have to drill it into ourselves and Benedict. Make a game out of it. If we are going to get through this, we have to use all our wiles. Play the game."

This is getting really serious now. Darn it! Do I have what it takes to deal with such violence? Can I be less intelligent? How do I act stupid? How does Sapphira act stupid? What do we do with our new Land Rover? It shines. It has been the envy of our neighbourhood - what about now?

"Ma, how does one act stupid?"

"*You don't have to worry*! Just act your normal self, brother____"

"Sapphira! *That is untrue, uncalled for and hurtful*! How can you even think of being the world's best lawyer when you lack basic integrity! Luther, apart from greeting, just look blank and say nothing. Pretend to be a *marty,* in a new country, who knows only how to say hello, but does not know the language."

∞

We continue to crawl along. Nearly there.

I begin to see more and more of the cathedral spire ahead. Papa mentions in passing that the British built a cathedral in every city in Juxon, the smallest and most recent one being in Carton. I wonder how Ellie and Grandma Meertel are getting on. Is Ellie having fun? Is she missing us as I am missing her?

I still remember the story I told during our story time session in class. I was six years old when she was born. We had been to the hospital the day before to see her and Ma. I was so happy and proud when she curled her tiny hand around my little finger, as if she knew I was her big brother! In class I told them how my little baby sister Ellie smiled at me at less than one day old! All the children clapped their hands after I had told my story. I went home and there was Ellie and she did it again - curled her little hand around my finger! We have been friends from that day, and she is closer to me than Sapphira. And now I am missing my little sister so much.

Eventually we reach Hamilton. It is now 17:58, making it ten and a half hours of travelling. The sun is beginning to drop behind the cathedral spire and tall buildings. The evening sun creates an absolutely stunning glow in the sky. The birds are flying home in their perfect V formation. Is anybody else seeing it? Appreciating such exquisite beauty?

It is a very small dusty town on the border with Belling. During one of our many unavoidable stops, the Wiggins family, including young Benedict, sent out a huge prayer for the best accommodation to be found.

I see people standing beside their cars, looking lost or undecided as to what the next step is, while policemen are bossily and persistently directing them away from the market. The day market is closing for the night, and being replaced by the food traders, who have just started their small fires.

Papa and Ma are praying quietly for somewhere to stay. Papa says we are very conspicuous with our new gunmetal grey Land Rover and we might have to stow it away as soon as possible until we can use it again.

Just then a policeman starts shouting at Papa to get out of the car. A small noise escapes me. *Nobody* speaks to Papa *like that*! He is, after all, Dr. Wiggins, Head Master of the most prestigious high school in Juxon. How dare a mere policeman!

Papa takes a deep breath whilst we collectively hold ours. He unfolds his tall dusty crumpled self from the car and looks at the policeman.

"*Cecil*! Greetings! How can I help you?"

"Er, Sir! Good evening Sir! Greetings to your family!" He puts both hands over his heart now. Papa also responds with *Kelsho*.

"So! Cecil! I am happy to see that you are keeping on the right side of the law! Very glad indeed. It shows that your integrity has grown and grown. Congratulations! Well done! I am very pleased for you! Come and meet my family."

"Er Sir. Yes Sir!" Sergeant Cecil shuffles after Papa. Ma greets him, and then Sapphira and I. He keeps his eyes downcast, does not even look at Papa when Papa asks him, "Sergeant Cecil, as somebody who works in this town, do you perhaps know of anybody who may be able to help us with some accommodation? It will be *good* to have the recommendation coming *from you*, then we are certain and reassured that it will all be *above board and safe*. Do you know of any such person?"

Eyes remaining down and constantly shifting from one foot to another, still not looking Papa in the eye, Cecil stutters to Papa to wait just where we are and he will return with good news.

When he is a distance away, Ma asks "Frederick, I don't remember Cecil. Which one was he? What did he do that you remember him so vividly?"

Papa chuckles. "He was in my last year at Parrish High before I left for Montgomery. The school thief and bully. If anything was missing, our first instinct was always to find Cecil. And his excuses for having whatever was stolen in his possession were legendary. It was quite fun getting him into the office just to hear his bizarre excuses. Then one day we decided to take a huge gamble. I taught him the rudiments of bookkeeping and put him in charge of the tuck shop. We thought giving him this responsibility and knowledge would stop him stealing from the tuck shop and anywhere else. As Headmaster, I announced his promotion at morning assembly, so everyone would know. We lavished praise on his perfect bookkeeping and his honesty. I am sure he sweated the first few weeks, as we did. But we were always there to support and guide until gradually people came to respect him. Now, I was almost sure he was stopping us to impound the Land Rover. Fortunately, I recognised him before he could do anything to tarnish his reputation with me. He has to behave now. I hope."

Papa, Sapphira and Benedict wander around the food traders. The delicious smell of food starts to permeate the whole area and waft into the car as well. I realise how hungry I am, again. All Jolene's sandwiches and knickknacks have been nibbled on throughout the journey. Ma and I remain quiet, watching the comings and goings of everyone else. Ma says the majority are professionals like us. "Always first to leave, because we have the means and the knowledge *and* we are the first targets. We will leave our mark here! Raise the level of this little place - you'll see."

I smile at Ma, ever the businesswoman; she can see a business opportunity everywhere!

Twenty minutes later Papa returns bearing gifts of grilled meat and chips and salad wrapped in bread. Delicious! As usual I finish Benedict's leftovers.

Afterwards, we sit quietly in the car, drinking hot sweet tea, hoping for the best.

Cecil returns. Eyes still downcast, and continuing to shift from one foot to another, he says the two large hotels are full so he has found us a self catering one bedroom holiday flat in a large house two streets away from the market. He has also found a place to conceal the vehicle for a weekly rent. Papa thanks him effusively and hands over the extra ration of supper. "Here you are, Cecil. If I remember correctly, it's not the first time I have shared a meal with you. Thank you and go well. I always trusted you would do well. Thank you for being here. No doubt we will bump into each other again. We *do* need to agree a weekly rental for the safekeeping of this vehicle, don't we? Will tomorrow do? Good. See you tomorrow then, Sergeant Cecil."

My head thumps the headrest in front of me as I struggle to hide my disappointment. One room! For all of us?! Even when we stay at Auntie Kathy's in Stonehouse, I have my own room. It's just a given! Now in this mess called Hamilton, I have to share with my whole family!! How can a growing man share with his sister *and* his parents!

This is unacceptable! *Unacceptable! Totally, totally so!* Darn, darn, *darn*! Hell! This is a joke, a sick, *sick* joke.

Chapter Five

"Why do we have to stay in one room? Surely there are other places? What if Cecil is revenging his school days? What if there *are* rooms in the hotel, or even a house and he is not telling us because he can get more money for it? Why can't we see for *ourselves* what good accommodation there is?"

Ma turns in her seat, grabs my arm and demands I look at her. Her look warns me of an impending volcano. But *I have to say what I feel*! Why *should* I smoulder?! I *hate* this bloody dump of a place. It's a great disillusionment and *I want out*!

Ma shakes my arm until my teeth rattle. "Listen! Do you think any of us wants to do this? Or wants to be here? You have seen the news, listened to the bulletins, seen the people pushing and shoving to get onto the boats. You have observed the traffic, heard what people said. Add all this together – what do you come up with? *Tell* me? That we will be safe in Parrish where they have burnt the university library and stolen from the cathedral? *What* is it you *don't get*, Luther? *What more* has to happen to get through to you that this is not some grand adventure we planned, a surprise for you? *Get real*! Now!" She glares at me for a moment, then continues.

"I promise you now that when we return to Parrish, you and Sapphira will be doing weekly volunteering for charities we select. Sapphira! Listen as well! *You are spoilt*! Your father and I are to blame for that. We wanted to give you everything we never had, so that you would never want for anything. *A big mistake*. Because you have never *ever* had to learn to manage and plan for something you really want. To dig deep. To wait. To work. To value!

And now, now you are unwilling or unable to face reality. Luther, you can't hide behind us anymore – there is *no more hiding*. Deal with it! The flat will be our home for however long it takes to return to Scholar's Close. It's your *Onashi* in two week's time. You still have *plenty of time* to reflect on what kind of man you are choosing to be."

I hear Ma turning back in her seat. After a few short breaths she continues on a calmer note.

"I *know* that I would wish every son of mine to stand firm and strong in times of crises, to be a *leader,* to be the *best of the bunch,* always. I *know* that *all* my children are strong beings, *leadership* potential. It's your choice to sink or swim. We are here, will always be here to support you and help you get through this as we *all* have to."

The space in the car is far too small to contain my anger, my heaving mass of emotions. I implode, sink my head down and stay that way until we reach the house. Benedict takes my hand, strokes it. I breathe deeply into the dusty evening air. *Crish! Flunking Crish! Whatever* that means!

∞

It is a sizeable room, until we bring all our stuff in. We have a huge en-suite. Ma is clapping her hands. She says she really didn't expect to have running water.

I wonder aloud why ever not, as Hamilton is part of Juxon and we've *always* had running water!

"If I had a choice, I would probably have opted to stay in a hotel. And I accept that all the best hotels are full to overflowing, and that they are probably charging an enormous rate. This, however, is so much better than I had envisaged. With this large room, we are saving money *and* we have a kitchen to cook our own meals. Much more economical this way. And we are all together, instead of maybe having to have two rooms and not being able to cook in our room. The mirror is cracked. A minor detail. As your father says, a mirror is a looking glass, not a place to have plastic surgery! The window overlooks the front porch. Yes, we have a good room. I am pleased. A prayer answered. I feel we will be safe in this flatlet and other good people will occupy the vacant flat next door. All in all, a good and promising start."

The evening light bathes the room, showing dust everywhere. No electricity at present though. Sergeant Cecil said vandals cut the electricity last night. The engineers have not yet repaired it. I'm glad we can use our wind-up torches at last, Christmas presents from long ago, played with then put away for exactly this kind of situation. A smaller flat next to ours is empty. A group of women nurses and their children share the third flat, which is bigger than ours; but then there are more of them. We all go to greet them. They tell us that they arrived here on one of the last few buses allowed to leave Queenville, early this morning. They say rebels demanded that the medical staff not treat the injured, and when they started negotiating with them to at least treat the worst cases, the rebels killed two doctors and three nurses. One of the doctors killed was the husband of one of the nurses here now.

∞

We return to our new abode, the Wiggins Headquarters, WHQ as Papa has named it. We stand in the middle of the room and hold hands as Papa says a heartfelt prayer. "Dear God, thank you so much that we have reached our destination safely. Thank you for our humble abode. Give us all the courage to face our difficulties, whatever they are, to ask for what we need and to help others less fortunate than ourselves. Keep us together in spirit if not in form and guide our leaders to respect differences and find a way for harmonious living soon. In gratitude and love, Amen.

"Cecil has done us proud" Papa remarks as we survey the three wooden single beds, a heavy old table and a full-size wardrobe. We work quickly to push two beds together for my parents, Sapphira and Benedict and the other bed for myself. Sapphira is not happy with this arrangement. I haven't even thought about it. "Why can't you and I and Benedict sleep together, Ma?"

"Because I say so! Do you want your father and Luther to sleep on that narrow, single bed?" Ma shouts as she busily damp-dusts the surfaces. I look at Sapphira, silently urging her to just accept things as they are for the moment. But she gets into a huge huff and mutinies on one of the beds. Benedict is crabby and tired and Ma is rushing to get him into bed.

"Listen, girl! I can't be a flash of enlightenment now! There are other priorities. I don't know all the answers to all your questions. I never will. And, on occasion, you too will be wrong. Sometimes one just has to accept certain things and, if this is not one of those moments for you, you'll just have to live with it, whether you sulk about it or accept it! Now please will you help me make the beds and make our new home liveable! There's a time for asking questions, relevant or not, and a time for work. Know the difference. We will find another bed tomorrow. Bear the discomfort for one night!"

Papa comes in. He starts to whisper. "I was outside and I heard everything you've just said. I know I am louder than all of you put together. We *have* to be very careful from now onwards. We just don't know who is friend or who is foe. I suggest we become the 'Whispering Wiggins'. What do you think?"

In the end, Sapphira, Papa and Ma share the two joined beds whilst Benedict and I share the single bed. I have a fleetingly guilty thought of being glad Ellie is not with us – where on earth would she be sleeping tonight? *And* Grandma Meertel?

Benedict is very restless during the night, tossing and turning and kicking and lashing out with his little arms.

∞

I wake up when Benedict starts using my arm and torso as a road for his little red Mercedes Benz. I must have slept! I *actually* slept! Wow! And

I thought I would be awake *all night*! I must be tougher than I think; than *everybody* thinks I am! Swimming... Great! I start tickling Benedict until his giggles put a smile on everyone's faces as they potter about the room. I sincerely hope we can find another bed today. Benedict can play football in his sleep with his parents!

I stretch lazily as I greet my parents. "Where's Sapphira?"

"In the bathroom. Isn't it wonderful to have our own bathroom? You know Professor Marcus, don't you? He and his wife and daughter arrived last night. They are in the smallest flat. Their bathroom is miniscule."

After a long pause, Ma speaks again. "We might have to think of having a kitty and cooking collectively. Every third day. Be good not to be doing the cooking every day."

"Is it proportionate?" I ask my mother as she snuffles around in the many plastic bags Jolene had managed to pack. She does not answer immediately.

"I mean, there's three adults eating in Professor Marcus' room, we have four and a half mouths to feed here and the nurses have four and three halves. Who is giving what so that we all give equitably?"

"My son, the accountant! An accountant with integrity! I am impressed! Very impressed. What I said yesterday has sunk into fertile ground.

Well done. Here's a piece of paper and pen – do your maths and see how much each family has to contribute. Remember, this is not set in stone. Prices are sure to rise.

Now let's have our first breakfast. Your father went out early this morning to buy some rolls and marmalade. Your father and I have decided we will listen to the news *after* breakfast. I would like breakfast to be a time of serenity and family ordinariness, yes?"

∞

When a Carton President was elected for only the second time since independence, Royce came to Juxon to cover the inauguration. We had just moved into Prestige Street. He stayed with us in our new home. Having recently bought a new 'top of the range' Panasonic shortwave radio, he gave Papa his old one, the smallest, most compact short wave radio I had ever seen then. A small Sony, only four and a half by three inches. It is this tiny radio that we tune into now. It picks up BBC World Service as clear as a bell in our room.

We listen to the eight o'clock news on Sunday morning.

"This is the BBC World Service from London. After the assassination of the Juxonese President Jameson Welter on Friday night, the President's body is now lying in

state in Queenville Cathedral, heavily guarded by the military. Although heads of states have sent messages of condolences, not one world leader has condemned the assassination nor has any government or organisation come forward to act as an intermediary between the two factions in conflict in Juxon.

Unrest is spreading in this former British colony. The main towns of Tomsdale, Chessletown and Parrish have all seen an escalation in violence, as well as looting and burning of institutions.

In Mogadishu, the capital of Somalia ..."

"No mention of Carton, so Carton is still safe. Let us ring Ellie before we go to church and then buy the bed after the service," says Ma.

Ellie tells us Grandma Meertel's cousin, Uncle Herrin, and his wife, arrived last night and are staying with them. They speak with Papa, then we all speak with Ellie again before going outdoors.

"These older folk! Just like my mother, they too refused to go. All their children are now in Ushquel. Last night Uncle Herrin was coshed over the head as he returned from his friend's house in Tomsdale. He thought no harm would come to him, being such a stalwart Carton supporter. So now he is angry and upset about the whole debacle!"

"Frederick, I am worried Ellie is with all these old folks."

"And I am so grateful she has more people around her. Yes, Uncle Herrin can be rather miserable much of the time, but Ellie will probably be spending more time with my mother and Auntie Annie. Both are young at heart and love adventure. She'll be fine. Our daughter is a bright shining light, remember that." Ma cries twice a day, after each phone call.

We attend the nine o'clock service at the cathedral. I spend more time scanning the congregation than listening to the bishop. Then I see Father David, our Parrish Cathedral priest, sitting on the side of the altar. He is here as well? Was he forced to flee or did he come here because some of his congregation is here? How did I not spot him before? I nudge Ma and point my head towards Father David – she nods and smiles. She saw him earlier? I don't feel so guilty now about missing most of the sermon – *everybody* else seems to be looking for someone familiar!

∞

After the service, we hang around outside the main cathedral door, hoping to see and chat to familiar faces. Parrish Cathedral faces that we see on a weekly basis, at the very least. We meet with Father David.

"Father David! I was not expecting to see you here, although now it does not seem so surprising after all. When did you arrive?"

Ma is, as usual, looking magnificent in her snugly fitting designer floral outfit, the front a high neck, showing no 'lungs' - Sapphira's current reference to breasts - to uphold pious decorum. Ma calls it one of her 'cathedral' outfits. It does not prevent Father David's eyes searching around that area, though. He abandons his search with a sigh when he notices me watching him. Father David is young and unmarried, and many young women in the congregation have shown a fevered keenness to fill the vacant position of wife. Ma loves teasing him about his reluctance to choose one amongst the many. "Sampling the wares takes time, Angelina Wiggins," is his usual answer.

"Angelina Wiggins! Glad to see you safe and sound. Where's the illustrious Dr. Wiggins? All the family here? Yes, I see Frederick. Ellie? Where's young Ellie?"

"Long story, Father David. Tell us about you first, then come to tea and we'll tell you our story. When did you leave? When did you arrive?"

"Hooligans, that's the only way I can describe the rabble that entered the cathedral! They burst into a special service on Saturday. Fortunately the cathedral was less than a quarter full. There had been trouble around the cathedral all afternoon, but the police had managed to move these hooligans to another area. Jolene and Jacob were there. They told me you had just phoned them to say you had arrived here.

Anyway, these thugs were high on drugs and drink when they returned and demanded money and booze. They were not Carton protesters; they were simply louts taking advantage of the crisis. I endeavoured to reason with them, to no avail. Then, out of sheer malice, they just set my church, our cathedral, on fire. Probably hoping it would be seen as Cartons protesting.

Everybody escaped by the rear door. The smoke then attracted the Carton protesters who decided this cathedral was only used by the Frees, so they started destroying the pews and the font, and beating me with whatever they could lay their hands on. They were bent on killing me as a Frees' priest. With the help of the police, I managed to get to my car before they could inflict mortal damage and fled here. I arrived here at midnight. Fortunately Bishop McGregor is a very good friend of mine, so I am staying here for a while. Goodness knows what Bishop Thomas will be feeling about our cathedral. Then again, how fortunate that he and his family were invited to Westminster Abbey the week before. At least he is safe there."

We chat for a little while longer before he sees another member of the Parrish Cathedral congregation. After chatting with a few more people and exchanging addresses, we leave to buy a bed at an even cheaper price than we would have paid in Parrish, according to Ma.

Leaving Ma, Sapphira and Benedict chatting to a group of women, Papa and I amble around the market area, the hub of Hamilton, open seven days a week, unlike Parrish which closes for Sundays. For a few brief moments it seems just like when we are strolling around the market near our home in Singapore. When life feels so carefree and sunny and predictable and safe. Almost holiday mood.

Chapter Six

We have been here for less than twenty four hours now. The newness of it all is still tingling and scary. It's Juxon, but not quite. They have a shopping mall with all the familiar shops. I see the same shops along the road, the same people, and yet it is not the same.

We Juxonese love chatting, greeting everyone we meet, spending a few minutes catching up on news. Nobody is laughing now; the smiles are brief and disappear after the initial greeting. Anxiety hangs in the air like the smoke after a long, major firework display. People's eyes dart furtively, unlike the usual relaxed 'who else do I see on this beautiful Sunday morning?'

As we chat with yet another colleague of my father's, four truck-loads of soldiers arrive, plus two jeeps. They seem to be installing themselves in the huge Civic Centre. They are the only ones laughing and joking as they carry their bags and boxes of supplies into the building. Lots of ammunition; boxes and boxes of it. Conversations stop as we watch them unload.

"Papa, why are they not going to the barracks at the border? Why right here in town? The Civic Centre is on the way to Tomsdale. Are the soldiers at the barracks preventing Belling people coming over the border, and the Civic Centre troops protecting us from attacks from the Tomsdale side?"

"Just a precaution, son. A show of force can be advantageous at times - stop those marauding gangs in their tracks. I see the cinema is still going strong. We might take a look and see what is playing there tomorrow. Give ourselves a treat. What do you think?"

I heave a sigh of relief. Easy explanation. I smile and nod as we wander about, bumping into many of my parent's friends and colleagues. Many are from Tomsdale, Chessletown and Queenville, a few from Parrish. It is like a constant reunion: brief outbursts of joy, back slapping, hands crossed over the heart saying '*Kelsho*' and then quickly descending into their stories of horror and flight. All the collective titbits of news are traded around, much is speculated, even more is theorised; after all, they *are* the country's intellectuals.

Someone advises us to break into smaller groups so as not to attract attention. The stories all begin to sound the same, like the news bulletins. I search and search for someone I know. Anybody! No one. I see no one I know. Where have they all gone? Parrish is burning; how did people manage to get to Ushquel, or abroad? I thought leaving at seven thirty on a Saturday morning had been pretty early.

Another thing keeps bothering me. If the President was killed at ten o'clock, surely Ma and Papa were still awake? Sapphira and I went to bed at nine o'clock so that 'we can have some time together, remembering,' Ma said. *What were they doing?* We had no visitors. The party was to be on Saturday evening. Hmmmm, puzzling.

∞

I half listen to some of the conversations. People had headed to the airports or Ushquel border as soon as they heard about the assassination. So, why didn't these people leave? Why didn't anybody ring us? Whenever something happens, the phone is usually red hot with people phoning and discussing motives and betting on outcomes. Why not Friday night?

Did *none* of us hear the phone ringing? *Impossible!* Did they switch off the phones? They *must* have done, someone would surely have phoned Papa! If we had left on Friday night we would have been in Singapore by now. Surely!

Well, as Ma, says, we're here now, so work from *this*, not from 'should have'.

∞

I keep my eyes peeled. I am absolutely certain I am due for a surprise *any* moment now! Nobody. Soon it is lunch time and we return to WHQ. I have seen nobody of my age that I know. I spend the afternoon texting my friends. Two replies. Disappointing. Even my best friend Dexter hasn't texted me back, just two of my *Onashi* group. Where have they all disappeared to?

"What the matter, Luther?"

"Nothing Ma."

"Let's add to our ground rules. If something is bothering us, we need to find a way of dealing with it as soon as possible. Living in such a small space we are going to get on each other's nerves. Fact. Also, the situation might get worse before it gets better. We need to help each other deal with these issues, rather than bottle it up and explode at an inappropriate time or place. Agreed? *Right*! Now, Luther, what's up?"

"Dexter hasn't texted me since I saw him at school. Nobody has texted me and I have just texted them, except Colby and Baron from my *Onashi* group. Both of them are in Ushquel. Where have they all gone, Ma?"

"Well, Dexter's family has probably arrived in Perth, Australia by now. I told you Caroline is in Singapore. Graham's family's on their way to an uncle in Norway, both Theo and Kennedy's families have gone to their holiday homes in Bali and the Proctors, Baileys and Denningtons have all flown to London. Anybody else, I think, is waiting at the Ushqueli border with flat batteries in their mobile phones. So, wait a while and check again tonight or tomorrow."

∞

It is Monday evening. We have been here for two days now. More and more people are arriving. We're developing a routine. Papa, Benedict and I fetch the warm big flat rolls for breakfast. We listen to the eight o'clock news on the BBC World Service followed by the eight thirty news on QV radio. We call Ellie. Ma cries. My parents call friends and family, especially those they have not been able to contact yet. Many are sleeping in their cars. In their cars! *Phew*! At least I have a bed of my own and we have a bathroom and kitchenette. Where do they go if they want to go to the toilet? The solid matter toilet?

Ma's, and sometimes Papa's tears let us know someone dear has died or been badly injured. We hold hands around the small kitchenette table and give thanks for our protection and pray for safety and sanity for Juxon.

We go to the shopping mall, the main gathering place. Nobody is buying anything, apart from small amounts of food. With the banks still closed, every cent is being turned over and over again. McDonalds was among the first shops to close; nobody wants to splash out, not even on their cheap deals. Or maybe the rumour is true; as a Free the manager feared for his life and fled with his family to the seaport of St Giles in Belling? Who can blame him?

Ma says to use our mobile phones for as long as possible because nobody will be sending out bills just yet. The damaged power lines were repaired on Monday evening so we have electricity again. We also have a curfew at ten o'clock now. Police and the army have orders to shoot on sight anyone or anything that moves after ten o'clock. Boy! Are they strict! At night we hear many gun shots and screams within the first five minutes after the ten o'clock deadline. We Juxonese are learning fast to be less flexible about a curfew – ten o'clock means ten o'clock - not a minute afterwards! Ma has made Papa promise to be home by a quarter to ten.

∞

Ma's suggestion that we should have a rota with the other two families does not work out – the nurses say they prefer to cook for their children, as they know what they like. Ma hates cooking, so she has made a rota for the four of us to take turns to cook. I love it when I manage to budget a main meal *and* a dessert for my turn! I lap up all the praise from Ma. Sapphira is much more suspicious, feeling Ma is grooming the two of us to take over this role.

Sapphira and I usually take Benedict for a walk to Hamilton's periphery along the road to Tomsdale. The more people I see moving towards Hamilton, the more scared I feel. I feel that they are acting like magnets, drawing the Carton protestors towards Hamilton and my family.

Many more people are travelling on foot. There is a deeper sense of urgency now. Cases and clothes and other belongings are strewn along the roadside whenever people find it too heavy to carry all the things they thought necessary when they left home. We move slowly and watch others picking through these items and taking whatever they feel they need.

We observe an old man bent double carrying a table on his back from goodness knows where. He pauses often, comes out from under the table, stretches for a while, then goes back under the table for a few more yards. The table is quite distinctive. It has a broad shiny black stripe running the entire length of the table. I laugh when I describe this spectacle during our after-dinner discussion time.

After smiling at my rather exaggerated depiction, Papa says: "Purely as a matter for discussion, for stretching your mind: Luther, what if this table becomes an extremely valuable asset to him here in Hamilton? What if he has this conviction, and he is doing everything to get himself and his table here to Hamilton? Think of all the different uses the table may have for this man, especially if this is all he thinks he has as a valuable asset." I never thought of it that way; it just seemed such an unwanted burden to me, at a time when others are jettisoning their overload. I wonder if I will ever see the man or his table again.

∞

Despite what Ma said about keeping a low profile, people instinctively see Papa as a learned man. Must be the way he holds himself: tall and dignified. And Ma's eye catching designer clothing is a huge attraction as well. I speak about it after supper.

"It's the way both of you move."

"How *do* your father and I move?"

"Like you are walking in your boutiques; like when Papa walks about the school. Like you *own* that space. But you've said repeatedly that, if anything stands out, it is targeted. I thought we need to keep a *low* profile, not announce our whereabouts!"

Ma points a finger at me: "We also need to talk about a fourteen year old boy, a man-child, nearly six foot tall, who *struts* around with a *distinctive swagger*, as if to say 'here I am, girls, look at me'. Is that what we're talking about?"

"I don't!"

"Yes you do!"

"Ma, I *don't*!"

"Luther, come on now, be honest ___"

Papa interrupts. "Let's not argue about whether you 'walk with attitude' or not; I'd rather discuss ways and means of not drawing attention to ourselves, especially as muggings and shootings have increased here by a thousand percent in the three days we have been here. What do you suggest, Luther?"

I loll a while in the delicious knowledge that they *have* noticed! My family has noticed my stroll, my strut! Then others must be noticing it as well....

"Well, we should practice walking like the downtrodden, the scared, the poor. We see them every day. They walk slowly, eyes to the ground, as if they do not want to be noticed. They pass the checkpoint into town and the soldiers as if they are shadows. Maybe we should do this as well."

"So! Show us. Tell us how to walk, how to change our demeanour, to walk more humbly, with less or very little intention."

Each one has a chance to practise. All this is done in whispers. We end up rolling about in silent laughter, tears streaming down our cheeks. Ma is by far the best. She could have been an actress any day! So we follow her movements whilst bumping into each other in the confines of our minute space. Head down, shoulders rounded, stooped, walking slowly, shuffling more than walking. Practise, practise, practise!

∞

It is Wednesday, day four of our stay in Hamilton. I have still not heard from Dexter or anybody else. I am bored! Bored and anxious. Things are 'hotting up'. In our household, our pocket money has been stopped. Sapphira and I spend hours afterwards whingeing and grumbling about it, bonding at last on a single issue. We *know* our parents cannot withdraw any money and we have to be careful, but the pocket money was a small symbol of our independence. *That's* what we are surrendering: our independence.

In contrast, Benedict is as happy as a lark with his new playmates in the house. The younger ones call him Bendy. They play in the small yard and there is much laughter and shouting. I watch them at play. They seem to change rules a thousand times, every time to the changer's advantage. Sometimes they fight; most of the time they simply accept the changes and play again. *Sooo* flexible. Can't be reality, *not that*, surely? When do they learn that rules can restrict you, can stop you from doing what you want? On the other hand, Sapphira has *never* let a rule stop her from doing anything she sees as advantageous to her. Why, when I break rules, do I always get caught? Is it as Papa says, that I don't weigh up the end result beforehand, that I fire first, then aim? Sooo much to learn, sooo little time!

WHQ is too small to contain my restless, unhappy self, so I spend ages dawdling in the market or in the town centre, or the mall, looking for familiar faces. I spend a lot of time at the only Internet café. Just waiting. Waiting for one of six computers. Papa has decreased my time there to only *one* hour a day. That's not enough at all! The games only start to warm up after half an hour! I complain like mad. Ma says we have to all tighten our belts. Everything is rapidly becoming more and more expensive. I *know* that, darn it! I know the money situation, but this is just another relentless appropriation of my independence! So many changes and I am expected to kowtow to all of them, *immediately*! That's what slaves do! Not an independently thinking young man! How on earth do I maintain a sliver of independence during this crisis? I'm having multiple crises within this crisis. Huh!

∞

I can't even pick a fight with Sapphira because she has found a classmate. Funny that, she could never abide this girl Savannah before, never *ever* acknowledged her, yet *now* they can't stop visiting and talking with each other. Savannah comes to our flat, stays for ages. 'Sapph and Sav' Ugh! Makes me want to *puke*! All over them. *Ugh*! Every time I ask her something she giggles! How can Sapphira stand that?! She must be desperate! Boy, am I desperate for some boy-bonding as well!

∞

Another day passes before I eventually see three boys from my class, two of whom attended my *Onashi* preparation class as well. I used to find them boring guys, not my type. Now, on day four and a half of our stay in Hamilton, we are greeting each other like long lost brothers! Suddenly Chandler and I have a connection we'd never had before.

"When did you get here?"

"Five days ago. You?"

"Last night."

"*Only last* night? Where were you all since the assassination?"

"Well, firstly to Queenville airport. Left the house at eleven o'clock on Friday night. Booked flights, everything. At the check-in desk we discovered my father's passport had expired a week before. Long story short, my parents became rather hysterical and threatening, to put it mildly, so they arrested both my parents. Us kids stayed at the airport and watched everybody leave. We were going to go to Perth. Man! We were so sooo angry!"

"You stayed at the airport for five days? Hell!"

"No, three days. Five kids! We had nowhere else to go! They took pity on my five year old twin sisters. Then Ma was released first, after two days. She was a *mess*, I tell you! Then, when my father was released hours later, they had *another* fracas at the airport because no more flights were leaving that night; they wouldn't transfer us *and* wouldn't give us our money back! Boy! Did the police beat up my father! You should see his back and legs and arms. Covered in bruises. So, anyway, we went back to our car we had abandoned in the airport car park and drove to Tomsdale."

"No more flights? Awesome! Who had you booked with?"

"British Airways. BA. Bugger All. Actually, to be fair, no other flights were allowed to land either. Only those taking the *marties* away, back to their countries."

"You spent two days in Tomsdale?"

"Yes. The car broke down just as we got into Tomsdale. I tell you! Never drive anywhere with a hysterical woman! We kids were doing OK at the airport, but *as soon as* we left, seven of us stuck in a car, my mother made us nervous wrecks! Then the car had to break down as well."

"Talk about bad luck."

"Hmmm."

"Then what? Why all that time in Tomsdale?"

"My father found this mechanic, exclusive to Volvo and other deluxe cars. He had about seven cars there and everybody wanting their car the day before. So we *just had to wait*. Our nerves were ratted! Every day we saw streams of cars heading towards Hamilton. For those two days and nights we heard gunfire, screaming, more gunfire. Hell! It was awful!"

"Where did you stay?"

"We stayed with the garage owner; the mechanic and his family. His garage is called Dennis Deluxe, so we called him Mr. Deluxe. Weird man with one grey and one brown eye. I could never decide which one to look at. He was a huge bear of a man; an absolute softie in the house, but in the garage he worked like one possessed!

We stayed in their cellar. My mother and older sister Janine were going mental, absolutely mental! My elder brother Galen and I helped out in the garage, just to get away. My father was nursing his bruises and couldn't be bothered. Imagine having traumatised parents before we even started out. And my father a psychiatrist!

Galen is an adrenaline junkie, so it was good hanging out with him. He made life bearable. At sixteen, he's our unofficial head of family now; our parents are too messed up to do anything."

"Isn't your mother a surgeon? Is she helping out at the local hospital? We have nurses staying in the flat next to us. From Queenville. They got jobs straight away at Hamilton General Infirmary."

"At the moment, my mother says she needs to recover from her airport experiences, then maybe she can help others."

What a story! We all then talk about our leaving Scholars Close or Parrish, striving to outdo each other in the drama of our unexpected departures.

My story pales into insignificance beside Chandler's. I give it a go though, embroidering tension and grist into it. It seems we all wanted to head off abroad or to Ushquel; Hamilton being such an inferior alternative. I listen to all the excuses we make to justify our coming to this bucolic, 'nothing' kind of town. Really backward – *one single* Internet Café here! What are we going to do?!

"Did you see what they are doing to the cinema? Right now? They are removing all the seats in this town's *only* cinema to prepare for masses of families still making their way here. So, no movies either! Man! Is Hamilton *truly* a part of Juxon? There is *nothing* here!"

We groan and bemoan our boring downgrading for as long as we can, each saying what he would be doing had he been in Parrish or abroad right now. *Yes!* Sometimes catharsis is good for the soul! It seems absolutely certain we are going to be extremely bored here, waiting and waiting through boring days to return to civilisation! At least there is no school. Then again, that could make our computer-less days go slightly less slow!

"Hey Sidney! What's happening with your *Onashi*? We're supposed to have it in nine days' time!"

He shrugs. "Been delayed until further notice. Yours?"

"We will be having a little ceremony. Father David is asking around for more boys. Shall I tell him about you? Where are you staying? I tell you, that priest fancies my mother something rotten! All those single young women throwing themselves at him and he is after *my* Ma. Imagine! Any excuse to visit us. He knows I know. Did your parents bring your bauble for your *Onashi*? Mine's a Tiger's eye. Made by one of my mother's designer friends. Cool, eh?"

"Wow! That *is* virtuoso!" Sidney's exclamations of awe at my designer *Onashi* stone make it irresistible to embellish, just a little.

"Uhuh! Specially imported stone. It's going to feel *sooo* good against my skin. Even now I can feel it moving against my chest when I walk. Makes me feel *really cool*! Am I going to be the only new man amongst you lot? Respect man, respect!"

Chapter Seven

Day six and I am left to baby-sit a sleeping Benedict. I lie on my bed, fingering my Tiger's eye. Harry Potter is smiling down at me from the wall; my space. I reminisce about my speedily organised *Onashi* ceremony, squeezed into a very busy day for Father David, and within minutes of returning home after connecting with Chandler and the other guys. Less than an hour, yet utterly life changing. What a wonderful ceremony my *Onashi* turned out to be.

Eventually. Because, when I zipped up my brand new specially tailor-made pair of trousers, my world collapsed. It can't be! It is impossible! Not now! In my finest moment! My trousers hovered inches above my ankles! This growth spurt Ma was always saying I was going to have, arrived and I hadn't even noticed it! Now, on this very special day, my new pair of trousers was too short! I can feel my eyes welling up, even now. I wanted to weep with shame. Why, at this special moment! My finest moment so far in my life and my trousers are inches above my ankles!

"MA! My trousers! They're too short! *Ma!* Above my ankles! I can't wear them. I *can't*!"

"Well, I don't have time to take the hem down now. We have ten minutes before the ceremony. Wear your clean pair of jeans. It's not the trousers that make you a man. Today, you will be welcomed into the men's' world. With or without a pair of trousers, you are still a man. Whatever you wear, wear it with the dignity that befits this occasion, Luther."

I continue to whinge. "This was going to be so perfect! You would never have allowed me to wear these trousers in Parrish. *Never*! It should have been perfect! Now this! What else is going to go wrong?!"

Papa interrupts my tirade of self-pity. "Stop that 'shoulding' Luther! It has taken so much effort to organise this ceremony. We've scraped money together to have this small celebration sooner than planned. For whatever reason, no other parent was able to continue with their son's *Onashi*. This *Onashi* is for *you* alone; an absolute exception.

Your short trousers are your first hurdle, and you let it affect you *this* much! None of us knows how many more hurdles and obstructions we face. We all need to learn how to react to these hurdles in a *positive* way. Find a way around it or through it or over it. Perhaps you might consider being grateful that you have *three* other pairs of trousers to choose from, two of them freshly ironed. There are people out there in *rags*."

I feel ashamed at my outburst. A reality check. Papa always has a way of making me see things from a more positive angle. Practise, practise, practise.

I still refuse to wear the trousers, though; there are limits! And I *know* Ma would *never* have let me out of our home in Parrish with trousers as short as that. Funny how quickly Ma has changed. To *even* think I could wear these trousers, even though they are brand new *and* tailor made. *Huh*! Standards are slipping. Mine aren't though!

Or, perhaps I am taking too long to adapt to new circumstances.

Am I? Do I? Always? Usually?

In the end, I forget that I am wearing my clean pair of black Levi jeans. This ceremony is e*specially* for me. We have a private celebration in a small side chapel. My family and Father David. Friends of my parents who had been invited chose instead to offer support and discuss the new development of clandestine arrests of their colleagues last night. Phew! Scary, very scary indeed. Is Papa an even bigger target than we think?

Ma has filled the chapel with candles and draped one of her floral dresses as a cloth. I can still feel shivers going up and down my spine. I jiggle my toes to stop the shivers. Father David speaks first.

"We are gathered here to continue our tradition of witnessing the rites of passage from boyhood to manhood. Because we are in unconventional circumstances we are going to approach this *Onashi* ceremony unconventionally. Nevertheless, the focal point remains the same: witnessing the ritual passing of boyhood to attain manhood.

The candles represent the fire. Fire is hot; fire is dangerous and can kill when not contained. It is rather apt that we speak of this now, because you are witnessing, day by day, fires that are out of control. These fires are causing so much damage, physically, culturally, emotionally, mentally and spiritually. If these men are true Juxonese, they will all have passed through the preparation for this ceremony. Luther, you know that the classes you attended taught you how to manage those fires without causing destruction to anyone, least to yourself. The classes informed you of your connection with God. And yes, there are only six evenings in total for you to learn all this knowledge and more. You have not had the guidance of the last two weeks. However, this is not the end! This is simply another part of your journey. A special trip that has been designed uniquely for boys."

Father David pauses for a while, looks at all of us, eyes Sapphira, then continues. "Girls get to see their magnificence and their roles as well, so this is not a time when we will feel superior because we have a recognised ceremony. Believe you me, girls have constant teachings from birth on how to manage us men folk. They need it!

We have merely developed different roles. And now that this heartlessness is upon us, we may already have had to change roles. You may have witnessed some things women have to endure *and do* on a daily basis. You too may have had to do all the work womenfolk do in order for you and your family to survive. I don't know what the future holds for you, Luther. We may all see our skills in cooking, cleaning, dress designing, rearing babies flourish! Remember this: bear your burdens lightly, knowing that they are always there to teach you something.

Do not ask to have your load lightened, to have your troubles disappear! NO! Ask rather that you may be given the courage to face whatever stones and rocks of trouble are flung at you.

May you be man enough to ask for help, and may that be sooner rather than later.

May you stay connected to the Divine force and may you always be grateful for whatever you have and are given.

You have many resources now; build on them. Know that these resources have always been there; you were simply unaware sometimes of how to apply them, to use them. It may take a lifetime of practice."

Allows this to sink in before he continues. "Luther, always strive to be resourceful rather than resourceless. Remember that you have all the resources you will ever need. I say again: they have always been there. Over the years you have found these resources worthy, worthwhile and useful. *You* created them in the first place! All you have to do from now onwards is to *remember* that you have these resources and to choose the appropriate one. Of course, sometimes you may need more than one; something I am sure you have discovered already."

He smiles at me as he says this, then Papa continues.

"Above all else, Luther, find and hold onto that deep, enduring, unconditional love your mother and I are always showing you. Know that whatever we do or don't do, we are always worthy of love and prosperity, even and *especially* when it comes in unexpected forms."

I feel as if an electric current is running through me, making every cell come alive and tingling. I'm still moving my toes to stop myself jiggling about. It's like ants running through my veins, arteries and capillaries!

Then Father David speaks again. "And as your father puts your necklace on you, think of it as a symbol of the responsibilities of a man. Of course this does not mean you will be in competition with your father or mature men. You still have *much* to learn.

What I want to really stress is that you are very much at the first step of manhood, learning and practising, observing, discerning the good from the bad, infusing the good into every cell of your body, listening to people's motives and values and seeing them from their point of view, so as not to judge them. We all have reasons for doing things, good and bad. It may not always be for the reasons we think are correct. It may be that we are using the right resources at the wrong time. It may be that we have forgotten that we have these resources; we all become forgetful sometimes! Now, how can we judge another's behaviour unless we can walk a mile in that person's shoes?"

The talking continues, Papa alternating with Father David. My mind wanders. My Tiger's eye feels cold to the touch. It feels wonderfully weighty; I will always know it is there. Ma has tears in her eyes and a wide smile when we look at each other. Father David then blesses the necklace and me as one. This necklace is for life. I am swept away by the significance and power of the occasion, short trousers long forgotten. And I *can* feel the necklace becoming part of me. I am a tiger! My necklace is one huge Tiger's eye. It is exactly the colour of my eyes! Bingo! A real tiger! Swim.

Chapter Eight

Day six and life becomes increasingly scary as well as rather surreal. Little incidents here and there are on the increase. A small fight here; a loud disagreement there; someone stealing from the market trader. The people from Hamilton, now in the minority, are blaming all the incomers for the trouble.

People are hanging around in groups, watching and, mostly, silent. There's another scuffle here, another robbery there, stealing from stores, meaningless attacks on the elderly, the young, women; anybody and everybody is a target. Two more of Papa's group have been arrested; that's six in total now. I am so scared for Papa; I wish he would just stay indoors; but then, they can arrest him there as well. Every trip to the police station to discover friends' whereabouts is to no avail. At night, Papa and Ma's whisperings are too low for me to catch and I fall asleep while struggling to stay awake.

Still more and more people arrive; I mean hundreds and *thousands* more people. The cars are a steady, constant stream. They keep arriving all day. The town is jam-packed with vehicles. No more buses are connecting the towns, not even mini buses or taxis.

A few journalists pass through. I keep looking out for Royce, but his daily calls to Papa shows he is in the thick of it in Queenville. Ma is always urging him to come to Hamilton.

The new arrivals fill the market square and then fill their days just standing around. They look haggard and travel weary; they seem lost and without direction, until Sergeant Cecil and his team force them to leave the square to I don't know where. The army is still keeping a low profile here, allowing the police force to handle things. Must be in 'back-up' mode at the moment.

In the mornings when we go to buy the bread, our porch is filled with people and their few belongings. We have to tread warily over sleeping children and goats and chickens.

∞

During our whispered meetings in our room, Papa warns us again and again that we don't know who is friend or foe anymore. He reminds us to politely greet and walk away from strangers. "We know there is no physical difference between Liberal Frees and Conservative Cartons, no specific way of dressing. We know that the difference is a belief system. Evidence continues to be gathered about people betraying others to the authorities for a huge reward; those whom they don't like or are suspicious of, or whatever. Ultimately, no reason is actually necessary, is it? So, although there is nothing much one can do when someone has a grievance against you, it is better that such a seed is not sown in the first place. And, to be honest, I don't know what more to do that we are not already doing now. Apart from the people we know, I suppose dozens more have been arrested and secreted somewhere. I pray for courage to face whatever comes after the arrest and I want you all to be strong and resilient, so that I don't have to worry about you not coping here. And you all *will* cope, won't you? Good."

We continue to visit the people we know all day long. There is nothing much else to do. Everybody is on tenterhooks and the smallest thing brings about a massive overreaction at times. At other times a huge issue, such as a killing, will cause people to walk away, numb and silent. An itchy, edgy kind of silence.

Papa and I visit and Ma and Sapphira and Benedict visit. We are checking to see any newcomers we may know and get the news they bring.

The gatherings in the evening are growing larger and larger. Papa and the other men suggest breaking up and meeting in smaller numbers so they don't attract unwelcome attention.

The newcomers and the BBC World Service news at six o'clock every evening inform us how bad the situation is becoming.

"...... Queenville remains a battle ground as the army tries to bring order. Small pockets of fighters are creating diversions. A number of buildings have been damaged with homemade incendiary devices.

The Juxon-Shenroth border in the north is heavily policed by the Juxonese army to prevent the Conservative Cartons pouring back from Shenroth where they fled over four years ago, before the last election. The Shenrothi government is known to be sympathetic to their cause and from Shenroth the Cartons have amassed other outside help. They are heavily armed and determined to kill all those who pushed them out years ago.

Elsewhere, the Cartons are killing everyone who does not support their cause, including the intellectual and professional Cartons whom they accuse of persuading the people not to kill the Liberal Frees ..."

It is all becoming so confusing for me. I don't understand who is killing who anymore; I don't think anybody does. Papa says this confusion is part of the game because confusion increases fear and distrust. Yet the Frees too are arming themselves and there are increasing reports of them fighting the Cartons supporters with all kinds of the latest weaponry. I am scared, really scared now. Who is the army supporting? Is it a three for all having a free for all? I don't want to fight – I would prefer to talk!

When are the *marties* coming to help us? Surely they could make more effort to get here and help us?

∞

Day by day we hear of Papa and Ma's friends who have been killed or injured. Ma seems to be constantly crying. Those few friends who have been released from police custody are a mess, physically and mentally. They tell of being tortured into giving names of Free perpetrators, leaders and those with influence. I pray Papa's name *never* comes up! Both parents continually warn Sapphira and me to keep a very, *very* low profile. We are targeted by both sides.

I make huge efforts not to show how scared I really am. What do I do with Sapphira and Benedict should Ma and Papa be killed or tortured into a blubbery mess? Will Sapphira listen to me? Can we really look after three year old Benedict? I break out in a cold sweat every time I think about it.

I seem to be doing a lot of praying these days, begging prayers. Please, *please*-keep-all –of-us-safe-and-together-please prayers. 'Swim' prayers, whilst I feel myself sinking into I don't know what. I should be more street-wise! Too much school education and far too little *real world* experience. Pathetic. I am utterly resourceless when it comes to surviving on instinct. I think Sapphira is right when she says instinct is behaviours learnt until they become second nature. Is that what criminals do?

On the other hand, I must admit that I do like that feeling of excitement, of unexpected expectation, of a touch of danger – so long as someone is with me. I see other boys walking alone and I wonder what it would be like to walk the dusty streets of Hamilton on my own, touching shoulders with the military stationed here.

We see more and more military arriving. Sapphira says it makes her feel more secure; Papa's friends think their increase in numbers mean they are preparing for trouble.

∞

Saturday morning. We've been here a week now. Ma and I are at a market stall, buying some pasta and tomato puree and powdered milk. Ma and other buyers' voices rise in anger.

"Two days ago this pasta cost two and a half Kutek. And that was bad enough. Now you've increased it to five! In two days! Scandalous! How do you sleep at night?"

"Like a worried man, Madam, a *very* worried man. Have you seen any lorries enter Hamilton in the past few days? No food supplies are coming this way. Soon there will be nothing. So, pay for it now because soon you won't need your money, because there will be nothing to buy!"

It is my turn to cook tonight. While Ma is paying for these purchases and reminiscing to me in a quiet undertone how she used to buy food by the trolley-load before, I watch a young man slow down his 125cc motorbike. He parks the bike right next to me. A beauty. Exactly what I had asked for my eighteenth birthday. A Honda 125cc. Royal metallic blue.

A soldier with two silver stars, wearing large mirror sunglasses and a huge grin, swaggers up to the young man, inches from me, with Ma slightly behind me.

"Hey Brother! I need your bike. For *official* reasons, you understand?"

Silence descends. In that very instant everything stops, even my heart, I think. I feel Ma's breath on my shoulder.

The young man looks at the soldier. The soldier unclips his holster, removes his pistol from the holster, languidly touching and holding his pistol, caressing the short barrel, swirling it around his right hand, palming it between hands. All the while he has this grin on his face. I smell the earthiness of his perspiration. There is something rather manly about his sweat. As if he has earned it, is worthy of it. Time stands still while we all wait and watch.

A jeep screeches to a halt. Dust settles. The jeep is filled with soldiers wearing their own brands of fake designer sunglasses. Smoking cigarettes.

"Hey! Master Bato! Need assistance?"

"Nooo. Just negotiating a fair deal here. You go on. I'll catch up with you in a minute on my new Honda 125."

"125! Surely there's got to be a bull of a bike around here to match your size, what?"

"Hey! This one's for our country, man, not for me! If it was for my personal use, I wouldn't be seen dead on this baby bike."

They scoot off with more laughs and suggestions. I don't quite get what they're saying. Master Bato continues to smile at the young man, mesmerising the young man and myself by caressing and playing with the pistol, aiming it at his feet, at a bird, then back to moving it from hand to hand.

"Come on! Come on now, young man! See how busy we are? I am *certain* I need this bike more than you do! I am from Queenville and we have *proper* roads there, not these single lanes you call roads! I *need* to get around *faster* than you do to *protect* all of you standing here now looking at me. You are *helping* me in my work." He casually points his gun at the young man. "Now, do you have *anything* to say *against* this?"

Another long silence. The silent young man is still staring at the soldier, growing paler and paler, still mesmerised by his hands on the gun. "No? Oh, so thank you, *thank you* for helping the military in their work. Will send you the necessary paperwork." He blows the length of the barrel then puts his gun back in its holster, gets on the bike and with a cheery wave throttles away, leaving a cloud of dust for us to inhale.

Still nobody moves. Hmmm, that was close, *very* close. And quite exciting. My adrenaline is still pumping – it could have gone either way! It could have ended up with me being all blown to bits, severely injured!

I'm all shaky as I say this to Ma.

"Why are you getting all worked up about things that did *not* happen? Letting your imagination run away with you? See Luther, sometimes we are very lucky. Yes! As you say, that could have turned out much worse, and guess what, *it didn't*. So let's just concentrate on the positive, shall we? The young man lost his motorbike, *not his life*. And yes, had he been able to sell the bike, he would have had sufficient money to live from it for a little while. It didn't happen that way and now he has to look for alternative ways of buying food. He is safe, *unhurt*! I want you to always to be able to look at the realistic side, not what might have happened, or what should have happened, because it didn't, did it now, Luther? You need to start thinking on your feet, young man!"

I nod and as we walk towards WHQ, adrenaline still coursing through my veins. My arm touches Ma's. It is cold and shivery and dripping with sweat! *Huh!*

∞

How would I have reacted if it was my bike? I know the bike owner was older than me, but that doesn't matter when one has to deal with the same issue, does it? I *did* like the soldier's total self confidence, his swaggering, as if he was merely playing a game, even though I feel it was wrong of him to have taken the bike. But, if you are afraid, bullies pick on you. The law of the playground. If I swagger, they will think I am a confident chap..... And like Ma, I won't show fear.

Swimming. I'm *ready* to swim! Oops! Not allowed to swagger; have to keep a low profile... Think again. Plan once more.

I would let the soldier have the bike, before he loses face and feels he *has to* shoot me. It's about losing face; I don't think it is about the bike at all. I pray that I never have to lose face with all the public staring at me. Never.

Chapter Nine

During our evening whispered meeting Papa demands yet again that Ma wears something much more humble. He says he is afraid that all her dresses are so flamboyant; she stands out a mile! Hostilities are increasing and he wants us all to be safe, to lessen the odds. He feels she continues to attract attention, and the last thing we want is to attract attention, isn't it?

Ma is outraged! "But Frederick, this is who I am! This is my *identity*! These are my *least* colourful dresses! You *know* this! I chose them *specifically* because they are so much less eye catching. You mean I have to dress down *even further*? Become a *nobody*! Become like the rest of these poor displaced people, become a poor villager in everyone's eyes? The *me* will die. I know, I know, *I know* that it makes perfect sense. I am just not quite ready to do that yet."

"Angelina, Angel, surely it must make good business sense to you to adapt according to the circumstances? So, as one of Juxon's best businesswomen, isn't *now* a good time to adapt to these vital changes? We are constantly saying we have to keep a low profile, and yet my exceptionally intelligent wife is having so much difficulty letting go of her designer wardrobe in order to keep us all safe? Angelina, what dire incident *has* to happen before you can do this?"

It goes back and forth, all in intense whispers of course. Ma alternates between pleading, 'shouting' [even in a whisper she manages this], flattering, cajoling, wheedling, sweet talking, all to no avail. Ma is repeating over and over again that she understands it all; she just cannot make that vital next step.

Papa remains unrelenting; he won't budge.

"Angelina! I can't believe you can even consider not doing so this minute! Look at your children! Do you want them to be orphans? Do you want me to be a widower? Do you want to be arrested and then disappear, never to be seen again? Do you *never* want to see Ellie again? Aren't you worth more than the latest designer dress? Aren't you worth more than the measly amounts of blood money people are receiving to report you to the authorities?"

Ma eventually concedes to swap her dresses for something less eye catching. Sapphira will go to the market tomorrow and find suitable dresses to *blend* in.

Then Ma says to Papa: "And I think you shouldn't wear your spectacles outside, because they give others the idea you can read and are intelligent. Remember the Vietnamese." Papa looks at Ma, sees that she is serious and starts to mutter and mutter and click his tongue. I see that he is finding it increasingly hard to contain his temper.

Normally, in our home, when Papa and Ma argue, the whole house shakes, it is *that* explosive. Then, half an hour later, they are drinking tea or dancing around the kitchen. Now neither Papa nor Ma can let off steam; what is he going to do? My father absolutely *hates* being told what to do. Whatever is he going to do? He is fit to burst!

He stands there, closes his eyes and lets the rage shake his body. *Awesome*; every part of his body shakes. It is really, *really* scary to watch. Perhaps he will explode! I can't take my eyes off him. Everything about him says he is like a volcano about to blow up: his bulging eyes, his throbbing neck veins, the sweat pouring from his face, his clenched fists turning white. I want to shout out; to tell him to stop, but I can't, because I'm holding my breath the way he is.

A few moments later, or is it a lifetime, all sweaty, he smiles, takes a deep breath and says "Phew! OK. Really only need them to read anyway. It's just that, well, when I wear them, I know where they are."

"And to think I suggested you were an intellectual!" Ma dares to tease so soon after his rage! Brave woman; but he merely grins sheepishly and starts caressing a sleeping Benedict. I hope someone will make me *sooo* angry so that I too can strive to do what Papa has just done. That was awesomely awesome!

∞

Ma is crying and crying as she sits in our room wearing one of the two dresses Sapphira had bought in the market. Ma has not left our house. She has washed the second-hand dresses twice already. Papa is becoming increasingly perplexed and Sapphira plain impatient. We all say the same thing. "*We know* you are still who you are. It's just the packaging that has changed. *And* it is a wonderful survival technique. We want you alive."

"At the moment, *this* is not *I*. *You* may find the packaging agreeable, I'm still working on it! Of course, intellectually, I know you are all right. Emotionally, this adjustment needs a little time. So, *please*, bear with me as I adjust. I can now see how difficult some of the things have been for all of you to adapt to. Forgive my previous impatience. I am, *nay*, I used to be a walking advertisement for chic; I own boutiques; I used to inspire women to wear clothes that make a statement about them! Now I ___"

Just then Benedict wanders in from playing outside, stands for a while looking at Ma with his head to one side, and says "Jolene?", making Ma burst into a fresh bout of tears.

Papa continues the conversation as if Benedict had not uttered his ill-timed and inept remark. "Angel, they will see that yet again you are a *true pioneer,* leading the way to show them once and for all that, when drastic and far-reaching changes need to be made, you have the guts to be the first to do so. What a wife I have, what a woman!"

After a few more sniffs and a few more deep breaths, Ma continues, "of course I am! And if this is the worst thing I have to contend with, well, then life is going to be just *wonderful*. I have overcome. I can now see some things take a little while to adapt to. Thank you for bearing up with me. What a family!"

∞

Later that day Papa and Sapphira return to the market to buy some 'ordinary' shoes for Ma, as her own shoes were not made for walking any distance at all. Twice she sent them back and eventually surrendered to wearing flip-flops, like everyone else. Apart from barefoot or slippers indoors, I don't think I have ever seen Ma in anything but high heels.

I worry about what *I* have to give up.

I do notice the change though; Ma is just like any other woman now. She doesn't flaunt as she walks and she walks more and more like the village women who have done a hard day's work and still have to go home and do the housework as well.

This is swimming. Huh! Tough strokes. I feel like a beginner competing at Olympic level.

Chapter Ten

The eighth day here and the news bulletins become more and more grim. Even more people are pouring in; Hamilton seems to be the last refuge. We hear them say they have been moving around the different cities and towns. Every place they've been to has been full of angry Cartons and thugs on wild 'free for all' rampages and lootings.

The newest arrivals have told Papa and his colleagues they have seen increasing evidence that both the police force and military are from Carton families mourning their President's untimely death. They think the police are just not interested in protecting us non-Carton supporters.

I am scared, very scared. This is not Juxon, police not doing their proper impartial duty are not like any I've known before, except in films. Are they imitating the films?

Later in the afternoon Sapphira and I decide to walk outside Hamilton's periphery on the

Tomsdale side once again. This time we continue a further five minutes than our usual turnaround place. We stop dead. A massive camp has sprung up right under our noses – as far as the eye can see. Apart from the river, there is nothing else here!

So this is where Sergeant Cecil and his men chase the people to! My God! The makeshift shelters are not the sophisticated things we've seen on television! All neat rows and spaces in between. Oh no, *not at all* the case here! These shelters are a few branches on two or three sticks, crammed together. Compared to this, sardine tins look luxuriously spacious!

"God, Saph."

"Lu…"

Little spirals of smoke curl upwards from a few fires as people cook their meals. People are chopping down the bushes and trees for firewood.

Sapphira mutters. "With all these people, soon there will be no forest! What then?"

"Well, the way things are going now, they will run out of things to cook *way* before they run out of firewood."

She picks up a stone to throw at a mangy dog. "Huh! Where are all these aid agencies? Surely they should be here? Why can't they come via Belling - Belling's safe. This is going to be a dreadful catastrophe, an absolutely *avoidable* catastrophe, in my opinion!"

There are a few people along the road, selling their meagre belongings. Almost everyone looks grey and dusty, thin and filthy. Eight days, and people already resemble those pictures we've seen time and time again on television of Ethiopian or Sudanese refugees. I thought it took longer than this, *much* longer. They must have fled without anything, and nobody here able to give them anything. Boy! Do we need help very, *very* soon!

∞

We have people not only sleeping on our veranda, but also living there now. Sergeant Cecil and his team have a constant battle moving them on. They return after a short while. More killings everywhere too; even military interventions now; more unrest all over; more fear. There was another ugly scene this morning; two farmers bringing their produce to the market were given a severe beating by an angry crowd. Sergeant Cecil and his team were there in an instant and then the army came as well, standing on the periphery, ever at the ready, it seems.

Whilst both my parents were keeping a low profile, Papa's colleague and our Scholar Close neighbour Dr Paul, was certainly not. His angry eloquence reverberated across the market.

"Sergeant, the prices of dry commodities have increased tenfold, because no stock is coming in. Although we may not like that, we understand that thinking. However, here, the farmers are taking unfair advantage of the situation by rocketing vegetable prices for no honest reason.

Number one: there is no problem transporting their produce. Number two: at present, it is harvesting time and there is a *glut* of produce. So tell me, why are they capitalising on this astronomical scale? A fair increase, yes, but this is *preposterous,* unfair and so unJuxonese! This is why the people attacked them. If they were to raise their prices to an *acceptable* level, this attack would not have happened. They are being greedy instead of smart!"

During the momentary silence, I watch Sergeant Cecil take the time to scan the crowd. He is looking at Papa. I freeze, then pray frantically: 'Don't involve Papa, *Please*! Leave him alone, a low profile!' I see Papa imperceptibly shaking his head. Sergeant Cecil takes a deep breath and turns to the group of farmers.

"You are a war within wars! This is greed! Why are you doing this? Tell me! Have you ever before shown such greed to others? NO! Because if you had, you would have not have been so stupid to hike up the price so astronomically! So why do it now? We are all Juxonese; I beg you to remember your fathers and your fathers' fathers and behave as they would have you behave! *Please*. Let us show that this part of Juxon still lives and breathes Juxonese values. Come on friends. Be fair. Remember, God is watching you."

I breathe a long, long sigh of relief as we all silently disperse.

∞

We listen to the news every waking moment, it seems. Part of me does not want to listen; it's the same thing over and over. Yet my 'new man' role demands I listen. The whole country, except Hamilton and Kavari Quay, has been affected. They *really, really shouldn't* have mentioned Hamilton as a safe place! Now, *even more* people will flock here. There is no more place here and they are going to make it *even more dangerous* for us!

I wonder if the boats are still taking people away – and to goodness knows where. The newsman says ….. *"The international agencies have begun working on the Ushqueli side of the border and are providing the refugees with food and non-food items, as well as health care. However, after a week of allowing the Juxonese to cross into such safety, the Ushqueli military has new orders to increase security by not allowing any males over sixteen years into Ushquel at present. They don't want the trouble to spill over into their country. Juxon is still far too unsafe for the international agencies to assist inside …"*

We are alone. What will happen to us? Why can't we cross into Belling? Does the government of Belling have to give permission?

Tonight, Sunday night, still day eight of our being here and the tension in Hamilton is even more palpable. I always thought 'you can feel it in the air' as merely poetic and unworldly. Now I *know* tension can definitely be felt.

It reminds me of when Benedict had a chest infection as a baby. We all stood around worried and helpless, willing him to breathe. Now we are willing the attackers to come to their senses. My father is with the other men figuring out what to do. I hope they find a very good solution.

Papa and his friends are saying it is just a matter of time before the rebels get to Hamilton. They know that the military and police are supporting the late President and therefore Cartons, and that there is increasing evidence showing them to be quite unsympathetic towards the Frees or the non-Cartons. The reports of the army and the police not doing anything when Frees are beaten up, are growing. I think Papa and his friends must deeply regret not fleeing abroad. We need to leave Juxon as soon as possible. What about a silent night flight? Would we be able to quietly make our way over the border to Belling? On our few walks to the border, Sapphira and I have never seen many border police on the Belling side. If the adults know this and can't do a thing, what can *I* do? These thoughts make me feel quite panicky. What to do? We are sitting ducks! I *must* think what we could do, apart from rushing into Belling. There is even less than nothing there! They are a very poor country. Most of their people seek their fortunes in other countries including ours. Do we have to be even poorer than we are now? Not only that, but it is going to take us even longer to return home, isn't it? Can I think of nothing else but a 'worse case scenario'?

I better think what I can do to swim; otherwise I will sink with the rest of them. A very, very strong prayer, I think. What else is there? Pray the soldiers are fair and humane? Pray for international support? God's ears must be red hot, His post box full to overflowing; and these are only *my* prayers!

Our family prayer before sleeping this eighth evening of our stay here is for Divine protection and for all to be safe here in Hamilton.

I am lying in my bed with Benedict. He has chosen to sleep with me tonight. I feel quite nervous and start adding to my marathon prayer. "Please, can all Juxonese men come to their senses, look into their tool bags, select the right resources for the right occasion and bring peace to this beautiful country again." It isn't much to ask, is it? I mean, they *all know they can do it*. They have been through the *Onashi* ceremony. Or have they forgotten?

∞

I am awakened from a restless sleep by the sounds of gun fire. Machine guns!

It is sudden and it instantly brings back that old burning in my guts. Not now, please, not now. It's past midnight. Then my prayer is answered; there's silence. I doze off again, only to be awakened, yet again, by gun fire; this time more prolonged – and with shouting.

I hear high pitched screams, running feet, trucks passing, shouting commands. The nurses start shouting hysterically. Papa's deep boom commands them to be quiet unless they want to inform the rebels of our whereabouts. I clutch Benedict to me, heart racing, stomach rumbling, sweaty. He begins to struggle in my grip. I can hear the sounds coming ever nearer. I feel they must be in the market square. We are only two streets away from the market!

Papa whispers loudly. "Luther, Sapphira, you OK there?"

"Yes, Papa." Both of us.

"Get under your bed! Now! Take Benedict with you. Quick! Are you there yet?"

"Yes, Papa." Both of us.

Under the bed and I don't move a muscle. I can't! Stiff as a board, holding onto Benedict who is squirming and squirming and starting to protest loudly. I can hear cars and trucks driving around and around, men shouting, "This is Carton land! This is Carton land!"

Shooting. Sudden long bursts of gunfire.

Outside people are shrieking and screaming and shouting. People are banging against our porch window. The window rattles, the whole room shakes. Both Sapphira and I crawl from underneath the beds and dive under Ma and Papa's bed. Benedict still squirming in my arms; wanting out. He shrieks and shrieks. Papa takes him and comforts him. There is panic out there.

I am praying silently; mumbling all the time. I feel hysteria rising. I clutch Papa's arm. I hear the crackling of fire and smell burning. The flames from the fires light up the room through the window. Oh God! We are going to burn! This must be Hell! They are coming closer and closer to us. I keep praying, "please don't let us die tonight!" A new man for less than a week!

Papa is saying "Luther, know that you are loved, Sapphira, you are loved, Ellie, you are loved, Benedict, you are loved, Angelina, my Angel, you are so loved." We all say 'I love you' to each other; I even feel a deep sense of love for Sapphira. To me it sounds as if we are preparing to die – I don't want to die *or* get hurt here! I have things to do and places to go!

I am *sooo* scared! I hold onto Papa like a lifeline! Papa continues his 'I love you' theme. He is mentioning everybody: his brothers, sisters, Ma's brothers and sisters, cousins, colleagues, neighbours, people I haven't heard of! I think he is even sending love to those long underground. Ma is also muttering, but I can't catch what she is saying.

It is boiling hot underneath the bed with all of us bunched together. I am perspiring from terror and heat. I am too scared to move a muscle. This is tough, *very* tough. It goes on and on and on. We cling to each other. Papa is still finding people to love. I want him to stop.

Unexpectedly there is a break, a sudden silence. Papa says in a normal voice "All of you alright? Well, just sit tight. It will soon be over. They are going to go on their lunch break soon. A Juxonese never misses his lunch break, you can count on that!"

Ma starts sniggering, Sapphira gives an exasperated grunt and I start to giggle softly. I can feel Papa shaking with silent laughter. We must be mad to laugh amid this pandemonium. Or is this the hysteria Chandler said his parents had after the airport saga? Is Papa mad? Whatever it is, it helps relieve some of my tension.

Suddenly I feel it is all going to be alright with the Wiggins family. I relax a bit, enjoy the moments of silence. Yeah! Not that scary after all. I wonder what they are eating? Eating? Food? Oh food, *yes please,* I can eat any time of day or night!

And there *is* a lull. Papa was right - maybe it *is* their 'lunch time' - my all-knowing hero. In the movies, soldiers don't stop for lunch breaks; must be a Juxonese thing. We continue to lie under the bed, savouring the moments of relief. Phew! I need to sort out some strategies here – I am a man after all and running to my parent's bed is not a manly thing.

The 'lunch break' lull lasts only a few minutes; then I hear helicopters and gun fire above our roof. We have never heard the helicopters at night before. During the day yes, their noise has been almost constant. Now they sound terrifyingly close, right above our heads.

Benedict and Ma and Sapphira start to scream. Benedict climbs over Papa to me. Ma is shouting for Ellie. I don't think anybody out there can hear. I shout as well, but nothing comes out. My boy-to-man voice breaks up. There is *sooo* much gun fire with bullets smashing into our walls. A window in the bathroom shatters. Too close! *Far* too close!

There is *sooo* much screaming and shouting going on just outside our room. People outside are still pushing against the window as if they want to come in. It holds. Thank goodness. I hear heavy thumping in the corridor inside; whatever could that be? This is *war*! My heart just keeps thumping against my chest as if it wants to leap out. My mouth is like sandpaper. The noise goes on and on *and on*. Benedict wets himself, all over me. I just let go and do the same. I can always blame him.

It is quiet at last, except for moaning and the screams of people. My watch shows 02:38. Papa and Ma say a short prayer of thanks. Exhausted, I fall asleep.

Chapter Eleven

Monday morning. There is a stillness in the morning, despite the constant keening by women and a few shouts now and again. I look very carefully out of our window with a sense of disbelief. What a rude awakening; the war has come to Hamilton. Yet it is such a beautiful sunny morning. The sky looks a particularly beautiful blue. A wisp of a cloud floats by. I don't think I've ever heard the birds sing so melodiously before. I feel I've just been given a second life. My heart suddenly wells up with gratitude for being alive. I look at my family with love; even Sapphira, who is lying curled up against Ma.

When eventually we hear movement outside, Papa and I venture out very tentatively. There are soldiers everywhere!

For once the dusty market place is not dusty. Blood has seeped into the sand. As if it had rained. Small rivers that stop abruptly. I imagine all the dead and injured bodies that had lain here. The soldiers must have removed them all.

We venture rather tentatively towards the baker to buy our morning bread. There is no bread for breakfast this morning. However, the soldiers are allowing the traders to set up their stalls in the cleaned up area of the market. Life has to go on. The soldiers seem to be in charge now; very few blue police uniforms are visible.

We return to our house to report to the others. The nurses go off to the hospital to help with the injured. Ma starts cooking breakfast using our emergency rations whilst Sapphira and I clean the room. The floor has huge damp patches, not just where Benedict and I had been lying. I put an extra handful of washing powder into the bucket of water. Yes, life and washing continues as usual.

∞

I'm in the bathroom combing my hair and examining myself in the full length mirror when I hear Ma's *"Oh NO!"*

"What now?"

"No signal. The mobile phone's signal is down!"

Ellie! I rush into my shoes. Halfway out of the door. My father grabs my arm. "Tell us where you're off to?"

"The hotel! They have a *landline*! I've still got the bread money! There's always a long queue. I'll wait there and you can come later."

"What if the queue is short – then you will be the only one talking to Ellie." Sapphira, being a pain as usual.

"Just let me go! Check it out. If it is a long queue, I'll ask the person behind me to hold my place while I run back here to fetch you. OK? Just let me go. *Now!* Ellie's *waiting*."

I sprint the to The Hamilton, the four star hotel. I count ten people ahead of me. No longer than the usual number I see when I sometimes stroll around the foyer. Good! Nobody else thought of this yet. There is a new sign up though. THREE MINUTES PER FAMILY. Three minutes! Ma is not going to like this *one* bit. I wait for someone to queue behind me, then beg them to keep my place while I rush home to fetch my family. I remember I have not eaten my breakfast yet; first time that has *ever* happened.

∞

Only when we return from calling Ellie, does the scale of the devastation begin to dawn on me. I feel weak, anxious and extremely sad. It has been a massacre. The tiny police office is inundated with people, inside and out.

The army is all over the town. They tell us they have killed all the insurgents and set up more road blocks on the roads both to Tomsdale and to Kavari Quay. I'm sure Papa and his friends do not believe this story – Papa and his friends believe they are one and the same, working hand in glove! Is our army so corrupt or sneaky as to allow the rebels to do all their dirty work for them? Do they pay them well? Is this what is known as 'blood money'?

How do we get out of such a mess when we don't know who informs whom? So I too act grateful even though I am *very* scared indeed. Are the roadblocks there to keep a check on us? How have I suddenly become so cynical, so disbelieving? What happened to me during last night? If they are all in it together, who was shooting at whom? Were these the few dissidents or the breakaway army? Too many rumours, too many theories.

Royce's last call to Papa said that the military are divided between Carton supporters and Frees. According to him, the Frees have external military support and the brains whilst the Cartons have the masses and their fear tactics. Do the military know who they are targeting – is it all friendly fire? Phew! I am now beginning to understand Papa's theory of the use of fear to manipulate the masses. I'm definitely a part of the masses.

∞

The police and army are directing people to the cathedral, where the Bishop, Father David and others are dealing with the dead. Papa and I head there as well. Keening and wailing fill the air as people identify their dead, and sympathise with the bereaved. Whole families have been slaughtered! Many were the families seeking shelter in doorways and in the market. There are also many of Papa's friends amongst the dead.

Papa offers to sit in the cathedral and write labels for the dead, so that the identified ones can be moved to one side for burial. Father David is around comforting survivors. Will this compromise Papa's low profile? Will the police and army remember him? Can I trust Sergeant Cecil? We are still paying him rent money for our Land Rover.

I look at the dead. Some are disfigured and maimed and gruesome; I can't take my eyes off them. When my father looks up and sees me there he demands I leave immediately to help dig graves.

Suddenly the beautiful morning is turning into a hot and nightmarish day. I finger my Tiger's eye for comfort. For normality. For Juxon.

∞

At lunch time Ma arrives with a huge pot of stew and a bag of bread. Huge flat rolls particular to Hamilton. Four of my newly met grave digging mates and I find a quiet patch to eat our stew sandwiches. None of us have had any casualties in our family. We are simply here to help out. We are new men.

"Last night, when you heard the gun fire, what did you do?"

"I uh, I didn't hear anything. I slept."

"You slept?! It woke the dead!"

"When I sleep, I sleep."

"Man! You missed something awesome. Wasn't it dead awesome, guys?"

"When that helicopter came, it was as if it was hovering just above our roof. Dust came flying from the ceiling."

"One helicopter? There were at least three, man! *And* about a dozen trucks. That was some noise last night!"

"Were you scared?"

"No, not me. We fled from Queenville when they were massacring people all over the town."

"Yeah, but they didn't have the helicopters there, did they?"

"No, there was no army there either. That's why we fled."

A long pause.

"I was really scared. I mean, *really* scared?"

"You were? So was I, man. I thought we were all going to die. One of the rebels ran into our house and the soldiers came after him and killed him just outside our door. The door was shaking. We were all screaming until the soldier banged on our door, told us to shut up because the man was now dead. We could hear them dragging him away."

"Awesome, man, awesome."

Chapter Twelve

There's no rice anymore. Well, only at unaffordable prices; way out of our budgets. How can we survive without rice? Everything goes with rice; it's not a proper meal without rice!

Neither is there affordable powdered milk, nor any tinned fish. The other day Ma was giving Professor Miles' wife some of our supplies. When Papa heard about it he was really angry; he said our family comes first from now onwards, no matter what. Sapphira and I tell him that Ma is eating very little, giving all of us the food. This makes Papa even more incensed. He asks her if she wants this family to be without a mother, and who will look after Benedict and does she not want to see her youngest daughter again?

Apart from Benedict we are all eating one main meal a day now. We have bread for breakfast; a roll with the thinnest of thin layer of jam on it. That kind of layer that puts jam on the bread and then scrapes it all off again - a smidgen of jam.

We all take turns eating Benedict's half roll. Papa told Ma again that we don't have enough food for ourselves and we cannot afford to feed Professor Miles and his family as well.

On the other hand, the nurses are getting paid to work at Hamilton General Infirmary and Papa does not want them to feel obliged to share their meals with us. My parents have accepted with much gratitude their offer to share their midday meal with Benedict. I can smell their meals. It smells delicious! It reminds me how hungry I am and how small my portion of food is going to be this evening and how my stomach is going to continue rumbling for the rest of the night until I eat my fresh roll the next morning.

∞

It is late afternoon on day nine of our stay in Hamilton, the day after the night of hell. Benedict and I are strolling through the market, just to get out of the confines of the flat. Suddenly three soldiers out on patrol pull at Benedict, intending to get him off my shoulders. I hold onto a screaming Benedict for dear life.

"You are *not* a nanny! Enlist now! What kind of *effing* coward are you, not fighting for your country? Do you want to be a nanny looking after a child instead of being a proper man?! What's in your pants, huh?"

I cling to Benedict, crushing him against my chest. Holding on tightly. I am struck dumb; cannot utter a word. Dry, dry mouth. Benedict has stopped squirming, his arms like a tourniquet around my neck.

I wet my pants. Everyone can see the growing dampness. The soldiers laugh and laugh.

"Look! He's pissed his pants! Ha! Ha, ha! Too much education, and not smart enough to do something manly! We'll make a man out of you, Nanny! Make you street-wise!"

A crowd gathers, including Sergeant Cecil and two other policemen. He talks with them; "Look at him! Look at his face! He's a *boy*, a child! Probably no more than fourteen years old! Leave him alone. He's just a child." They let go of their vice-like grip on my arm. Still laughing.

I walk home, shivering and shaking, sobs racking both my little brother and me. The wet pants now cold against my legs. I reach home to find Professor Miles and his wife and my parents *and* Sapphira are all there, sitting around the kitchen table. I stand there, huge sobs shock-waving my tall frame. Ma takes a now crying Benedict from me. Shock, shame and horror keep me rooted to the spot. Ma hands me a pair of boxer shorts and a clean pair of jeans. Pushes me towards the bathroom, saying as she goes: "Frederick, go and talk with him."

"No. We will *all* talk about this. This affects *all of us*. Come sit here as soon as you've had your shower, Tiger."

The last thing I want is all this exposure. Why couldn't Papa do as Ma asked? The shame of it all. I stay in the bathroom for ages. Then there's a knock on the door; Papa. "Luther, come on now, let's talk about this."

Five minutes later, Papa is still coaching me out of the bathroom. Eventually I allow him in; cling to him while I sob and sob. I can feel the warmth of Papa's tears on my shoulder. After a long while we move to the kitchen. Professor Miles and his wife are still there. I'm that low I'm past caring now.

Sapphira gives up her chair for me.

"What happened ...?"

For a while I remain silent, still confused. Stunned. Shocked. Unbalanced. I still want to cry. Take a deep breath. "It was far too sudden. Totally unexpected. I just couldn't find anything in my tool box that quick." I shudder again as I tell my story but play out *the hero* for not letting go of Benedict.

My father opens his arm and gives me his famous crushing bear hug. He says nothing, just holds me. I feel his heart thumping against mine. Gradually both our hearts become steadier. The sob in my throat disappears. The shakes go. Sapphira pours some sweet tea for all of us. We each have one biscuit from the emergency rations.

"Ok! What do we do now?" asks Papa.

After a long silence I say: "Walk around with a photocopy of my passport so that they can see my age. Speak with Father David. He has been accosted many times before. Run away, if I need to."

"Miles, what would you suggest?" Ma asks everyone around the table.

"Angelina, I haven't the foggiest idea!"

"Well, what if this happened to you? It might, you know. Conscription for every male aged eighteen to sixty years."

An argument between Professor Miles and his wife follows. She is still unhappy that they ended up in Hamilton instead of abroad. Professor Miles says he had to finish his experiments first. Now he has a stack of papers with him and very little money. They have already started to sell some of the stuff they brought in order to eat. They eventually leave to go next door without suggesting any strategies.

"Hmmm. See, when he was a brilliant scientist, she glowed in his limelight, did everything for him so that he could do his research. Now times have changed and we all have to adapt and she does not like what he has become." Ma observes wryly.

"Angelina, I think we are all in that boat. We all have to be open to learn new skills."

"What about Benedict? Look at him now. He must be *sooo* traumatised." Ma says as she strokes his hair.

Benedict has been quiet all this time, savouring a long denied treat - a biscuit from our emergency rations.

"Benedict?"

"Papa?"

"What did you do when the soldiers grabbed hold of Luther?"

"I scweamed and scweamed! I put my arms alound Luther's neck. Luther is stwong. Vewy, vewy, vewy stwong." He puts his arms around Ma's neck and squeezes her until she begs for air, dramatising the effect until he giggles.

"And if this happens again?"

"No! Frederick! NO! He is too young!"

"Too young to learn, or too young to teach others?"

My mother merely shakes her head, wiping tears from her cheeks.

"Papa, I go with Luther, because he is stwong!" Again he chokes Ma until she laughingly untangles his young arms from her neck, allows him to finish his now-soggy biscuit.

"It's the way you framed the questions, isn't it Papa? Like the lawyers." My sister smiles knowingly at our father.

"See, he is already looking on the positive side of life."

Benedict, having eaten the rest of his biscuit, suddenly stands up and starts dancing and singing. "*Always look on the bwight side of life. Ohoh, ohoh, ohoh.*" We all join in until Prof Miles' wife bangs on the wall.

∞

I can't sleep. My watch shows 01:27. That fear keeps coming back. Makes me shake and shiver. Thoughts grip me, and especially that inability to control my bladder. That shame, that utter, *utter* shame. That humiliation. Oh God! Why me? It was so sudden; it happened so quickly. I froze; except of course for my bladder. How could I let myself down like that? I'm shivering and shaking, near to tears. Miserable. Benedict! At least I held onto Benedict – my only saving grace. Yes! I held onto my brother!

I go over to my parents' bed, see Benedict lying on the edge of the bed. I pick him up. Papa stirs, opens his eyes, looks at me, winks, nods, loosens his arm from around Benedict. I take my sleeping brother to my bed. I need the comfort, that supportive, comforting feeling of another body against mine. I fall into a dreamless sleep until Papa wakes me for breakfast.

Chapter Thirteen

After breakfast, I remain seated, unaware of the bustle of family life in the small confines of the flatlet. I am smiling, somewhat tentatively, as I finger my Tiger's eye. Manhood: I will walk down that street with my head held high. Courage and alertness: a true tiger.

Eventually I become aware of Ma talking, "Sapphira, just in case, *just in case* a time may arise when you are *sooo* angry, you might be goaded into teasing Luther about this incident, what would you have done if this had happened to you? Being so scared and many people seeing you wet yourself?"

Sapphira looks at me. I really can't imagine Sapphira being in such a situation. Can she? And if she *does* mock me about it, how will I react? I stay still whilst we all await Sapphira's answer. Actually, I don't care if she should tease me. She *wasn't there,* keeping Benedict safe, like I did!

"I don't know what I would do, Ma. Scream so loud, people will come running. To tell you the honest truth, I don't know what really nasty thing could happen to me."

Ma looks at her. "I know of things. Maybe we will talk about what might happen to us women this evening."

∞

My teachers duly come to teach me how to deal with my new situation. In droves, it seems to me.

First teacher comes the very next morning. I rush back from the bakers. "Ma! Papa! Sapphira! I've got a job!"

"What, what, what?"

"I accepted the baker's offer to deliver bread every morning. Two free breads for the Wiggins household; that is all he can guarantee! I asked whether we could use his phone to phone Ellie every day. I said five minutes, a minute each. He is thinking about that."

"Wow! That's great!" Exclaims Ma, adding "It would have been nice to have discussed it beforehand; but sometimes, I know, if opportunity knocks, you just have to accept it, there and then. Well, done. More money for food. Good negotiating the phone call as well. Well done. Which area do you deliver?"

"Don't know yet, Ma, I just wanted to come and tell you first of all. I have to start at six thirty until eight thirty every morning, that's all. He is baking so many more of those special Hamilton breads now that he needs an extra delivery boy."

"Interesting. Yesterday you couldn't enlist in the army because you are too young; today you get a job!"

"Oh! Come on, Sapphira! That was sooo different yesterday. Today I am helping our family get food – and, hopefully, a free call to Ellie."

"Just checking. And Ma, how does this fit in with our plan to never go out singly, always in pairs?"

"Well, answer your own question; are you offering to deliver bread with your brother?"

"Certainly not! It's just that we made this rule and now it's being broken already."

"Let's wait for your father and discuss it as a family."

We wait, we discuss and the verdict of the family discussion is that I can do my delivery alone. If I've not returned by nine o'clock, two of them will go to the bakers. Yes! We can eat two meals a day again.

∞

My second and third teachers come as a package.

It is taking much more courage to face the many soldiers present everywhere. Much, *much* more courage. Every time I see a soldier, my heart thumps up against my ribs and I become an instant sweatbox. I panic. I want to run home, except it seems that I can't move. I am terrified. This is not good, not good at all.

A group of laughing soldiers come towards me and I rush into the cathedral. I sit in the pew, cold and hot, sweaty, terrified, feeling utterly helpless. Father David looks up from what he is doing and comes towards me. He sits down in the pew next to me. Just sits.

"Luther."

I swallow; swallow again. Merely look at him. He puts his hand on my shoulder. Eventually my breathing slows down, so does my heart. I become calmer.

"Every time I see a group of the soldiers, I want to hide."

"What else?"

"I am still utterly terrified of them – of not being able to cope should they grab hold of me again, or mock me. I can't do it."

"What else?"

"I don't know how to stand up to them."

"What else?"

"I want to be brave, so I can face them with confidence."

A long pause. I wipe the tears from my face. I'm glad his hand is still on my shoulder. I need the human touch, the sympathetic, kind human touch.

"As a boy, can you remember a time when you have felt confident facing someone fearful?"

"Can't remember."

"Think again. Take your time."

"Don't know; really."

"What boy do you know who has faced someone or something fearful?"

"Nobody."

"Dig deeper; I'm sure you know of someone."

Another long pause – has this incident made me incapable of thought as well? Dear God No! Imagine Sapphira taking control!

"Harry Potter!"

"What does he do?"

"He uses his wand to disempower his adversity."

"How can you use that?"

"I can't. He's fictional."

"How many sticks are out there? Let's just count the ones in this church yard."

"Dozens. Hundreds. Loads."

"How many does Harry Potter have?"

"One."

"Good. What do you want to do: find a stick or use your finger? Which do you choose?"

"My index finger."

"Wise choice. It is always there with you, a part of you."

He pauses. I wait. I don't quite know where this is going – can he do magic? Is it allowed – a priest doing magic?

"OK. This is how I have coped when faced with someone who is attacking me. You know they say animals can smell fear? And that's why they sometimes attack? So, we need to change your fear into something positive. Something that does not attract. I know that prior to this incident, you were not afraid of them and yet it happened. Well, now, we are taking precautions against further attacks. This row of hymn books here represents a group of soldiers coming towards you. *You* have *all the power* to control this situation towards a positive conclusion. What positive conclusion do you wish for?"

Mmmm. I think I get the idea. Maybe.

"That I walk past them with confidence. They cannot touch me. In fact they are so engrossed in their conversation, they ignore me."

"Excellent. Now, close your eyes and see that in your mind's eye. See yourself totally confident and fearless, walking nonchalantly towards them. Feel that. Really *feel* that confidence and moral fibre and guts. See them walking towards you, seeing you, but laughing and joking and completely ignoring you. How does it feel?"

"They look like a small group of school children coming towards me. It's no big deal at all."

"Wonderful! I saw you wag your finger. And I know Harry Potter and his entourage say a word. Do you think a word might be apt for this change?"

"Hmmm. Transform! In another language. To give it a sense of mystery and increased power."

"Brilliant! Your special word can appear later. For now, look at this group of soldiers, point your power at them, then at you and say 'transformation'. Tell me which one works best."

"Wow! When I point at me, I feel a surge of energy! I can do it! They've changed into manageable school children."

"Well done, Luther! You know you need to keep practising, to maintain the momentum until it becomes second nature. You do know that, don't you? Good! So now, tell me, how will you integrate this in your daily life?"

"I will transform everything fearful or dangerous or difficult into something easy, manageable and safe. Thank you so much, Father David."

"Hang on, not done yet. What will you do when they are actually threatening you? Because, given our circumstances at present, it might just happen."

"Run away."

"What if they say: Stop or I shoot?"

"I stop. Hope for the best. There's nothing else I *can* do, is there, Father David?"

"I merely wanted to point out to you that a blanket solution may not be sufficient. That we need to be realistic in the face of real danger. Good thinking. I pray none of us will need to use it. Sit with your family and discuss ways of dealing with worst case scenarios like this. Be prepared."

"Thank you, Father David. I do feel more confident now….."

"Of course, all you have to do now is practise, practise, practise!"

Chapter Fourteen

I am awake way before six every morning, planning my route, seeing where I can reduce time, how I'm going to pack these flat round breads, as big as my hand, to evenly distribute the weight. Sizzling with impatience to get up and out to the baker's.

I do the rounds in the richer part of town, although few are left. According to the baker, most have left by sea. However, since so many people have come to this small town, the bakery is doing four times the amount of baking. Soon there will be no flour. Maybe the baker can get some flour from Jamari? It's only about twenty minutes' walk away from the Belling border. He tells me he has had to do so twice already since the President was assassinated.

Against Ma's wishes, Papa and a friend went to Jamari the other day, crossing the border to do a 'recce', a reconnaissance, around the town to see if we should move there or stay here. Papa was all for going there, especially after one of his best friends mysteriously disappeared a few days ago. Despite many visits to both the police and the military, he appears to have vanished into thin air.

They returned and said it was very poor there. He found a few Juxonese families already there. They found no rooms to rent, even though Papa volunteered to teach at the local primary school.

After many discussions amongst ourselves and with my parents' friends, we decide to stay where we are for now, even though everyone keeps saying that it is only a matter of time. I can't understand this 'sitting duck' attitude; I would have gone to Belling immediately and be one of the first Juxonese to move. It's like waiting for an earthquake by waiting in its worst area of destruction. Why? Do they hope everything will subside now that the President has been buried? Doesn't that increase the chances of anarchy?

Papa feels the people there were a little bit suspicious and not very friendly. He thinks it is because they don't want Juxon's troubles in Belling, particularly not there in Jamari. Better to stay in the cramped apartment than risking 'not knowing' on the other side of the border. I'm all for going way beyond Jamari, maybe to St. Giles, the seaside port - the place the ferries were taking the people when we were on our way here. Many of my parents' acquaintances surreptitiously moved to Kavari Quay and shipped out to St.

Giles. Isn't life funny; then I couldn't bear to even *contemplate* boarding the ferry, now I wish to be exactly where those people are now. Where's my 'ready, fire, aim' attitude when I need it!

∞

Each morning Ma and Sapphira leave soon after I do, to buy vegetables from the farmers at the market. We haven't eaten meat in days, not since my *Onashi* all those days ago. What a lot has happened since then! Rather than risk more beatings and mob anger, the farmers *did* reduce their prices, and people queue from early morning to buy their supplies, but everything has gone by nine o'clock. At the moment there are tomatoes, spinach, and pears.

∞

I think of food all the time. The baker smiles and shakes his head when he sees me eating the crumbs from the loaves. He says he remembers his own son going through this phase and gives me a crust dipped liberally in oil and black pepper; manna from heaven.

We are lucky. I say a truly heartfelt 'thank you' every time I eat. Thanks to the baker, the Wiggins family is eating one and a half meals a day now. Rather than a roll, Sapphira and I share a small loaf and so do Ma and Papa. From each loaf we cut a small portion for Benedict.

The bread doesn't fill me though, merely puts a small plaster on a big hole. Still, as Ma often reminds me, most people are starving. We haven't actually seen a truck bringing supplies since that night of hell. We hear rumours that the soldiers guarding the road blocks take the bulk of any supplies for themselves first.

The shop traders have also increased the prices so that almost no one can afford to buy the very few dry goods. Everybody is waiting for the prices to fall again. Traders cross over to Jamari, but there's nothing much to buy there. Our household supplies of rice, oil and sugar are gone and our money is disappearing fast. The wads of money in our money belts are thinning day by day.

So, no food. No petrol. No mobile phone. No nothing, except insecurity.

What will we do?

Chapter Fifteen

Today is day ten and the whole Wiggins family is standing outside the police station. A massive crowd is gathering and the soldiers are out in force to control the crowd. Two dusty and muddy white trucks are parked near the police station. There are *marties* at the police station and at the health clinic. They came across from Belling in the two huge trucks. It must be food!

We plan our roles carefully so that each one can get something from the trucks. Sapphira and I move quickly to the front. Someone has tapped onto the side of the trucks and says there are boxes and boxes inside. It must be food!

Sergeant Cecil brings out two chairs. He stands on one, holding his hands up for silence. He introduces the *marties*. Next to him, a small thin woman stands on the other chair. She puts her hands over her heart, Juxonese style. Says *Kelsho*. She smiles at the instant response and starts to speak.

Her voice is strident for one so tiny; Sapphira is taller than her. A little smile plays around her mouth. She scans the crowd, looking people in the eye and nodding her head in greeting. She must be the boss – like Ma.

They need an interpreter. Professor Miles is nearer to the front than Papa; Sergeant Cecil calls him forward – and he begins to translate her words.

"The *marty* gives greetings to all of us. She is called Lydia. She hopes that we are as well as can be expected given the circumstances under which we living at present. They have come to help us. They are called MSF. It means Doctors Without Borders. They provide care to all in immediate distress. That is why they could cross from Belling. They have come to help the sick and the injured and provide safe drinking water. Also to do a survey to assess what else is needed and bring in the necessary supplies and staff. She is in charge. There are five of them at the moment. A doctor, two nurses, an engineer and herself, the administrator."

There is a great cry of protest from the ever increasing mass of people pushing closer and closer. They shout that they want food. One woman is shouting "What's the point of medicine when we are dying of hunger? We need food, not pills!"

Professor Miles quickly translates this for her.

The small thin *marty* woman merely stands there, staring out across the crowd, the slight smile on her face. Stands firm on the wobbly chair. What courage!

We Juxonese don't behave like this! We don't welcome *marties* with shouts and demands! Politeness breeds politeness, that's what we are taught from the cradle! But man oh man! I am always hungry! And there is less and less food in the market these days. Tomatoes, spinach and pears are just not enough!

Professor Miles, now standing on the other chair, holds up his hand for quiet. He starts interpreting again. "The *marty* says that by next week they will have a centre where children under five years old can receive food."

Even Ma is shouting now, saying "Thank you very much, but babies are no good when their parents have starved to death! We all need food, *please, please, please.*" People take up a chant again of *food, food, food*.

The *marty* woman talks with her friends.

Professor Miles's hand goes up and he starts interpreting again. "She understands our plea and is very sympathetic towards it. She says this is what they do; other *marties* deal with food. She hopes, like we do, that these people will come as soon as possible."

People are angry and disappointed. They don't want to listen any more – what's the point when there is still no food coming. They leave the police station area and a few vent their anger on the market traders, beating them up and taking all their meagre, over-expensive supplies of flour and oil and sugar and anything else they can get their hands on. The police and the army chase people out of the market area, firing into the air to disperse the crowd.

A litre bottle of oil rolls my way. I pick it up quickly and hide it under my huge shirt. Then I see the battered trader on the ground. I can't take this oil. I *can't* take this oil! I buy stuff from him all the time. I like him. He is an honest man and treats me well. He knows me!

Ma needs oil. I am starving! There's nothing to go with the oil. Oil keeps for a long time. Papa and Ma will be so mad with me. Damn! I am so hungry and this came my way – I didn't steal it, it chose me! My gift! I *can't* take what isn't mine! What to do? We *need* that oil! We need the energy from the oil. It came my way; it is mine. The trader has tripled his prices over the past weeks. He has lots of money; he is rich, robbing the poor. We deserve this oil! He is greedy. I cannot take what isn't mine. I want it. I don't know what to do. I know what to do, I just cannot do it. He is injured and scared. He cannot work. I am starving, but I can't take his oil. I didn't pay for it.

I go to the trader, still lying moaning on the ground and hand him the bottle. We look at each other in silence before I walk away. It feels better inside, *and* I'm still hungry. *Darn*!

∞

I tell Ma when I return. Ma takes in a deep breath and lets out a long sigh. "That was good Luther. The emphasis is on *was*. That rule and philosophy *was* when we had, when we could afford to be magnanimous. New rules now, Luther! Changes according to the circumstances we are in at present. Now we have to see to ourselves first, otherwise we die! Always see to yourself first, otherwise you will be unable to look after others. How can you care for others when you are weak? Strengthen yourself first! That bottle rolled towards you – it was *meant for you*. Next time, say 'thank you' and walk away with gratitude. You can always repay him another time in another way."

In bed that night, I wonder what else I will have to unlearn. Transform. Hey! The *marties* will have a different, more exotic word for transform. I will ask all of them!

∞

Good news! Papa has a job with MSF. Professor Miles was recruited right after he'd finished translation on the day of their arrival and he recommended Papa and told all the nurses to present themselves.

Now Ma is looking for a job as well. Sapphira and I will care for Benedict and do the cooking and cleaning. I don't like this idea at all, so I too present myself at their gate. I speak my best English with confidence. I have a long conversation with one of the *marties* about life in Juxon, specifically Hamilton. I can see he is impressed. Then he asks me how old I am. When I say I am fourteen, he says he cannot employ children.

"In Juxon I am a *man*!" I say indignantly.

"Young sir, you may be a man in your culture, but according to international employment law, you are under age. I am sorry. Also, you say your father is working for us? It is our rule to give as many families as possible the chance to earn some money, so we employ only one person per family."

I can hardly wait for my turn to speak at our evening family meeting. I have been kicking at everything in my way, shouting at everyone, been shouted at by every one!

"Papa, you went through hell organising my celebration into manhood and here this man says I am not a man! What was that *Onashi* ceremony all about then? In my eyes and the eyes of Juxon, I *am a man*." Because it is the evening family meeting, we are whispering. It makes it all seem so much more poignant.

"Tiger, I was rejected as well, although I do see that we should not be greedy and allow others the opportunity to earn some money as well. The nurses too were rejected because they are already employed. MSF says it is not their policy to deplete functioning local resources." Ma says.

"Ma, I am not *that* bothered about the money. I feel I have been rejected as a man!" I look towards my father for support, but he has a headache and is not supporting me. He says his eyes hurt because he has been staring at a computer all day. They are showing him how to record every item entering and leaving the large warehouse.

Papa gets impatient when he can't grasp things quickly enough, so he is in a bad mood. He says the small print on the screen is hurting his eyes and giving him a headache.

"Papa, enlarge the view to 125% or 150% or more. To whatever is perfect for your eyes."

My father looks at me and smiles. "I knew that computer of yours would come in handy one day. Thanks, Tiger."

Ma suggests that he sees an herbalist to get some treatment for his eyes.

"I don't have time for that! I'll be working all day, every day. They say it is the setting up period and everyone *has* to be prepared to work flat out so that the clinic and other activities can get started." Papa and Professor Miles arrive home minutes before the new curfew time of seven o'clock.

Ma says she can't wait for Friday when Papa will be paid. It is not a huge salary, only an 'incentive', but at least we will have money for food again. Although we all still have money, we are keeping that for dire emergencies, which I feel are pretty close.

Sapphira and I go wandering around the spartan market the next day, making a dream list of all the food we would love to buy with Papa's 'incentive'.

∞

Papa and Ma are arguing about our Land Rover. It has become the rule in our household that serious discussions take place around the kitchen table, just as it used to in Prestige Street. Also, when two people are having a disagreement, everybody else is silent and does not participate at all.

This rule applies between Sapphira and myself, between Papa and Ma: any two individuals. Sometimes it is *sooo* difficult to keep quiet; I find it really stressful. At home I could go to my own room, or put on my music, or play outside. Here everything happens in this small area. And life has to go on. Arguments happen. And it is all in whispers. So Sapphira and I are listening while Papa and Ma are having a heated whispered discussion about the Land Rover.

"The Land Rover, which is still safely hidden by Sergeant Cecil in exchange for his regular fee, is exactly what MSF needs. If we rent it to them we can have a regular income *and* we can increase the rent when everything else goes up."

"Frederick! This is not a good deal for us. Believe me! We don't know how long they will be here or how long we will be here. I feel it is better that we *sell* it to them and use the money for food and other things. Unless food comes, I think people might turn nasty and force the *marties* to go."

"Angelina, they say other *marties will* come with food and kitchen utensils and things like blankets and soap and what not. Other aid agencies *will* come. We just have to be patient for a little while longer. They won't come if it is not safe here. However, with MSF here, others might deem it safe enough to come as well. I think we should dedicate tonight's prayer to safety and the swift arrival of other *marties*."

In the end, and it takes several days of discussion, Papa takes Ma's advice and sells the Land Rover to the *marties*. Each of us receives some money to safeguard. 'Not putting all our eggs in one basket' Papa and Ma say in unison.

∞

I am filled with trepidation, with volcanic anger, with absolute frustration. This democracy thing does *not* work! Especially when someone like me is vehemently opposed to the final solution. How can I accept this decision as a group decision? It is *sooo* wrong!

How are we going to get back to Parrish if we do not have a vehicle? Has anybody thought of that? We are stuck in this dump of a town, this dusty place with one road, no school, no food and since yesterday, no electricity as well! It's more than a fortnight now and it feels like twenty years. And the incentive Papa gets from working with the *marties* is *sooo* little, what with the prices rising all the time, we have nothing spare and there are still ages to go before the next payment. Ma says she used to pay Jolene more in a week than Papa receives in two weeks. This is getting more and more terrible.

In our whispering meeting, I say my say, staring at my father. "It was a *big* mistake to sell the Land Rover, a huge, massive mistake. How are we going to go home now? Have *you thought* about *that*?" I spit it out to my family.

Papa looks at me for a long time before answering. I am sooo angry I don't notice the silence. All I want is an apology, telling me that I was right!

"I don't not want to hear this moaning ever again! Do you understand? The family made this decision. As a family, a unit. Accept it. Because that's how decision making works. Decision made. Deal done!"

Another long pause while Papa continues to simply look at me. "I accompanied the engineer Marcus to two huge camps today, one on either side of Hamilton, just a few miles away. He plans to bring water to the camps. They call the people there IDPs. It means internally displaced people. In fact, that is what we are all known as. Those people are drinking filthy water and there are no latrines. People, especially children, are very, *very* sick. Many are dying daily. And, as if that's not bad enough, they have no food *and* the farmers are shooting anyone who comes onto their land, so we are extremely lucky to have running water as well as a roof over our heads and some food twice a day. You have a job. I have a job. Both keep us alive. I want no more of this moaning and groaning. Cut it out! Go and look at those poor people in the camps. Get some perspective on your blessings!"

Much later I do my 'transform' exercise again. Point my index finger at my heart. Close my eyes. See a never ending convoy of buses filled with singing Juxonese returning to our homes. Jolene and Jacob are there. Ellie is standing with them, waving and jumping up and down as we alight. Yes! For the moment, at least....

∞

There are now two different families living on our veranda. Where have the others gone? The tiny rear area where Benedict and the nurses' children used to play is heaving with three large families. There is no place to move even a grain of sand. Now all our conversations can be heard on all sides. At present these families have no shelter from the hot sun. Soon the rainy season will come and they will have no shelter from the rain. At night we hear the babies crying almost constantly. Is it hunger or sickness or just plain misery because they are not in their cosy beds at home?

I know all these things. But as Ma said to me after the bottle of oil incident, we have to look after ourselves first, in order to take better care of others. So, why the sermon? *Huh!*

∞

MSF is new on my delivery route. I deliver to MSF their daily basket of bread. I want to show them that I *can* work, but they are sooo busy with other things, they just about manage to mumble 'Thank You' for the bread. So engrossed in my ego trip, I nearly collided with a truck this morning. More *marties*! Wow! *Yes*!

During the day five different groups arrive. I go to each one to present myself. They are still looking for accommodation, so we patiently line up at the front of the first truck. There are long queues; *everyone* is looking for a job and some income. At three of the *marty* places, they put people in two different queues; one for those who can speak and write English, the others for cleaners, drivers, guards and such like. They give us paper to write our résumés. I have not much to write on mine, but I am confident of being able to persuade them! At each one they say I speak fluent English, but I am too young for employment.

OK! OK! OK! I *get* the message! In your world, I am not yet a man. They ask me many questions about the town though, and if there is anywhere to stay. I direct them to the baker who knows all the empty houses where the rich had left. I also tell them my sister will know better, because she has been visiting friends and they might know of someone. I run home to fetch her. Sapphira offers to take them to a few homes. She has been telling us that her friend, Savannah's parents, know about all the rich people who have left their huge houses to flee by sea to St. Giles and beyond. Many of these houses are unoccupied except for the guard. They seem perfect houses for the *marties* to rent.

I decide to advertise for Ma, telling what a wonderful businesswoman she is. I run home to fetch Ma's résumé, which Papa had printed, then back again to give each group Ma's résumé.

They are impressed. Very impressed. I run home and tell Ma she has three interviews the next day. I am becoming a businessman! Not a scientist, not a dreamer, but a businessman, following in Ma's footsteps. I have the flair! Entrepreneurial life is for me! And I was ever so magnanimous by giving Sapphira an opportunity as well. That's what I call networking. We Wiggins are a force to be reckoned with, especially this young Wiggins *man*.

And every time I speak with a *marty*, I ask them what transform is in their language. I now have a list of words for transform in seven languages. So many *marties* from across the globe! Disappointingly for me, transform sounds the same in many of their languages. Eventually I choose the Danish word '*Forvandl!*' It has the right feel to it. And I like the Danish man, Theis; he treated me with respect, as an equal, man to man.

Chapter Sixteen

The town is now filled with the intrusive noise of generators chugging non-stop until way past eleven o'clock. We never know silence before bedtime again. We go to sleep with the noise and we wake with the noise. Lights show where the groups of *marties* are living, in the affluent area just to the left of our place.

Sapphira asks Papa how they could get housing so quickly when we have to live in a cramped room. "Well, they have a regular income to pay for the rent. Apparently, some people are moving out of their homes into the camps or squashed up with friends or relatives so that the *marties* can pay a 'very healthy' rent to them. Professionals or wealthy people own these particular Hamilton homes. The homes are huge and they have considerable space to park all their vehicles. For security reasons the *marties* install high corrugated iron fences. You have seen the massive recruitment drive for cooks, cleaners, guards, nurses, interpreters, engineers; anybody who can speak English. These queues are long and the people wait patiently and tirelessly outside each groups' house. Who wouldn't when there is a chance of an income? I would!"

"But Papa, why can't they *share* some of the light? We have all the noise and no light! When I am a lawyer, I will make sure that there is fair distribution!"

"Sapphira, I feel life is not always about fairness, but about balance. Look at it from different perspective. Their presence here decreases the violence, and increases our safety, decreases our illnesses, and increases our food supply, decreases our dependency and despondency about how we can earn a living and increases our independence and selfworth. Can you see the balance that is being achieved? Strive to see life as a balance, like summer and winter, because what seems unfair to you may seem perfectly fair to someone else. Can you see that?"

"I see, Papa, but I still don't see why they can't share some of that light!"

"Probably because they have different priorities and comfort needs at the moment. I think, and this is only me thinking this, that we are better off than they are, actually. Who needs light when you have your family around you to be the light? They are also working very hard indeed to prepare everything in order to start work as soon as possible. There is an awful lot of paperwork involved! They do this at night when all of us 'locals', as we are called, have gone home to their families. For this work they need light. I also think they need to feel comfortable and surrounded by familiar things. Wouldn't it be nice if you had all your music with you, all your books, favourite food, favourite clothes, huh? Well, you know, when it comes down to basics, those material things fade into nothing. Who of you would rather have Ellie here with us than another book to read? Or light to read the book by? *We* have each other; *they* have light and a computer! Want to change with them?"

Sapphira does not answer; she's not convinced, as usual! I am. Although a teeny bit more jam on a piece of toast would be so delicious. Just a bigger little blob, thinly smoothed over a slice. Grandma Meertel's apricot jam. *Mmmm,* now that would be utterly divine. I'd move my tongue over it ever so slowly to savour every little bit of sweetness. And then leave the sweetness there and go over it again and again until the jam is drenched into the slice. Oh! Heaven!

And one of Jolene's roast dinners now and then would be so *awesomely* awesome, the juice running down my chin as I chew the delicious meat. Best *not even* to think about *that*! It makes my tummy grumble....

Sapphira has thought of another issue. "Papa, can we not have had *marties* stay in our house whilst we are away? What do you think?"

"I think my two eldest children have inherited their business gene from their mother. Perhaps we could have rented our home to *marties*. Who knows? It is still a possibility should they go to Parrish. However, I don't think the *marties* are anywhere else but in Hamilton at the moment. The reports suggest that it is still too unsafe in Juxon in general. Hamilton is close to the border should insecurity become a problem for the *marties*. The last news I heard was that more and more Juxonese are streaming over the borders. The news says that of the three million Juxonese, one million are registered in Ushquel with a half million here in Hamilton. There are two hundred thousand dead. Imagine that! Nonetheless, I will ask at the office and find out whether the aid agencies are in Juxon yet – or preparing to come. *If* they are thinking about it, someone will surely know. No one has said anything so far."

∞

The next morning when I return from my bread delivery round I hear much shouting and arguing in our building. The nurses, Professor Miles, his wife and daughter, and my parents are all crowding around a man. A rather small man. Weedy. Professor Miles and Papa tower above him. He is keeping his head down, refusing to look them in the eye. He shifts from one foot to the other, outclassed and outnumbered, repeating his sentence with ever decreasing confidence until it is a mere stutter. I cannot hear what he is saying; it sounds more like Ellie when she is begging and begging to get something she wants but is told she cannot have. A whiny voice.

Then Ma smilingly pushes the two big men aside to stand in front of the man. She bends her tall frame down to his eye level, puts her finger under his chin, raises it and gently shakes it until he *has to* look her in the eye. Voice dripping with the sweetness of fresh warm honey that sets all my alarm bells ringing, she says in a calm voice. "So, let me get this absolutely clear. You want *us*, fellow Juxonese, *professional* fellow Juxonese, to *move out* so that you can rent this place to the *marties*. *Or* you want to raise the rent from near impossible to out of the question, so that *we*, the displaced Juxonese, pay the equivalent of the *marties*? Is that right? Tell me, *how* will you sleep at night knowing that your greed has pushed *three families* out on the streets so that you can be even greedier in what you get for these rooms? I am appealing to you as a mother, as a woman, as a fellow entrepreneur and as a fellow Juxonese, who has been raised to be helpful to those less fortunate, the needy, the dispossessed. *Who* are you shaming right now? Whose kind support and upbringing are *you* ignoring? And what will you be *spending* it on? How will you be *guarding* all this money from those who have none and wish to take some, if not *all*, of yours?"

When Ma does this voice and attitude to me, I always buckle and give in. You just don't know where the blow will be coming from! This is merely the preparation, her introduction. The kill will come from a totally different direction. I see Ma seeing the man hesitate. Oooh! She goes in for the kill!

Papa is smiling gently at Ma. He catches my eye, winks at me then tells me to fetch Father David.

I really don't want to leave; I want to watch and learn from Ma. Yet I feel good. I am a man again. Going to fetch the priest is *very* important. And yes, I know Ma's tactics; it makes me squirm even if I am not in the direct line of fire!

∞

I find Father David at the side of the cathedral. He is just completing the burial of a small child. It is a small gathering, much smaller than it would *ever* be in Juxon. There, the whole community would have been present to support the family in their loss.

A small gathering is an indication that the family is not an active part of the community. After a burial as small as this one, Father David or any other priest would be bending over backwards to bring this family into the embrace of the whole community, so that they always feel supported and know that they have somewhere to go and someone waiting to help them.

Burials are huge social events. I remember Sapphira and me taking cakes and food around to one of the neighbours after their eldest son died whilst studying in Singapore. Papa and Ma also went along later in the evening to pay their respects. It's what everyone does.

I wait impatiently. By the time Father David and I reach our building, the deed is done. The landlord has accepted Papa, Professor Miles and the nurses' status in the community; accepted that it would be a huge show of 'beneficence' to allow us all to remain here. In any case he is already renting a second house to a foreign group.

Father David listens to both sides and then says a long prayer. He praises the man's business acumen, forgives his greed, prays for us to be more generous and asks us all to promise to help each other endure this difficult period more effortlessly and wholesomely whenever we can. The man leaves with the adults – all except Ma.

Sapphira and I breathe a sigh of relief. Ma is strutting around like the winner she is. We high five several times. Yes! My Ma. How I love this woman! What a negotiator! Sometimes she is absolute fire, a volcano erupting, and sometimes she is pure honey. She knows exactly what to use when. How and when do I begin to practise my negotiating skills?

Papa returns to our flatlet during his lunch break. "Angelina, my angel, what a performance! Hollywood has need of you! Thank you so much. That was an Oscar winning performance. Let's dance."

"My dearest, darling Frediddy, you ain't seen nothing yet!"

That night we give thanks for our room, for the rent staying at the same price and for Ma's skills at negotiation. And the fun we had doing so. I hear Ma's suppressed throaty gurgles as I float into a dream.

∞

Ma has a job! Ma is working as second in command to one of the *marties* at Save the Children Fund. Benedict calls them Save – and so do we. In fact, everybody seems to call them that – now how did Benedict hear of that? They are running a feeding centre for the smaller children, the ones five years old and younger. Even though MSF is doing the same, both places are filled to capacity, according to Papa and Ma.

We visit Ma's place of work. Ma has a beautiful desk. The man we had seen carrying his table on his back all that time ago, very proudly sold it to Save. How patient he has been! He is also working for them as a warehouse manager. I ask him about the desk.

"I reckoned I would need some money, something to live by, for a few months at least. The table is my most prized possession. My father and I made this table from two trees the government felled to make way for a road. Both my father and I used to climb these trees as a child. We wanted a good remembrance. So, I brought it with me. See all these scars? I had to defend it from people wanting to chop it up for firewood. What battles I had protecting it. Now, look, I have a good job; good fortune, eh?"

∞

Ma, who shies away from anything that hints at domesticity, has a job organising the workers to prepare the special food. She is also in charge of distributing the dry rations of high protein, high energy biscuits for those children who are able to stay at home. Plus, Ma interprets for the *marty* called Linda. Linda is in charge of the feeding centre. She is Belgian. They also have Nurse Clare who is in charge of the section for malnourished children. She is from Jamari.

Ma loves the work. In no time at all she has organised the whole place, bringing in the healthier children who visit daily, getting them singing and dancing, as well as networking to find the best tailor to sew clothes for the *marties*. Ma becomes a mine of information, Mrs Fixit, the person everyone goes to when they want to know anything.

Every night she has wonderful stories to tell us. "Story of the day. I petitioned for burial cloths for the dead children *and* I am once again leading the grieving processes, just as I did in Parrish. You see, this job is like *any other* business, and I'm going to improve it to my high level. This is going to be *the best* feeding centre Save or any other agency has ever had, believe me!

What I've discovered is that Linda and the whole of Save are all very keen to maintain our culture; they're very sensitive to cultural values. So, I've decided that whatever I or the women feel is necessary, will be deemed a 'cultural necessity' because I have observed that Save and the other *marties* respond very quickly and positively to those words."

She also brings home the broken bits of special biscuits for Benedict, which Sapphira and I eat as well. They *really* fill you up.

Chapter Seventeen

Before Ma started work, we had a family meeting to discuss 'changing domestic dynamics', as Ma describes it. So now, whilst Papa and Ma are at work, Sapphira and I care for Benedict and do all the housework and cooking. Ma leaves the room everyday with the warning: "Now you two, I don't want to see a *single mark* on Benedict when I return! You care for him properly!"

We are doing the work of our housekeeper-cum-cook, our cleaner, Benedict's nanny and a washing machine. I find this work extremely boring. It's not what I was born to do, of that I am absolutely sure! Businessmen don't do domestic work! They have others do it for them. Sapphira doesn't like it any more than I do.

"This is not women's work! This is domestic work; genderless! *Both* of us have to do it, so equality reigns in the Wiggins HQ. In fact, this is by no means equality; I vote for it being proportional.

I am younger, therefore I need to do *less* washing and cleaning."

I had used this argument with her before, suggesting that, as I am bigger and older than all of them, I need to have more chocolate ice cream and bigger slices of cake. Now she is using it on me. I am doubly annoyed because I cannot use this argument any more; I hadn't realised it would backfire on me so soon!

This new arrangement does not sit well with my image as the daytime man of the house. I was leaning more towards it being me telling Sapphira what to do and checking up on her later, whilst I go walking around the market place, meeting up with other young men and discussing the 'situation'. Some dream!

This new plan is far too restrictive; I can't move! We have to stay indoors or in the small back yard guarding the washing until it dries. When going to the market, we *have* to go together to buy the day's supplies. We are *stuck* together. We are not allowed to move without the other. We, who have been used to a considerable amount of space and freedom, are suddenly shackled by domesticity.

In addition, until Papa and Ma started work, we always had them around to entertain us. Sapphira works on my nerves! All this questioning all the time! I don't have Papa's patience.

Our squabbling increases to all out war; we are getting physical! Today was a particularly bad day, and Benedict tells Ma as soon as she walks in the door that we have been hitting each other. Now we are having a special meeting.

"I know it's difficult! You don't have to tell me – I know! You have too much unstructured time on your hands, and you know what that means don't you? You are bored, uninterested in domesticity and not using all the resources you have. It *is* true, isn't it? None of us in this family wants to do this work, and yet, it *has* to be done. We cannot afford a cleaner at present. And, if we could, what would you two be doing with all the spare time in such a restricted area? The cleaner would probably be acting as referee! As you two cannot earn a wage and your father and I are blessed to be employed, it is up to you two to take on the responsibility of the housework.

I know you hate this domestic arrangement at the moment. And do you know what; research has shown consistently that it is these little routine things that help to keep us sane. We all need normality within this chaos, like getting up every morning, instead of lying in bed until goodness knows what hour. *Everybody* finds that doing the mediocre chores in times of stress gives us the strength to continue, to give our lives stability when everything is falling apart around us, when others are going mad with grief. These daily routines are a godsend, a blessing. The sooner you realise this the better it will be for you.

It is this very lack of *more* routine things that is causing you to quarrel so much. I think if you had more structure to your day, this wouldn't happen. Apart from your delivery round, structure comes in the shape of domestic routine. Rise, wash, eat, wash dishes, do the laundry, buy food, prepare food, care for Benedict. What I propose now is that we set you a task every day to keep your mind occupied as well. What do you think, Frederick?"

"I think that is an excellent idea. How about us giving you some money to buy an exercise book each? Wouldn't it be a good idea to write about anything you witnessed each day? Keep these diaries – see them as history in the making - something to look back over years later, something to cherish. Write at least a half a page of story. The other half of the page is what positive learning you have gained from the incident and how you intend to integrate this into your life.

In fact I think all four of us can do this. I too am learning so much every day and then I forget some of the insights, or I have been remiss in integrating the learning into my life and teaching others about it. What wasted moments! Never mind, we can start now. We will then discuss these insights every night. What if each of us has ten minutes for their story, their insight and how they intend to integrate it into their life? Daily teachings; isn't that inspiring? As you can see this is merely another routine and one that keeps your mind sharp and active."

My father remains deep in thought for a long while, then continues in the same vein.

"Yes, I see where your mother and I went astray. We were so busy with our new work that we did not pay attention to your needs. When we speak to Ellie, we will instruct her as well. To repeat, your learning is very much part of a routine; normality within this chaos. Do you two understand this? Good. "

Sapphira and I nod our heads in agreement.

Ma continues: "I see the *marties* have many technical books. Is it so at your office as well, Frederick? I will see if I can borrow one book at a time, one per week. Bring it home each evening, return it every morning. Maybe negotiate the entire Sunday. Each evening one of you will read the book, study it, write about it, and discuss it."

Papa laughs: "I can see us all becoming experts at digging the best latrines, as the *marties* call toilets, immunising children, making special feeds, providing water, and so on. Soon the Wiggins family will be setting up their own emergency agency! So you two had better become absolute experts in each of these. What do you think?"

We both nod, smiles on our faces; an absolutely brilliant idea.

"What will we call our agency, Papa?" Sapphira asks.

"I don't think it should be an acronym. It will simply be known as Wiggins. At least they will remember that it was started by the Wiggins family."

"Wow, Ma, that is *sooo* cool. We don't need an explanation. We can do some research to see where there is a niche." Sapphira is all excited.

Ma smiles. "Good. So, from tomorrow, when you go about all these routine, normal tasks, say a huge thanks for them, because it gives immense structure to your day."

Papa adds, "Remember also to be grateful for living in a house that has running water. The people in the camp have to fetch and carry the water from communal standpipes that come from huge bladders filled with thousands and thousands of litres of water. Now, sometimes, there is no water because the trucks that fetch the water are held up or broken down. People stand in long, long queues waiting and waiting for water. Please remember these things.

As for the daily writing that we do, I hope to see a change in all of us. It is my hope we can *all* see how blessed we are, even in these circumstances. The intention of the writing is to gain an insight into the events and to take all this attention away from ourselves. Serve others - and learn how we can use these insights in our daily lives, by *teaching* others as well.

At present, all you two children are concerned about is yourselves. Yes? Well, from now on I hope you see that there are others around you that need care and attention. I am sure this will change your constant squabbling. Do you understand?"

"Yes Papa," we say in unison.

∞

We are frequent visitors to both my parent's places of work. Nobody seems to mind. We only stay a few minutes, then go. The *marties* like Benedict's lisp, so we use him to gain daily visiting rights.

Sapphira is intrigued by how they do things. I like their busy-ness; the ambience; the words they use; their accents and their hand-held radios. These radios absolutely fascinate me. We, too, decide on our own call signs; Sapphira's suggestion is that we use the first two letters of our names.

"Lima Uniform! I don't want to be that. You would be Sierra Alpha and Ma is already Alpha One. It will confuse Benedict, won't it? What if we choose our own? Let's write down three choices and choose from there."

"OK. I am now Victor Oscar"

"You can't be! Victor's a man's name!"

"It's not about gender, is it, and it is *my first* choice! Stop wanting other people's!"

I can't make up my mind. My father's call sign is Foxtrot Romeo. All of theirs seems so *apt* for them! Mine has to be fitting, personal as well!

An hour passes. I still can't decide. Benedict comes in from playing with his friends.

"Benedict, your call sign is Bravo Echo."

"No, it isn't! I'm *not* Bwavo, I'm Bendy. Chiya and Gwace call me Bendy."

"But that's not part of the call sign!"

"Doesn't matter! I'm *Bendy*!"

"But it is *not* the international code."

"Doesn't matter! I'm *Bendy*!"

"OK! OK! So Bendy Echo then."

"No, no, ***no***! E is for elephant. *It's in my book*. A is for apple, B is for ball, C is for cat, D is for dog, E is for elephant. I am Bendy Elephant!"

"But you can't be!"

"I AM! I AM! I AM!"

OK! **OK**! Bendy Elephant!

Of all the call signs left over, I eventually decide on Tango Zulu, a dancing warrior! Yes!

∞

"Victor Oscar. Victor Oscar from Tango Zulu. Over."

"Tango Zulu, this is Victor Oscar. I copy. Over."

"Location of Bendy Elephant. Over."

"On toilet. Over"

"Doing what. Over"

"Number two. Over."

"What is our ETD to the market? Over."

"Two minutes after final evacuation. Over."

"Do I copy two minutes? Over."

"Affirmative. Add two more minutes post evacuation. Over."

"Don't copy. Over."

"Job's not finished until the paperwork's done. Over."

"Roger that. I copy. Over and out."

We see young boys in the market with their own hand made radios. We search and search for something to make our own as well. After days of searching we hit gold. In MSF's rubbish bin we find three tiny empty tonic water cans, like the ones they serve on the aeroplanes. The Wiggins offspring each have custom made radio sets.

Chapter Eighteen

Papa and Ma work long hours helping to set up and run their offices. Despite all the observations I am doing, looking after Benedict the whole day is sometimes both onerous and boring.

It is taking sooo much effort to restrain this compelling urge to go wandering around the camps and see who is there. What are they doing? How on earth do they live like that! This huge mass of people living so close together, having nothing, so grey and dusty and bent over. I am intrigued by my parent's stories at night. *I* want to do something as well, instead of merely being a *nanny*!

The *marties* are all working in the camps, but Papa forbids me to go to the camps. I argue that I could increase my knowledge for our Wiggins agency much sooner if I am allowed to go to the camps. I am going to be a researcher, of course; but Papa remains adamant - the answer is no.

Papa, Ma and the nurses tell us that some of the Jamari residents have crossed the border and taken up residence in the camps to get food rations and all the non-food items. They feel they are missing out on all these free handouts when they too need these items.

The Jamari residents live in both the camps and their homes across the border, and they, like us, have special cards from MSF giving them permission to stand in endless, timeless queues and be given all sorts of things. They are called NFI's - non-food items. We guard this special card with our lives; without them you cannot get *anything*. So far we have received cooking pots and spoons and plastic bowls and a jerry can to carry water from one agency, and three months' supply of rice, beans and oil from another agency. We really have no space in our room now.

To receive each of these items I have to stand in a queue from early morning, immediately after my bread round. Sapphira has to care for Benedict - Papa's instructions. Ma also told me to wear my clothes for at least three days so that I can blend in and the *marties* can see that my family really need these items. Well, we *do*! But every so often a *marty* will remove someone from the long queue because they look as if they don't need the handouts. I tell you: *we all* need whatever is been given! We left so many things back home; *nothing* is spare. Why should they judge us by the clothes we wear! What if many in the queue have special 'distribution day' clothes, all tattered and torn?

∞

Standing in the hot sun from eight thirty, after a hurried breakfast, until perhaps three o'clock or longer is hard work.

We go through stages in the queue. Initially, everyone is silent, anticipating, doubtful, hopeful. Some of us sing and dance, as if to energetically draw the supplies towards us. I think we are all hoping there will be enough supplies until *after* we have collected ours. Then I feel guilty at such selfishness and pray that there *is* enough for everyone in the queue.

We watch the trucks arrive, park and open up to reveal their contents. We watch the men unload; their bodies glistening with sweat and dust. Each item is stacked in a specific section so that we can move along the line from registration to receiving every item in turn. Today we are receiving three blankets and soap and salt; three sections only.

I watch the *marties* talking on their radios, shouting at some of the workers, talking and laughing with others. I wonder what they are saying. I find them fascinating and a weird group of people. It is so hot and they are wearing *boots*. Very few wear hats and their faces become blistery in the heat of our Asian sun. And do some of them smoke! I count the number of cigarettes they smoke; they must be burning their mouths to cinders!

Papa never smokes; it's not that important for anybody I know. Except the poorer people, although neither of our gardeners smoked. Maybe these *marties* are really poor and are sent by their countries to work here? I must ask Lydia, the lady boss of MSF. Her ashtray is always overflowing, no matter how often the cleaner empties it. She's not poor, is she? She wears lots of gold jewellery. And the doctor can't be poor, so why do they behave like our poor people, I wonder.

When everything is back to normal, I must check to see whether rich and educated Juxonese smoke. A researcher! That's what I will be. Sociology or anthropology? I can research all the different behaviours of people - perhaps why people smoke so much - or maybe research why there is war and conflict, why people have to fight about politics. So much research to do! Maybe I should just concentrate on one particular thing? Find my niche, as Sapphira says – perhaps.

Waiting in the hot sun makes my mind tour around a myriad of other things; friends, family, what Ellie is doing right now – I didn't talk with her today, I don't have the time on distribution days. The baker has reduced our calls to Mondays, Wednesday and Fridays. I miss her; *really* miss her.

More waiting, just standing or sitting in the queue. Even the women behind me have grown weary of chatting. I scratch the scabs off my hands and arms. Three days ago, Sapphira and I took

Benedict for a compulsory immunisation jab at Save. Ma showed them that he had already had the measles jab, but they insisted, saying these are unsettling times and there's a huge risk of him dying from a measles epidemic. Benedict did not want an injection; he said he wasn't sick! He kept running away. In the end, both Sapphira and I had to hold him whilst he scratched and bit us. It was his fourth birthday; he's probably going to remember this for the rest of his life!

I hope he also remembers the wonderful party he had. Both Ma and Papa brought presents from the *marties*; they like him. He insists they call him Bendy Elephant and doesn't respond when they call him Benedict.

When they heard it was his birthday, they gave him lots of sweets and biscuits, even two tins of canned fish. I never thought I would give those two tins such a warm welcome! We never used to eat them at home, only when I used to go on outings with the cubs and scouts.

We added some bottles of fizzy drinks and Sapphira put jam on the biscuits and invited all of Benedict's new friends from the yard. Everything, including crumbs, vanished before Sapphira had time to light the single candle. "Faster than the world's best magician's sleight of hand." I told our family around the evening discussion. The next day we took Benedict to both offices to say 'thank you'.

At last I reach the registration table. The man writing down the details on my card is from Parrish; I have seen him many times before. One of the many of Papa's ex-pupils before he moved to Montgomery. I look down and have no eye contact after a polite greeting. I don't want him to recognise me, just in case he thinks we don't *deserve* the blankets and soap and salt.

Suddenly I feel ashamed to be standing here begging. I have never felt this way before, why do I feel so now? Because he knows that I come from Scholars Close? Knows Papa? That we were richer than him? Now *he* is giving *me* and my family things.

What if he feels we don't deserve it? What if he thinks we can afford all these things, expensive and unobtainable as they are right now? He seems to be taking *ever* so long finding our family's details.

I don't breathe. I am *really* scared. Did he like school? Did he, does he respect Papa? Was Papa good to him? Of course, he *always is,* but particularly so? I can't *bear* to have others think we don't deserve this. The shame of walking away empty-handed and them screaming after me that there are others who are more deserving. Please, *please, please,* let me pass along.

Breathe. Papa always says to breathe deeply. I do so now. Oh! How to swim through this? Take another big breath. Stand tall. I, we, my family, we deserve this!

After centuries of waiting, he says softly "So, Mr Wiggins, hard times, eh?"

"Yes sir" I reply, looking straight at him, managing a small smile. He looks down again, ticks besides our name. "Go well" he says and hands me our card. I breathe a huge sigh of relief and move along the line to receive the three blankets, then the two double bars of soap and lastly a small bag of salt. I say "Thank you" for all three items, then head home.

∞

I reach home to find Sapphira in a thoroughly bad mood. Benedict is near her, playing with his toy car.

"What's up?"

"You dawdled and dawdled, wasting time. You could have been home *ages* ago to help do the cleaning."

"What? You're talking rubbish, as usual! Your supersonic eyes have let you down, yet again! I came home directly! What's this rubbish about dawdling? Your delusions of persecution are taking over your life again."

"Oh *shut up*! *You know nothing*! I've done most of the washing. Finish it!"

"*No way*! I *refuse*! Why should I?! It is three o'clock and the washing should have been dry by now! I was as busy as you!" I say as I hold out the blankets and soap for her to see.

She is not impressed with these gifts. Shouts something and rushes out of our house. Ugh! Sisters!

At first I refuse to do the washing. However, when, after fifteen minutes she still does not return I, having already done a day's hard labour waiting in the never-ending queue for the blankets, complete the washing like a supreme martyr. I figure it is better to do the washing than get a tongue lashing from Ma and a long lecture from Papa. There were only a few small things of Benedict's anyway. It's the *principle*!

I give one of the children in the yard a very precious half of a Save biscuit and ask her to guard our washing as before. There are now three families living in the yard and each of us living inside give them a plate of supper. She is the child of the family we feed. Sapphira argues that this small amount of food, which is feeding the whole family, is slow death, but as she cannot think of an alternative, we continue to provide.

I return indoors. Stand still. Benedict! Where's Benedict? I call and call. Did Sapphira take him with her? She was so angry at the time! Knock on the nurses' door. No Benedict there, Sapphira had fetched him ages ago, after his lunch there. Oh God! Ma is going to kill me, us! Rush to the porch. Ask the people sitting there. They shrug their shoulders, their own anxieties leaving no time to observe little boys taking walks on their own. Where is Sapphira? How *dare* she just walk out like that! She's supposed to be looking after Benedict. Now both are gone. What to do now?

I can't go to Ma. She will skin me alive. Besides, she is working. They are very busy there. She cannot leave her work for something I am supposed to be responsible for, can she? I walk towards the market, fine-toothcomb the place. *Definitely not here*. I return to our place to see whether Sapphira has cooled down and returned yet.

My watch shows 16:00. I remove the dry washing from on the line and still Sapphira has not returned from wherever she went. Damn! Please keep Benedict safe. And give Sapphira whatever she deserves! Make her realise what she has done! And please give me some inkling where my little brother is, please, please, *please*.

Deep breath, then another few. Close my eyes and I imagine that, when I open them, Benedict is sitting with Sapphira in the kitchen. I see him, with his red striped T-shirt. Open my eyes. OK. No, not quite the instant magic I had expected. Maybe retrace steps.

Sapphira and I are arguing. Do I really see Benedict still sitting there? Yes? No? Don't know. Did he leave before Sapphira rushed out? Ask the people on the porch again. Still shake their heads. Go to the yard.

"Bendy Elephant. Bendy Elephant. Tango Zulu to Bendy Elephant." Wait. Repeat. Wait.

"Tango Zulu, this is Bendy Elephant. I copy." A little red T-shirt emerges out of the shelter of the girl guarding our washing. Thank you God, Buddha, Allah, Gandhi, Mandela, Jesus, Einstein, everybody!

Benedict is telling the toddler a story. He closes his book as soon as he sees me. I scoop him up into my arms and take him home.

"Benedict, we *all* have to tell someone where we are going at all times. House rules! You know that."

"Yes."

"But you didn't tell us where you were going!"

"I did so! You and Saffy were scweaming and I don't like it. Sowee. I was telling a stowee to Luke. Maybe I should …"

Suddenly there is a loud bang. Explosion. Screaming and shouting. Guns being fired. Benedict shouts "Saffy!"

The noise, the mayhem is coming from the market. What to do now? Take Benedict with me and see what is happening? Where the hell is that bloody girl?! Do I now wait here for Sapphira to come home? Is it safe to take Benedict with me to the market? Do I leave him with the laundry guard?

I rush to the market, piggy-backing Benedict. The soldiers, who are using a petrol drum as a shield, stop us. I kneel beside them, Benedict in my arms. I shout that my sister is there in the market. I really don't know, but there is really no other place to go. Unless she went to Ma's work to complain there? I hope not. Still I have to see.

The soldier won't let us through. They are still shooting. Rebels have thrown two grenades in the market and now they and the soldiers are having a shoot-out. I am really worried about Sapphira. I don't feel safe here at all. In fact, I am terrified. Still, I beg the soldier. He says he will knock some sense into me if I don't leave! What to do? This is an *emergency*! I am allowed.

I run with Benedict to Ma's work, praying as I run. Is this God's answer to my prayer? I didn't mean you to kill her, God! How on earth can she learn the lesson when she's *dead*?

Ma takes one look at me, shouts something to Linda and we run towards our home. I am crying. Ma tells me to shut up until we know what really happened.

We wait and wait and wait at our house for the shooting to stop. Ma is sitting down, Benedict on her lap. She is breathing heavily, not saying anything, not looking anywhere. I keep starting and attempting to explain what happened, but Ma is not responding at all until she shouts, *"STOP!"* I stop. I'm nervous and guilty and I can't bear this waiting.

∞

The shooting stops – eventually. All of fifteen minutes of mayhem. A soldier shouts over his radio that all the rebels are dead. How did they sneak in here, or were they here all the time? Are they the 'breakaway factions' we keep hearing about now? Once we see others running towards the market, we follow. People are looking at the injured and the dead to see if they can identify anyone. Papa and MSF are there, plus all the nurses.

Papa sees the tears pouring down my face, shouts "Sapphira?!" and starts rushing around searching the market for her. I stay with Ma and Benedict. We can't find her! Where is she? Ever so often we meet up with Papa, but he too hasn't seen her. Panic is rising in me. Ma has gone from silence to hysterical in a blink. Papa is shouting Sapphira's name like a madman, Benedict is screaming. I am paralysed by guilt. Where is she?! Was she here in the first place? I promise to be friendlier towards her, *please* let her just be safe!

∞

The MSF medical staff has taken all the injured to their hospital. Papa stays with us. We check all the dead again. Gruesome bodies. I don't see the full horror of it; I'm just praying that Sapphira is not among them.

No Sapphira. We have scoured the market. She's not here! Papa and Ma are too distressed to return to work without knowing where Sapphira is. It's nearly going home time anyway. We decide to go home and wait for her there. Visitors come to offer support and sympathy. Papa and Ma barely talk. Both just sit, their bodies occasionally wracked by deep sighs and sobs. I am *sooo* scared! I am begging Sapphira to just turn up.

We hear the main door of the house click open and shut. We think it is one of the nurses returning.

It is Sapphira, sauntering in at five thirty, just before Ma would normally arrive. She is puzzled to see Ma *and* Papa already at home.

We all shout at her. "*Where have you been*?!"

"I went to Savannah's place. Luther was horrible to me. He wouldn't help me with all the washing. So I was annoyed and I left! When I heard the fighting in the market, I stayed with Savannah until everything was quiet and now I've come home."

It all sounds very logical and sensible and carefully planned. The *complete* opposite of our turmoil! *All the more* reason to be irrationally incensed with her! Papa's low, deep bass measures out in slow bulleted tones. "We spent the whole afternoon looking for you. We didn't know where you were; we thought you were in the market. We searched and searched and searched, fearing you were injured, if not dead. And now you walk in here, brazen as hell and tell us you were safe all the time! Did you tell Luther where you were going? Can you see that rules have been broken here? Can you see what happens when rules are broken?

You were inconsiderate. Yes! You were angry! Yes! You felt you had to get away. Did you consider what would happen by breaking the rules? Next time, obey the rules and please tell someone in the family where you are going. I don't want to go through another afternoon like this ever again."

Sapphira is silent. Papa gulps and gulps before talking again.

"Did I not say that we *always* have to know where the others are, for this very reason? We searched and searched the market, our hearts heavy at the thought of you injured or dead. Thank God you are safe. We did not need to have gone through that."

There is more talk, much more talk of us being more tolerant towards each other. It is as if relief has made Ma and Papa eloquently garrulous. All the pent up feelings are being spent now. I accept part of the blame. I don't know why, when I don't think I have done anything wrong! Apart from being intolerant and impatient towards my sister. I have very mixed feelings: grateful she is alive and resentful that she left the house and was safe whilst we went through all kinds of agony. I don't even mention Benedict's disappearance. I hope he learned his lesson as well! Neither do I mention that I went to the market *with Benedict* at the height of the shooting. Why on earth did I do that? Because my concern for Sapphira overshadowed my survival? Wow!

Nobody even looks at the blankets and soap and salt I waited in line for, for over six hours. I'm so ashamed to be thinking of Sapphira lying ever so slightly injured and I look at her and say, "I told you so." No. Not a good thought.

Chapter Nineteen

After this incident, security is stepped up. Curfew is now from seven o'clock in the morning until seven at night. Anyone that moves, the soldiers have authority to shoot to kill. Sometimes during the night we hear the soldiers shouting and then shooting. These gunshots really scare me. I don't like not knowing what is going on, who has been killed or injured, if more splinter groups are forming and intent on invading Hamilton, and when we will all be safe again.

These worries make my heart thump in my rib cage. Some nights I'm too scared to sleep, just in case we are awoken by gunfire. I figure it's worse being woken by sudden blasts of gunfire. Makes my heart thump like mad and it takes ages to become calm again. During these times I just lie there, soaked in sweat and sending prayers for our safety, *and* that the outside world's experts and negotiators come to our rescue like they did in other countries. Why not here? We are or were British after all! Surely all English speaking countries should be helping us, and encouraging all other nations to support them as well! Why is this not happening? I'm getting no answers to my questions. No more calls from Royce either.

These uncertain times also stops Ma's and Papa's whispered giggling at night. I lie curled up around Benedict. Sometimes he sleeps with me, sometimes with Sapphira, most times with Papa and Ma.

Sapphira whispers to me, "Are you all right, Luther?" Of course I say I am all right. But I'm not. I can't wake up in the mornings because I can't sleep at night. Ma notices my sleepy head and says, "Never mind, many people can't sleep at night. What we need to do is send each other silent messages of courage. That way we know we are not alone."

I keep praying. I seem to have formed a more frequent discussion pattern with God. Well, begging actually; begging Him to keep us safe. We *have* to get back to Ellie, haven't we?

∞

Few of those displaced to the camps come into the town these days. Besides the soldiers keeping them out of the town, they have no money to buy the stuff that is there now. Since the *marties'* arrival the traders are very happy. They make their money from all the *marties* now. All the *marties* working in Tomsdale have to pass through Hamilton on their way there. They have decided it is safe enough to set up their work there as well.

Lots and lots of traffic; fast moving traffic. The *marties* and the military are putting people's lives at risk with their reckless driving. Is this how they drive in London, or Paris or wherever they come from? Hamilton is not Queenville; it's a sleepy little backwater place, not used to so many vehicles. The children and adults now living in the camps are not used to such fast driving vehicles. Many road traffic accidents are happening.

I see our Land Rover now and again. It has MSF stickers on the sides. How did they manage to make our new vehicle look so old and battered *so quickly*? It always fills me with concern about how we are going to return home without transport. Will they just say 'thank you' and return it to us? Will they take it back with them? Will we need to buy it back from them?

Fortunately for me, the Land Rover has moved to Tomsdale with the MSF branch there, so there is no daily reminder for me. Still, I see it often enough to start the wound bleeding again, to remind me of what we had, of starting me to worry and think how we are going to return home.

Twice now the agencies have had to hastily withdraw to Hamilton due to 'insecurity' in Tomsdale. I have discovered that it means they were shot at or threatened. How can people shoot at those coming to help them? How can they steal all the supplies the people in the camps need? How can they call themselves Juxonese?

∞

While Sapphira and I walk around the stalls with Benedict, we do our own pretend shopping. We keep tabs by making an inventory of all the new wares brought in especially for the *marties*; instant coffee, beer, different cigarettes, powdered milk, cornflakes, chocolate spread and many more exotic and expensive things. We used to eat all these things at home, now we can only look at them, imagine tasting them again. It makes me even hungrier and after a short while I decide not to play this game anymore.

I leave Sapphira and Benedict to play while I ponder more serious questions; questions like: when are we going home? How are we going to get there? Every time the *marties* rush from Tomsdale to Hamilton for safety, I am so downhearted because it means that Juxon is not safe enough yet for us to return. Papa hears from Royce via emails at the office. He has been back and forth twice now. The view from Juxon continues to look depressingly bad.

Occasionally, Sapphira and I take Benedict for a walk to the outskirts of town. Well, to the outskirts of the Kavari Quay or Tomsdale camps. We check to see how much larger they have become since our last visit.

I see more and more stalls all along the road. People are selling their wares, even the donated stuff. Papa says it is to get money to buy special or different foods for their families. There is even fresh meat. They must have gone hunting in the great forest near the border. We haven't eaten meat for a while now. In fact, I can't remember when last we actually ate meat. It's beans and rice with a bit of vegetable most days. I, who hated beans so much that I gagged on them, now can't wait for the evening meal. We buy peanuts and sunflower seeds to add to our meals. There's a lot of it around, so it is cheap. Ma says to buy as much as we can and store it. Both Ma and Papa eat lunch from the stalls outside their offices, and we share Benedict's high energy biscuits and milk. I am as tall as Papa now. But my answered prayer to be as tall as Papa is creating a few more negative effects.

One of them is that all my trousers hover above my ankles now. Lydia, MSF's administrator, says it is all the rage in Europe; both she and Marcus the engineer are wearing their calf length trousers today.

"See, Lydia, personally, I don't like it. I prefer it to be ankle length. I am a new man and these three-quarter length trousers seem so *undecided*! I want some certainty in my life and wearing ankle length trousers is one of the few things that provide me with that 100% certainty."

"Then you will have to stop growing or become rich enough to buy yourself some longer trousers!"

∞

The *marties* from both Ma and Papa's work lend Sapphira and me some of their books to read. My parents inspect the contents first to see whether these books are suitable for us. I read the back cover of some of the books Papa rejects. They are sooo violent. Why do people, dealing all day with violence, still read books on violence? I must ask them one day.

I read as voraciously as Sapphira. We read *everything* allowed, including old English newspapers from England, Australia, America and Canada. Both Sapphira and I use our Latin to speak Spanish and Italian. It doesn't always work but it does provide some fun and laughter. I didn't realise I know so much Latin; I hated the language so much when I had to learn it!

We read their field books about toilets, clean water, immunisations, monitoring the under-five year olds, how many calories we all need daily – I disagree with this! I need infinitely more food and calories than they are giving us.

I prefer their 'off duty' books. I enjoy reading about quantum physics and such like. Sapphira argues it is not factual and 'all in the air'. Maybe I like 'all in the air' stuff. This synchronicity stuff makes sense to me. Ma says it is no good for a businessman. Papa argues that it has meaning in *everything* in life.

So what am I going to be eventually? Thank goodness for this present mess – I don't have to decide just yet. There is so much more choice than I was aware of, which makes it even more difficult to decide. I want to do a little of everything!

∞

Later that week when I use the flimsiest of excuses to visit Papa's work, Lydia calls me into her office. She gives me a parcel.

"Do you mind if I open it immediately, in your presence? It is a Juxonese custom to open presents in the presence of the person who has given it to us."

She laughs. "Go on, my constant teacher. Open it now."

I fumble a bit out of sheer excitement and nervousness. Whatever can it be that she is giving to me? Material. A pair of trousers. A *new* pair of trousers. I hold them against me while saying 'Thank You' and *Kelsho* over and over again.

They're about two inches too long. I look at her, a little doubt creeping into my eyes. There *are* shorter trousers. I have been checking the market and the shops. She laughs at my confusion.

"Luther, I do not want to be buying you a new pair of trousers every other week! You can grow into these. Surely it is OK to walk around with turn ups? See, they have pockets all over the place, even more than some of your own pairs. I thought you might like that – very functional."

Boy! Do I feel good! After many more thank yous from me she laughingly shoos me out of her office.

I go to the bathroom and change trousers, turning up the extra two inches. It feels good. I swagger a bit around the office – I don't care how amused they all are. At home I put my comb and toothbrush in one pocket. In another pocket I secrete my portion of cash from the Land Rover. Since my parents started working, we haven't had to use either Sapphira's or my portion, yet. We all keep saying, "It's not quite an emergency yet, is it? Not yet dire; we can still make do." Now, look, I received a gift of a pair of trousers!

At our evening meeting that night, Ma makes a suggestion.

"Tiger, how about selling your two pairs of Levi jeans? They are still in excellent condition. Use a quarter of the money to treat yourself, Sapphira and Benedict and save the rest. What do you think?"

Brilliant idea! The next day Sapphira and I check out the prices of jeans in the market. We double our price, then add twenty percent more, in case of haggling. These are Levi jeans, after all!

Soldiers come and finger them; they're too expensive for the poorer ones. More soldiers come, higher up the pay scale. Finger them; check the size; check them against their bodies.

Haggle.

I can't see their eyes behind their mirror sunglasses. I put a finger to my heart -'*Forvandl!*' Take a deep breath. Wait. Heart stops thumping. Sweat dries. Tongue is moist again. Normal.

They want to pay the same price as the new jeans in the market.

My deep voice booms out in annoyance. "These are *genuine Levi* jeans. Quality. You won't find these anywhere else. The *right* person will come and buy them for the right price. It's a *very fair* price for such quality." They leave. Obviously not the right person.

Master Bato and a colleague stroll along. I have a sharp intake of breath as he fingers the jeans. Thank goodness they're far too small for him, otherwise he would probably take them, like he did the motorbike!

Master Bato's colleague, a tall, thin, absolutely skinny man, buys one pair with minimum haggling. He pays the price we asked, then says: "Levis were going for double your price a few days ago. Check your market man!" Darn! Never mind, it's still a huge amount of money for us rookie salespeople.

The other soldier, who had been haggling and wanting to lower the price, now agrees to buy the other pair at our original price.

When they are out of sight, we hug each other. What a good partnership!

We go shopping. What a thrill! We spend a quarter of our newly earned money on a big scrapbook and a set of coloured pens for Benedict, some hair clips, baubles and a hairbrush for Sapphira and some batteries for my MP3 player. Best of all, a jar of chocolate spread and some biscuits for the family. We buy an extra loaf of bread and rush home to have an early lunch of warm bread and thickly spread chocolate.

"Marvelicious." Benedict says whilst licking the spread. He has chocolate smeared all over his face.

"Heaven," I say while nibbling slowly, savouring every lick.

"Paradise," says Sapphira as we smile at each other.

"Fantabulous!" We remark in unison.

∞

Nipping in and out of my parent's office for various mundane excuses, I begin to learn a lot more about these *marties*. Many of them don't greet each other in the morning. And the man who is the accountant at Papa's place has music plugged into his ears all day. When he takes them out, it is to swear and growl at everybody and anybody. Such rudeness! Such foul words! Violent words with a violent temper. They fight *worse* than Sapphira and I could ever have imagined.

When Lydia sees me looking at their offensive interactions, she tells me they are stressed - that is why they fight so much. I tell her to talk with Papa because he has many ways to deal with stress.

I had asked my parents before about this issue of not greeting; it is of huge importance to every Juxonese. I ask my father again.

"What about us respecting their customs?" I look at him in amazement; is his reaction merely to provoke a different viewpoint from me or does he, after all his reminders to us, accept such rudeness?

"But, Papa, they are in our country!"

"So, Tiger, does that mean that if we were to go to one of their countries, we should only be doing what they are doing?"

I am stuck. I have not thought of that. I can see now that they bring their customs with them, the same as I would take my customs with me. "But Papa, how then can we do things that would help us to respect and accept each other even though there are differences? I mean, we go to Singapore and our customs are symbiotic, aren't they?"

"Well, from the questions you say the *marties* are asking you, I think it would be fair to say that we *are* learning from each other to see what is acceptable. What do you think? Do you think we could learn some things from them as well that would enhance our lifestyle, our way of thinking, and make life easier? After all, we have already adopted some British, and a few Singaporean habits, haven't we? Do you think they learn things from us for the same reasons? Observe and see what positive things they do that would make your life easier, or positively different. Use that as your story for the day and see what insight you gain from it. Your mother and I will do likewise."

∞

Now that I am watching everybody like a hawk, I don't think my father really likes working here. As headmaster, he is used to being in charge. And he used to have a secretary to do all his paperwork. Now he has to do it and accept orders from less experienced people who are disrespectful to our culture and to each other.

This stress thing really messes people up! Maybe they need to talk with Ma as well. Ma 'clears the air' there and then; she doesn't allow things to be stashed away.

"Do you want to be happy or do you want to continue being miserable? In my home there is only cheerfulness. Where will you go with this misery? Come and let me help you to be happy." And she would prise the reason out of you in multiple ways until you are dancing with her. My Ma!

I am also concerned about Lydia and all this smoking. I know she has given me the trousers and that I shouldn't abuse her hospitality, but that gift was a few washes ago, and now I am really *sooo* curious as to why they smoke so much, all the time. The time to ask is now – today seems a slow day.

"Lydia, I am really curious about this issue – why do *marties* smoke so much?"

She takes a long drag at her cigarette before she smiles and looks at me. "Why are you so curious about it?"

"Well, I don't know anybody in our family or my parent's friends who smoke. Maybe I haven't really observed this before, and if they do, maybe they only smoke one or two. I can't say I have noticed. I have never, *ever* seen people smoke as much as in these offices here. Why?"

"Well, do you have a bad habit? What do you do when you are stressed?"

"Those are two questions! A bad habit? I suppose blaming my sister Sapphira first for everything even though I know it wasn't her – does that count? When I am stressed I go to my father or mother and tell them. Do you have parents you can go to?"

"No. They live far away from me."

"So, who is there to help you?"

Lydia shrugs, takes another long drag on her cigarette, but does not answer my question. Instead she asks me about the word *marty.*

"It means foreigner, that's all. My grandmother and her friends use it for people behaving like foreigners as well. Sometimes it's offensive, like when they are doing something alien and shameful to our culture; sometimes it's a compliment, such as the person being very rich and charitable. Both my mother and my father are sometimes called marties".

"I know - I've observed that. I've worked in many countries before, and they all have a name for foreigners. Not only that - they also, like your grandmother, label people who behave like a foreigner."

"It's not offensive, nor derogatory."

"Oh, I know that. Not initially though. I used to get so upset when the children would be constantly calling out 'foreigner' to us. I used to tell them my name, and then of course all you would hear was 'Lydia, Lydia, Lydia'. No, I know it is merely the word some nations use to describe us. After all, we do call you 'locals' – do you find that offensive?"

"Well, what else would you choose to call us, or the people you work with in all these countries? If you don't call us 'locals', you call us IDPs."

"We have discussed this so many times, in many different countries, and all we come up with as agreeable to both sides, is 'local' We have experimented with several other words, but the people working for us prefer the word 'local' when we ask them for a more appropriate word."

Chapter Twenty

I begin to think seriously about my life. I want to do something useful. I want to work like a man, earn like a man, and be respected as a man. I tell Papa and Ma I have decided to help Father David. The ministers still occupy a few rooms at the back of the cathedral. The UN food agency WFP is using the cathedral as a storage and distribution place for their food. Church services are now held outside in a huge hollow.

I feel it's OK to learn stuff from the *marties*, but I am not gaining that much from them. I don't actually like their behaviour; it's not the Juxonese way. I prefer Juxonese ways. Neither do I like all this uncertainty. Mixing with the *marties* seems to involve a lot of uncertainty: the way they talk, the statistics I read on odd bits of paper lying about, some of their behaviour. I want to reduce my uncertainty as much as possible. There is enough uncertainty at present here in Juxon – I don't need to add to it. In addition, helping Father David provides me with different news that I can share at our regular family's after-dinner meeting.

∞

It is a beautiful sunny Sunday morning. We are all washed and dressed in our clean 'Sunday best' clothes. Ma says she is feeling defiant and wears one of her own dresses, adding the handbag and a small stole as well - chic! We, and many other families, are on our way to church for the weekly Sunday service.

We go to sit on the far side of the cathedral, under a tree, in the shade. I don't know what is going to happen when the rainy season comes. Hopefully, by then, we will all be back at school in Parrish. How are we going to get home? All these people here, with no buses? How many days will it take to walk home? Papa should only have rented the Land Rover to MSF.

Ma says she feels something strong is going to happen today; she feels it deep within her. Ma is usually right about her intuition, but as she can't pinpoint it, Papa says let us all go to church and ask for divine protection and safety.

There are a few soldiers in the grounds of the cathedral. They are always around when a large group is gathered. Father David says we are probably about five hundred parishioners. We sing a few hymns and pray, then we sit on the grass looking uphill to the bishop. His sermon is about the miracle of Jesus feeding a group even bigger than us with five fishes and two loaves of bread. His talk about food makes me think of our breakfast this morning. Ma gave us bowls of scrumptious cooked oats with honey. We're keeping the bread for lunch, so we can have three meals on a Sunday. Papa went on a field trip a few days ago to some of the outlying villages and returned with this wild honey - delicious. Now this talk about food is making me feel hungry again.

I watch the birds flying around in the sky, all very effortless and magnificent, such exquisite grace and ease. I watch the clouds lazily drift across the sky. My mind wanders all over the place. It's better than listening to a sermon about food!

I look up and observe that Father David, who is standing near the bishop, is staring at me. Has he noticed I am not paying attention? He does that sometimes. There is a look of horror on his face. I can't be that *bad*! No, he is not looking at me; he is looking beyond me, *beyond* us. Is God coming? He should be pleased! The birds scurry away. Something is frightening them. At that moment shooting starts.

I look back and see two soldiers fall. A huge group of men in tattered clothing, holding rifles, are shooting at us sitting in this hollow. We're sitting ducks. My family is near the front. Papa shouts for us to get up and run. Everybody else is running all over the place, bumping into each other. It is mayhem. Women are shouting and calling for their children as we run away from the town towards the border.

We keep together and we run. Ma has her shoes in her hands. Sapphira and I are ahead. Papa shouts for us to stay together. I turn around to wait. Papa changes Benedict to his other arm. A split second later a bullet flies past where Benedict's head had been and finds a woman's head. The family drop to their knees around her; reluctant to leave her behind, shocked by the suddenness and violence of it all. We were attending church, for goodness sake! There is much shouting and screaming and bullets flying. People are calling each others' names. Wild staring eyes. Chaos. Noise. Shock. Disbelief.

More people drop dead around us, their family staying with them and risking death as well. Some have lifted the dead and are carrying them to bury elsewhere. And yet, even in my fear I find it amazing that I am not as shocked by this scene as I had been the first time I witnessed it. Am I getting tougher or just more accepting of such violence, I wonder?

Numb. Numbed out. Otherwise my pants would be wet again. Not prepared for this. Is anyone?

We keep on running: over farmland, then over stony, thorny ground. Ma is holding onto Papa's jacket. Papa is shouting encouragement to

Sapphira and myself. Benedict is confused and crying. I feel bullets whizzing past. God help us! We run and run. All that exercise and outdoor pursuits in Parrish have paid off: we keep on running. Blood from others spurt onto us. We slalom through the injured, the dying, the dead. This run, such a short distance from the cathedral, seems like forever.

Despite the indescribable cacophony of noise, of shock, of panic, the Wiggins family is silent. The only sound is our jagged breathing and Papa's occasional encouragement. We are all concentrating on crossing the border. My mind is endlessly repeating 'safe, safe, safe, safe, safe…. I keep looking back to see whether Papa, Ma and Benedict are still right behind me. Sapphira, as is her habit, keeps on running, expecting others to keep up with her.

The sound of gunfire continues. Increases. Grows louder. They're chasing us! There can be no stopping.

A lifetime passes.

Our soldiers have left their posts at the border to deal with the rabble faction. It is they who are shooting amongst us. Friendly fire; wounding and killing friendly fire.

We cross the no-man's-land with leaden legs and gasping breaths into relative safety.

Chapter Twenty One

The Belling soldiers guarding the border are not at their posts on this beautiful and warm Sunday morning. Thousands of us surge into the small border town of Jamari. We stop only when we reach their tiny market place. Empty. Except for three border soldiers, hands holding their plates of breakfast and steaming mugs of coffee - rooted to the spot, open-mouthed, staring.

∞

Sunday. No food in the market. No nothing. Still, we are so grateful for having fled from that unprovoked carnage. My chest is still heaving. Ragged sobs escape. I am shaking. We huddle together, arms around each other for support, love and comfort. What to do now?

A lone *marty* driving past sees us and immediately reaches for his radio. Within ten minutes there is a muddle of agency vehicles. Hundreds of people mill around the cars, the *marties*, burying them from sight. We see many people have been wounded, even though, in our panic and fear, we did not even feel it. How some people managed to run with such horrific injuries is a miracle, beyond our wildest thinking. Now the numbness is wearing off and being replaced by pain and shock. Some people have started screaming and groaning. The less wounded are taking those now unable to move towards the agency vehicles.

Papa has a long bullet graze along his left upper arm. Ma's feet are a mess of cuts and bruises from running over stony and thorny ground. Sapphira has a bullet lodged under her skin in her upper arm. Benedict is unscathed. I felt the bullets passing around my head, but as Papa says, 'Thank goodness, no bullet passed through your head!' I have a few bullet burns and a few grazes. Lucky, compared to others.

In a wink, the *marties* set up a first aid station in the market place. Take the seriously wounded to the hospital in their Land Cruisers. Wow! To be sooo prepared! To be willing to work on their day off. To be so organised! They are like a dozen Ma's and Papas, different agencies all working together. No fighting. Is this what our Land Rover is sometimes used for? *Wow!* Our Wiggins Agency is going to be like this! Prepared. Professional. Compassionate.

Apart from Sapphira who is asked to go to the hospital in a few days time, all our wounds are cleaned and dressed here. Afterwards, Papa leads us to a more private place and we say a prayer of thanks for our safety. "Our prayer has been answered. We had asked for divine protection and we were protected. Apart from a few minor injuries, we have survived intact."

Except, now we are on a different path. We have nothing apart from the clothes we are wearing and the wages paid on Friday, partly used. And the money from the sale of the Land Rover.

What now? How do I – we – get word to Ellie?

CAMP ALPHA

Chapter Twenty Two

Everyone fled with nothing. Sapphira calls it a level playing field. We Juxonese are no longer classified as internally displaced people. We are a new category now: refugees.

We have refugee status because we are seeking shelter and refuge in another country. Does the new label make it better or worse for us? Will we be like the people in the camps just outside Hamilton? Please God, *NO! Not that!* How will I - we - survive that?

Father David's arm is wounded. We gather around him. Heavily bandaged, he completes the sermon he had started earlier today. A kind of normality descends during the sermon. Was it only this morning? I wait for the fishes and the bread; nothing comes. We have nothing except ourselves. We know whom to trust and we can provide support to each other.

The cathedral parishioners move to our own special area, staying close to our shepherd, Father David.

While walking around we discover that Professor Miles and his family are not here. They sat next to us during the service. We don't see the nurses either, but we find other familiar faces. We hug and hold onto each other, crying with sadness and joy. We are the survivors! But where are the others?

We walk around and find many more acquaintances whom we had merely greeted before. Now we greet them like long lost brothers and sisters, constantly retelling our stories, asking where so-and-so is, crying when we hear of someone's friend, neighbour or relative who had died or not made it across the border. So much emotion - like a constant see-saw; gratitude at being alive and sadness for those who had died. I feel such a strong connection with fellow Juxonese, from the humblest to the most educated; as Sapphira says, truly a level playing field.

Darkness falls rapidly. We have congregated with fellow parishioners from Parrish Cathedral. Papa, Father David and a few other church leaders thought it a good idea to keep our cathedral community together. Before lying down to sleep under the stars, our family hold hands and quietly pray for anything better than this.

Father David had said to be thankful it is not raining. To be thankful the rebels have not followed us into Belling. To be thankful the *marties* are here and have the hospital in place. He suggested that we pray that the *marties* are busily organising plastic sheeting for shelter and food and clean water. To thank them for giving up their well deserved day of rest to help us. We all pray for these.

We sleep on the hard dry earth. We sleep huddled together, Ma's stole covering Benedict. As far as the eye can see in the sickle moon darkness, I see little clumps of humanity huddled together for safety and support. Moans and coughs and sighs travel over us.

What about Ellie? No more baker to call from. Can we use some of our money to call from somewhere in Jamari? "Ma, Papa, tomorrow I'll go and search for a phone to tell Ellie, OK?"

∞

The next morning at eight o'clock, the *marties* from the International Committee of the Red Cross, the ICRC, direct us to a place where we have to register. We have to walk a few more miles because it is further from the border, closer to the forest. Papa says it is because they want a safety zone away from the border. They are in charge of this camp.

After registration they distribute readymade packs of plastic sheeting, buckets for water, blankets, soap and kitchenware.

I see Papa talking to one of the ICRC men. They talk for a long time. He then speaks on his radio. Papa shakes the man's hands. Papa turns away with tears in his eyes and a smile on his face.

"Blessings, blessings, blessings. I'm to go to their office tomorrow. They need to recruit more people. Another prayer answered. This is what a man does when he has a family to feed and care for. Take action. Take heed, Luther and Sapphira – grasp opportunities and remember what your mother has been instilling into all of us – see opportunities in every situation. Be one or two steps ahead. Always. Now we have to build a house in a camp."

We have no sticks to make a frame. We have no axe or machete to cut bamboo. Papa has to pay a Jamari man to fetch bamboo for us. It takes the rest of the day.

∞

We are proud of our new home, built entirely by ourselves. We made it as big as the plastic sheeting would allow. It is low and broad. All of us, except Benedict, have to bend, 'be humble', inside. But we can do nothing about the bumpy ground, or the lack of ventilation in this thick white plastic tent. We leave a little door flap open so that we can breathe. Thank goodness Ellie and Grandma Meertel are not with us. There is *very* little space here.

Ma says to us in general "this is the most spartan house I have ever seen. Even when we moved into our house in Prestige Street, it looked less bare than this. And yet, this has a feeling of hope in it, a feeling of love and support, doesn't it? And it is all of our duty to keep it so. Rough times may be ahead; remember this is our home, like any other home, because we are here."

Papa holds Ma's hand, then we all hold hands as Papa says: "This is where we will learn true humility. In this home we will learn to rise above petty issues, live from the heart, be grateful for every morsel we receive, help others. We have nothing but ourselves – we live from this now, and we will, won't we?"

We all say yes, as if Papa is our inspirational coach at the beginning of a very important game. I suppose he is – and the game is the game of life; it couldn't be more important.

We can actually talk in low voices as the next tent does not touch ours. The camp is all well prepared: designated plots for our tents, and signposted. Ma says they must have been anticipating our coming. They must have known! Could we have arrived here sooner? I don't think so; the place was completely unoccupied.

All those things we had read about in the textbooks of the agencies are all here. We have pit latrines near us; a deep hole in the ground and we have to squat to use it. It's the VIP kind, the ones with ventilation. There's a smaller one for Benedict and other children – our deep hole is far too wide for them to balance squatting on. There is also a place to shower. A huge water bladder is just a little distance to our other side.

Next to us is Kelvin, one of the boys from my *Onashi* group, which seems like eons ago. He too had his ceremony. They are looking for his father who did not attend church and now they don't know what has happened to him. Kelvin says the ICRC has a woman who sends letters and enquiries to families separated by conflict. I speak with Ma about this; maybe we can send a letter to Ellie?

"What? Never! Kelvin is talking nonsense; nobody can do this."

"Remember Angelina, whatever you say is impossible, someone is already doing!" After a long pause Papa continues. "I have accepted the position of Field Officer to the Protection Team at the ICRC, starting tomorrow morning. For this I am very, very, *very* grateful. Sooo, I will enquire at my new place of employment tomorrow. I have a full day of briefing on communication. Perhaps this issue comes under that heading."

∞

The next morning, I wake up early and hungry. Starving. Famished. Ravenous. There is only water to drink.

It is quite early, yet Papa has already walked to the ICRC office in town. Papa reckons it is about a thirty-five-minute walk. Ma accompanies him into town; she wants to go to Save in Jamari's town centre with her identity card and see whether she can get a job here in the camp.

This camp is called Camp Alpha. Are they hoping for more? What happens when we get to Camp Omega? Sapphira and Benedict and I wander around to the newly opened camp office to ask when there will be a food distribution. The man says the ICRC is planning on distributing food today. The word spreads quickly. A queue starts. We wait in the queue.

The ICRC workers begin to rope off areas. Stage one of distribution. First Sapphira, then I, go with Benedict to drink some water from the sets of taps attached to the water bladders the *marties* had set up yesterday evening.

The morning sun is hot. I think the water in those bladders must get really hot as well. I suggest to Sapphira that we need to fetch water in the morning when Papa leaves for work; that way we will have cool water to drink.

We hear Save has set up an emergency tent for the under five year olds. Sapphira and Benedict rush towards it while I wait for the food. We know the routine by now. I will wait for them to return and help carry our food supplies.

Such a busy day!

∞

We wait. Old people, sick people, tired people and the injured sit down on the bare dry earth.

We wait. Nobody talks. We are too hungry. Still shocked after yesterday's escape. Occasionally there is gnawing doubt and people talk quietly to each other about what might happen – but it's all rumour; after all, no-one has made any announcement, like they did in Hamilton.

How did they know we were coming? Why did they not give us this food before? We were starving and they hoarded the food here? We hope there will be food for all. I mentally prepare to run to the front.

Eventually eight huge trucks arrive. One is to refill the water bladder, the others must have food! The queue stirs into an active line, then immediately into chaos. People surge forward. We are going to be trampled! The doors stay closed. People are getting impatient and angry! What is the hold-up?

A *marty* and a Juxonese man climb onto the top one of the trucks with a loudhailer. The *marty* greets us in Juxonese. We all return his greeting. The Juxonese worker starts interpreting. "The ICRC says there is food for everyone. Food will be distributed to all in an orderly line. If there is any pushing, or chaos, or cheating, this emergency distribution will stop. Is that clear to everyone? I repeat. There *is enough food* for *everyone*. We have worked deep into the night to sort out the numbers according to your registration yesterday. We will open the trucks only when an orderly line has been re-established. Please remain within the roped boundaries. My people, am I understood?"

We all shout, "YES!" We laugh. We cheer. We clap our hands. People start talking to each other.

There's an instant buzz of excitement now. We are ready! We are *patient*. Now that everybody knows that there will be sufficient for everyone, there will be no need to fight for food. The Juxonese show they are a disciplined and well-mannered people.

A few women start singing some lovely old Juxonese songs. The songs are sung all along the line. A few loaders smile broadly, raise their hands in acknowledgment and move at a jaunty pace with fifty kilogram bags of rice to the distribution area. Their bodies become ever more sweaty and dusty as they move from the truck to the holding area. We cheer as they return faster and faster to the truck. How do they do that? They must have had a hearty breakfast this morning!

Sapphira returns with Benedict from Save's distribution tent. He was weighed and measured and given a pack of those biscuits. Sapphira and I halve one to ease our hunger. My mouth is so dry it sticks to my palate.

"I wonder why they are weighing a bag every so often."

"Remember how Ma told us that a few of the workers took maybe one or two biscuits from each pack for themselves? I think they are checking to see if the bags have been tampered with as well. That *marty* at the scale, she checks every tenth bag. That is some stringent checking, huh? At least we know we are getting our full share. That is what I call meticulous attention to detail! I'm glad Papa is working with them. They are fair." My sister, the ever-present lawyer.

They do the same with the beans, then the salt. The oily cartons of oil are the last to leave the trucks. The trucks move away, hopefully to bring more supplies. The sun is extremely hot. The songs have stopped a while ago. The whole area is roped off with many guards. We all know the procedure by now. Wait in the queue. Walk between the roped walkway until you reach the registration table. Show your ICRC card. Pick up the bag of rice, beans, salt and oil. Say 'Thank you'. Carry it home.

∞

The distribution centre is a quite a distance from our tent. The salt is in one of my many pockets. Sapphira and I first carry the bag of rice to a spot, then return for the beans. A very heavy load. Benedict has been assigned the container of oil. On his fourth birthday Papa and Ma told him that he is a big boy now and he has to help and do his duties as well. We are all struggling and resting often, most times helping Benedict with the oil. I am weak from hunger after two days without food. Water only: Biblical.

We *have* to get the food home *and* cook. After a while, Benedict does not want to play this game anymore. Neither do I, actually, but I know that when we get the food home, we will be able to cook and eat. Eating is my main focus; my driving force!

We rest a long while near water taps. Drink our fill. Watch others making their way, ever so slowly, back to their tent. Nearby, four little girls are also struggling with the heavy bags. They are singing action songs. It will take them forever. *But,* they are *happy*!

I start to sing too. Benedict and Sapphira sing along. *YMCA. Make Some Noise. I wanna break free.* ABBA songs. Nursery rhymes such as *From the tiny ant to the elephant, Ten green bottles.* We put the bag down and do all the actions that accompany the songs. Guitar strumming, hips swinging. Jumping around. Elephant walks. Our own invented moves. We laugh. We carry. We stop.

Benedict is very eager to put down his can of oil and do actions, any actions that will allow him to let go of his load. We laugh. We carry. We stop.

Eventually Sapphira and I carry the can of oil on top of the beans until, finally, we have all the food in our tent. After resting to drink some water, we move on to our next task. Now we have to find stones to raise the bags from the ground so that the mice and rats don't eat our supplies; it says so in the books.

We also search for stones on which to balance the cooking pot. We rummage around for twigs and dry wood to make a fire. When Ma arrives from the town late in the afternoon, the food is cooking beautifully! Those books are certainly coming in handy.

"My children! Where did you learn all these survival skills? My city children who have had domestic help all their lives; what latent talents are within you! Well done, all of you! I am *sooo* proud of my children – true leadership qualities! You even knew how to get the fire started and the food cooked. Amazing. I have truly amazing children."

∞

Ma cannot stop smiling broadly. When we nag her for the reason, she says to wait until Papa returns home and to stop guessing why she is so happy. When Papa eventually arrives, also smiling very broadly, she bursts out saying she starts work in the camp with Save tomorrow. They are setting up right here in the camp. We go inside the tent and do a little boogie together. A bit of bended-knee dancing on the spot. Then we kneel and say a huge thanks for Ma's job.

"Frederick, it is thanks to these money belts we had made in Hamilton. I always carried my identity card in it, so, all I needed to do was show my photo identity to Save here; they told me to start work tomorrow."

Chapter Twenty Three

That night we sit and have a quiet discussion about our family. Big stuff. Papa and Ma include Sapphira and me; I feel *so* adult. We all have a chance to say what we feel and what we would like to happen now.

Papa starts the discussion. "I know we have just arrived, yet I am worried that my bright, intelligent children's brains will rot in the camp. There is nothing to do here at present and it is far from the town. Also, the townspeople might not want a huge population of impoverished and idle Juxonese walking around their town. I suppose they would also want to be the first to be employed by the *marties*. As far as I can remember from my recent little recce trips here, there did not seem to be much here at all. It is quite under-developed, a true border town. Everybody expects to be merely passing through. On the other hand, you need to keep occupied."

Both Sapphira and I say we want to earn some money to help the family. Ma nods and continues the discussion.

"We need to grab the short window of opportunity to target the camp. Those with money would, like us, have carried it around with them all the time. So, there *is* money here. Learn what they would want to spend it on. I will instruct you on how to be business people in the camp. Firstly, stroll through the camp and use your eyes to see and your ears to listen to what the people want or need. Then we will have another chat as to how we can ease their pain and solve their problems."

I feel very adult about this. I am to some extent grateful that we are here in the camp. If we had stayed as we were in Parrish, we would never have had the opportunities to do all we are doing now. We would have been told to concentrate on our studies and be grateful that we are able to get a good education. I feel quite exhilarated. This is a lot more exciting than school! I will be contributing to our meals. I've accepted the agencies won't give me a job, but I know I can work here, so I *will* work here in the camp.

After a long pause, Papa continues with a broad smile. "I am inviting you children to come with me to work tomorrow morning. Angelina, I would love it if you could come as well. Ten minutes – twenty minutes maximum. I have something to show you there."

∞

We all leave fifteen minutes earlier than Papa would normally do. Ma is annoyed she has not managed to wheedle the surprise out of Papa yet. Papa looks very pleased with himself for holding on to his surprise.

We enter the gates of the ICRC office and go into Papa's office. We open the door and – huge intakes of breath and shouts of joy. Ma reaches him first. Almost floors him. We all hug him. Ma is crying.

Royce is smiling broadly through his tears.

"My God, Luther! Luther Royce Wiggins! Look at you! A man! Your father told me last night that you are as tall as he is, but I could not visualise it. So handsome as well! The girls must be swarming around you, eh? And Sapphira. Another Wiggins beauty. I hear you are still on track to be the world's best lawyer? Well done! And master Benedict. The last time I met you, you were still in your Ma's tummy! Despite all the problems, you all look fine; better than I expected."

"I am Bendy Elephant. Not Benedict. He stayed at home."

"Oh! I'm sorry to hear that. Can you tell him I have a little gift for him?"

"You can give it to me! *I'll* take it for him. He loves me. Thank you!"

We chat and laugh for another ten minutes, until it is time for Ma to leave for her job in the camp. Royce bends down to Benedict. "Bendy Elephant, will Benedict mind not being part of the family photo? Can he come tomorrow? Because I will have a special surprise for him."

After Benedict first shakes, then nods his head to the questions, Royce takes a few photographs of us on a new tiny spy camera. He certainly likes gadgets!

He also hands over an ordinary small black plastic bag to Ma. Inconspicuous. We each say 'thank you' and a fond 'see you' and leave Royce chatting to Papa.

"I would really have loved to stay the whole day with him." I say.

"Yes, me as well. I wondered whether we would see him. We have so much catching up to do. The last time we spoke was the day before the mobile phone network went down in Hamilton. That's a while ago. Your father will probably tell us tonight how long he will be staying."

"Why can't he come here, to the camp, Ma?"

"It's too dangerous for us, Sapphy."

"How can it be dangerous coming to us here, Ma?"

"Well, we have to continue keeping a low profile. We don't know who has fled with us. I remember those conflicts in Rwanda. They reported that the rebels and their families fled as well and regrouped in the camps. We still don't know who to trust. If we were seen to be talking to journalists and *marties*, we might be a target for abuse, injuries, or worse. So far, we have been blessed with safety. I'd like that to continue."

We leave Ma and the mysterious plastic bag at Save's office and set off on our 'research of the camp activities.'

∞

The three of us spend the rest of the morning wandering around the camp. I did not realise how huge this camp is. It stretches far away from the main road. It is all clearly marked with road numbers. Sapphira thinks these signs are more for the *marties* to locate various areas; the English is written in large words and the Juxonese words more as an afterthought. I comment: "Probably because they are driving and have to see things at a distance, whereas we are walking and are much nearer the sign." She merely humphs, looking, as usual, for a deeper meaning.

As we stroll around in the early morning, we notice people are already setting up their small stalls. Three onions, six potatoes, some sweets, a few packets of washing powder, loose cigarettes, soap, and a few medicines. The first thing I notice is that there is no bread here. Not even a roll.

"Sapphira, I feel some of them may be able to afford bread; at least for the moment. When the money stops, we would already be looking for the next venture. What do you think?"

"Is that what they need, or what you want to give them?"

"What would you do? You have money. You are homeless. Maybe, like us, you stayed in a house rather than the camp. Haven't quite worked out how to do the cooking from a single pot or use an open fire. Haven't yet collected wood. You *know* you will be eating the *same* food every day. Sometimes, I think, we don't always know what we want, until it is presented to us. That's what J K Rowling said about her Harry Potter books. If she can do that, so can we, can't we? I am going to test the water with bread. If you can think of something else, we can do that as well. Why not? We have the whole day. Huh?"

When we have our evening talk, I tell my family. "I will go to the baker's in town tomorrow morning and tell him about my delivering bread for the Hamilton baker. I'm sure they must know each other, don't you think? Then I will buy a few loaves and we can sell them in the camp. Just a few loaves, to test the water."

Ma says, "Fine by me. Sounds good. There is only one rule: No credit! Cash only. You can give them as much sympathy for free as you want, they *have* to give you cash. We are all hungry and dispossessed here!"

∞

Discussion over, Ma eventually brings out the plastic bag. Sapphira and I have discussed the contents over and over and *over* again. We know there are gifts for all of us; we just can't imagine what Royce has brought us. We know that he had returned to England while we were still in Hamilton, and had just arrived back here last night. English things! How wonderful. Chocolates? Does England have good chocolates? Maybe. That's probably Ma's present.

Every gift is beautifully wrapped. Papa stops us from opening our presents. "Let us take a moment to honour Royce. To me, this is what friendship is all about; support, love and kindness in your darkest hour. When life buries you with rocks, there's your friend digging you out with his bare hands, risking his life for you. May you all know such friendship. I hope that all of us also *provide* such friendship."

Both Sapphira and I have wind-up torches. These ones are much smaller, more compact than the previous Christmas gifts we left behind in Hamilton. Ma is delighted with a tube of her favourite face cream. Papa receives a solar powered watch, insignificant looking so that it does not attract attention. Benedict has a new pair of sturdy sandals. Perfectly timed. And there is a small box of Thornton's chocolates for all of us.

"One each; savour it. We will make it last for as looong as possible."

Except for Benedict, who guzzles his chocolate down, we smile and giggle as we quietly let the chocolate melt in our mouths. Savouring the taste, the flavour, the richness. Melting manna. Ma puts the box under her pillow of cardboard.

"Ma, why can't I have another one? Please?"

"Because Benedict and Bendy Elephant, these treats are rare and we have to take pleasure in each minute morsel, make it last and last and *last*. That's why!"

I look at Benedict's crumbling face. "Ma, why can't we just *celebrate*? There's only another one each. Let's just celebrate. Then we can remember this night, as the night of the Thornton chocolates! Ma? Papa? *Pleeeeeeze*?"

Ma and Papa look at each other. Keep looking, smiles growing broader and broader.

"Oh alright! Luther, you're right. Let us *celebrate*! Let us *indulge*. Let us live in this moment!"

"And Ma, I am *not* cleaning my teeth tonight! I want to wake up with the taste of chocolate in my mouth."

∞

It's the next morning and we're back in Papa's office. Royce hands Papa another gift. We are all silent as Papa opens the A5 envelope. Extracts a photo. Takes a huge breath. Then tears start pouring down his cheeks. Still silent, he hands the postcard size laminated photo to Ma. Similar reaction. Ma hands it silently to me. I too am speechless; filled with heartache, longing, joy. I hand it over to Sapphira who covers her mouth with her hand and starts to cry. She passes it to a worried looking Benedict. He looks at the photo and bursts into laughter.

"It's Ellie! Ellie! Look Ma, it's Ellie! Ellie is with us in the photo!"

Torrents of questions rain down on Royce. We have only ten minutes before we must walk back with Ma to the camp. And Ma wants to know everything immediately!

"I have an appointment with Save today, so I'll see you in the camp. For your security you know that we have to behave with circumspection. I don't want you hounded and beaten by the authorities like some of my previous informants or interviewees. Please Sapphira, Benedict, Bendy Elephant and Luther, stay away from Save today. It is going to be so difficult to pretend I have never seen your mother before. It will be even worse to pretend with you. OK?"

Very reluctantly, we nod.

"OK! Long story short and I'll fill Frederick in on the other details. I arrived via Parrish airport, went to Prestige Street, then Carton and hiked a lift via Kavari Quay to Hamilton. Crossed the border. Scholar Close is essentially unscathed. It has literally *just* become the homes and offices of the international aid agencies. Yes! They are starting their business in all areas of Juxon now.

Your home is being rented by the very organisation you work for, Frederick. ICRC. Your home and the ones on each side of you are offices and residences for the staff. They arrived about a week ago. Because Parrish airport is near Ushquel and safe, the organisations bring in most of the supplies from there. This attack on Hamilton was confined to Hamilton. Juxon was unaffected by this crisis. In fact, things are at last beginning to ease up there. Talks are continuing, and there is hope.

Jolene and Jacob are there. Jolene gave me this letter to give you. Very much the confident entrepreneur! She wants to know what to do with all the money. The deposit is in your safe at present and, according to the staff there, she says she will count it weekly!"

More stories. Grandma Meertel, Ellie and a few more aged relatives are still in Carton. They are safe there. "Ellie was really happy to see me. Here's her letter as well. I didn't want to give these letters to you last night, as I wanted to see if

I could fiddle around on the laptop and insert her picture into yours to make a family picture."

∞

I accompany Papa to his work again the next morning. Royce had asked to see me. Sapphira is quite peeved that she has to mind Benedict and cannot see Royce again before he leaves later in the afternoon for Juxon. Still, he has letters from all of us and a drawing from Benedict for Ellie and Grandma Meertel as well as Jolene. We are so happy with our laminated postcard size photo of our family. Even Benedict has his own copy. Treasureable. Mine is already filed into one of my trouser pockets.

After greeting us he says: "Sorry folks, I have to rush. I have an appointment with the UN in ten minutes. OK Luther – down to business. You do know how I like gadgets, don't you? Well, I've replaced my small spy camera with an even smaller, *more* unobtrusive one; the one with which I took your photos yesterday, so, I'm giving my old one to you, Luther.

Your father and I decided that it would be better to give it to you. I know ICRC's policy that their workers do not use cameras in most areas they work in, but I want you to know how it works, Frederick. I know you've seen it and played with it before, Luther, but I would like to go over a few things again. This is for family photos, OK? In your tent only, yes? Any abuse and your father throws it away. This new battery will last around a year, by then you should all be home and settled back into Juxonese life again, I hope.

Frederick, you know you can download the photos onto the computer here, send it to your and Luther's email address for safe keeping, then remove them from the computer.

And Frederick, I know we have discussed this yesterday, but if you have *any* qualms now about Luther having this camera then tell me now and I will keep it for you until everything is safe again. I don't want you to lose your job because of a camera."

"No. It is small and unobtrusive. Luther has shown admirable decision making skills in when to do or not to do something. We'll be fine. And as I am able to use the internet here at the office, I can let our families know how we are. Thank you so much."

After much back slapping and bear crushing hugs, he leaves Papa's office. Papa and I look at each other, tears hovering, and throats too thick with emotion to say anything. I give Papa a hug before I too leave the office.

Chapter Twenty Four

At night I actually miss the constant noise of the *marties'* generators that used to lull me off to sleep in Hamilton. Here it is exceptionally quiet. And just before the new moon it is black. Disorientating.

When a dog barks or a baby cries, the noise is sudden and startling; as the gunfire was. I am glad we are all curled up together, stifling though it is. I feel safer this way. During the day I can be a man, but at night I need the reassuring firm body of Papa and the regular snoring rhythm of the man next door.

I lie in the darkness, my mind wandering over the events since leaving Parrish. It's amazing how my need for my private space evaporated into a need to be near my family as often as possible. Clingy, as Ma sometimes would say of Benedict.

We are so busy surviving that I don't really miss my Parrish friends. I think about them occasionally, vaguely wonder where they are, but more in a curious kind of way than in a desperate longing for them. My whole life revolves around my family.

I love the evenings because we sit around chatting to each other. In Parrish I would have been playing on my computer, Papa would be at meetings, Ma on the phone doing business deals, and Sapphira on her bed reading.

Even Sapphira and I are closer now, especially during these times of crisis. She is sooo unruffled, sees things from a distance, sometimes looks down on things; has a clearer perspective than I do. She expects the worst and is constantly prepared for it. I hope for the best and then struggle to deal with a crisis; never fully prepared for it. All the same, I am learning. Three months ago in Parrish, I would never, *ever* have coped with all these issues the way I am doing now.

When I tell Ma this a few days later, she tells me it's OK to ask for help.

Papa too says, "it's OK to feel insecure and ignorant at times; I do. Remember, there is always someone out there with the wisdom and farsightedness to assist you. Sometimes it may be your sister, because that is who she is. You are both wired differently. And guess what? Sometimes it is *you* offering the wisdom." I am listening to what Papa is saying and adjusting to all of this; some things take longer to accept than others. What am I good at? How do I help Sapphira? She doesn't buy this 'first born and male, you *must* respect me' malarkey.

When I ask Ma, she says: "Maybe you open doors for her. Even though she is my beloved daughter, I notice that her standoffish attitude, her 'I'm an authority on this' attitude does not warm people to her; I think she takes after Grandpa Justus, he was the same. He was quite a lonely man; he just could not bring himself to break the ice. He expected others to come to him. And when you break through that icy exterior, you find a heart of gold.

All Sapphy wants to do is help others get a fair deal; she is passionate about this and she has chosen her career well. With her attitude, she will serve them best by being their advocate, their lawyer. You are much more sociable, so you are Sapphira's icebreaker until she learns to do so herself. Have you noticed how she tags along with you and gets to meet people she would never have approached herself?

On the other hand, she is your warning system. Until you learn to size up a situation quickly and use your intuition about an issue, Sapphira will be there to warn you. You might not like it, but she is there as damage limitation for you! You balance each other.

Ellie is there to show us lightness of spirit and to dance through life. In other words, not to take life sooo seriously. I am sure she and Grandma Meertel are having a wonderful time, both have a lightness of spirit. Papa is here to teach you wisdom, get a deeper meaning than the shallow issue that shows on the surface."

"So, Ma, what do you teach me most?"

"Me? Oh! I am here to let you see and grab the advantage of every disadvantage, to help ease the pain of others by offering them a cure, and to be richly rewarded for this. Look how well your bread business is doing." I nod.

Ma continues, "I have this constant strong urge to tell the baker I want five percent of the business I have put his way. After all, it was *my* idea to approach the agencies and deliver their hot bread every morning. He is a rich man thanks to me! Now you see Tiger, that was almost an opportunity lost. Always be at least three steps ahead of your game.

In this instance I allowed the move here to get in the way of my business acumen. Now that you know this, always be prepared, no matter what! That part of your brain has to be constantly ticking; it is your other heart. And let them always work together. Never *ever* do things you will be ashamed of. I'm not talking about failing; that is mere learning when you rise above it. Always act with integrity.

See, we would never have had such wonderful conversations back in Parrish – we would all have been too busy.

∞

Life here moves at a slower pace and we develop our routine. Sapphira and I fetch water first thing in the morning, then I leave with Papa to take the baker his money from bread sold the previous day. These loaves are twice the size of the Hamilton bread; a proper loaf. I am given a free large roll for myself, which I dip in the oil at the bakers. I eat my half.

Having eaten my breakfast, I carry the sack of loaves all the way back to our hut. I am gone for about an hour and a half.

During this time Sapphira and Benedict clean the hut and wash any clothes and cooking utensils. I much prefer this routine to the one we had in Hamilton. Sapphira and Benedict eat the other half of the large roll, then off we go to the market area to sell our bread.

Ma advised that for the moment, we have less bread than we can sell, to keep the customers eager! Besides which, I cannot carry more than twenty loaves and the baker can't supply me with any more. Nor do we have the capital to enlarge our enterprise – now that I know what that means.

We sell out quickly. I have my regular customers as well as 'first come, first serve'. It is wonderful to know we can expand. Sapphira and I are so busy running our business that we have no time to squabble.

∞

Ma and Papa arrive home tired. Ma is home first because she works in the camp. Ma has only been at Save a few weeks now and already has a most profitable network. Whatever the *marties* want or need, Ma is able to supply top quality. She has reclaimed her 'Mrs Fixit' title.

I know.

As part of her recruitment assessment, I had my hair cut by a barber who Ma deleted from her list! I had to go to another barber to sort it all out. Was I mad! I can't remember the last time I had been that angry! And all Ma did was dispassionately remove the man from her list, like a beetle off her arm; job done. *Huh*!

Thus, any hairdresser, dressmaker, hair removers, shoe makers on her list, Ma guarantees their quality. She takes ten percent for her recruitment, of which she gives half to Father David for the congregation, we save thirty percent and spend twenty percent on toiletries and extras. These crumbs here and there gradually fatten our purses.

"Good housekeeping, children, that's all it is. We never know when we might really need it and, of course, we can't go spending and living too high a lifestyle here or we'll be targeted. So, a low, comfortable profile. The least I want is for my family to have toothpaste, soap and other toiletry essentials."

"You know, Ma, money-wise, it gives me a huge degree of confidence knowing we have something to fall back on. And because you distribute it amongst our money belts, wherever we are, or if we become separated, we all know each one can survive."

Benedict continues to receive his portion of special biscuits and milk that we share. Papa is happy in his work at last. He has a very important job. It's called Protection. Most of the time he comes home just after dark. Ma worries that he has to walk the thirty five minutes in near darkness.

He travels around with a *marty* to present talks to both the military and the rebels. They talk about humanitarian law and how each side should treat the enemy humanely. It is fascinating, a new concept to me. Why do we have to treat each other humanely when they kill us and beat us and steal from us?

Sapphira, our future lawyer, asks Papa tons of questions as soon as he sets foot in the door. She wants to know about women's rights, children's rights, refugee rights. Papa says they talk much more about neutrality and rights for everybody than specifically women or children.

Sapphira argues with this concept. "But Papa, if women had rights they would have more equality and *then* we can be neutral!"

I don't always follow. After all, I am aiming to be a scientist, I think. At the moment I have the business bug and I love being a businessman and negotiating prices. Still, she is insatiable with her questions until Papa begs for a break.

She wants Papa to organise a meeting with his boss as she says she has some very important questions to ask him. Papa says they are too busy at present. When things slow down, he will ask Alain. Every evening he brings home some leaflets for us to read. Sapphira keeps all of them in her special plastic bag; her personal belongings.

My special plastic bag contains all the paperwork for the bread business. I tell the baker I think we can ethically increase the price. The price of potatoes has risen along with the price of flour. If we don't raise our price, we will be losing money. I also check with Ma. She smiles and says it sounds like a sensible thing to do. I smile too. A few weeks ago I didn't even know the price of a loaf of bread!

∞

Growth spurts are wonderful things. There's a certain confidence in my step, as if I have crossed the bridge into permanent manhood now. My voice is deep. I practise making it *even* deeper. The bass comes from deep down somewhere in my feet; my huge, manly feet – bigger than Papa's – toes curled over the front of my sandals.

My face still looks young on top of my bony six foot frame. Ma says this is a very good thing, as the military may want to question my not being enlisted again. Outdoors I walk with a slight temporary stoop, telling myself this shrinkage is for my own good. Indoors I stand tall. Well, not in our hut, because it is not six foot high. I am grateful to Lydia for the added two inches on my trousers. Now it is at its full length, covering hairy manly legs. It's my mobile office as well as my personal wardrobe; truly multi tasking. My Levis would never have been able to fulfil all these criteria.

∞

Occasionally, like tonight, we have heavy outbursts of rain, even though it is much too early for the rainy season. I lie awake waiting for the next roll of thunder. It feels as if it is rumbling through the ground beneath our tent. Benedict is absolutely terrified of the thunder and is being comforted in Papa's arms. I worry whether the plastic tent will keep us dry, especially our food. We have found weevils in our rice before; we don't want it ruined by rain as well!

The rain comes down in sheets. The sound is thunderous and earsplitting through the reinforced plastic, right above my head. Nature going wild – I like it – the feeling of imminent danger lurking. It goes on and on and on. The whole tent seems to be electrified by all this energy. As we cannot leave the flap open, it is extremely humid inside.

Papa says that waking up to our stale household smells is far better than gun fire.

The next morning, we wake up wet through and through. A little river runs through our tent. We open the tent flap to let it flow faster. The whole camp is a quagmire; outside we are ankle deep in mud. Fortunately Ma had brought home extra sacking to cover the food and, because Sapphira and I had spent hours searching for large stones to keep the rice and beans off the floor when we first built our home, now it is safe and dry. But we, and the sacking on the floor, are absolutely soaked.

Papa is *absolutely* beside himself with rage and frustration. "How can I meet the chief of police when all my clothes are soaking wet?" The tent shudders with his anger.

We are all in his way! He doesn't know what to do. Sits on his haunches and shouts at all of us. We can't go and sit out in the mud, so we shrink into the corners, shivering in our wet clothes. Papa's ranting and anger continue until it feels the tent will lift off.

Ma shakes her head, goes to him, kneels in front of him, holds him close, whispers to him as if he was Benedict or Ellie in distress, holds him until he takes a few deep breaths and calms down.

Then Sapphira and I go to hold him too. He is conveying what we are all feeling. Are we sinking down to a new low? Swim! We ought to *swim*.

After a while Ma takes a deep breath, says: "We need some enthusiasm here! *Right now*! This minute! We can't all be on the same side of a balance. Tip the balance. Come on! Come on! Someone be enthusiastic! Luther! How's business? Benedict! Sing! Come on! Dance! Let us all clap hands! There you go! Beautiful day. Thank God we are all safe and have food to eat tonight.

Frederick! It is not your wet shirt that will do the marvellous interpreting! It is not your soggy trousers that will define your dignity! Rise above this. Rise high above this, where your spirit can soar. NOW.

Excellent. Now let me dress in my finest damp and creased dress and go to work as well. And I bet you we will *not* be the only soggy workers around. We will merely be the *same* as the others. Come on Luther, young man! Let us walk forth with confidence; it is after all, only rain! Only water!"

Papa looks at Ma with that look that usually starts them dancing, shakes his head with a smile and off we go to the town, huddled together under a large sheet of thick plastic. I am singing in my heart. My parents. The best!

∞

It has been raining in great sheets of water for three days now. Sapphira, Benedict and I had to move our tent twice. Both times our food remained dry. We feel *sooo* good about this, high fiving, doing little jigs despite the mud and the mess. A really good thing accomplished. Papa and Ma say a big 'thank you' to all three of us.

"How did you manage to save *all* our dry rations? It is sooo wonderful that our children can work together in times of emergencies. Congratulations too on your lack of squabbling. Both your father and I have noticed a distinct lack of warfare since our escape to Jamari. We are sooo pleased about this. Now, what have you learnt, and how can you apply this in your everyday life?"

Benedict says, "It was fun, Ma. Lots and lots and *lots* of fun." Naked Benedict has been refusing to wear clothes; he says they will just get wet.

Sapphira says, "It was because I had planned everything in my head well beforehand and knew *precisely* what to do and how. Besides, both the boys collaborated with me."

What did I learn? I hadn't realised until Sapphira mentioned it, that I had followed her orders. Me, being told what to do by my younger sister! I remember her telling me that I was the strong one and that I could carry the bags of dry rations more efficiently than her.

Funny how both of us agreed instantaneously on the right spot to place our 'home'. I lay in bed that night thinking things over. Sapphira is sooo like Ma – I hadn't even realised I was doing what she asked me to do. I remember the many times Ma told Benedict and Ellie how wonderful they were and the happy look on their faces. After this, they would rush and do whatever they had not wanted to do before. When Ma praised them again for having done it, it seemed as if they grew taller – they could not contain their happiness and joy. Is this a woman thing?

Does Papa do this as well? Perhaps, but not as often as Ma. Papa uses the moral issue more often, such as his famous saying: *How would you be feeling tomorrow when you see the positive results of others and know you too could have achieved this?* Is praise - massaging our egos, as Sapphira describes it - is this how the women persuade us men to do things we are so reluctant to do?

I can do Papa's approach; I've heard it often enough. From tomorrow onwards I am going to watch the women and learn from them –

this is *definitely* something I can use. Is it manly though?

∞

Our new home is on higher ground. Our whole cathedral community moved with us, so we are still an enclave, a small village.

What a sturdy place Sapphira and Benedict and I have constructed whilst Papa and Ma were working. Sapphira and I are extremely proud of our house.

After our first move, Ma was not happy with our site at all. She said we had not considered all the angles. "This is far too conspicuous a site. We are right next to the road! You know the thieves are lazy and attack the homes nearest to the roads. Why not look for somewhere more unassuming and unobtrusive, safely in the middle of the site? We will be surrounded, much safer, don't you think?"

Given the number of crimes committed in the thick of the night, we have to agree. Now, third time round, we are aware of this. We choose a spot in the middle of our community and feel this is the perfect place for our home. It's a little bit further from the water taps and the toilet and shower places, but it is safer in the dark.

By the third time, we also know exactly what to do. We sit together, Benedict included, and plan everything first, then go looking for an agreeable site. After this we go to Ma's work and fetch her to double check whether she likes the new site. Papa always says he is happy wherever we build; he trusts our good judgement. A bit like Ma's praise – I hadn't noticed before.

Again, now that I am conscious of it, everything is achieved through collaboration and cooperation and fun. We use a piece of plank to level the dampish clay; no more bumpy beds for us! Papa and Ma bring home anything they think would be useful, any bag or piece of plastic or wood or cardboard the *marties* discard. Ma says they have to ask first, in case someone perceives it as stealing. Now we cover our floor with thick cardboard on top of the plastic. We also have an excellent covered lean-to to keep the wood dry. Sapphira has a shelter for cooking. She shares it with Kelvin. They have still not heard from his father.

Each time, after completing our new home, we go to Ma and Papa's work to escort them to our new address. Each time we move we also have to inform the ICRC so that they know exactly where everyone is.

∞

I hope this is the last time we have to move and rebuild. I pray that next time we go into a home, it will be our own in Parrish. I think I have learnt enough now and can implement all of these learnings in Parrish.

Business-wise, in eight weeks we double the number of loaves we sell. Fantastic! I have managed to do two rounds every day so far. Our share of money goes to buy clothes. I am the last on the list for new clothes. As a team we decided that Sapphira and I do not need any more than one change of clothing; Papa and Ma need more due to their work and because sometimes it rains and rains and their clean clothes do not dry soon enough.

Benedict is four years old and is soon dirty when he decides to wear clothes. Ma promises us that once back in Parrish, she will find her friends and have beautiful clothes designed for all of us. Papa remarks "Maybe our priorities will have changed and clothes may not be so important when we get back to Parrish."

Ma looks at Papa as if he has gone mad. I laugh. I cannot ever see Ma dressed in less than elegance and style once we are back home again. As she says, she is merely tolerating this difficult time with constraint and dignity.

∞

This week is my turn for a new shirt. My T-shirt is mere threads.

I had received a shirt from one of the *marties* at the ICRC office, but he was smaller than me and it was far too tight. Now Sapphira wears the very colourful striped shirt.

I rather like my shredded look; I can see strong defining muscles underneath. Thanks to being outdoors most of the day, the sun has turned my skin to a deep golden brown. I like that. I like the way the girls surreptitiously look at me as I walk through the camp.

I am working on my walk now. I watch one of the *marties* at Papa's office. He walks with an easy strut, as if the world belongs to him; such confidence. I'm working on it as I walk around the camp every day. This is a very large camp: where are all the girls though? I want their reaction to fine-tune my walk. They like my height and my muscles – that I know. I just love their attention, silent as it is.

Chapter Twenty Five

After many months in the camp, Benedict becomes very hot one night. He is sick over all of us. Ma gives him water, but his temperature remains very high. Ma is worried. She says when I was Benedict's age, I used to get convulsions whenever I had a high temperature.

We all have a very wakeful night. We sleep with the flap wide open. Ma takes him to work with her at Save's feeding centre in the camp. They have a small ward for sick children. Sapphira goes along as well. Once I have sold all the bread, I go there too.

Benedict is in the small hospital section. Sapphira is sitting with him in a long tent. I have never been to this area of Ma's work before. There are eight beds in the tent. Everything is spotless. Benedict is still looking very sick; he is just lying there. They say he has a fever and they can't fathom why. It's not malaria or anything they can test for. He is receiving intravenous medicine via a drip in his right hand.

I give Sapphira her share of the bread and half a special biscuit. She has not eaten since a hasty breakfast. We decide quietly who stays with Benedict and who goes to cook the supper. Now that she has eaten something, she wants to stay here. Ma comes to check on Benedict every minute she is free.

∞

I observe the mothers or carers sitting with the other sick children. Nobody talks much; the sick children take our chattiness away. I watch the refugee Juxonese nurses, who, like Ma, have found work with the foreign agencies.

They are not the nurses who shared our house in Hamilton. I ask about them. They tell Sapphira and me that those nurses were working the day of that massacre. They managed to shelter at the hospital. The sister who cleaned and cooked for them and the two small children, Benedict's little friends, were all killed. I am sad. More deaths. I'll never see them again.

I pray that we all go home to Scholar's Close soon; our whole family intact, meeting up with Ellie again. Suddenly, I miss her very much.

This ward makes me dwell on sad things, probably because this is an unhappy place, filled with sickness and death. I feel quite helpless. We can't really do anything except wait until the medicine takes effect and Benedict improves. I really don't like him looking so pathetic and motionless. I can't remember him ever being this sick since he was a baby.

I find it quite distressing, seeing him just lying here, no energy at all; he does not even want to drink the oral rehydration solution Sapphira is constantly struggling to persuade him to drink. She looks up at me, frustrated. Hands me the cup and spoon. We swap places.

I sit next to my little brother; hold his hand whilst Sapphira takes a break. I mop his hot brow with his damp comfort blanket that Ma had earlier soaked in water. Later, I feed spoon after spoon of oral rehydration solution to him.

"Bendy Elephant. Bendy Elephant. This is Tango Zulu. Do you copy, over."

Slight, slight nod.

"Bendy Elephant, water lorry arriving. Open your tank to receive your quota."

He drinks it and does not vomit. Good! And a tiny, minute 'gone in a second' glimmer of a smile. I am going to be a world class father, right up there with Papa and Dick Hoyt that I used to watch so often on Youtube. I wonder fleetingly what else can be hitting the million mark viewings on

Youtube. Then back to the present. I am going to use Ma's tactics of praise – look how well it works when I tell him how well he is doing!

∞

Whilst Sapphira and I are sitting beside Benedict, a baby dies. The room transforms instantly into shock and sadness; a heavy stillness. It makes the hair stand up on the back of my neck. Although I have seen so many brutal deaths since leaving Scholar's Close, I have never seen a baby or anyone actually die. Switch off. One minute the baby was there, and the next he was gone, forever. Phew. These people, like us, have lost everything and now they have to lose a precious family member as well.

Will this be in our future as well? I couldn't bear it if anyone of us dies……

Sadness creeps into my cells, my bones. I stiffen and my heart, my body, everything, become as heavy as lead. Sapphira and I move closer together, quietly supporting each other, comforting in our touch.

The father comes, tears streaming down his face. We cry for him. For us. For life. Sapphira and I had sympathised with the family, now we go to sympathise with him. I stand in front of him, covering my heart with my hands, *Kelsho*. No words are spoken, sadness shared in tears.

The family wrap the baby with so much love in a small sheet provided by the feeding centre. They say 'thank you' to the sad staff. The father carries his little bundle to the graveyard outside the camp. I turn back towards Benedict.

I have to walk past the graveyard daily when delivering bread. I see new mounds every day; big ones and small ones. People are dying every day. I used to barely glance at it when passing. Now it has significance; I know a little boy there now.

I pray that Benedict comes home with us and remains very healthy. I don't want him to be a mound here in this country – he is Juxonese and should be buried in Juxon as an old, wise man.

Within minutes of the dead baby's departure to be buried, another very sick baby occupies the dead child's now cleaned bed. Wow! Such speed! How quickly that other baby had to be forgotten; to be replaced. Benedict becomes all the more precious to us. Very reluctantly I go home to cook the family's evening meal.

∞

I haven't cooked on my own here yet. Kelvin comes with me to fetch the water we were unable to fetch this morning. He also sits with me while I cook.

This is the 'nth day we are having the same meal. When Sapphira moaned about this monotony earlier, Ma had said to be grateful we have food; can she remember how hungry and desperate we felt when there was no food? Nevertheless, the next day Papa bought some spices at the market to change the flavour a little bit.

Kelvin and I chat about this and that. His mother and older sister are working for other foreign agencies in the camp. He is in charge of the house.

"It's amazing. You are so matter of fact about your missing father. I don't think I could be so nonchalant if Papa was missing. Then again, it *is* weeks ago now, isn't it? Months! Do you think your father is dead?"

He turns away from me, one foot making patterns in the dirt. I take it he does not want to talk about this subject, and I, having just witnessed the death of the baby, am quick to change the subject to something less painful. Even if it is mundane, it is not about sadness, death and dying. I moan about the lack of meat.

"Oh, I usually go with other boys to catch rats and mice and frogs. We have been eating meat almost daily."

I gag when he tells me that this is the meat they eat. He is so matter of fact about it. Ugh! At home I avoided the kitchen when Jolene was cutting and cleaning chickens and things. And now frogs and mice! How hungry am I for meat? Very hungry! Would I eat rats or mice or frogs? No, thank you! Not quite yet. Perhaps? Er, NO!

Whilst all these thoughts are stampeding through my mind, Kelvin continues to talk about these things as if it is our daily diet, our norm. He is saying the supply is running low, probably because there are so many boys out hunting.

I wonder aloud why Sapphira has not given us meat. Perhaps I *have* eaten it and not known? Sapphira is not squeamish about such things; she would probably weigh the pros and cons and decide that if rats and mice and frogs are to be an extra source of protein, then it would be fine. All these things are making my mind dizzy and I feel quite nauseated. All the while Kelvin is continuing his story. He says the reason why Sapphira does not have these meats is because this hunting is only for the boys. The girls pick the fruit and they have picked the last of the berries ages ago.

∞

Once the beans are cooking over a low fire, I accept the challenge and we go to hunt some meat. My first hunt. I feel extremely squeamish about killing and handling dead animals. Not quite how a budding scientist or surgeon should behave! Maybe I have to delete these careers from my list? We had our cook Jolene do all this for us. I used to only touch the meat I was about to put a fork into it on my plate!

Kelvin had set traps. Wow! Proper hunter. We find two big rats in one of his traps. They must have been chasing each other. What luck. Rather tentatively, I offer to carry the animals while we check his other traps. Fortunately he has a bag for his dead animals. I don't need to see them or touch them. "How do you know how to make these contraptions?" I ask him.

"An older boy had injured his arm when we fled and he asked me to help him set the traps. He showed me all the tricks." Kelvin passes this information on to me as well. There's a whole new world out here that I didn't even know about.

Back at the camp, I swap some wood for a big rat. Sapphira and I together can carry more wood than he can alone, so our supply is quite good at the moment. I offer to chop the wood into smaller pieces while he prepares all the meat. By the time I see the meat, it looks like small bits of meat, not rats, thank goodness. I much prefer fetching wood to hunting meat.

∞

These days Sapphira and I have to go further away each time we need to replenish our supply of wood because there are so many of us needing wood now. The camp continues to grow. In fact, Papa says five camps have formed since we fled all those months ago. None as large as Camp Alpha. I wonder why my bread-round has not increased – could it be that those arriving now have less money? I must ask Papa – at the office they keep track of everything; maybe they keep track of people's neediness when they arrive so late in the crisis? I invite Kelvin to accompany us when we need to gather wood, so that each one gets a chance to rest between carrying the heavy load.

I had recognised some herbs whilst we are out hunting and put that in the pot as well. This food is beginning to smell exceptionally tasty today. I caution myself not to overdo it, as Sapphira may just decide I should share the cooking more often.

∞

When Papa comes home, earlier than usual, he tells me that the ICRC has a holiday on Saturday, so we have all been invited to lunch there. That is in four days' time.

We both say we hope Benedict will be heaps better by then. As we go to the hospital to fetch the others, I ask Papa about Switzerland. All I remember about the country is that we are better off than the Swiss because we have a few miles of sea. They don't have any sea and are completely surrounded by other countries. Papa says they speak four different languages.

"Papa, what do they do when there is conflict in their country?"

"Well, they practise neutrality, so don't interfere in other countries' conflicts."

"But, Papa, what about fighting amongst themselves, as we are doing now?"

"Tiger, they don't seem to do that. No bloodshed. If they do have disagreements, I think they sit around a table and talk it out. It does not get physical."

Hmmm. They speak four different languages and they don't fight? No one wrongly interprets what another is saying, or meaning? We have one language and there's always something to misinterpret, to fight about, to shed blood. Maybe they are not as passionate as us Juxonese are about their politics. Or maybe we should also sit down together and respect each other and talk things out, like Papa and Ma does with us.

I wonder what they do to *not* become so passionate about their politics? I will ask Sapphira to ask them about their politics. She has read everything there is to know about neutrality. She has exhausted the supply of books. She is always asking Alain, the *marty* in charge of the legal side of the office, how it works and so on and so on. He gives her countless internet downloads on the subject.

I am not interested in politics. Grandma Meertel often made a huge effort to interest me in Conservative Cartons history and politics. I am interested in the history, but definitely not in being an active politician. At the moment, I am beginning to struggle with my bread business, so I'll leave politics to Sapphira. She will fill me in when it is necessary, as she always does.

∞

When we arrive at the feeding centre, we see that Benedict is still not well enough to be discharged. However, there are no nurses for the night. Every child is sent home. He and all the others are to return tomorrow morning. They disconnect the intravenous infusion and Papa carries him home. Ma carries the medicine they gave us, Sapphira the biscuits and I the special milk.

It is a sombre supper even though the food is so delicious. Ma congratulates me. But Benedict's laughter and constant interruptions are absent. Papa and Ma would continually tell him to wait his turn to speak, and now we miss his interruptions! He is sleeping. Ma wakes him for drinks and medicine that he does not want.

Sapphira tells Papa that one of the mothers at the hospital says they saw the rebels come during the night and they planted mines on the border *and* on our side. She says it is because they don't want us to return to Juxon. Papa's face is grave. He makes us promise not to go near the border for any reason. "Mines can blow your legs off, even kill you."

How on earth are we going to get home when they are intent on keeping us out? I am so glad now that Papa sold the Land Rover, because we would not have had all the money from renting it.

If only I could see a little bit into the future! Will we return home this year? Will I be a scientist? Or a businessman? Will I go to university? Will I forget all that I have learnt? Will the ICRC have meat at their party?

Ma wants me to buy a shirt on Saturday morning. She does not want me to go bare-chested, which is what I do now. I am disappointed that I haven't found that special girl who is utterly impressed by my sunburnt torso – yet! Still, a flamboyant shirt might do the trick.

∞

It is Saturday afternoon. All the chores are done. Papa and Sapphira and I are off to ICRC's celebration day. Ma is working and Benedict is with her. He is much better.

Today Ma and her team are measuring the under-five year olds' weight and height to monitor malnourishment. It is the first time she is working the whole Saturday. She says Linda told them it is an emergency, because many children in the camps have been reported with malnutrition.

We go to Papa's office via the market so that I can buy my new shirt. The one that I like is fifty cents over budget. It has two huge chest pockets. It is strong material. It is a brilliant blue with a thin gold stripe. I can see it on me, matching my blue multi pocket trousers. I turn away and look at a cheaper, very colourful one. This one is far too 'busy' for me. Flamboyant, but no class. I need both. The blue and gold stripe shirt fits the bill.

I haggle and haggle. I don't want the trader to see how much I *really* want the blue one. I am aiming to show a high level of nonchalance, but I begin to suspect that he probably sees my eyes flicking constantly to the blue shirt. It is a game.

"Luther! Are you hungry or not?" I glance at Papa's face.

The trader doesn't budge.

"Can I pay off the extra fifty cents over the next two weeks?"

"Young man, I don't know what will happen in two weeks' time. Business is business."

Now I am in a dilemma. I agree that is how I run my business as well.

"Tell you what. I will give you the shirt, short of fifty cents, if you deliver my bread as well in the morning. For a month."

For a month! I am so busy already! I will have to leave the camp before Papa.

"No! That deal is unacceptable to me, Luther. It is unsafe. I will loan you the fifty cents. You can pay *me* back over two weeks."

"Thanks Papa; deal done!"

I wear my new shirt to the party. Boy, do I feel good.

∞

There are three foreign visitors in the ICRC compound. They are from the main office in Switzerland. They have come to see how things are going here. One is the president of the ICRC. Wow! He came all the way to see us! I would have preferred that he see us in Parrish. But, as Ma would say; deal with the present moment, not the 'should have been'.

Dealing with the present moment, I see a huge open-sided tent with mountains of food on it. Chicken! Meat! Plates and plates of chicken and meat. And mountains of rice and potatoes. *And* a brightly coloured vegetable mix. And a mixed fruit salad! Where did they buy these things?

I don't know if they could hear my stomach rumbling, because they serve the food before any speeches. I am so grateful for the plate of food handed to me. It's just as well that we weren't able to help ourselves; I might have disgraced Papa and the family *and* Juxon by putting a few extra pieces of chicken and meat on my plate. Papa has told the kitchen staff about Ma and Benedict working today, so we have a plate for them. I can eat *all* of my food without having to keep aside for others. Magic moment!

After the meal, the speeches begin. Papa is interpreting.

The old, wise men speak. The *marties* call them 'elders'. The elder's speech is very long; it takes twice as long with Papa having to interpret. Soothed by the extra pieces of chicken and meat I have managed to eat and the delicious pieces of chocolate, I daydream. I sit very contentedly next to Sapphira who is being rather annoying by translating everything the old men say before Papa is half way through. Actually, her habit is not annoying me half as much as it used to.

Must be the Swiss chocolate. I remember when Papa used to bring Ma bars of Swiss or Belgian chocolate on special days. Some special days I could not fathom. I mean, it wasn't Ma's birthday or any special day I knew of. Both Ma and Papa would have that certain twinkle in their eyes as they fed each other little blocks of chocolate, while at the same time keeping us children happy with tiny morsels.

I love their chocolate – it slips sooo effortlessly over my tongue, lingering a bit before it disappears, leaving a rich, sweet, creamy taste on my tongue that lasts as long as the next piece of chocolate. I love it! Ma says the Belgians make better chocolate. Well, at the moment, I am in ICRC's compound and this Swiss chocolate tastes pretty good to me. I don't need better, perhaps just a few blocks more!

After the speeches, photographs are taken. Then we head home. During the thirty five minute walk, we talk about all the discussions we had with different people there.

"I spoke to a woman who was very interested in my income generation scheme. She asked if there were many boys and girls doing this. I said I don't know, I am too busy focusing on my struggling bread business to network much at present. I also mentioned the rat catching and berry picking and all these other activities we do."

Sapphira says "I spent ages with the man from Switzerland. He told me he is the head of the legal department. I interrogated *him*. *Well,* I asked him to explain some things more specifically. You know Papa, as yet, I am not completely convinced about their ways. I need *much more* information on everything. I told him so. He said I have valid arguments. He told me he would send me a few books and to remind you to print out all the articles on their website about international humanitarian law. I asked him to write down the name of the books."

Boy, what cheek! Or courage. I too am eager to learn again. Maybe then I will know what I really want to do. "Papa, when will we ever be going to school again? I am losing so much time!"

"Be patient, Tiger. There's an agency called Unicef. They will be setting up a school shortly. Just be patient a little longer."

∞

Ma is not home yet. We decide to go to her. We reach the tent where Ma and her group are measuring the upper arms of the children and weighing them. We can't see Benedict.

Sapphira asks Ma where specifically Benedict is. She is so used to looking after him, she wants to see him. "He met his little friend from nursery school in Parrish and they are playing with his new ball." Sapphira wanders off to find him so we can go home. Just then a child runs up to the tent to say two small boys are in a small field where someone is saying they saw men planting mines there early this morning.

One of the workers laughs and says: "It can't be. They would never *dare* come so near to the camp. This is right by the camp. They must have seen something else. This is just scare-mongering. We have enough rumours – tell them to take their stories elsewhere. Imagine! Scaring people like this. They ought to go to prison for causing more stress!"

Suddenly Ma looks up at us. There is a look of horror in her eyes. Before I can even think of what the woman had said about scare-mongering, Ma is out of the chair, out of the tent and running. She knows something. Mothers know. Ma knows.

Benedict! Where is he? We run towards the area where no tents have been constructed. We have had so many talks, lectures and plays about mines and other exploding devices. UXOs – unexploded ordnance. *Everybody* knows they are not supposed to go into an area with even one UXO. Benedict knows. But this area adjacent to the camp perimeter is not known to be a mined area, unless the rumour is true and the person *did* see men planting mines early this morning. Why didn't she tell someone before? That's what we are all supposed to do! Had she said something to someone this morning, the area would have been cordoned off this very morning. There would have been huge signs up forbidding everyone to enter this area. Benedict knows about these signs and to stay far away from such areas.

∞

Benedict is in there. He has his new ball in his hand. His little friend is waiting a small distance away from him. He sees us all and starts to run towards us. We all hold our breath – he could be running his last step! We tell him to stop. He doesn't. Benedict is running as well. Papa shouts at him. "Benedict! *Stop*! Stop right there. *Now*!"

Benedict stops. His little friend has seen his mother. His little friend continues to run despite everyone shouting at him to stop. Everyone is petrified: he is so near. Then he is at his mother's side. She crushes him to her. Now we all look at Benedict.

Ma and Papa shout together. "Stop, Benedict. *Stay* right there!"

In an instant, the air becomes tense and on edge. Apart from hushed "What?" "What?" What?", there is an eerie silence. It is smothering me. I can't breathe. I feel my heart thumping inside my chest, as if it is something alien. Women start wailing.

"Shut *up*! He is not dead yet!" Ma screams at them.

She calls back to Benedict, telling him again to stay exactly where he is. He is so near, we can see him shaking, I can hear the little whining noise he usually makes when he wants to cry, but holds back. His eyes are darting from Ma to Papa to me and Sapphira. We all stare back at him, stiff smiles on our faces, willing him to stand absolutely still.

I hear Tom, the Save engineer on his radio, "Tango Five to Bravo Uniform. Bravo Uniform, do you copy?"

"Urgent. Field Four. Bring the robots. Bendy Elephant in field four. Repeat. Bendy Elephant in field four. Do you copy?"

"Roger. Over and out."

Tom comes over to us. "They are on their way. Will be here in minutes. Just had the reports of UXOs in this field. They were already on their way to set up barriers and clear it."

For me, each minute is sixty seconds too long, *much* too long. Benedict cannot stand still for *one* minute. If he is not dancing around, he is hopping on one foot, or running around, or climbing. He looks beyond us, at the gathering crowd. Papa turns to the crowd, uses his hands to stop them from pushing forwards.

I shout "Benedict! Remember we 'tossed in' to play 'statues'? Now! Statue to you!" Benedict lifts his finger and says: "Statue to you too!"

Silence.

Only Ma's voice breaks the silence. Ma's voice is strong, strident. She is standing slightly apart from me, yet I can feel her energy like an intense presence. As if she knows she is here to perform a miracle. "Benedict, if you stand absolutely still, Tom has called for a *very special* robot to come and fetch you. It's new, brand new! This is a *very special* prize for a *very special little boy*, because you are listening and obeying Papa and me, aren't you? This is your prize for being such a good boy. I am *so proud* of you. Look at *all the people* come to see you get your *special prize*. See, they too are standing like statues, so that *you* can stand like a statue. Aren't you sooo clever to make everyone play statues? Soon now, very soon, your very special robot is coming to you. You have to stand still until it says you can move, OK?"

Ma continues talking to him just as she would normally talk. I remain ice cold. It is only my heart knocking against my ribs that reminds me I am alive. All I feel is ice. Will he? Can he? I feel dread. The ice is in my guts. My baby brother. If only there was a Harry Potter way to change places with him. Despair keeps overbalancing my hope. I've got to believe! I've *got* to trust he will soon be in my arms. Dear God! Help me to trust! To believe. To know for certain. *Please*.

Ma continues to talk with him, telling him a story. Hansel and Gretel, one of his favourites. Everyone is listening and waiting, the under-five assessment abandoned. When Ma pauses for a moment, Sapphira nudges me, tells me to tell Benedict the story he likes so much. My voice croaks. Nothing comes out. Ma shakes my arm, shouts at me. "Luther! Bear up now!" I take a deep breath, find the courage.

"Bendy Elephant. Bendy Elephant, this is Tango Zulu. Do you copy? Over."

"Tango Zulu. Tango Zulu, this is Bendy Elephant. I copy. Over." A little, wobbly voice.

"Bendy Elephant. Everything is Charlie Charlie. What's your agenda? Over."

"A story. Over."

I am surprised at how calm and normal my deep voice sounds. I tell him his Roald Dahl story, The Chocolate Factory. I stand firm, strong, my full height. Light-years go by. Four minutes, I hear someone say.

Knowing Benedict hates stories that stop midway, I continue when the de-mining team arrive with their new remote control de-mining gadget. Even as we are all moved further away, I continue the story. Tom Yon, the engineer, winks at me, gives me a thumbs up, gives me strength to continue. He and Benedict are firm friends. Benedict calls him Tomyon.

I had watched the de-miners before with this amazing contraption. I have seen it work *all* the time. I trust it. I *have* to! I continue with the story; Charlie is now in the chocolate factory. The de-miners work fast, quickly putting the machine into action. Is it fast enough? Can Benedict be a statue for another minute or two, or more?

I look at my father, standing next to me, a mountain of stone. Just looking at Benedict. Willing him to stand still. Papa does not utter one word. Just keeps looking at Benedict. There is so much love in that look, it takes my breath away.

I let out a small sob. I take another deep breath. Ma says again to bear up. Benedict looks at Papa, takes a deep breath, smiles. Gives an exaggerated wink. Waves. Still standing still. This *is a miracle*. May it continue until I feel him in my arms again. PLEASE.

∞

The sky is darkening rapidly. Soon the rain will come. De-mining work itself is slow, precise and methodical. Beeps let everyone know there is a mine very close to the machine. The deminers then defuse the mine by remote control. The beeps start. A UXO between the robot and Benedict. *God! Nooo!*

Silence.

I begin telling Benedict another story. "Wow Benedict! The robot is telling you it's coming closer and closer to you. Soon it will be there! Right next to you. Then you can run to Ma. Not yet, though. Stay where you are, Bendy Elephant."

Sapphira takes over the story. The beeps remain loud. Benedict is half listening to Sapphira, watching the robot and checking with Papa and Ma about the noisy beeps. God help us, *please*.

Six and a half minutes have passed now since we first arrived here. This is an absolute record for Benedict to be still. A record too for the response time of the de-mining team; thank you *sooo* much. How much longer can a four year old stay still?

The robot is inching its way towards Benedict. Father David has arrived and stands by Ma as she now keeps talking to Benedict, just saying soothing things to him. Just talking; mother stuff. People are praying quietly.

Father David starts talking to Benedict, telling him a story about a little boy called Bendy Elephant and what a good boy he is, what a brave young man he is, how God is smiling upon him.

The robot is about eighteen inches away from Benedict. I can see the loud beeps are scaring him. Now Tom, the Save engineer, starts talking to Benedict, pretending he is on his radio.

"Tango Five to Bendy Elephant. Bendy Elephant, do you copy?"

He relaxes a little now. The robot continues to inch its way towards him. Puts his hand up to his mouth. "Tango Five. I copy. Over."

"Roger. Special robot approaching you. Keep still. Over."

"I copy. I'm keeping still. A statue. Over."

"Roger that. You've just been voted a champion of champions. Over."

"Tango Zulu. Tango Zulu. I can nearly touch the robot ____"

"Let it touch you first! Bendy Elephant, it has to touch you first. Stay still! Do you copy? Over."

"I copy. Over." Giggle, giggle.

Six inches to go. Beeps at its loudest. The source is right next to Benedict. *Please God!*

Raindrops start to fall here and there. I don't think I am breathing any more. I don't think anybody is. The robot stops. Starts poking around. We are *nearly* there.

Benedict is going to be safe!

Lightening suddenly smacks the sky.

Benedict hates it!

He jumps!

His foot hits a mine between him and the robot. That short, *short* distance. He and the robot fly into the air, exploding, splattered all over the place. I see Ma running towards him. Everyone is shouting at her, *screaming* at her, *begging* her to stop! She is running towards where she last saw her baby son. She hits a mine and is lifted way up in the air before falling to the ground like a sack of donated rice.

∞

Strong hands hold Papa, Sapphira and me. They needn't bother; Papa and I remain stone statues, turned to cold, cold ice.

Only a small part of my brain remains functional. I can hear Sapphira screaming hysterically. I can hear the thunder and lightning continue, and, as if to prolong the drama it has just exacerbated, I can feel it is starting to rain heavily. A cloud burst: an instant massive tepid waterfall. I can hear *marties* forcing people away from the scene. I can hear them wanting to push Papa away. I can hear Papa giving one long deep shout of NO! – the shout that usually makes mountains rumble and wobble.

We stay. I can see Papa has one strong arm around Sapphira. I can hear she has stopped screaming. She is now merely shuddering, like Papa and me.

What now? The de-mining robot is broken and Ma is lying in a mine field. Puddles are growing bigger and bigger. I hear a noise behind me. Turn around. The older de-mining robot! They had brought both! Thank you, thank you, *thank you*. We now watch the robot inching its way towards Ma. Nobody can give her first aid, nobody can stop her bleeding, nobody can hold her hand until a path has been cleared. All eyes are on Ma and the robot, this worker of miracles. I am going to be an inventor one day – inventing life saving gadgets.

∞

The rain eases off as quickly as turning a tap, leaving behind a heavy mist raised by the humidity. Just above a whisper people are beginning to sing ancient Juxonese songs that Grandma Meertel used to sing to us. Softly. Gently. The sound is a merciful breeze, caressing me, calming me, filtering into my cells, sustaining me, giving me hope.

The only other sound now is Father David's gentle voice praying. While some people continue to sing above a whisper, others follow Father David's prayer. My lips move. I don't know what I'm saying, just a begging noise. Papa, Sapphira and I continue standing together, holding each other, an island in hell.

More light years pass. Father David begins to sing. The chorus of one of Ma's favourite songs by Brendan Graham. Our whole family loves to sing it, especially Papa to Ma.

You raise me up, so I can stand on mountains

You raise me up to walk on stormy seas

I am strong when I am on your shoulders

You raise me up to more than I can be.

People are singing the chorus over and over again. Their heart and soul in the singing, soothing, balm on my petrified soul.

Eons pass. Then Ma raises her right hand, a mere half inch from the ground. Those who see this minute motion raise their singing to an instant crescendo which then continues at this louder level. There is joy in their voices now. A prayer answered. She is alive. She is acknowledging their singing.

∞

Eventually the path is clear and safe. The de-mining team take the stretcher to her. They signal she is alive. People are still stuck on the refrain. It is filling us with hope.

Papa, Sapphira and I go into the vehicle to the recently constructed British military hospital. Part of Ma's left lower leg has been blown off. Her right foot is injured as well. The de-miners cover her leg; put a drip in her arm. She is moaning quietly, not quite conscious. Thank God for moaning – it shows she is alive. She is holding Benedict's red toy car in one hand. God! How did she get hold of that?

Why Benedict? Dear, dear God, keep Ma safe, PLEASE, please, *please*!

∞

We sit like statues while she is in the operating theatre. The staff brings us mugs of tea with lots of sugar in it. My mind remembers in passing how Ma hates mugs, always insisting on a cup and saucer. Well, she is asleep at the moment, having her leg and foot 'cleaned up', as the surgeon said.

We wait. Staff from ICRC and Save come for a few minutes to give us strength. Father David and other leading community members all come to spend a few minutes with us. They are a blur.

My baker comes as well. A few of my regular clients. Kelvin.

Ma is wheeled into the ward. Her right foot heavily bandaged. Intravenous infusion in her right hand. A hospital gown covering her. A big emptiness where her left leg should be.

That night Papa sleeps at Ma's bedside. Sapphira and I curl up on the other beds in the small ward. The doctor gives us each a tablet; Papa refuses, yet demands we swallow them. I don't remember anything after that. I wake the next morning. Papa is sleeping at Ma's bedside, her arm across his shoulders.

∞

None of us talk when we are alone in the ward. Words are so inadequate to communicate our grief, our pain. When Ma's colleagues visit from Save, or Papa's colleagues from ICRC, we smile and make polite conversation. Their presence temporarily eases the profound melancholy of the Wiggins family.

After Benedict's funeral, Papa returns to work. I can't begin to describe *that* farewell. My feelings. Papa tells us before we left our tent, his deep bass hurting out each slow word "Benedict is up there, happy. He wouldn't understand us being so sad. Let us be happy for him. Remember something he did that made us smile. Keep that memory and the feeling alive in you."

Nurse Clare came to pay her respect. So too Linda and Tomyon. Alain and the Head of Papa's office attended as well as the Cathedral community. Afterwards Papa, Sapphira and I went to Ma. I sobbed and sobbed into Ma's blanket until I temporarily drained the well of pain.

The hospital staff on duty brings us hot sweet tea.

∞

Sapphira and I spend our days at the hospital, going home with Papa at night only after the medical staff becomes very stern. They tell us they are there to look after Ma and everybody needs to rest.

We cry together at Ma's bedside. At night, Sapphira and I lie on each side of Papa. We sob and cry and hold onto each other for dear life. Sometimes when I close my eyes, I see Benedict exploding in the air. Nightmares torture us at different times so that our whole night is more about wakefulness.

The visiting psychologist of the ICRC speaks with all of us separately, then at Ma's bedside. I don't hear much. All this talk is not going to bring Benedict back, is it?

∞

We spend all of our time with Ma at the hospital. There is nothing else to do. I spend my fifteenth birthday at the hospital. Sapphira had told the medical staff it is my birthday. I remember Benedict's fourth birthday. We spent it fighting with him to have his measles immunisation. Now this. Is this how all birthdays are going to be now? Ma's and Sapphira's were fine. Nooo. This is negative thinking. I put my index finger on my heart for *Forvandl!* I see us all celebrating my sixteenth birthday in Prestige Street. Yes! We are *all* going to get out of here!

Later in the evening one of the surgical staff gives me a box. Inside there are many little things. Chocolates, biscuits, a packet of five razors, a small magnified x 10 mirror, four guest soaps, some money, a bright green polo shirt with a four leaf clover emblem on the chest, a comic and a penlight torch, just like the one the doctor used when he looked into Ma's eyes. A little note says: "Happy Birthday Luther. May your light shine forever."

∞

Days go by. Ma can't walk yet because her right foot is still healing. Her only foot now. I can't bear to look at that space, that space where my Ma's foot, used to be; should be.

Ma doesn't particularly want to do anything, merely lie there with her eyes closed, holding our hands. Food from goodness knows where is brought to us. People come and go. Comforting. Father David stays for long periods. We pray together at Ma's bedside.

As he leaves one evening, about a fortnight after the incident, Father David asks me about '*Forvandl!*' I had quite forgotten about it.

"Wouldn't *now* be a perfect time to practise it, Luther?"

I nod. All this misery and I could have used my transformation to change things sooner, more easily.

∞

I hate seeing Ma like this. She is usually energetic, flamboyant and vibrant. I search and search for a way to bring some hope into our lives again. Instead, all I see is Papa's silence and faraway look, Sapphira's lacklustre, shrunken self and Ma, just lying there. Welcome back, *Forvandl!*

So, on Sunday, before the church service, I ask Father David if he could bring the congregation to sing a particular chorus outside Ma's ward after the service. After the service, where I represented the Wiggins family, I rush back to be in the ward with my family.

They duly sing the chorus of a song Papa usually sings to us when he is away from home attending conferences and whatnot. He sings Lonestar's chorus over the phone to us. Just like the choir is doing now.

I'm already there, take a look around

I'm the sunshine in your hair

I'm the shadow on the ground

I'm the whisper in the wind

I'm your imaginary friend

And I know, I'm in your prayers.

I'm already there.

They sing the chorus over and over again. Each word fills me with a warmth so comforting, so healing, so loving that all I can do is stand with my hands over my heart in deep gratitude. *Kelsho.*

With tears running down our cheeks we look at each other around the bedside. Smile. *This* is what being Juxonese is all about. Love and support to ease us out of our darkest hour. This is *Forvandl!*

∞

I hear the birds singing, the special bird whose chirping Benedict thought he could imitate. I smile when I remember his efforts.

"Ma, remember Benedict's efforts to imitate that bird's song?"

Ma emerges from her reverie. She smiles and nods.

Sapphira starts to talk about his speaking to the *marties,* refusing to be called anything other than Bendy Elephant. Their disappointment when he started talking without his babyish lisp.

Papa joins in.

Soon we are all smiling, even laughing at some of his antics we remember. Some of the memories I didn't even know about; some I had forgotten. A peaceful feeling cloaks us. Afterwards we hold hands and give thanks for all the good memories, thanks for the medical staff caring for Ma, thanks to Father David for holding us in his loving embrace when we were so angry, so hurt, in such pain.

We leave the hospital much more light-hearted. Ma shouts after me to start my bread round again! I smile as I wave. I love that woman!

Chapter Twenty Six

Life goes on. Ma has commenced work again at Save. It is a ten minute walk to the clinic. Sapphira accompanies her to work. Save had given us a thick foam mattress for Ma, as a 'welcome home' gift.

"I'm hoping I can persuade them to donate another one. It is lonely up there with all of you sleeping below me!" Her gurgle is back again. She walks around with a grand pair of crutches.

The surgeon said that Ma can easily have a prosthesis fitted to her stump just below her left knee once her leg had healed. Nice people, the British military. Ma particularly enjoyed their cups of tea. "Proper tea in proper cups and saucers!" We loved their biscuits that seemed to be made of pure butter. They also used to give Sapphira and me their old newspapers. We read every word and chatted to them about it later.

"You know, the stories in your newspapers would never *ever* be allowed in ours. Is this truly freedom of speech? It is *far* too damaging. It's impolite, rude actually. How does this story benefit your society?" I had to drag Sapphira away from this discussion with the anaesthetist. Nevertheless, we cut out 'interesting' titbits and filed them away in our special plastic bags. The rest of the newspapers were used for so many different things in the tent.

∞

Ma is managing very well, now that she is 'back in circulation', as she calls it. Keeping her hand in entrepreneurial ventures, however small. Doing her networking.

Only one major issue persists. Going to the latrines is a nightmare for her. She cannot squat, cannot balance herself. Sapphira has to go with her. Even then it is difficult. The enclosed area is very small, thus difficult for Papa or me to help her. The bandage on her below knee stump becomes filthy. I really don't want her to get an infection.

I am thinking of having a special seat made for her. There are ironmongers in the town, but we don't have sufficient money to pay for it. They want us to pay *marty* prices!

During our chat in the evening, I ask Papa and Ma whether we can get someone to make her some kind of sitting 'thing' she can place over the latrine hole. "Can we not ask Tom to make something? He likes pottering about. He has been asking constantly what he can do to make your life easier."

∞

Another of life's little coincidences: Tom is driving around in the camp just as Sapphira and I are sitting outside with Kelvin, guarding the washing. He stops by. I show him a drawing of a seat to place over the latrine and ask whether he could do that for Ma. He smiles. Takes a piece of paper out of his back pocket. Similar drawing. Much more sophisticated than mine, though. We laugh and high five.

"I was on my way here to see which latrine your mother uses and check out dimensions and so forth. The women were discussing your mother's dilemma in our compound last night. Got me thinking and planning. I'd love to do this for Bendy Elephant and your mother. He was so special and so is she. All of you.

I know Save looks after the under fives, but if this works for your mother, we can sell our patent to another agency who would like to help other amputees. We'll be in business!"

I am going to be a creator, an engineering creator!

In less than a week, Ma has her throne. Photographs taken for the family records.

Forvandl!!

Chapter Twenty Seven

UNICEF started the school in the camp while Ma was still in hospital. Papa asked ICRC if he could transfer to the school. He feels he wants to return to his calling as a teacher. The Red Cross are reluctant to let him go. Papa argues that he is beginning to feel unsafe walking the thirty five minutes each way, especially now that sun is beginning to set earlier. They eventually concede and give him a glowing reference for UNICEF.

It had been good having Papa working for them. We learnt so much. Sapphira continues to go there; Alain, in charge of Protection, invited her to come and chat with him. He told Papa he found her inquiring mind razor sharp and has to hone *his* to keep up with her. This message continues to delight her immeasurably. Her books from the head of law in Switzerland arrived and she has more ammunition to fire at Alain now. He'd better be on his toes; our Wiggins women are a force to be reckoned with!

Secondary school classes are in the afternoon. This suits me fine as Sapphira and I usually sell our last bread before one o'clock. Thick soup and bread are handed out before the lessons. The younger ones get a thick porridge and milk in the mornings.

The lessons are boring; things I have already learnt, but it is *sooo* good to just be in a school again. I never *ever* thought I would be saying that!

We also have after school games. I find some boys from Parrish and we visit each other after school. We catch up on news. Since Ma's accident, I have been out of circulation, and listen to the gossip and news they have. It is nothing much, nothing different from before: fighting is now sporadic, there are an increasing number of *marties* working in Juxon now, especially in Queenville and the major towns. Families are returning from Ushquel, but we cannot, as we have to get past Tomsdale and Hamilton, the only towns that remain unsafe. 'They' think it is because the many factions of rebels commute between the camps and these towns.

The *marties* in Tomsdale have withdrawn yet again, all the way back to Jamari, due to increasing dangers. There are strong rumours that we all may have to move away, away from the mined areas.

Move? We are practically on the edge of the forest already! Move where? Inside the forest? What next? Why can't the people start talking to each other like the Swiss? Surely we can do the same with one language? What is it that the one side does not understand the other side saying? How is it we know about collaboration yet persist dogmatically in power struggles?

We start to listen to the news on the BBC World Service again. One of the people at ICRC was leaving at the same time as Papa and gave his radio to us. Small and very, very clear.

"....the talks have broken down once again. Skirmishes and unrest continue in the western town areas, derailing the present peace initiative. People are returning from Ushquel....."

They don't say anything specifically about Parrish, or Scholar's Close. When we have our 'above a whisper' discussions at night, Ma says, "I am really grateful Jolene is renting out our home. It is being used. It is secure."

So, we know that life remains tense on this side in Juxon. In addition, people are still crossing the border. They bring with them stories of gross atrocities and massive destruction in Tomsdale and Hamilton. Every time there is a great flare-up, more people flee across the border.

∞

With people still crossing the border, Sapphira too found some old friends and made some new ones. One in particular sets my heart singing. The purest sonata. Slightly older than Sapphira, fourteen years of beauty. Called Cecilia. Just sort of slips over my tongue. She is graceful. Has poise. A bit like Ma, except she is thinner, quieter, even more beautiful than Ma. We seem to have a lot to talk about. Sometimes we just sit together looking out over the tents. We talk about our dreams, where we see ourselves next year. How we have changed. The things we have learned. What we dream of doing once we return to Parrish.

Sapphira starts teasing, but it is like water off a duck's back. Is this love? It's definitely something!

Papa is worried I am not eating. He says to concentrate on one thing at a time. No woman is going to look at me lying weak and thin in the mud! Frequent unexpected erections surprise and delight me. Pleasant. Very pleasant indeed. I walk around with a silly grin on my face. Can't help it. Life is good.

∞

The situation is deteriorating; little things and big things. A little big thing is that less and less people can afford to buy bread. I struggle to sell the reduced number of twelve loaves. The family decision is to start selling only eight loaves.

Big thing is that at night we hear more shouts and screams. It is pitch black at night and no-one ventures out. In the morning people are taken to the camp clinic or one of the priests are called to bury the dead. Papa is worried that none of these deaths are being registered anywhere.

We know that rebels have infiltrated our camp. Their families probably crossed the border with us. Others arrived later. We don't know who they are, so, once again, we are suspicious of everyone. This suspicion grows.

I am the only one to leave the camp now. Early one morning, half way back from the baker's, a bunch of men grab my bag of bread and beat me with thick sticks and kick me with their boots. I protect my head. Feel the thud of the boots and sticks hit my ribs, my back, my legs. I lay dazed on the ground. Nobody helps me. I limp slowly back to town. No one looks at me or offers help.

This assault takes me by surprise. I did not even see or hear them coming. Perhaps it was because I was thinking of Cecilia; that must have made me less alert. I go to the baker who sends me to the MSF clinic to have my wounds treated. He tells me I am his third worker to be beaten in three days. The men take the bread and run towards the border. He thinks he will stop his delivery for a while and see how it goes. At least he does not ask for his lost payment. I am grateful for that.

At the clinic, MSF is interested in my beating. They are keeping a record of all such incidences.

It doesn't make me feel so vulnerable anymore. I am not alone! Others have been beaten as well. For me it is somewhat comforting to be a statistic and not 'special'. In fact they say this kind of violence is growing daily.

Nothing is broken, merely severely bruised. I feel pain more than fear – and sadness that no one is helping one another anymore.

I don't go to school that day, but sit at Ma's work bathing in the staff's sympathy and eating a few of the special biscuits. I thoroughly enjoy a special herbal concoction rubbed into my body by one of the nurses there.

That night Papa and Ma agree that I should stop my business until things calm down again. Maybe I should look at something else; selling bread is not profitable any more, anyway. I smile.

"Do you remember the first time I was grabbed by the soldiers demanding I enlist? When I wet myself out of sheer fear and terror? Well, this attack, I think, was infinitely worse and yet I don't have any of that emotional baggage that I had had with that incident. Strange, huh?"

Ma answers first. "That was more than a year ago. We have all changed. You have become a strong young man. Not just in body, but in mind and spirit as well. Well done for looking back and seeing the giant leaps you have made. There is stuff that is still the same, though, such as your family being your greatest priority. Your dedication to finding ways to stay in contact with Ellie, and helping us to heal over Benedict. All these things are appreciated. Also still being the dreamer, every new interest an idea for a future career."

Papa smiles as he says:" I wonder what career you will eventually choose. Or will be chosen for you. I am very proud of you."

"You know Papa, you both say that there's always a compelling lesson in every experience. Now that it is so ingrained in my molecules, I can see that if this crisis had not happened, I would still be a spoilt brat, expecting Jolene and Jacob and you to be doing everything for me while I concentrate on my studies, which I wasn't *that* interested in when we fled. I was much more interested in girls than geometry, in kissing than in thinking about a career. What about you, Sapphira?"

"Well for me this crisis opened a whole new world in law. Especially when Papa was working with ICRC. They treated me like an equal – with respect. They listened to my questions and provided me with *sooo* much information. I really don't see the need to go to school any more; I feel I could easily enter law school with the knowledge I have now. Do you think Queenville University will allow me to study law when we return?"

"It's possible and it will not happen. Meaning, as your father, I will not allow it. Remember how I am always speaking about balance? Yes? So you have this excellent brain for law school. What you lack at thirteen are the social skills and maturity of the nineteen year olds entering law school. That is most important."

"So what would the balance be? Because I know, I *just know* I will be *sooo* bored in school – like I am at the UNICEF school now."

"Well, you know, part of the intention of the school in the camp is to get you all together again; socialising, supporting each other, helping to heal and doing 'normal' things. School is never solely about learning mathematics and writing essays. It's also about socialising, being with your peer group. So, I suppose, a balance would be to attend university for law studies and Montgomery High for Latin, mathematics and whatever else you feel you need to become a more rounded person. That way, your ego remains steadfast and you mature with your peers. It might seem so unimportant to you now, but believe me, the research has shown time and time again that this is a very important part of maturing holistically."

Sapphira's eyes are shining. She is laughing at the sheer joy of this balance.

"Do you know another thing I really like about this crisis?" I ask the three of them. "It's this togetherness we have here. I thought it was the pits when we first arrived in Hamilton and I had to share a room with all of you. But now I like the way we weave in and out of each other's way in this confined space. We *do* give each other space.

I particularly love the closeness of the family. If we were in Parrish now, Papa, you would probably be at a meeting, Ma, you would be on the phone networking, Sapphira, you would be reading in your room and I would be playing games on the Wii. Here we talk to each other. I think, apart from Ellie not being here and Benedict in heaven, this has been an excellent learning for me. And, it can stop now."

"Wonderful words, Tiger. I am grateful to my children for keeping our home so clean and tidy. Here, in this tent we call home, there is order within chaos. Not just in the tent, but as you two mentioned, in our lives as well. I think it comes partly from dealing with things in the moment, rather than harking back to how it was or wishing for how it should be. That shows real maturity."

Ma asks "Frederick, if it is only partly that, what is the other part or parts?"

"Well, it is the love we share. It is us as parents striving to be excellent role models the children can emulate. It's listening to them, treating them how we wish to be treated. It's that deeper being inside us. It's the support for each other and for others. It's thinking of others, of being of service. It's love. Thank you so much."

Chapter Twenty Eight

It is Papa's birthday today; he is forty years old – a stately elder in the *marties'* eyes. He doesn't look old to me, just special.

He used to be one of the tallest men in Parrish; when he walks into a room people stop and look. They listen to his deep bass voice that starts rumbling from his boots. He loves being centre stage. He loved the interpreting at the Red Cross. He likes being out in front there, fighting for the rights of others, being the voice of others. And when he gets angry, boy! The earth rumbles. Except for Ma.

When they argued at home, I used to see Ma almost preparing herself for a good fight. She used to say he was all mouth and heart; all she had to do was get past the mouth part. I never knew what she meant; I quaked when he rumbled! And yet I used to run to him first for anything: my great protector.

Ma wants us to have some meat tonight to celebrate. She asks Sapphira and me to buy a good piece of meat. Papa says no, this is too ostentatious; just buy some bush meat. We have to keep a low profile. People know both adults work and they may be envious and target us. Best to give the money publicly to Father David so that others can see we are sharing our wealth. I see the sense in that, especially after my trip to the MSF clinic.

We have a lovely little celebration for Papa. Ma had asked Sapphira and me to come to the clinic. She has a foam mattress for Papa! Well, for all of us now. Both Sapphira and I work hard to clean the hut, and gather some herbs to make the meal as delicious as possible. We eat by candlelight, previously by choice, now by necessity. We still talk in low tones, and it makes the occasion all the more intimate.

Before eating, Ma says a long prayer of thanks for our family. We are all tearful that Benedict and Ellie are not with us.

The meal is delicious. Afterwards I take a few photographs and then Papa recites a poem by William Blake:

Love seeketh not itself to please,
Nor for itself hath any care;
But for another gives its ease,
And builds a Heaven in Hell's despair.
So sang a little clod of clay,
Trodden with the cattle's feet;

But a pebble of the brook,
Warbled out these metres meet.

Love seeketh only self to please,
To bind another to its delight:
Joys in another's loss of ease,
And builds a Hell in Heaven's despite.

Just before dropping off to sleep I hear Ma's suppressed giggle. Hmmmm. I *know* what that is all about now. How on earth do they do it without moving? With Sapphira close up against Ma and me next to Papa? Mmmmm.

∞

Benedict would have been five years old today. We are sad. We still have his little red Mercedes Benz car. We hug each other and Sapphira and I plan a lovely supper for our family that night. We did this with Ellie's ninth birthday as well. Benedict is the first to have two birthdays celebrated in exile. As usual, I take a photo of the occasion. Royce's mini spy camera remains a pot of gold for our memories. And well hidden.

∞

The unrest continues; little incidences here and there. I am back to being in a constant state of alert. Edgy – *very* edgy; I think we all are. We become jumpy and a bit irritated with each other. Sapphira and I are fighting again. Not as bad as before, but niggling issues become inflated.

It seems everybody is suspicious of each other. Murders and rapes and beatings become regular news. We can do nothing but pray. Ma says the feeding centre has double the number of children it had the previous month. There is also cholera in the camp. Papa and Ma tell us to always wash our hands after going to the latrine and before dealing with any food. All around us people are dying, though not so many in our Parrish community.

Another foreign agency arrives. They are very active in the camp. They go to each hut and check our water containers to see whether they are clean or not. They have a high pressure cleaning campaign to stop the cholera. In our community, people volunteer to continue this work. Both Sapphira and I volunteer for our section of the camp. We tell them of our rota for families to keep the latrines and shower areas clean. They are pleased.

We still go to school, where we learn about many health promotion issues. They ask us our opinions to see how we all can cope with what we have and still remain healthy. Our class makes a poster for washing hands and keeping the water containers clean.

∞

Sapphira and I have just returned from collecting yet another three-month supply of rice, beans and oil. I *never* thought we would have to do *this again*. I had prayed and prayed and dreamed and dreamed that we would be back home now, eating at our own table, Jolene serving a delicious meal of roast meat and potatoes and vegetables. With ice cream. Now, here I am once again. How many *more* times? Will this be the last time? I send a silent prayer asking that this be the last time I stand in a queue waiting for a food distribution.

Although it is not the rainy season, another bout of unseasonal rain makes the whole distribution process that much more taxing. We stand for hours in the rain. The vehicles arrive late. It is not the Red Cross carrying out the distribution; it is a different organisation.

Suspicion grows. People become restive; they wonder whether there is to be a distribution at all, and maybe that we are brought here for a different reason. Adults chastise children for playing while waiting. They say we have to show the *marties* that we desperately need the food; playing means we don't really need it. We sit, we stand. We wait until our turn comes around. All I can think about is that tonight we will fill the pot with food! We've had to decrease the amount of our dinner for a few days recently. No hungry belly to grumble throughout the night tonight! Others say they have done the measuring of the children, they know we need food.

The beans that they give us are foreign beans. They take forever to cook. Even soaking overnight does not shorten the time it takes to cook these beans. The elders complain. The *marties* say these are the only beans on the market at the moment.

We need more firewood to cook these beans. All the nearby trees and bushes have been chopped down ages ago. Sapphira, Kelvin and I have to take another day off school, this time to fetch firewood and dry sticks. It is that far to go now. We go with three other families; there's safety in numbers. Women have been raped fetching firewood. I stay close to Sapphira, on constant high alert for any danger. It's tiring. Very tiring.

Everyone is complaining about the beans. These beans are not good for our digestion. The wind! At night it is just impossible not to pass wind. Holding it in gives *sooo* much pain. What a smell! And the noise! We can hear neighbours farting!

One night Papa's fart goes on and on and *on*. Ma becomes annoyed with him; says he is letting standards slip.... Then *she* has to go and hers is even louder than Papa's! We laugh and laugh. Then Sapphira and I let go at the same time. *"Stereo"* Ma guffaws. What had been such unacceptable behaviour in our home before has now become a laughing matter.

∞

Sunday morning. Someone from our community comes to tell Papa that Father David has been murdered. To murder a priest! *Our* priest. He arrived at Parrish Cathedral on my tenth birthday. I become panicky. Who next? What will we do without our shepherd? Who will lead the cathedral flock now?

I hear the man asking Papa to lead the funeral service.

"No! I say *no*!" Ma shouts from inside the tent.

We all look at her. Papa has done so before. Why not now?

"We all agreed in Hamilton about keeping a low profile. You left ICRC partly because you felt you would be a target for someone thinking you know too much. Father David was killed because he was high profile. That is his job; was his job. He has no family. I want my husband with me to care for our children, to be there with me when we collect Ellie, when we start over again in Parrish. I *beg* you, Frederick, refuse this request. *Please*."

Dark grey eyes stare into tiger eyes for a long time. A long, long, silent time. Dark grey eyes turn to the man, says: "I will support anyone who takes over as priest. Support him or her fully, whilst I take care of my family." Turns back to his tiger eyes again.

∞

The cathedral community is now a shepherdless flock. Directionless. Stunned. Confused. Who to turn to now? Papa assists the newly appointed lay priest and her husband with burying Father David. So many good Juxonese people buried in foreign soil. Who will visit them? Care for them? Know who lies where?

Our family holds a long and sombre family meeting after the funeral. Papa says we *have* to be prepared for anything and everything now. Consider all previous preparations as null and void. We start afresh.

"I want to know each one's suggestions and thoughts. What are your thoughts, Angelina?"

"I have accepted that I cannot run. Also, that I may be raped and/or killed. I am perfectly OK with this now. All I ask is that you three run to safety *no matter what* and not look back."

I am stunned into silence. Papa lets out a long moan. Sapphira starts to cry. Ma is the only one that is calm. "I have accepted this since I lay in the hospital. I will *not* be a handicap to you. You will have a better chance of surviving without me."

Papa stares at Ma in the candlelit tent. He says in a very low, very deep voice, every word a single sentence. "Without you I do not survive. You are my life, my breath!"

"Frederick! Now is not the time for sentimentality! Hard facts! I cannot run far nor fast with crutches. Hungry lions take the weakest ones. I am the weakest here!"

"Angelina! We came as a family, we survive as a family! Besides which, I have carried you many times before, I can do it again."

"That was from the kitchen and lounge to the bedroom, hardly a marathon!"

"You didn't complain then, don't complain now. It's only a matter of stretching my mind. Sapphira! What are your thoughts and suggestions?"

I sit there amazed. Ma is preparing for death. Papa for survival. Do we *have to* prepare for both?

Sapphira is talking. "I suggest that if we should ever get separated from each other, we meet at Grandma Meertel's home. That way we all know exactly where to go. And if Grandma Meertel and Ellie have moved on somewhere else, we go to our house in Parrish." We all say this is a brilliant idea.

Papa's suggestion is that we continue to carry our papers on us. Thanks to his money belt, we still have our identity papers. Papa had photocopied them all when he was still working at MSF. "What I suggest is that we show our papers *only* to *marties* or those working with *marties*. I feel showing them to local people may mean they take them for themselves, or destroy them."

I had put mine in my leg trouser pocket. They're safe there. Sapphira had made a body belt for herself. She puts all her newspaper cuttings in there as well. Asked why she is carrying all this bulk with her, she says she left Hamilton without anything. She wants to own at least these papers when she returns to Parrish, or whatever happens.

I could not come up with any ideas, except to pray for safety and protection and courage to face what we need to. And to stay together for as long as possible.

∞

Papa has a huge smile on his face. Earlier in the day he had gone to the Red Cross office here in the camp. There, waiting for him, is another Red Cross Message from Ellie and Grandma Meertel! It had taken two months to receive a reply. He reads the short note, then rushes to Ma's centre. Now we are in school and he calls Sapphira and me to one side and hands us the letter to read. I read it again and again, then once again. Ellie's neat handwriting fills the small space.

Thank you for your message, and all the other ones. We received your latest one today. I miss you sooo much. We are well! We have moved to stay with a foreign agency called HelpAid Worldwide. There are four marties from all over the world. Grandma Meertel is the cook here. We share a small room. I brought the photo Royce gave me. It is sooo good knowing you all have one as well. I help Grandma Meertel peel potatoes and clean vegetables and things like that. We eat well. There is no school, but I'm teaching the children English. The rebels chased us out of Grandma Meertel's house. I have a new pair of shoes. Love and kisses. Ellie and Grandma Meertel.

That night we have a long prayer of gratitude that we have heard from Ellie and that they are safe. Two days ago Papa had gone to the market in town and swapped twenty kilograms of the farty beans for twelve kilograms of our native beans. Papa says it is worth its weight in gold. So tonight we are eating delicious beans and rice and a small piece of meat each. If Grandma Meertel and Ellie can eat well, then so can we!

The next day Papa checks to see whether HelpAid Worldwide is in Jamari as well. He is told they are a very small agency and they are only in Carton. A pity; we all thought of the joy of speaking to them via their phone. As usual, we all write a little something on a Red Cross Message to Ellie and Grandma Meertel.

∞

Cecilia and I usually see each other daily. The romance is blossoming and remains a wonderful thrill. Then a week passes and I don't see her. She does not attend school the next afternoon for the third day in a row. No questioning during mealtimes can take my mind off this worry. Ma tells me that I know what to do when something troubles me: take action. The next morning, before attending school, I go to her home. The hut is gone. An empty space. An old neighbour tells me her parents had been killed during the night two nights ago. They saw their bodies been taken for burial. The two girls left. They don't know where they have gone. Nobody asks questions anymore. Nobody asks *those* kinds of questions anymore.

I return to our home. I don't want to. I'd rather walk and walk until I can't think anymore, but I adhere to our family rules to inform each other of our whereabouts. Sapphira is impatient to go to school. I tell her about Cecilia. I tell her I am staying at home today. No school today.

I lay on the mattress, sinking into the foam, sinking into a heart that has splintered into a thousand pieces yet continues to pump blood around my body. I curl up, a puddle of pain. I cry for Cecilia, for this life, for Benedict, for fear, for all these unbearable events. Why do I have to lose yet another person I know and love?

I don't hear Ma entering. She holds me, stills my wracking sobs. I feel her warmth, her love, her life, life. Eventually she whispers to me: "Tiger, the unbearable in due course becomes bearable. Hang in there. We are here to love, guide and support you. Like we have always done. Always remember that."

Chapter Twenty Nine

It's Monday evening. Ma always returns from work on a Monday with heaps of weekend news, even though she only has Sunday off. "Wow! For once I am grateful that we live out in the sticks! Apparently, there had been a great disturbance in town last night. The MSF *marties* were having a party and the rebels turned up as well. Imagine that – inviting themselves to a private party! No manners!

There was much alcohol flowing. They helped themselves to the drinks and became drunk and obstreperous. Many became embroiled in a fight. The police were called. The military also paid a visit. While all this was going on, another group of rebels forced their way into the compound of International Aid, shot the guards and took all their computers, their money and whatever else was lying around. This morning ICRC found their smaller warehouse of medicines empty. A new consignment arrived just a few days ago and now it is all gone."

This news increases my level of fear. What does Ma and Papa say we need to do when panic overtakes us? Take slow, deep breaths. I do. Five minutes of slow deep breaths calm me down.

Sapphira cries: "I've had enough. I want to go! Now! *Anywhere* but here! This is becoming unbearable."

Ma asks while comforting her, "Sapphy, what specifically are you so scared of?"

"I'm scared of this not knowing. I need some *certainty* in my life. I hate this constant uncertainty! I just want things to be *normal* again. We've played this game long and hard, but it never seems to end! I want to know what is going to happen next! I want to get on with my life. This is strangling me, my future."

She goes to Papa who wraps his arms round her, burying her in his huge frame, and gently rocks her until she is calm again. I just pray that my parents never die! What do we do without them? Would I have been able to comfort Sapphira or Ellie the way Papa did just now?

∞

It's amazing how quickly parts of me get used to this new level of violence. Inured to it, I feel it's more a case of 'well, it hasn't happened to me or my family, so on we go!' I still walk around with a high level of alertness; quite tiring actually. I am really glad when Papa or Ma is around. Their presence reduces my stress level.

Sapphira and I have become inseparable, in an 'I need you, you need me' sort of way. I find it quite amazing that when bad things happen, we tolerate behaviours that would normally drive the other one crazy. And, when we ease out of the crisis, that behaviour becomes intolerable again.

She is such a smart ass when she emphatically tells everybody she is going to be a lawyer. Such certainty! And she plays the role of a lawyer *all* the time, questioning everything, looking at every argument from a hundred different angles when I feel one would be fine. Yet, when there is a lot of fear and abuse and killings, I ask her what the world needs to do; I actually ask her opinion!

∞

It's another Monday. Today Sapphira and I are going to school in the morning as well. UNICEF visitors are arriving from their headquarters in Geneva in the afternoon. We are going to help Papa prepare the welcome.

We all walk with Ma to her work first. Despite the dust and the smells of the latrines and the sheer poverty that is around us, I feel content. Ma is happy we are walking with her. I am looking forward to seeing these UNICEF visitors. I am still curious about all these *marties* who hail from all over the world.

Heading towards Save's clinic, we hear a huge rumble, like a strong wind on the ground. Coming from behind us. Earthquake of guns and grenades. Then we hear people screaming and running towards us. For a split second we stand still, then we all jump into our rehearsed action. Papa shouts "Run! Run!" He has picked up Ma and with her over one shoulder; he is running next to Sapphira, with me ahead. I keep turning to see that they are following.

There is absolute panic. Guns firing. Explosions. Missing us by inches, splattering other people's blood on us. We've been here before. Some things are familiar; the noise, the running, the terror and horror of it all.

People are running in all directions and screaming. The noise gets worse and worse, louder and louder – and still the shooting and explosions continue. People are blown up right in front of our eyes.

There are men in front of us, shooting at us! Have they lived with us all this time? Where can we run to? We are surrounded by rebels and the army. We are caught in the middle of the war. Oh my God, *help* us now.

I keep running. This was our plan; to keep running, no matter what. I am running. Automatic pilot. I breathe ragged breaths. My legs don't seem to be moving one inch forward; they feel like lead.

This feels much worse than all the other hostilities put together. I wet myself. Hold onto my bowels. Just. Have to keep going. People screaming. Mothers shouting for children. People running out of the latrines, their tents. Screaming for children, family.

Our clear path is blocked by such chaos. I am angry and panicky that the clear path is being sooo obstructed. Papa *needs* a clear path to carry Ma! More people falling about us. Some lifeless. I can't help but run on top of them. Others have to do the same, trample on them. Papa, Ma and Sapphira are still right behind me. I am the path clearer. I pick up a stick and hit people out of my way!

We are nearly beyond all the tents, heading towards the forest, a huge place to hide in. No more guns in front of us. We are going to make it. *Again. Thank God*. I turn around to see where my family is. Right behind me. Papa shouts again. "Keep running!" At that moment a bullet comes straight through Papa's chest. Blood spurting on me. Fascinated by the froth. Both he and Ma drop to the ground. People trample over them.

"Papa! No! Ma! Ma!"

I want to stay. Ma is motionless, just lying there underneath Papa. I can't see her face, her upper body; only the stump of her leg. I look into Papa's eyes. His eyes are begging me to go. Then his life just stops. Abruptly. No more. *God*!

I look for Sapphira! I see her, just ahead of me. I shout. I scream. She doesn't hear. Bullets are flying all over the place. People are dropping all around me. Where is she now?! I can't see her anymore! Where is she? Please God! PLEASE!!! I stop to look where I last saw her, but there are too many bodies on the ground. A bullet must have hit me; there is blood oozing from my arm. I feel nothing except a huge emptiness, a panic. This wasn't how we planned and rehearsed it. We are all supposed to be running together! Now I am running to nowhere with no one. Just get out.

Amongst the bodies, the limbs, the carnage, is a small boy, arms outstretched, sitting still whilst mayhem and panic engulfs him. Without thinking I drop the stick and pick him up to clear my path as I run. I feel nothing except a huge heavy emptiness, running to nowhere with no family. Just get out. I have to believe Sapphira is ahead. Then I catch a glimpse of her, now way ahead of me, right at the start of the forest. I run and run. I know I *will* find her again.

THE FOREST

Chapter Thirty

Confusion. Chaos. Commotion. People running. Backwards and forwards. Shouting, screeching, shrieking the names of their family members. I too screech for Sapphira. Until I am hoarse. Forced to stop. Constant sobs. Wracking my chest. This is useless!

She was way ahead of me. How can she hear amidst all the others yelling so loudly, so desperately? Will she wait as she was told to do, as we rehearsed in our tent time and time again? Will she?

The thorns of the bushes rip my shirt, tear my skin. All I feel is the dull thud of my heart, a colossal wretchedness that Ma and Papa are no longer here. I *need* to see Sapphira, to know she is safe. I am now the leader of the Wiggins family. My duty. My responsibility.

I start running again, the little boy in my arms, sobbing her name in the cacophony of others calling to their loved ones. I, like the others, am running around like a hurt animal, going goodness knows where. I feel I am going around in circles – all the trees and bushes and undergrowth and people look the same. My legs are heavy. I don't know what is going to happen now. I have the comfort and the burden of a little boy clinging silently to me.

What seems like hours later, another swarm of people arrive, eyes wild with fear, panting, hysterical, stumbling. Did we look like this as well?

"Rebels! Go! Go! *Go*!"

This terror, this immense sadness, this helplessness, drains the energy, the life out of me and forces me further and further away from Papa and Ma.

Exhausted as we are, we all rush away, helping the wounded, the aged, the smaller children. The little boy is still clinging to me. I think I need to hold onto something alive as much as he needs to. I continue to pray Sapphira is safely with others. She can be so arrogant and independent! I hope she is with others. She will be! She must! She knows! I too need to be with others for better protection.

I am thirsty from all the running. My watch says 10:30. Ten thirty! I have spent a lifetime escaping, searching and seeing Papa and Ma die and it isn't even lunchtime yet!

I run ahead of the first group. I see many of them are badly injured. From my first aid classes at home, I know broken bones need support, but there is no means to support these broken limbs. We have nothing! I can't help them. I do not want to be slowed down and caught by the rebels before I even see Sapphira. My mission is to be with Sapphira!

The forest is heavily wooded. Very little sun penetrates its density. It is a permanent state of that time just after sunset: deepening dusk.

I continually bump into other small groups. Ages later, a group of people from our Parrish Cathedral is calling to me and I go towards them. I recognise one or two. They are near a small stream and the boy and I drink thirstily from the stream. We exchange news.

"I saw my father shot through the chest. He fell on top of my mother."

They mourn my parents' deaths. I ask after their losses, sympathise with them. It comforts me for a while, just being here with them, continuing habits and rituals in a world gone mad. This tenuous semblance of normality revives me. They scrutinise the boy, checking to see whether he resembles anybody they know. He doesn't. He hides his face in my chest. I comfort him. He feels a bit like Benedict. Probably as old as Benedict would have been as well.

I ask about Sapphira. They say they call all of Parrish Cathedral people to them; Sapphira has not passed their way. I earnestly pray that Sapphira joins a group. Ma talked about females being raped. It sends a shiver right through me. I will *kill* the man who does that to Sapphira. I love her so much now – she is all I have here now.

An older man says he feels we need to move further into the forest. We nod but continue to sit or lay around, stunned.

I can feel my own and the others' tremors of reaction. Every so often someone will let out a sob, or wonder aloud what has happened to so and so. This sets off the whole group again. The older man shouts at them. "Stop this useless worrying. *Trust* that you are being cared for, whether in this life or the next. We have been protected this far, continue to trust every step. I suggest again that we move a little further inland. It would be far enough so that the rebels would tire before getting to us and near enough if the army or aid agencies call us back."

As a man, I agree with them. Papa would have done the same - taken charge. Now I have to emulate him. I help the injured to move a few hundred yards deeper into the forest. After that, we simply sit around again, not talking, too shocked and dazed to do anything; I don't even think. I am like stone, inside and out. Even the small children and babies are quiet. The forest too is eerily quiet as if helping to protect us. No bird sounds, no nothing.

I say to the older man. "I read somewhere that when the animals are quiet, then danger lurks. Like the tsunami when the animals went very quiet and moved away from the danger. Should we follow suit?"

"Young man, the animals are silent because we have eaten them all!"

I don't entirely agree, but I remain silent. Respect his opinion.

We are on high alert for every twig that snaps; every sound makes us jump. This high octane alertness saps us, makes us super-terrified beings. Nobody mentions food. We are waiting for safety, for a helping hand.

∞

During the night it starts to rain, gently at first, as if giving us fair warning, then torrential. The little boy is lying almost under me. Yet not a whimper escapes his young lips. Has he been shocked into silence?

Our group is silent as well; it is no good moaning about anything – there is nothing anyone can do about it. The rain is actually a blessing. It has been so hot and steamy in the forest; I watch a myriad of little heat blisters popping out all over me. Now it is cooler. The stinging water also eases the burning from a few bullet grazes I seem to have. I remember the searing pain of one near my right eye, but I don't remember the other ones across my left shoulder, on my right buttocks and right calf. My right eye is quite swollen and I can just about see out of it. I am glad to be alive, if only to care for my sisters.

∞

The next morning we are all still in shock. Everybody continues to sit about. The constant swarms of midgets are ignored. We're too scared to go back to the atrocities and too scared to stay in the forest where there is only water.

The older men say the fish in the streams are poisonous; that is why they are still there, otherwise we refugees would have fished them to extinction. So, we have nothing except water. We sit and wait. My mind remains blank – better that way.

Much later that afternoon, towards evening, the little boy and I are lying quietly in the leafy undergrowth. We hear someone speaking on a megaphone. They are repeating over and over again that it is safe to leave the forest now. We stay where we are; how can we trust that voice? Later, one of the woman who had worked as a health campaigner for one of the organisations says we should send someone from our group to do a recce, a reconnaissance, to check out what is happening. I don't volunteer – I have a little boy to look after, and besides, that would mean two of us are volunteering. I can't volunteer him!

∞

Hours pass. We watch others move back towards the camp again. I am too scared to return. What if Ma and Papa are still lying there? Would I have to bury them as well? I can't face seeing Papa or Ma lying there. I just can't. Impossible.

Perhaps I need to look after the living. I had helped to bury others. I *know* others will bury them. Besides, our drill was to keep together. No going back - Ma was empathic about that. What if Sapphira returns here and I am gone? I'll carry their memories with me, always.

Oh God! All I want is my family and you are constantly decreasing our numbers. Three gone! What more? Who else? Please keep Ellie safe until we meet up again, *please*.

All I want now is to find Sapphira so that we can go home to Ellie and Grandma Meertel and start a life together without Benedict, Ma and Papa. Yes! That had been our family plan. My mission is to find Sapphira, no matter what it takes. The

Parrish Cathedral group continue to persuade me to return. I am adamant that I must find Sapphira first!

"What if she returns, thinking that is the wisest thing to do?" One of the elders asks. It makes sense to me. Will it make sense to Sapphira? What would Papa do? Would he be confident we would stick to our plan? Would he wait here or return? What do I do? I know Sapphira. She will expect me to go looking for her. After all, she was leading. We were following.

I *will* find her. My decision! I'm head of this family now.

Chapter Thirty One

Another night in the forest; another silent-animal night. This time it does not rain. We remain very quiet. After those first few hours within the smaller group, there has been no reason to talk. Apart from prayers, there's nothing to say. Many return to the camp. Many also stay here in the forest, too scared to return. The health worker in a small group adjacent to me issues her health warning, requesting us to use the far side of the stream for a toilet.

I awake refreshed in a way but still gripped in a fathomless abyss of grief. Endless emptiness. I *know* I will get out of the forest alive and head home to Parrish. Home without Papa, Ma and Benedict. Phew….. Still, it's home; I have simply not quite sorted out the 'how' yet. I am conserving my strength. I am leaving the 'how' to develop as it will. I am merely going to trust and *know* it will happen. And the boy will be with me until we find his family. If ever.

Later that afternoon, we hear the megaphone again. This time it is a *marty* speaking first, then a translation.

"We are the UN, the United Nations. We are in charge now. We are ten thousand Peace Keepers. We have, with all the humanitarian organisations, prepared shelter for you. There is food for all. There is medical care for the injured. It is safe to return to Jamari now. The battle is over. The rebels have been rounded up. The Juxonese government is setting up again; a Frees and Cartons coalition. We are supporting them. Peace will soon be restored in Juxon. You are safe. You will be cared for and your basic needs will be met."

They repeat this message every fifteen minutes.

People are reassured. They start to help each other towards the voices with the megaphone.

I am rooted to the spot. I *cannot* go. Deep inside me I know I have to find Sapphira! I cannot return there only to discover she is lost in the forest. She was way ahead of me *and* she is an excellent runner. I just *know and feel* she is in the forest. I *cannot* leave her there! I can't. I just *cannot* leave her in the forest.

Once again the women and the elders of Parrish endeavour to persuade me to return with them, saying our God will care for her. That my father would have had the same thoughts as they, taken the same action as they are doing now.

I continue to stand there, shaking my head. I just *know*. The little boy refuses to leave me. A silent leech on my side.

I say *Kelsho* and walk away from them to find my sister.

∞

We have now been wandering for four days. The boy and I mark our passage so that when we return, it will be easier. He has started to walk. Holds my hand whenever he can. Where we find berries, we stay there until all the berries are gone. I figure it is best to eat when we can, so we stay in an area until the berries run out. I am a city boy, so I really don't know about eating forest food. It is pure instinct that is keeping us eating the right things so far. I see fish in the streams. We spend ages trying to catch them, even though the older men said they were poisonous. I'm not quite ready to eat raw fish yet. We are merely practising, passing time in the water. And keeping our healing wounds clean.

Darkness, as usual, comes quickly and dramatically. Everything is enveloped in blackness. I am a little scared of the night animals; I hear some rustling at night, a few calls from I don't know what. Nature was never high on my interest list in Parrish. I am, after all a city boy. I know dogs and cats. Perhaps a few birds, but they aren't the things I hear here.

I pray they are leaf eating creatures, vegetarians! Most nights I am too emotionally drained to care. And Ma always said that I'm a heavy sleeper.

The little boy hasn't spoken a word yet. He merely looks at me with the biggest eyes, his very soul pleading with me. I still don't know his name. It doesn't seem to matter. Nothing much seems to matter.

I speak with him, telling him stories, talking to him about anything at night. I need the companionship.

"Once there was a young man and a small boy, walking in the forest. They walked and walked all day, searching for the young man's sister. They had a soothing cold shower under a small waterfall. Because our mothers tell us to keep clean, is that not so? What a day we've had today, huh! All those groups we've met today? How many? Show me how many fingers? Four groups of people? Are you sure? Yes? OK, so we met four groups of people today. None from Parrish Cathedral. No one recognised the girl in the photo. No one saw a tall young girl with a gap between her front teeth and called Sapphira. No one recognised the little boy. Were they upset? Were they disheartened? Oh! No! They continued, searching for their families. Because their motto is: If not today, then tomorrow!

Because their motto is: If not today, then tomorrow! So, guess what the two will be doing tomorrow? Continuing as before. Their quest. So, before they go to sleep at night, what do they do? Yes, they put their hands together and the young man prays for divine protection, courage, food and certainty of finding Sapphira. The end."

It soothes me, and maybe him as well. I speak with him like I would to Benedict, telling him I have to conserve my strength and that he will grow stronger and stronger. I sing some of the songs Benedict liked; I can see that he knows them; he is simply unable or unwilling to utter them. That's OK! At least I am getting some response from him.

When the berries are too high up on the trees, he stands on my shoulders and picks them for us. I see he is happy to be contributing to the food gathering. Twice now I have found a bush of wild limes. Absolutely sour. The little boy puts his hand to his mouth so that I can't squeeze some of the juice into his mouth.

"I know it's good for you, even one drop a day!"

No budging. Definitely Benedict's age and behaviours.

We play little games. I learn that he is five years old. Well, he nodded his head when I asked if he was five fingers old. The age Benedict would be if he were still alive. Using the same finger activity, I strive to discover how many brothers and sisters he has, but he becomes stony, his breathing comes in short bursts and then he closes his eyes; closes out the world and me. I decide we don't need to play that game yet.

"What is your name, little boy? Master five years old?"

He continues to look at me with those huge black eyes.

"Adam?"

Head shake.

"John?"

Shakes his head with the tiniest of smiles.

"Harry Potter?"

A much bigger smile and a bigger head shake.

I go through all my classmates' names, my male family members' names, and still no positive response.

"How about George?"

A different response. A quick jolt. A fright. Hmmm.

"If Ma was here, she would say you are gorgeous, so, until you tell me your name, I am calling you George, Georgeous George! Is that OK?"

A small smile.

∞

Thanks to my watch, I know we have been walking around for a week now. We continue to pass a few straggly groups. I ask them about Sapphira; no one has seen such a girl. They tell me many of their group have died from hunger, disease and injuries. They share with me their experiences of what is safe to eat. I tell them about the messages from the UN, that Juxon is going to be peaceful soon and that many people have left the forest and returned to the camp. All are delighted by the news and eager to return. I show them George and my landmarks so that they can return more easily.

I quite like that, being the bringer of good tidings. One day, someone will bring me good tidings as well. I am sure. Please, let it be soon - very soon.

∞

Today, I have decided to change tactics. Every morning I used to have a small dilemma: do we walk as the feeling takes me, or do we walk in a fairly straight line so that others can find their way back to the camp more easily? I ask Georgeous George; he shrugs his little shoulders - the question is way too big for him.

I decide to go where my feeling goes from now on, for whatever reason. Part of me loves the adventure, the freedom to do what I wish; the bigger part of me wishes I could share this with my whole family. Most times I keep myself numb; I don't think about them, because when I do, the sadness overwhelms me.

∞

Ten days since the day of the fatal shooting, we meet a group of people wandering the forest. Young and old – an actual family. When asking about Sapphira, they say they spoke with her a few days ago.

I show them the photo. Yes! It is her. She was asking whether they had seen her brother. Oh! How my heart warms to hear those words! They point vaguely to the general direction of the endless forest behind them. To me it is as if they have given me an absolutely clear street map!

I am 'jumping out of my skin' happy. I am that much nearer to Sapphira! I say a huge thank you to the group and when they are out of sight, I dance and sing with George who smiles with delight. I laugh and say a thousand million thank yous to the squawking monkeys, the singing birds, the silence, everything, to God, to Georgeous George for sharing this journey.

I really don't want to stop for the night; I want to shout and call Sapphira's name as we walk and walk and walk towards her.

"Not long now, George, then we will be three, a crowd! Just a little further to go and then we too can head back to the camp."

At the mention of the camp, I see George changing into a scared little boy. I see it, *and* I am so excited about seeing Sapphira soon again. I ignore his fear of returning to where, I think, his entire family were slaughtered. Well, my parents were killed as well. And if we have to return, we will. I will teach him *Forvandl!* tonight, so that he too can practise transforming his painful short past.

At least I will have Sapphira next to me. He will have two of us rooting for him.

Actually, why am I using a foreign word for transformation in a foreign country? Why can't I use the Juxonese word? Surely, it will have even more *kick, more power*? Why did I think it *has* to be foreign? *Right,* from now onwards, I will use *Kiff*! Much more appropriate. Juxonese. Short, sharp and sweet! *Kiff.*

∞

The next morning George is upbeat and playful. *Kiff.* For me there are too many sobering thoughts that are taking away my joy. Even the midges are bothering me this morning - a bad sign.

I spend ages thinking. The group said they saw Sapphira about four days ago. If she is walking in one direction and I in another, the chances of us meeting are zero, nil, nothing. Dear God! I need some guidance here, please. What to do? Where to go?

What would Papa and Ma do? What would Harry Potter do? What does *Kiff* feel I do? Ma always said she did all her business through intuition, her gut feeling. I sit still and feel my guts. My guts are filled with fear and horror of maybe passing Sapphira at twenty paces in this dense forest and not seeing her.

Papa used to say; one has to have a strategy. My strategy is to walk wherever my gut feel takes me in the morning. Is that enough? Is that even workable? What to do? I need some serious support here.

All the while George is looking at me. I am talking out loud. I am anguished beyond life! Quietly George puts his hands together and closes his eyes. I do the same, the two of us kneeling there in this vast forest. Too tense too even pray, I simply remain quiet. After a long while I feel calmer, almost ready to accept once again this Herculean task. Deep breath.... Well, if Hercules can do it, so can Luther Royce Wiggins and Georgeous George!

We start walking again, instinctively, towards where the group had come from.

∞

We both have digging sticks and we dig out roots that a few passing groups told us are edible and also stops the hunger. One root lasts a whole day. It's fibrous and chewy. Sweetish flavour. Keeps our jaws working. Helps me to think I am actually eating. We stay within sight and sound of water so that we can drink. I am so thankful that we haven't come across any vicious animals. Maybe it is because there *had* been so many thousands of us living in the camp and depleting the wildlife, or maybe they have merely gone deeper into the forest. Anyway, as far as I am concerned, at this present moment, this forest has to end somewhere, sometime.

"Once upon a time, Georgeous George, two young men were walking in the forest, not seeking their fortune! Oh No! Not them! Nothing as feeble as seeking a fortune. They were searching for the older young man's sister, called Sapphira. And the forest was dark, like a constant evening. Sunlight seldom touched the floor of the forest. Both were walking barefoot, because, somewhere in their flight from menacing hordes of killers, they both lost their shoes.

But the ancient trees said: 'Fear not, because our forest floor is safe. Safe from broken glass or thorns or any other sharp things.' So the two kept walking and searching. Then one moment, *this* very moment, they saw a magical thing! Look! There are angel rays!

Look, Georgeous. See those beautiful rays of sunlight penetrating the depths of the forest? These are angel rays. That is a *miracle* sign! We are safe! We are protected. All is well! It is going to be *sooo* wonderful to feel the sun on my face again, to see a large piece of blue sky, to see shops and houses and cars and people who are happy. What do you think, huh? Story continues later."

A big smile and many nods. I take that as a definite yes. I take out my spy camera and take a photo of George standing in front of the angel rays. I sing *Make some noise* while George and I do exaggerated rock star actions. I sing Benedict's favourites, *The tiny ant to the elephant, Ten green bottles, Hey diddle, diddle, Sing a song of sixpence and add Georgie Porgy, pudding and pie* for George. He smiles. The trees applaud in their own inimitable manner.

Chapter Thirty Two

George points to a heap beside a tree. We move towards it. It is a man, as old as my father perhaps, his eyes watching our approach. My eyes go to his left foot. It is in a rotten state—blown up like an elephant's foot. I can smell the putrid smell even from this distance.

I nod my head and put my hands over my heart; he does likewise. It's then that I notice a gun in his hand. A revolver like Sergeant Cecil had. I become a statue. "It's OK. Not loaded. If it was, I would have used the last bullet on myself. It's empty, useless."

We say good morning, even though it is well past midday.

I introduce George and myself. "*Kelsho*. I am Mr. Dennis. Water, please. There is a small stream this way." Puts the gun down by his side. He needs our help.... He can't move. No point in shooting us then, is there? We'll give him the water, and then be on our way. No guns. Don't need any more guns. Ever.

We pick two huge leaves and make each into a funnel, then fill them with water, carrying them carefully back to him. He finishes both. Nods his head in thanks.

We sit near him, far enough from the smell of his malodorous foot, but for me, not far enough from the gun. His eyes are closed. What to do? We can't stay with him; I have to continue my search for Sapphira. She is *so* near. I cannot carry him or lend him my shoulder - I don't know how far 'far' is. What to do?

"It's OK. Just rest a while with me, if you can." As if he could read my thoughts......

I nod. Stay silent. Sometimes silence is a good thing. I look out towards the forest, George at my side. So, he knows we can't take him anywhere. Does he want us to wait until he dies? He looks really sick, in lots of pain. That short moment I looked into his eyes, it was as if all hope had gone.

Are there any berries or roots around here? George has eagle eyes for spotting berries. I turn to him – "Spot any berries yet?" He nods. We go berry picking. We use George's shirt as a container. We carry two big handfuls of berries back to Mr Dennis. The man gives his thanks and eats them as slowly as we do.

Still no talking. Do we stay the night? We could have walked another few hours today, perhaps bumped into Sapphira. Have to stay, haven't I? If this was me lying where he is, I hope to God someone would find me and stay with me! But then I wouldn't have a gun in my hand, would I?

We return to the stream, drink our fill, then bring water for Mr Dennis. We tell him we are going to search for roots to eat. He nods his head, eyes still closed. As we walk away, George looks up at me, his eyes asking I don't know what. I smile and wink at him.

∞

George and I sleep a little distance away from the sick man. I am not quite used to that sickly, putrid smell yet. As I turn and cuddle into George I think how weird life is: here am I wandering this great big forest, seeing fewer and fewer people, with a five year old who is unable to speak and staying with a man unwilling to speak. All this silence - to end up talking to myself like a madman?

∞

The next morning I am awakened by Mr Dennis' groaning. I see that his leg is swollen even more.

George and I relieve ourselves, drink from the stream, then bring water for him and sit together eating the berries we have just collected.

"I am going to hell," Mr Dennis says just above a whisper. The gun is out of sight, thank God.

I look at him. Say nothing. How would I know where he is going—I don't even know where I am heading.

"It is true. I have been a bad man, a truly bad man."

"What have you done?" I don't know what other question to ask. Perhaps this is the right one. Maybe I could be a psychiatrist - people can tell me their troubles, just like Mr. Dennis here.

"I killed many people."

Oh dear! Now what? I know he is incapable of moving. He said the gun is broken, not loaded. I have to believe him. George moves swiftly to my side furthest away from him, holds my hand.

"Why?" I can relax. I am almost confident he is harmless now.

He looks at me, takes a deep breath, closes his eyes. Silence once again. Keeping his eyes closed, as if he cannot bear to look into mine, he starts to speak very softly, just above a whisper.

His eyes. One brown, one grey. Who mentioned this to me once, long ago?

"I come from Tomsdale. I am a car mechanic, I specialise in Volvos. Well, used to, anyway. My own business and life was pretty good. Then the president got himself shot. People started going mad. I did not want to leave, run away like everybody else did. So I stayed. Life went on. People's cars still needed fixing. Money was still coming in. My wife and I and my family had a few scares, but we could cope with these minor law infringements."

He pauses for a long while. I think he has fallen asleep.

"Then one day, three drunken, drug fuelled, stupid idiots started breaking all the cars' windows, damaging all the cars, stealing my tools. In less than five minutes my whole life changed. While I raced after one of these hooligans with my crowbar, the other two went into my home, killed my wife and two young sons. Just like that. Four and twelve years old. They were watching television.

That's when I went mad. I killed and killed and killed. Anything that moved into my path: cats, dogs, people. I smashed them with my crowbar. Took whatever I wanted - some food and drink to drown my madness. Or maybe refuel it."

Breathless, he stops. I freeze.

"You are Mr Deluxe?"

"How do you know me?"

"One of my friends and his family stayed with you overnight. You were repairing their car. He said you had a grey and a brown eye. He said you were a huge bear of a man. An absolute softie in the house, but in the garage you worked like one possessed! They stayed in your cellar."

"His mother was a surgeon? Couldn't leave because of the father's passport? I remember. It was some months after this that those killers came to my home and ended our lives. So I became like them."

I am back in Hamilton again, seeing men senselessly hitting out at others until the police or soldiers kill them or they manage to escape. The horror of it all. How did this man survive? I really don't want to hear any more. This is atrocious! And now I have to stay here until he is dead? Phew.

"When I saw my father shot, I didn't even think of killing anybody else! I wanted *all* killing to *stop*! Why did you start to kill? Was it because you were angry and mad about damaging the cars and your house and killing your family? Why did I not have thoughts of killing? Because I was sad?"

He merely looks at me. Closes his eyes again.

Oh dear. Now we have to feed him and fetch water for him. I think George and I will be in his company as little as possible; perhaps only at mealtimes, and sleep even further away from him. His story is *too* bad. Perhaps psychiatry is not for me at all.

Hmmm. This is what Papa would call duty and Sapphira an 'undesirable obligation.' I think she may be right, as usual. Yet how can we leave him, knowing he can't even fetch water for himself? Then again, how long has he been lying beside the tree, all on his own? How did he walk all the way here? Who passed him by? Am I being too soft? Am I helping anyone in need, irrespective of his or her 'doings' as Grandma Meertel says? How can I leave? How long is he going to take to die? How bad will I feel tomorrow when I remember how I did not help a man who needed me? How bad will I feel in twenty years time? Who says I *have* to help him, be with him, care for him? And when he dies, George and I will have to dig a hole to bury him..... I should start now - he is a big man. That is going to delay us *even* more. And, if I do this, will I be rewarded by finding Sapphira sooner? He is a murderer - I have to protect George! He is dying, hopefully soon, and then we can be on our way again, knowing... knowing what? Is this compassion? Oscillating compassion. Nevertheless, compassion.

That evening, after our meal of roots and water, George and I lie down to sleep, even further away from him than before. Does he seem stronger this evening? Is all the food we are providing him giving him instant strength? Oh no, we will be delayed *forever*. Tomorrow I have to make a decision. Tell him I have things to do, to find my sister, get back together, get my education, find George's family, all these things; I can't be expected to stop here!

∞

It is morning. A safe night. Mr. Dennis starts talking again, as if his last sentence had been only a breath before. I am morbidly fascinated even though I want to cover my ears with my hands. George is still asleep, thank goodness.

"This killing spree seemed to go on for weeks. Weeks of not caring what I did because others had destroyed my life. Juxon was in turmoil and anarchy and so was I. I didn't care whether I was killed or not; in fact I wanted to die. I provoked people so that they could kill me, but I always ended up killing them instead. See, I had nothing more to live for.

I moved over the border to Jamari. That made me even angrier—a whole camp-load of people looking and behaving like victims! Pretending they are helpless! I couldn't bear this victim thing, so I provoked them! I killed a policeman, took his gun and started playing with it, harassing people, making them even more petrified. Whilst taunting them, I accidentally shot myself in the foot.

That woke them up. It woke me up as well, because suddenly there was an ever-increasing mob of angry people as well as the police chasing me. To tell you the truth young man, I did not even feel the pain in my foot as I ran into the forest. Suddenly, the reality of my life was a painfully lonely place to be. I found the stream and all these bushes with berries, also some wild lemons. Ate the fish I caught. I stayed here and my foot started healing quickly. Lying around forced me to begin thinking, reviewing my actions, my feelings.

What to do now that my foot is nearly healed? Where to go? I couldn't face life after all I had done - what I had done is unforgivable. All that killing was not going to bring my family back to life. It took me that long to discover that."

A long pause. I have nothing to fill it with, so I remain silent. Look at the trees, their tallness, their greenery, their solid trunks. Their roots must be deep to cope with such height. My roots must be sooo deep to be able to cope with this profundity of atrocities.

"I am going to hell, the only place for me. So I gave up. What's the point, eh? Can't live with myself. Can't live with others. And so, from then onwards my foot became steadily worse. I allowed it to become so, can you see? Absolutely painful. I couldn't move. I think a part of me wanted to feel the suffering of all of those I had hurt."

"Why don't *you* ask for forgiveness? Why don't *you* forgive *yourself*?" I ask him. Even a man heading straight for hell ought to have a few redeeming features, shouldn't they?

He is silent again. Did he hear my question or is he asleep again?

∞

In the morning, George and I go through our routine: toilet, drink, say a prayer for the day for safety, courage and gratitude that we are alive and able to look for my sister and care for Mr. Deluxe. Then fill George's shirt with berries, carry water to Mr. Dennis, have breakfast together, in silence, slowly eating the berries, one by one, chewing nothing much over and over again. After breakfast, when George goes looking for pebbles, remaining within earshot and eye contact, Mr. Dennis speaks again.

"I was here, in this spot, for about two weeks before I observed masses of people fleeing into the forest. I lay here, exactly as I am now. And do you know what, no one came my way. I could see them; I don't know if they could see me or not, but nobody came *near* me. I was out of their way. The gun was hidden, out of sight. A huge part of me did not want to shout out, to call for help. I was too ashamed and thought they might know as soon as they saw me, that I was, am, a murderer, a shameful murderer who had taunted them mercilessly. Of course a small part of me really wanted help. But how could I ask, when I had done such unforgivable things?"

Long silence again. I stay where I am; I have nothing better to do. George returns with five small round pebbles. I had taught him the five stone game Sapphira and I used to play when we were in primary school. George is becoming really good at it, except all our trouser pockets have huge holes in them, so we are constantly losing our small stones. We play for a long while on the soft ground; it certainly makes it that much easier to throw one stone in the air whilst picking up one or two of the stones on the ground. Sometimes, like now, I wish George would make a sound, especially when laughing. Just a small one will do.

He doesn't.

It is late afternoon, and before we go foraging again, Mr. Dennis starts to talk once more. What will we talk about once his story is over? Talk about me? I really don't want to share my story with a murderer, a mass murderer. Anyway, I am only doing my duty here. My oscillating, compassionate duty.

"I see you are wearing your necklace. We're both men. As one man to another, I am asking you forgiveness for all the sins I have committed. All of them. Please, can you forgive me?"

Me? How can *I* forgive? Murdering so many people is *unforgivable - he said* so himself. Why ask me to do something he cannot do? What to say? Help!

Unconsciously, my finger touches my heart. My overture to *Kiff*. *Kiff*. After a long silence I say: "Well, first you have to forgive yourself, haven't you? If you cannot forgive yourself, how can you expect to forgive others or for others to forgive you?"

Wow! How did I know this? It just poured from my lips; such wisdom. That *Kiff* came from deep down my soul.

After another protracted pause, he answers. "Forgive myself? True. I need to forgive myself. And, if I forgive myself, will you forgive me too?"

I nod my head. Of course.

∞

The next morning, I awake and turn to look at Mr. Dennis. He looks very peaceful lying there. No more groaning. Perhaps he has forgiven himself. I can still smell the smell. Strange how quickly I have become accustomed to it. I can't even remember when that feeling of wanting to retch disappeared and I can breathe normally close-up to him. Something makes me look closer at him. He is not breathing. Definitely not breathing.

Damn! I hope he forgave himself before dying. Is that why he died, because he forgave himself? I certainly wasn't expecting him to die so soon.

I'll forgive him anyway - should I have done so before? Does it matter whether I forgave him; isn't it heaps better that he forgave himself? Did he? Well, he can't do anything about it now; Mr. Dennis, Mr. Deluxe is dead.

∞

George and I spend the whole day digging a shallow grave for him. Our sticks break often. Digging makes me realise how weak I am becoming. In Hamilton, at fourteen years old, and after that first horrendous fighting during the night, I had dug a grave in the churchyard in three hours. Now it is taking George and myself twice as long. It is evening before I drag Mr. Dennis into his final resting place. Place the gun underneath him.

Look at his trousers. I need another pair of trousers. His pair is in better shape than mine. I don't need a pair *that* desperately. If not for the stench, then for the atrocities. My pair of trousers will survive until I meet Sapphira and head back to the camp.

We stand in silence looking down at him, covered in leaves. George nudges me. I look down at George; he has his hands together to say a prayer. I start to say a prayer. Whatever comes into my head. I hear myself forgiving him. It makes me feel better. Actually, it makes me feel strong and powerful. Hmmmm. I must do this more often - forgive others. Just imagine Sapphira's face when I forgive her there and then for her cattish remarks! Awesome. Empowering.

We really *must* be on our way tomorrow; I need Sapphira to practise this forgiving thing. George and I scoop the soil on top of Mr. Dennis. Pat down the earth to make it more compact. I hope any animals leave him in peace.

Too late to go anywhere, we head to the stream, first drinking from it, then washing ourselves and then our clothes. That night we sleep away from Mr. Dennis's resting place. Leave him in peace.

Chapter Thirty Three

It is now a month since that evil day. The day my parents died. My watch says so. Otherwise I would have lost count of the days. I have already lost count of the number of small groups we meet wandering around. The groups have changed. Many of these groups are kids - young adolescents, young people. Miniature families. A young girl, usually, but not always, in some visible stage of pregnancy, a young man like myself or younger, a few small children, often toddlers, occasionally a baby.

Some say they were in groups before the great escape from the camps, after they fled Hamilton; others had parents killed during the night. A few, like me, lost their families a month ago.

I am reluctant to join such a group. Firstly because they already have a young man protecting them. I don't want rivalry and conflict within such a small group. We have to survive together, not fight. A second reason is that I have a mission to find my sister. I don't want to be obliged to take responsibility of a group that might stop me searching for Sapphira.

This is what I care most about: getting my own family back together again. Then we can heal together. We can support each other. I am absolutely sure that my relationship with Sapphira has changed way beyond bickering and sibling rivalry.

I remain hopeful most of the time. Sometimes I feel I am quietly going mad and George is not able to stop me. At times I get so frustrated because he won't or can't speak. I need to hear someone else's voice besides my own – it seems as if I am constantly talking to myself. Sapphira would tell me there are places for people like me: they live in padded cells and eat with their hands! I laugh aloud at something that used to annoy me.

∞

George is standing on my shoulders, picking berries. We will probably stay here for a few days – there is a glut of berries. A bit overripe - nevertheless, it is food. The berries are becoming scarcer, so we stay where we find them.

He stamps on my shoulder, his way of alerting me of visitors. I look up at him. He is pointing ahead of us. I can see a small group coming towards us through the thick growth of bushes. I wait for them to draw nearer. They take their time; must be weak.

It is Cecilia! Cecilia in the distance, walking towards us. I let George jump from my shoulders and I run towards her. She is carrying a toddler, about eighteen months old. There is also a six year old boy with a mangled arm, rotting flesh that absolutely stinks, making me want to retch. He looks like the dead walking. Another Mr. Dennis. Dear God, his memory is still so fresh and here you bring us another one. Another grave.

I am so glad to see Cecilia. The first person that made me forget to eat. The first person that stirred me up so much, I didn't know what to do in bed at nights, crammed in the tent with no privacy. Feelings so sweet, I used to press the replay button over and over again. Then she disappeared. Never to be seen again. Until now.

We stand in front of each other, speechless, hands over our heart in our deepest greeting. *Kelsho*. What a beautiful miracle. What a delight. What a blessing. Or am I hallucinating? After all of the wandering, all the lonely times, all the silence, here is Cecilia.

We both start talking at once. Gibberish! I don't know what I am saying, and I don't understand a word she is saying. We stop, silly smiles on our faces. Is this heaven? It feels like a fizzy drink impatient to escape the confinement of a bottle. I touch her arm.

Everything stills; everything is just this moment, the bubbles quietly disappearing. I take a deep breath and say hello again. I introduce George. She introduces the little girl as Alice, her cousin's daughter. The boy is Neil, unrelated.

We return to where George and I had been picking berries. We pick more and put them in George's shirt for them. Cecilia and her little family are exhausted; they have not eaten for two days. Neil has become too weak to climb atop Cecilia's shoulders to pick the berries. Cecilia eats slowly, savouring every mouthful. Alice gobbles every one faster than George can offer her. Neil has to be persuaded to eat.

We fetch water in leaves for him and for the girls. George and I are so happy, I giggle and giggle. George remains as silent as ever, a broad smile on his face. I have taught him to wink; he winks when life is wonderful. I take a few photos. The battery still has fifty percent life in it. We'll be home long before it needs charging.

∞

After the first greeting, Cecilia and I don't speak much; we're so happy just to be, to have found a familiar face at last. I liked her before, even more so now. For me it is as if she has been sent to me. We will stay together, of course. She tells me she was with a larger group and when they returned to the camp, she refused. She feels safer in the forest. She sees me looking at her swollen belly. We look at each other.

"I see you see."

I nod my head, a thousand thoughts running amok in my head, confusing my heart, my senses. My first love, and she is pregnant! What now? I remember the sadness within me, the confusion when suddenly I did not see her in the camp anymore. Where had she gone? I would have supported her; comforted her like I would have done for Sapphira if anything like this had happened to my sister. Why did she not want to speak with me? I sigh. Explanations will come later, I am sure.

Her belly is big in her thin body. So that's why I haven't seen her for a while. I thought she had moved camp after her parents had been murdered. Whenever I asked, nobody was able to tell me where she was. Now I know. I sigh deeply. Or maybe I don't. I don't know what to say or do. I just sit. I look up at her again. Such sad beauty.

She nods her head.

"That's why I stopped visiting. The night they came into our tent and murdered Ma and Pa, they raped both my sister and me. Only I became pregnant. I did not want to see anybody again, especially you. I still feel so ashamed, so filthy. I was sure your mother would not have allowed me to visit, knowing this."

"I have two sisters. My mother was always worried about Sapphira getting raped. I can assure you she would have understood. Supported and helped you."

"Probably, but at the time, and even now, I still feel dirty, used, less than human, a dog that has just been taken."

I don't know what to say. What can one say? I look at her and smile.

"You're still beautiful to me, within and without. It's not your fault that the men chose to come to your tent, kill your parents and rape their daughters, is it? Did you know them, the killers?"

Cecilia shakes her head.

"Well, if you didn't know them and you didn't invite them into your tent and you were in shock because of the death of your parents, did you have a choice?"

"Yes! I could have fought them until they killed me as well! Now this is just killing me, day by slow day. I hate this baby, this growth! It's like a cancer, getting bigger and bigger and eating the life out of me. I hate it!" She starts to cry, more a whimper, like a badly beaten dog.

"Cecilia! Listen! I used to listen to Ma talking to Sapphira. In fact, she wanted me to be there to hear, so that I should never ever even think of raping a woman, taking any woman by force. I remember Ma telling Sapphira over and over again, that if a child is born from such an abusive act, then we will all send both the baby and the mother all the love in the world. The baby is innocent, Cecilia. How can you hate innocence? And if they killed you, I would have been very sad, very sad indeed."

We eat more berries for our evening meal. Neil is very weak. George fetches water in a big leaf. I feed it gently to Neil. Oh! To see a cup or mug again! Wouldn't it be wonderful! I will appreciate it so much, wash the mug as soon as I have drunk from it and say thanks every time I use it! Poor Neil has difficulty even drinking the water; it tires him out.

Alice is the only one expressing herself, rather volubly. She is completely naked; the forest's climate is rather unkind to clothes and too much washing or rain or the constant steamy humidity has made all our clothes threadbare. She is chattering and laughing and singing. George watches her, smiles at her, makes funny faces that makes her giggle deliciously. All the while he is his silent self.

∞

We settle down for the night. Cecilia lies next to me. Neil's stench seems more sickly sweet now, more bearable. Much like Mr. Dennis'. Alice has wriggled herself between Cecilia and me.

I lay there, in the pitch dark, a silly grin on my face. My future wife is lying beside me, with our children, a family. I wonder if Papa felt this way in our tent, all of us close to him. Well, most of us, Ellie–less, and then without Benedict.

The next morning, Neil is even weaker. He is dying. We can do nothing for him, save feed him the juice of the berries and carry water to him. We sit next to him, watching Alice and George playing. Sometimes we chat, make a comment; most of the time we are merely content to be together. Cecilia tells me she knows the baby is due in three months time. We hope we will all be in Juxon and reunited with our families. Cecilia has a sister. I invite her stay with us, whoever 'us' is.

I tell Cecilia about the man, Mr. Dennis, with his poisoned foot and leg. How it took me so long to forgive him. Now, here once again, is someone else with a body being poisoned.

"Well, you know, they say that if you do not learn the lesson the first time, it comes around again and again until you get it."

"What was I supposed to learn?"

"Luther, it has to come from you. It is *your* learning. What do you think?"

"Well, I suppose I thought what he did was unforgivable. How can I forgive the unforgivable?"

"What do you think I am dealing with now, with the baby growing inside of me, with this unforgivable act?"

"What do we need to do?"

A long silence. We each sit with our own thoughts.

Much later that evening, when the children are all sleeping, Cecilia and I sit close to them, close to each other but not touching. I am afraid to start that emotional see-saw again. Cecilia starts to speak softly.

"You know how your father used to say during assembly at school, that before we judge others, we need to walk a mile in their shoes?"

"Hmmm." I don't know where this is going. I keep quiet.

"Well, what do you think your father would have done if he had seen all of you killed?"

"I don't know. I would be dead, wouldn't I?"

"Luther! Just put yourself in your father's shoes. What was his highest value, what do you think?"

"I don't need to think, I *know* his highest value. His highest value was integrity."

"So, if someone stopped him from living his highest value, from maintaining integrity, for instance killing his family, what would he do, do you think?"

"Think of tearing the killer's heart out!" I say it with utter conviction although I had never ever seen Papa in any situation like that before. "Thinking doesn't mean *doing* it, though."

"So, perhaps Mr. Dennis wanted to tear the heart out of those who had killed his family. The only trouble is: he stayed in that mode. How does that sound or feel?"

"I think it is possible. I think any laudable explanation is possible. How are we to know? We are sitting here and I am listening to what you are saying, knowing it can be true or not. Frankly I haven't thought of it in that way."

Another long silence while we mull over all these deep things.

"So, what about you?"

"What about me?"

"What learning are you getting from the baby growing inside of you, that 'unforgivable' who is becoming more and more visible?"

"I don't know. I don't *know*. What would make a man do something like this? You are a man. Put yourself in this rapist's shoes. Why? Why did he rape both my sister and me, and how is it that I am pregnant and she is not?"

Another long silence. This is way beyond my thinking, way out of my knowledge zone. Besides which, she is asking me to wear too many men's shoes. I am not even wearing my own shoes at the moment, metaphorically and physically. I am just over fifteen and a half years old and still waiting for my first encounter with a woman, this woman sitting next to me. I haven't a clue. I want to love her, not force her. Besides, the legal age for consensual sex is eighteen years; two and half *loooong* years to wait.

Why do men have to rape? Maybe Sapphira would know; she would have read about it, I am sure. Oh no! I hope Sapphira has not been raped. Please, *please God,* not Sapphira. She would kill the man; he wouldn't stand a chance, he wouldn't even dare. Would he? What would I have to do or feel to rape a woman? Force. Take her by force. Where is the pleasure in that? Ma would be so angry! Papa would be so disappointed in me. *I* would be so ashamed. No! I could never do it. With Papa and Ma it was always about love and laughter.

"I think it takes a certain kind of man. A brutal man. My mother used to say it is a coward who does things like that. Brutal, coward, hurt, choose one. Why you? What lessons are you learning? Don't some lessons take time to learn? What if the lesson isn't learnt now, but when the baby is born? Maybe she is a blessing in disguise. I will take care of her. I will help you. I promise."

"No! I am soiled. The baby is soiled. I will *never* marry."

"Oh, oh, Cecilia, that baby is not soiled. It is only your thinking that makes it so. I remember when

Ma was talking to Sapphira of either or both of them being raped and becoming pregnant. Ma always said to think the best of the baby and themselves. Even when Papa protested that he and I should not be listening to such stuff, Ma insisted, saying we will *have* to be there to support them and love them, including any babies that may be born. I don't know. When reality hits you in the face, we find ways to deal with it in the right way. You are pregnant and I said I would love to share your lives.

I *know* we will leave this forest soon. I remain hopeful. I trust. If I didn't, I would have gone mad long ago, wandering around with a five year old who doesn't talk. Maybe I am mad. Maybe we met in order to restore my sanity and yours. Maybe we should just go and sleep. It is late. We are both tired."

We lie entwined. I am so happy to be talking to someone again and receive replies. How sensible I have become, being able to talk about things I would never have thought about had I not been through all of these 'challenges' as Papa called them. It is very quiet in the forest. Of your own accord, my hand moves to stroke Cecilia. Such silky skin. So warm. I feel good. She starts to giggle.

"What?" I whisper.

"It is merely physiology," she giggles again.

"What are you talking about?" This pregnancy thing, I think it is touched her brain,

her mind.

"These changes taking place down there with you."

"Merely physiology huh? Don't you feel it?"

"Uhuh."

"Well, how does it feel for you then?"

"It's kind of warm and pleasant and exciting, gives me a deep giggle down there and everywhere."

"Hmmm, I feel the same, except mine is more visible."

"So we lay here, all pleasant, okay?"

I sigh. Pleasant? Pleasant, yes! Frustrating, yes! Delicious, yes! Unfulfilled yet again, yes! Shall I move? No! Just another night of 'not yet'. Did Papa have these troubles with Ma? How many of my *Onashi* group have savoured the delights by now? Papa told me he was twenty four years old before he savoured these delights. It was the night when he married Ma. Do I really, truly have to wait that long? Can I wait until I'm eighteen – just over two years? Do I just practise on myself, by myself?

Times have changed, surely? Couples live together before they get married. I definitely *cannot* wait another nine years, like Papa did. A lifetime! It might all wither away and then I have *never, even* tried it, felt what it was really like. On the other hand, I don't quite know what to do? Will it all just fall into place? Hmmm. Did Father David die before he used his? Did he think about it while he was praying? How does one stop thinking about it? I fall asleep, my 'physiology' uncomfortable and uncomforted.

∞

These days and hours with Cecilia make me realise how little I do, how I have been conserving my strength. Cecilia says I am very thin. I know I am now using a third notch from the usual hole on my belt, but I admit not paying too much attention to it. It would add to the worries I have pushed out of my mind. I tell her I hope these berries and roots are 'complete' foods, filled with all the nutrients necessary for her and her baby.

I hope, for her sake, and the baby's sake, that the baby looks like her, so that she is not reminded daily of the abuse. That's what Ma said we should pray for if ever she or Sapphira became pregnant through rape. I remember the look of pain, anger, and disgust on Papa's face when Ma spoke of these things. He really did not like Ma discussing these things, but Ma insisted. She used to say one of the many things she learnt whilst in the hospital after her below-knee amputation, was the notice on one of the walls: *Proper Preparation Prevents*

Piss-Poor Performance. She changed it to be more positive and *Proper Preparation Promotes Powerful Performances* became a Wiggins motto. Now I am helping Cecilia to do likewise.

∞

It's four days now since our reunion. We are still at the same place. Neil is too weak to move. I am not strong enough to carry him a long distance. He just lies there, quietly; most times his eyes are closed. Sometimes he looks at us while we sit next to him.

I am sad about his dying, yet quite accepting. There is nothing more I can do under the circumstances, except fetch water, turn him, sit next to him, tell stories and let him know we are there.

I think back to the time when we were in the camp and Benedict was really, really ill. Our family was a bunch of nerves; Ma demanding the medical staff do more and more, even though they were doing their very best.

I think I am the way I am now because I have seen so much horror; I can be less emotional about death. It happens. Or maybe I have built a thick wall around me, to keep out all these horrible emotions until I can deal with them again. I don't know. At the moment it just feels right to be sitting next to Neil and not feel too much.

At night we all sit around Neil while I tell a story.

The berries have all but disappeared. Cecilia says they ate fish every day whilst in a large group. Nobody died. It wasn't poisonous as the older men warned us. I think the time has come for George and I to catch fish.

Georgeous and I spend a whole afternoon letting the fish slip between our hands. Eventually I catch one large fish – enough to feed my new family. I feel like a provider – the hunter.

Nearby is a small tree with a few wild lemons. The lemon juice on the fish reminds me of the Japanese food we once ate in Parrish; delicious. We take bites out of the fish like I've seen a pride of lion do with their kill. Cecilia bites off pieces for Alice. This is the best meal for weeks. Besides which, eating so many berries give us very loose stools, very often. They also make us thirsty and we have to drink more. Now we have meat to add to our bony frames.

∞

In our discussions, Cecilia feels we should head towards 'civilisation'. "I'm sure Sapphira will also see the pointlessness of staying in this huge, unending forest, looking for a needle in a haystack. And remember, the ICRC and Save are there to help us reunite with their Family Tracing and the Red Cross Messages."

I see her reasoning. Besides, I really don't know how to deliver babies; don't even want to think of the possibility. We decide to go once Neil has died. It won't be long now. He is getting weaker and weaker. He's unable to eat anything, just managing sips of water that dribble down his cheek. In the meantime, we are conserving our own energies. Our meeting has done wonders for our morale and I am now eager to get back to 'civilisation'.

Only one question: which way is it?

∞

The next morning, Neil is semi-conscious. Cecilia and I help him to swallow some water, just to make him comfortable. It just dribbles down his cheek. It's more to know we are doing something.

Alice and George are playing. Alice needs lots of diversion. Our meagre diet only manages to make her very angry. Temper tantrums abound, scaring the few birds I had paid little attention to. She wants more and there's nothing more to give her.

George is tapping on my shoulder. I ignore him whilst helping Cecilia to make Neil a little more comfortable. The tapping becomes a fist, demanding attention. I look up at him. He jabs and jabs his arm in Alice's direction.

Alice is eating mushrooms. The poisonous ones. Deadly poisonous ones. This much I know. I run towards a smiling Alice, opening her mouth. She starts to scream which helps to extract the bits of mushroom from her cheeks. Jaws clamp around my fingers. Holds her grip. Cecilia arrives, pushing her finger down her throat. Alice vomits.

"Water!" Cecilia shouts. I pick up the screaming child and race to the stream. We bathe her mouth with water. She chokes and splutters. We continue.

"What now?" asks Cecilia after a while. Alice seems fine, having had another monstrous tantrum. I shrug my shoulders. "We wait, hope and pray."

Cecilia starts to cry. What now? I touch her.

"You see! I am a useless mother! I can't even look after a child! I don't deserve to live!"

I don't quite see the relevance, the connection. Dear God, inspire me now – *please*! I am way out of my depth here! Right words! Right now, please.... I take a deep breath, then another.

"Cecilia." She is so deep in her stuff, she doesn't respond.

"Cecilia!" That sounds more demanding, like Papa! No! Like me. This is me! Deep bass.

She looks up. I look at her. Her eyes are filled with such hopelessness; I nearly lose my resolve. I hold her, her head against my chest. After a while I start to speak. My voice sounds unreal, not me. Well! I did ask for the right words! I don't quite trust my voice. Papa used to whisper in our ears when we were really upset. It worked then, might as well use it with Cecilia.

"Cecilia. I really don't see the connection. Alice is always hungry! We don't have the means to satisfy this hunger of hers. She doesn't understand this is all we have. I tell George that we are doing the best with the resources we have at the moment. And, at the moment, we have berries and roots and water. Also fish.

You want to do the impossible? Do you? And we are busy with Neil, caring for Neil. Does that make George inadequate as well? If anything happens to Alice, are both you and George going to blame yourselves for the rest of your lives, and Neil as well, for taking you away from Alice? Is this fair? Does it even make sense?"

I take a breath, continue stroking her. Start again. Still whispering, but in a gentler tone.

"You know, this wandering in the forest with silent George has given me much time to think about life, to sort things out. I have come to the conclusion I cannot do everything, be everywhere. And what happens, happens for a reason I don't always know or can't always see in the moment. So, I wait until it is revealed to me. It may take hours, days or even years, but of this I am sure, there's always a reason for things happening, or so Papa says. No! I've figured that out for myself as well. I believe this to be true."

I take a little break, all the while holding her, stroking her hair, her back.

"You are a beautiful person, inside and out. I want you to live. And you know why? Because you are going to be my wife, the mother of my children. We Wiggins men always choose the perfect wife, the highest quality wife. That's why I am choosing you."

I feel her snuggling up closer to me. Where, oh where did those words appear from?

She gives a small giggle. "Sapphira warned me about you. Said you were the smoothest talker she has ever met. She's right."

"*Sapphira said that* about *me*? You're joking! *Never*?!"

We both remain standing still, little tremors running through us like electrical currents. I can't believe *Sapphira* said that! About me! Wow! What *was* I saying just then? Phew! Me, not even sixteen years old yet, jobless, career-less, homeless, penniless, proposing!

∞

All forgotten and forgiven, Alice wriggles herself between our legs, breaking the spell. We move away, looking at each other. I touch her cheek: "I meant every word I said." I say before I pick up the leaf to fetch more water for Neil.

Soon afterwards, Alice becomes violently ill with diarrhoea and vomiting.

We look at each other. We know.

I turn to ice even though it is sticky hot. Minutes later she is convulsing in a strange, peculiar way. Soon she is unconscious, a rag doll. Remains that way.

George and I take the time to pick some berries, dig up three roots. He is holding my hand more than usual. I kneel down to his eye level.

"Hey, Gorgeous. I want to say a huge, humongous thank you for playing with Alice, doing *everything* to keep her occupied. You know she was always *sooo* hungry, wasn't she? Always wanting more than we had, more than we could give her. Do you understand, Georgeous? Alice is very sick because *she* chose to eat those poisonous mushrooms even when you told her *and told her not* to. Thank you for taking such good care of her. Do you understand, George?"

He nods his head, confusion leaving his eyes. I get up, walk to the stream. Sit there. Suddenly, I am blazingly angry with him. Why the hell doesn't he want to speak? He is making it *sooo* much more difficult! I can't deal with all this! Why can't he help me by talking? I am so overwhelmed by all of this. I lay face down in the stream and put my head in the water, cooling my anger, my frustration until I am forced to surface for breath.

I feel completely weighed down by all these events. Crushing me. Neil dying. Alice dying, Cecilia feeling worthless and wanting to die, George not speaking. Sapphira disappeared. Ma and Papa dead. What next?!

∞

After a while I calm down, take George's waiting hand. Return to Cecilia, Alice and Neil. Alice is still lying there like a rag doll, so small. As I look I see fresh blood start to ooze from her nose and mouth. Her skin is a strange bluish colour. As I continue to stare in morbid fascination at these rapid changes, she stops breathing. We wait, holding our own breath, until she breathes again. She never does. Less than two years old.

We are heaps of unmoving sadness, completely overwhelmed. I look at Neil. I see his small chest rising and falling imperceptibly. Dear God; soon, him too.

I move slowly to search for a strong digging stick. George follows. He holds my hand. I am unaware that I am crying until I taste the saltiness on my lips. Is this fatherhood? Is this togetherness?

What on earth is there to learn from this? I drop the sticks, walk towards Cecilia and enfold her heaving body in mine, open my arms wider to include George. Stay thus for ages. Sadness melted into one huge sobbing blob.

Eventually George and I dig a small grave for Alice. We are all silent, like George. Finally, I manage to say a few words, drag a few more out of thanks.

"Dear God. Thank you so much for this little ray of sunshine that sparkled for such a short time in our lives, yet long enough for us to feel the warmth and joy of her being. Give us the courage and ability to absorb her loving joyfulness into ourselves, so that we too can be a ray of sunshine to others."

Say a prayer as we all cover her with the soil. A tiny mound. Still silent, we move towards the small stream to wash ourselves. As though in a dream, we remove our ragged clothes, sit together, splashing water over ourselves when we remember.

Time passes. Sobs subside. Tears stop. A snake passes near us. Who cares. We are so immersed in our sorrow, it passes us. Probably can feel the sad energy soaked into the water – doesn't want to have anything to do with such immeasurable wretchedness.

Closer than ever now, we return to Neil. We sit, still entwined. I start talking to him, to them, to myself. Merely talking to let go of I don't know what. I want him to know we are still there for him. Tell him stories.

"Neil, once upon a time there was a little boy. We will call him Neil today, shall we?"

When I pause, Cecilia takes over, at the same tempo, talking about her childhood, her friends. Tells him stories of great love, tells him he is loved. I continue with her theme now, remembering stories Ma used to tell us, the ones Papa told to inspire us. George holds his good hand, strokes it. Neil does not move. He is past that stage. We are calm at last, or maybe simply out of emotions now. Rag dolls that reach out to each other for support.

That night, everybody merely picks at the berries. We drink water, turn Neil and retire, lying quietly side by side, touching, the heavy blanket of grief covering us.

∞

The next morning, I turn on my side. No Neil. *Neil!* My heart is pounding! What now! Has an animal sneaked up during the night and taken him away? How did I not hear? I look around. My heart stops. There, on the small mound that is Alice, lies Neil. A few pale rays of sunshine filter through the trees, shining on the mound, onto Neil. Angel rays.

Ceciliaalsoseesthis.Thisisfartooincomprehensible for us. We hold each other and cry and cry and cry. I cry for Alice and Neil's deaths, for Benedict, for Papa and Ma. I cry because life seems so unbearable at the moment, so draining. We are lost in this huge, unending forest. I feel weak and scared, everything.

∞

It takes George and me a whole day to dig a grave for Neil. We are worn out, physically and emotionally. Dear God, protect us; get us out of this forest soon, *please*.

Cecilia washes Neil's shorts and T-shirt. The forest is not kind to our clothing – we are all in rags. Later, George will wear the shorts while Cecilia keeps the T-shirt for her baby.

∞

It is four days since we buried Neil. We have decided to walk in an eastward direction, hoping we will get to Juxon or the sea. We walk slowly, amble, picking fruit and digging up roots on the way. Occasionally it rains heavily. Sometimes we sit for hours under a big tree, waiting for the rain to stop. We see no one. We keep our fears, doubts and worries to ourselves. Most times, Cecilia and I sing songs we learnt at school or church. We sing the action songs Benedict loved so much; *The tiny ant and the elephant, Ten green bottles, Sing a song of sixpence* and all the others. George knows the actions as well. We laugh as we all do the actions, over and over again. We sing *You Raise Me Up* to give us more courage, to feel protected, loved, to give us hope. We sing '*Make some noise*', *Hallelujah,* hymns *How great thou art, Swing low, sweet chariot, Kumbaya,* anything that comes to us. I take a few photos of George and Cecilia. She takes one of me and one with George.

At night, I sleep next to Cecilia. The sheer joy of it, feeling her next to me. The indescribable comfort of feeling the closeness of a loving body. I usually turn when I am aroused. 'Physiological' as it is, I don't want to upset Cecilia. Tonight, lying cosily spooned and feeling my arousal, I reluctantly turn. Cecilia's hand stops me.

"What?" I whisper.

"Stay."

I stroke her arm, her hand. I dare not stroke her belly, her breasts. I nuzzle her neck, move to her ear, kiss her shoulder. She takes my hand and puts it on her breasts. She turns towards me. We kiss. Heaven exploding. Deep warmth. Electric. She caresses me, strokes me, touches me. Voltages streak through me. I am afire! I caress her belly.

This is most wondrous, sublime. I am in heaven. At last. The baby moves, kicks.

Cecilia switches off, like the switch of an electric light I have not seen for months. Turns away from me. Starts sobbing.

"What?" I whisper in her ear.

"It's no good."

"What's no good?" I whisper.

"The baby is there to remind me. Always. Let it go, Luther."

Now, what do I do with all these aroused bits? I too turn around, lie there, concentrate on my breathing, listening to a very silent night. Dear God! What is this all about? Later I draw a sleeping George back into my arms. Some comfort.

After a restless night, I wake up, still confused. Cecilia refuses to have eye contact with me.

"What have I done wrong?" I ask.

"Nothing" she mumbles as she escapes to the toilet.

By mid-morning she cheers up.

And so it goes: during the day we hold hands and sing and chat, at night we kiss and caress until something happens inside her and the curtain comes down, swiftly, end of show. I remain confused; am I going too far?

Eventually, after much probing, she is able to talk about it. She says the baby makes her realise that she is not worthy of my love, that she is dirty, that there is a piece of dirt growing inside her.

Not worthy of my love? Love? This is pure and simple fifteen-and-a-half-year-old testosterone overflowing! This is wonderful! My hormones are taking over this previously wonderful relationship. Testosterone definitely gives me the 'up'. So near and yet so far.

I think of Ma. I am being the *ultimate* gentleman. No one else in this huge wide forest and *I am* a gentleman. I promise myself to be even more compassionate, caring and considerate with Cecilia and think of her needs. Yes!

And then the heat is turned up and my mind, my compassion turns to passion and stays at this level.

Chapter Thirty Four

My watch has stopped. We cannot figure out what day it is, or how long Cecilia, George and I have been together, or how long we have been walking eastwards. We haven't seen anybody for days now.

We still sing, although not as often. We are really conserving our strength. Food is getting even scarcer. Hardly any berries here. We don't know what to eat other than the berries and the roots. I manage to catch fish every day. Small ones, mostly. We carry a lemon or two to add to the fish. Sometimes, we just eat the fish without the lemon. Hunger does that. No, *desperation* does that. Or the will to survive. Having seen Alice die such a horrible death, we are too scared to experiment with other forest fare.

∞

We see tracks. The *first* time ever! A well-trodden path. Hope! Excitement! We are near somewhere! It gives us immense strength to continue with renewed vigour. 'Civilisation' is in sight. We follow the path eastwards. It takes us nowhere. Yet. We sleep near the path that night, eating the few berries and drinking from the nearby stream. No fish tonight.

The next morning, all three have diarrhoea. We can't think what we have eaten differently. We all feel weak and sick, me probably the worst. Still, we continue ever so slowly along the path.

I say, "Let's just keep going. I am *certain* someone will find us. All we have to do is keep walking on the path. This path is here to take us home."

By early afternoon, I am too weak to continue. Cecilia and George bring me funnelled leaves of water. We lay down on the path. I fall asleep. I wake to hear Cecilia talking to a man. With blurred vision I see he has a few children with him.

"Luther, Mr. Johnston here collects lost children for Save. Save then collects us from his home in the forest and takes us to their Children's Centre in Jamari. From there they take us to Juxon."

I smile wanly at him. Our saviour. He says he can't carry me as well as the two children he already has on his shoulders and in his arms.

"Go Cecilia, go. Take George." Both refuse.

"Mr. Johnston. Take them. Fetch me later." Both still refuse.

Eventually Cecilia is persuaded when Mr. Johnston says he will fetch me in the morning. George will stay with me. Of course. My faithful shadow.

"Cecilia. Remember my address for Carton and Parrish. I'll remember yours in Parrish. We know where to find each other. Go now."

Mr Johnston leaves a packet of Save's rich biscuits and a litre bottle of ORS, the oral rehydration solution, and two extra sachets. A bottle! I marvel at the bottle as if it is the first time I have seen one! Well, I have not seen one for weeks, or is it months? I am grateful for this. Before he leaves, I ask Mr. Johnston about Sapphira. Show him the photo. He has not seen her, neither have the other bedraggled children. Do I look as bad as them? Bony. More sores than skin. Grey. Ragged. Big eyes. Exhausted.

I go to sleep that night happy that I am near my journey's end. George and I still marvel at the bottle – our first possession in months.

∞

The next morning, energised and much better, George and I set off along the path. Soon we arrive at a fork in the path. Both are well trodden. Which one to take?

We choose the one going eastwards. I chat and hum now and again as we walk, happy in the knowledge that soon we will be in Juxon. Better not think of all the hurdles that will face us there. Let me simply concentrate on one step at a time.

Step one is to find Mr. Johnston again. I am so happy we have met up with Mr. Johnston; the berries are becoming even scarcer now and out of reach of George's little hands. We have eaten all the biscuits; rationing was out of the question – we are starving. We walk quite slowly. Although stronger than yesterday, I still feel quite weak. The sores that I had not noticed on my feet are hurting too much to walk too far. By late afternoon I am quite concerned that we have not yet met up with Mr. Johnston. Not another night in this forest! He promised! Please Mr. Johnston, *please* come; I feel I can't be strong for much longer. George has seen some berries. We move off the path to eat these few rather overripe berries.

∞

I am beginning to feel rather weak again. George is struggling as well. I cannot carry him on my shoulders. Not now! We cannot fall down now, so near to help, so near to Mr. Johnston. I think back of watching a Youtube clip of Derrick Redmond running his four hundred metres in the Spanish Olympics and pulling a hamstring. He continued even though he was in severe pain. *He* had *his father* with him to help him to the end of the race, though, didn't he? I *need* a father now; where is Mr. Johnston? I am becoming more and more distraught and it is making me lose energy. I need more of that rehydration solution. We can make it. We *will* make it! I decide to sleep here for the night; it's near water. I make our last oral rehydration solution with the litre of water. Allow George the lion's share. We curl up together once the sun goes down.

During the night it rains buckets and buckets. At least it cools us. Causes ponds where our beds are. We remain lying in the ponds – I merely make our leafy pillows thicker. Cools the many blisters I seem to have acquired that are becoming infected. My feet are swollen, not as much as Mr. Deluxe's though. That would be the end. Truly. I finger my Tiger eye for good luck, for comfort, for strength.

After eating a few mouldy berries lying on the forest floor, we search in vain for the path. It has been washed away. I don't know which way to go; I haven't been that observant because I felt Mr. Johnston would find us on the path. Now there is no path. Just a muddy mess.

"George, what now?"

George looks up at me so full of trust, merely shrugs his shoulders. George looks a bit like a skeleton – like those children. He is quite weak. Just sits. Too weak to move.

Well, we came this far; *we will* make it to Juxon. Dear God, what to do? Send me on the right path, PLEASE! *So* near and yet so far.

After a long rest, we give it another go. Walk slowly around in ever widening circles; surely the berries were not *that* far from the path? I have more bouts of severe diarrhoea. Precious water being lost from my body. This medicine is not working! We soldier on, find the berries again, or is this a different tree with berries on it? I don't know, just grateful George can reach it without my help. He picks the berries and brings some to me. I eat a few, knowing I *have* to. We curl by the berry tree; it is near a stream.

I don't know how long we stay here.

THE CHILDREN'S CENTRE

Chapter Thirty Five

A woman is sitting at my bedside, holding my hand. Tears in her eyes.

"Good morning Luther! At last you are waking up!"

I look around. Through a dense mistiness I see Robin Hood and Ivor the Engine painted on the wall. Spartan. Quiet. Specific smell. Distinctive. Unfamiliar. Clean. I feel exhausted. That tiredness that closes your eyes when you're still looking. I squeeze her hand; a pathetic effort. I drift off again.

Next time I wake up, a nurse is standing at my bedside. I nod my head. Say '*Kelsho*'. A whisper. No sound.

She puts her hands to her heart and says "*Kelsho,* Luther. Welcome. How are you feeling today? Your little brother refuses to leave your side. I hope you can stay awake longer today?"

Benedict?! Benedict is dead! Am I in heaven? Very ordinary, very poor for heaven. Not what I had imagined at all. Can't be!

Just then George enters the room, comes to my side, finds my hand. George! It's George!

"George."

"Pardon, who? John?"

I shake my head. Close my eyes again. Too much effort. George is with me. My shadow. That's enough for today.

∞

"Good morning Luther! Let me talk before you drop off again. Do you remember me? My name is Nurse Clare. I used to work with your mother Angelina at Save's feeding centre in Camp Alpha. Now I'm working here at the Centre. I am your assigned nurse. You are my very special patient. Do you know where you are?"

I shake my head, ever so slightly. Up until this moment I can't say I'm too bothered at all about my whereabouts.

"You are our guest at the Children's Centre in Jamari. You are in the Feeding Centre. In Room One, where the sickest children are. You have been here for ten days, coming in and out of a coma, getting stronger every day, thank God. Tell me, what is the name of the little boy who is like your second skin?"

"George." Still a whisper.

"George?"

I nod.

"Never mind. We'll get the whole story later, when you are able to talk. Mr. Royce left a message for you. He had to return to England on the very day he brought you here. He told me to tell you he will be back to visit you as soon as he can walk again. He left his satellite phone number for us, for you. Sends his love. I know it sounds a bit confusing, all this information, but I have been waiting and waiting to tell you.

I am feeding you special milk. Put some flesh on your bones. You are so lucky to be alive, to be here. All will be revealed later. Mr. Royce found you, you know. He is probably itching to hear your story.

I, too, am intrigued and eager to hear your story. Now! It's rest time. For as long as you need to gather up your strength. George comes and goes. That's his little bed there. We only managed to persuade him to sleep there since Friday, two days ago. However, in the mornings, we find him huddled in here with you.

No! No, no, no. I'll hold my horses. Your story can wait. Especially as young George refuses to speak at all. Does he speak with you?"

I shake my head.

"*Oh*? Well, that's fine then! *And* a pity. See you later."

"Thank you" Still a whisper.

∞

My first morning awake. Alert. Aware. I lie there all snug and cosy, knowing there is no need to get up or do anything. A Saturday morning feeling. I look around. My family photo is taped to the wall, next to the window. I look at my family. See their smiles. Heavy sadness descends. Drag my eyes away. Look at the rest of the room.

Apart from my and George's beds, there are three other smaller cots in the room. Two have little bundles in them. Quiet and silent. Just then Nurse Clare enters with a tray, as cheerful as ever as she greets me.

"It's weighing day! Are you awake yet? Typical teenager! Come on! Wake up! You can go back to sleep again as soon as we are finished."

"I can't stand." My whisper is stronger, not quite a voice yet.

"Ohhhh! Young man, we have ingenious ways of weighing you. Effortless on your part. Effort on my part. I weigh myself, that's the most difficult part because I have to reveal to the world what I weigh! Then I weigh us together and deduct my weight to get yours. Thanks to this high calorie milk, your weight has been increasing steadily. I can see you have gained weight today! You have decided to have cheeks again! Not quite as 'pinchable' as George's, but soon, *very soon*.

Come on now! Let's get this going. We need to weigh you before your next feed. I'm going to call Barbara to help. She always does."

I take full advantage of the few extra minutes of sleep it takes to fetch Barbara.

∞

"Luther! Oh Luther!" Nurse Clare is laughing and clapping her hands in glee at my expression. Before me stands a vision.

"Well! Hallo! Welcome back! I am fine, how are you?"

A tall, large woman is looking down at me, a huge smile on her face. Amazonian. Colourfully dressed. Clashing bright colours. Same age as Nurse Clare, I suppose. Younger than Ma.

I continue to stare at her. Her long dark and blond streaked hair looks as if she has forgotten to brush it this morning. Her wide smile shows front teeth smudged with lipstick; bright red lipstick. I look at her eyes. Her brown eyes are smiling and filled with happiness. Tears are running down her cheeks in rivulets of mascara. Next to her Nurse Clare is wiping her tears from her cheeks, a huge smile on her face.

Slowly I bring my hands up to my heart to acknowledge her. It's a very slow process until my shaky hands reach my heart. *"Kelsho"* This makes the two women cry even more.

Eventually the tall woman speaks again.

"Hello Luther. My name is Barbara. I replaced Linda. You remember Linda? I have been waiting for this moment for *weeks*. *At last*. What a fighter you are! So strong. Nurse Clare and the team here are *so* dedicated. It makes my heart burst to see how much they care for you. Nurse Clare worked with your mother. Told me what an amazing woman she is. And that handsome man Royce! Yes. I believe he promised to return. I am going to do my best to be around. Is he married, single, or gay?"

"Barbara! That's rude!" Nurse Clare can't stop laughing though.

"Well, I've got to check whether I have to put some effort into this or go read a book! He will be staying at our compound again so I want to be prepared. Luther?"

"Divorced."

"Well, well, *well*. I'll certainly organise myself for whenever he returns. Come on, let's weigh you."

Eventually she takes a breath, wipes her face with the back of her hand. This gesture spreads the blackened bits of mascara all over her face. I lie there, just looking at her. What energy! She talks the way Benedict's first nanny did. Non-stop. Eventually, even young Benedict used to crawl away from her. She had a heart of gold, though. Papa used to say that if we could bottle all her words we would be billionaires in a month! I smile at the memory. This 'crack your lips' smile brings fresh tears to Barbara. I am so busy with my memories; I haven't heard one word she was saying.

"Nurse Clare here has been your special nurse. She recognised you immediately although she couldn't believe it really was you. She weighed you when you first arrived. She cried when she you weighed you, because we could hardly see whether you were breathing or not. You are so tall; we had to have a special bed made for you. And of course, your little shadow, George is with you all the time. We are all hoping you will gain lots of weight, so that you can reclaim your own shadow. Because, at the moment, without George, you have no shadow!"

She guffaws loudly as she helps Nurse Clare carry me and step onto the scale. When Nurse Clare feels she is holding me safely, they read the scale. Do the deductions.

"Another two kilogram gain in one week! Well done! Well done, Nurse Clare and well done,

Luther! You see, Nurse Clare has probably mentioned this already, but I'll tell you anyway. It bears repeating. We are working towards you gaining two kilograms a week until you are a minimum of sixty eight kilograms. That is the absolute minimum we are hoping for your height. We prefer if you would weigh seventy or more kilograms – it gives you more breathing space, so that you do not slip back so quickly – do you see what I mean? Good. Nurse Clare will explain all this to you over the next few days, so that it doesn't tire you. We want you to conserve your strength. And no, Sapphira hasn't passed this way yet. Remain hopeful.

Well, 'bye for now, Luther. It is so wonderful to see you awake – a truly beautiful miracle. See you later."

The mere effort of being carried a few feet to the scale and listening to Barbara exhausts me. I spend the rest of the day napping.

∞

Days pass in routine and caring and chatting and resting. I can now feel my stomach filling up with milk every time Nurse Clare feeds me. I can feel the hard plastic of what Nurse Clare calls a urinal between my legs. Nurse Clare says soon I can have it at my bedside, when I am strong enough to use it myself. I love her talking to me when she is feeding me or tidying my bed.

Sometimes I wake up to her voice, just chatting away as if I have always been attentive. Once she was just sitting there, mending some clothes, gently humming a tune. Peaceful. I liked her before, when we were in Camp Alpha. Now, I like her even more, knowing that she has been here all the time.

"I thought you must be *so* lonely, so I'll just be here, soothing you, letting you know you are not alone. I would love to hear what has happened to your family, but I know it is early days yet. It needs time.

This is where the most malnourished children stay until they have reached a target weight, before they leave the high dependency area. Then they move onto Room Two, and then eventually Room Three and out of the Nutrition Centre. You too will be progressing that way. Ninety nine percent of the children in Room One are under five year olds, and ninety nine percent of *them* are under two years old.

"I don't hear much crying." I whisper to her.

"Like you, they are too weak to do so. Do you know, you are the oldest, tallest, most underweight person we have *ever* encountered? *Ever.* I only recognised you thanks to your photo we found in your trouser pocket. I could not believe it when Mr. Royce said it was you. The foreign doctor is writing up your history and progress. He plans to publish it in international journals.

You remember Tom Yon, the engineer? Made the throne for your mother? He is here as well. He extended his stay here when Mr. Royce and Nurse Winnie brought you in from the retrieval team. We sort of filled in the background to the doctor's case study. He will ask your permission to publish it when he visits you.

Now, Luther, all I and everyone else want you to do is to lie quietly and regain your strength. If and when you can, I would also like you to talk to me about whatever is troubling you, because troubling thoughts might stop you from gaining weight. I learnt that from your mother. Might that be true?"

I nod.

"You will be using your energy to sort out your thoughts, rather than to get better and gain weight. I know, or can put two and two together, from what other children have told us, that you, like them, have been responsible for a group of quite vulnerable little people, yes?"

I nod. She knows. I remember Papa telling us of adolescents caring for a bunch of children even while we were in the camp.

"Well, Luther, I can only guess at the weight of responsibility that you have been carrying, even if you didn't think, feel or know it as such. I mean, you still have George, right? Right! And you probably want to know what has happened to the rest of your family, aren't you? So now, what we would really wish you to do, is let go of all of these responsibilities, these responsible thoughts. Let us deal with them. Tell us. Tell me. It remains with me. Confidential. All we want from you is to lie here and regain your strength. Simply be a fifteen year old again. Is that a deal?"

I nod and say 'Thank you'. Sounds wonderful to me; like it used to be at Prestige Street with Jolene always at my bidding.

"You were so very sick when Mr. Royce brought you in. Then he had to return to England because he had fractured his lower leg in an accident in the forest. He promised to be back again. To see you. He said your father and he were bosom friends. He wants to look after you and George. He said your father had emailed him about Benedict and your mother in the minefield. I told him a few stories about your wonderful mother, about Bendy Elephant, about all of you. I shall wait until you are ready to tell me what you know. Just take your time, although I'd prefer it to be sooner rather than later!"

∞

Over the next few days, she starts reading Harry Potter's The Chamber of Secrets to me, but when she notices my heart starting to race at the excitement of it all, she stops.

"No, Luther. This is not a good idea! Not good *at all*. I want you to *relax*! Don't worry, we will find another way. I'm sure you will be able to read this book soon. Soon, but definitely *not* at this moment."

I don't spend much time feeling aggrieved at the loss of this single bit of diversion I have, notwithstanding Nurse Clare's chatting and Barbara's morning round. It doesn't seem to matter to me.

For a brief moment I think back to my life at Scholars Close where, if I could not play computer games for *at least* two hours a day, I would feel so restless, argumentative and lost, not knowing what to do. Now, those computer games seemed so distant, so alien to the life I was leading, am still leading. Will I ever be so involved in computer games again? Who knows. Then again, the first few pages of Harry Potter made my heart go racing away! For now, sleep is my main occupation.

I am fed this special high calorie milky feed every three hours day and night via a tube in my nose to my stomach. I can sip water if I wish, otherwise I simply sleep and sleep. Glorious sleep. No need to think, worry, remember. Blissful escapism.

Occasionally I feel George sleeping next to me, or just holding my hand. My little shadow. We look at each other, deeply, in the eyes. We smile at each other, wink.

∞

A few days later, Barbara bounces in like a friendly whirlwind. She never needs to announce herself - I can hear her laughter and happy voice as she greets everyone on her way to Room One. She is holding a small MP3 player in her hand.

"For our special guest, my darling friend. Good morning Luther. How are you this morning? Slept well? Nice smile? Thank you! Here, all the way from Holland! Nothing but the best for you! When Nurse Clare told me we needed something more calming and restful for you at the moment, rather than the excitement of Harry Potter, I e-mailed my friends all over the world to ask for help. One friend suggested affirmation CDs. Do you know what 'subliminal' means?"

I nod.

"Of course you do, an intelligent fifteen year old, of course you *know* about such things. Anyway, my friend sent this small MP3 player. I listened to it last night. It is simply sounds of nature. Try as I would, I could not hear any messages or affirmations in it. And *of course* it will be so, because it is subliminal! But I needed to check it out. We do have the words that are being said. It's all very positive and about healing.

It says you need to listen to it constantly for about three weeks, preferably a month. And Linda sent rechargeable batteries and a battery charger from Belgium. Aren't they all wonderful? So now we are ready. Listen to it as often as you wish, even when you are sleeping. I will collect the batteries every morning and return them recharged the next day."

"Thank you. Thank you so much. *Kelsho*" I hold my hands over my heart. I am filled with gratitude for the efforts of these wonderful people. The joy of having familiar faces around who knew me, Ma, the family in the camp. I have tears in my eyes. Both Nurse Clare and Barbara's eyes start to glisten with tears. Nurse Clare, too, has started to wear mascara so both their faces are blotchy with mascara now. I make a silent promise to myself to buy these two wonderful ladies waterproof mascara when I am in Juxon again. Ma wore waterproof mascara all the time - haven't they heard of it here in Jamari or wherever all these *marties* come from? I wonder why she didn't ask her friend to include waterproof mascara with the MP3. And waterproof or whatever lipstick that does not go on the teeth.

After a while, I smile at myself. These thoughts about the mascara and lipstick - I think they are my first thoughts again! Wow! Must be getting better! YES!!

∞

I listen to the music. It is easy listening. Reminds me of the forest, in a good way. The sounds of the birds that I took for granted and stopped hearing.

Now I remember how I used to feel comforted by sounds other than my voice. There were the sounds of a waterfall. I remember the fun times we had, when George and I were alone and we were stronger physically. We had such fun, playing in the water, standing under the waterfalls, washing ourselves. We found five in all; one was quite high. We stayed there for days.

The sound of crackling fire. I begin to remember the wonderful winter evenings at Scholars Close, all six of us cosy on the huge deep sofa, the crackling fire blazing away. Sipping hot chocolate. Roasting nuts. Ma putting aromatherapy oils on the coals, making the room come alive and cosy with the smell of sandalwood, or jasmine or others I can't remember now.

Sometimes Papa or Ma would tell a story. Sometimes we would simply be sitting there, staring into the fire. I can feel the camaraderie and contentment and cosiness of it all now. When there was thunder, Ma or Papa would choose some music so that Benedict wouldn't be afraid. We would sing along with their songs, until one by one Ma or Papa would take us to bed, even when I was nearly fourteen years old. Of course, being the eldest, I was the last of the children to go to bed.

I had forgotten, or maybe never even realised, how wonderful these times were. Snuggled between Ma and Papa, simply sitting. Being so proud to be the oldest of their children and feeling the privilege of having that special extra time with them. Once I had forgotten my book or something and returned to the lounge. There was Ma and Papa, snuggled closely together, so cosily, their favourite music playing. I hope Cecilia and I will have as loving a relationship as Ma and Papa. Hope she is doing well in Parrish.

∞

Nurse Clare tells me one morning that tomorrow it will have been one month since I arrived. As usual, while she is giving the feed through the tube, she chats to me.

"I looked in the workbook at all the things that have happened since you arrived. Some are small, others big. Actually, reconsidering, they are all *massive* events."

"Like what, for instance?" I ask, not remembering much of what has happened since my arrival here.

"Well, let's look at George first. Physically, he recovered within five days. Of course, he wasn't in as bad a state as you. You must have been looking after him very well indeed. After a week of persuasion, he was able to leave your side for two minutes only, gradually staying somewhere else for half an hour. Now, look at him, the only time he is with you is when he comes to see you before his meals and when he sleeps with you! In between these times he is playing with the other children. Isn't that *wonderful*? Of course he is still silent, still not uttering a sound, and yet in himself he looks fine and happy. He is participating in the games, dancing, doing drawings, happy drawings, going to his carer Lucy for cuddles. Huge progress there."

She pauses, looks at me. "And you, dear sir, look at you. I think his happiness is having a positive effect on you as well. It has allowed you to concentrate solely on yourself now and you are making rapid progress. Although not smiling as much as Barbara and myself would love you to, you are lighter in spirit. Your skin is also so much better. All those old scabs and ulcers have healed. Your feet look like feet again. You are back to being that handsome young man that used to practise his charm on the Save female staff! I'm sure you knew this before! You know that Linda is still absolutely in love with you, don't you? It's those huge tiger eyes that are holding her in bondage!" I smile. I love her gentle giggle.

"Now you have Barbara constantly thinking of what little thing she can do for you next! Such power!"

"And you?"

"You cheeky devil! I am a married woman! You *are* getting better!"

We laugh silently. Wink at each other.

"You have been gaining weight, steadily. You talk, although not much, but you do talk. You listen to us. You smile at us. You listen to the music. You sleep well. Now you're sleeping less and listening to the music more. Your beautiful tiger eyes are bright, your hair is growing. There is some flesh between your skin and your bones!

And tomorrow – tomorrow is D-Day; decision day. Tomorrow, after weighing – and I am sure it will be another gain – you will be moved to Room Two.

It is a huge, auspicious and very important day for both you and us. There you will be able to sit in the chair. Barbara and I will help you to walk again. Because you are so tall, I feel I need someone to support me supporting you until you are steady on your feet again. And as Barbara is almost as tall as you, and has been helping me to weigh you these past few weeks, she seems to be the ideal one. What do you think?"

"I agree. Thank you so much, Nurse Clare. I am really grateful."

∞

The next morning, I am awakened by activities going on all around me. Those kinds of activities that are fully intended to be quiet, and end up making much more noise. Reminds me of Jolene who sometimes used to start working far too early on a Saturday morning.

The noise is coming from Room Two. I think they are moving cots so that my long bed can fit in there. There is bumping, crashing, falling of items onto the floor, a broom banging against the wall, someone shouting quietly and urgently to be more careful because the floor is wet, twittering and tittering when all are making a great effort to be quiet, and then banging into something.

It's like Christmas morning when we kids used to go to the Christmas tree very early in the morning, struggling to make as little noise as possible so as not to wake Ma and Papa, and yet that air of excitement filled the air and wafted all the way to their bedroom.

I pretend to be semi-asleep, knowing I will receive a hundred apologies otherwise.

Finally, I feel it is safe enough to proclaim myself awake. Despite all those little noises, I must have dozed off again, because when I open my eyes, Nurse Clare is sitting at my bedside, tidying up my paperwork.

I smile a morning greeting to her, give a little stretch. She hands me my toothpasted toothbrush and I start to clean my teeth - about the only thing I am allowed to do, apart from washing my hands and face in the morning and after toilet.

She combs my hair and puts cream on my skin in companionable silence. She goes to fetch my ten o'clock feed, places it at the bedside and brings the scale. That feeling of twittering excitement is still in the air.

"We are just waiting for Barbara to finish what she is doing. Then we will weigh you and take you to Room Two where, as you know, you will be allowed to sit in a chair. We will move with your bed and then have a small celebration, like we always do when children are transferred from Room One to Room Two."

I nod. I have heard the nurses and carers sing and dance. Only vaguely though. I did not realise it is about this 'promotion'. I have not heard them that often. I gather the promotion from Room One to Room Two is not so often. I have also heard them cry and support each other. Must be when children die.

I hear Barbara progress towards the Feeding Centre, the chirpy sounds of laughter drawing nearer and nearer. Then she stands in the doorway, tall, round, a big woman in a big brightly coloured top - huge flowers all over it, lips as red as ever, lipstick already on her teeth, damp hair simply hanging down.

"Luther! Good Morning! I am fine - how are you?" I smile at her usual greeting, said with huge conviction and a mighty big smile and personality that dynamically lights up an already bright room.

I see a tall *marty* standing behind her, smiling the biggest smile at me. Coming towards me. *Royce*! Royce. Holds me in a bear hug, just like Papa. I hold onto him for dear life. Another connection with a loving past, with people who I have loved forever, who loved the same man as I did.

His tears mingle with mine. We stay like that until both have calmed down. He takes a deep breath, holds my face between his hands. Looks at me.

"Luther! Luther Royce Wiggins. My best friend's son. My son. I am so very, *very* glad to see you. God! You'll never know!"

He turns to the staff, now all teary eyed. Puts his hands to his heart. "*Kelsho*. There are no words to express my thanks. *Kelsho*."

While he is talking, something stirs in me. I remember his voice in the forest. Long-ago memories come back to me. I remember his voice just talking to me, the rich, soft timbre of his voice, so reassuring. Gentle. Soft. It was shortly after Papa and Benedict had persuaded me to come into the light with them.

"In the forest, I vaguely remember you talking to me, very quietly. Perhaps before I came here? Thank you, it made me feel everything is going to be all right. Thank you". We look at each other and smile quietly.

∞

With a clap of her hands Nurse Clare interrupts. She is eager to give my ten o'clock feed on time and Barbara is excited about the weighing and the moving to Room Two. Nurse Clare claps her hands again and we begin. The scale is placed on exactly the same spot as it has been for weeks. Everyone checks it is calibrated correctly. I feel like an actor on the stage of a little drama being played out. Like everybody else, I too play my role.

With a serious look on her face followed by a little smile for me, Nurse Clare stands on the scale and her weight is measured. Then she picks me up, all six foot one of me, holds me in her arms, steadying herself, carefully adjusting her balance. It is silent inside this little theatre. Outside I can hear the other children talking, shouting, laughing.

Nurse Clare walks all of three steps towards the scale, carefully stands on the scale. Barbara reads the weight, writes it down. Nurse Clare puts me back on the bed. They deduct our combined weight from Nurse Clare's weight.

"Sixty four kilograms! You have gained another two kilograms this week. Well done Luther. *Well done* team! What a wonderful achievement! Our targeted weight for Luther to move to Room Two. Thank you one and all. I think we will aim for seventy kilograms now with ease."

The nurses and carers clap their hands and cheer.

"Now, folks! The next stage. Luther's promotion to Room Two. Nurse Clare, as his prime carer, will you do the 'upgrading' ceremony?" Barbara asks.

Nurse Clare stretches to her full buxom height of five feet three inches, smoothes down her clothes and hair, clears her throat, looks at me, smiles and starts to speak in her professional voice.

"We all know the story, except maybe Luther. So let me begin from the beginning. When you arrived, when Mr. Royce brought you here, we didn't know whether you were alive or dead. We all held our breath to see if you were breathing. You were our tallest, oldest, and sickest fifteen year old we ever had. We couldn't, really *would not* let that record disappear into the wind! We stood around your bed, held hands, yours as well, closed our eyes and prayed and asked that you survive. Not just survive but also truly live! I asked that all of us see you walking healthily and with a confident gait towards the gate, towards the weekly bus to take you back to Juxon, back to a magnificent future.

So that is what we all visualised for you, and that is what we have worked towards, are still working towards, step by slow, patient step. The weeks of wandering in the forest, eating poorly were exacerbated by a very bad bout of diarrhoea. When Johnston found you, he carefully carried you all the way to his home. And another record, perhaps one that we would have preferred not to have; you were so anaemic; you were one of the most anaemic children we ever had.

We did not fear the worst, because *we* had this vision for you. We could transfuse only very small amounts of blood; otherwise your heart would fail. Many of the people gathered here today, Luther, are your brothers and sisters; they willingly offered their healthy, compatible blood to you. They were *so* eager to help, to be part of the vision, I had to keep a rota of all compatible donors so that every one gave at least once."

Nurse Clare pauses, blows her nose, takes a few deep breaths, and continues.

"We fed you, day and night, we fed you. We washed your body that seemed to have more sores and scars than skin! We massaged your body with special herbal oils, gave gentle passive exercises, let you sleep and rest. We prayed for you, sang for you, talked with you, willed you to live. We didn't need to do too much willing for you to live. And do you know why? Because Luther, you have such a great, tremendous will to live. It is awesome and humbling to observe. You are not moving to Room Two today because of what we did, Luther; we were here, mere helpers.

And do you know why? Because, if you hadn't had such a strong will to live, whatever efforts we made would have counted for nothing.

You taught us so much, showed such quiet tenacity. I, personally feel very privileged to have known you before, observed the caring and charming, handsome young man.

So, today, we leave behind this room to be swept and washed, all the pain, the agony, the weakness, the suffering of the past. We take with us to Room Two the present and the future, full of vibrant health, a bright fortuitous future. Let us go now, to Room Two, step one of the future. And, of course an additional two kilograms! Everyone who wishes, please say their aspirations for Luther now, while I give him his feed. Thank you."

All want to say a little something as well. Each one tells a small personal tale of their involvement with my life. Every story makes my heart grow bigger. Even Tom the engineer speaks! "I told Luther once, while we were quietly making his mother's 'throne', that I am someone that observes rather than talks. You know that of me as well. Luther is someone special. Makes me break my habit for a short while. I knew him and his family in Camp Alpha. I witnessed his great courage, and the courage of the family, when Benedict had his fatal accident. The privilege of helping with Bendy Elephant and the family will stay with me forever. If I could be more like you, have a son grow to have your qualities, I'd go to work on an egg right now!"

Huge guffaws of laughter. Applause. Women raising their hands. No one has probably heard Tom speak so much or with such emotion and wit.

I acknowledge each one with a quiet *Kelsho,* hands over my heart. I am quite overwhelmed; all this was going on and I was not even aware of most of it. I feel a deep gratitude towards them. How can I ever thank them for such dedication?

While the others tell their stories of how each helped me stay alive, Nurse Clare completes the morning feed, gives me the little water to drink - she says in order to reassociate my drinking with my stomach filling up. Barbara is the last staff member to talk. She clears her throat.

"All of you present here, plus all the others working in the centre, I am so grateful to be here, so humbled by your dedication. You all seem to do every task, major and minor, so effortlessly, so uncomplainingly. You simply get on with it. Such committedness blows me away.

Likewise Luther. I will tell my grandchildren about this day. My parents and family already know so much about you, thanks to my long e-mails to them. They would love to have more photos of all of you, and especially one of you, Luther. My mother keeps asking: has Luther smiled yet? Every e-mail she asks whether you have smiled yet. Yes, I *know* you *smile,* Luther. But we are not talking about those polite smiles, we are talking straight-from-the-heart-brighter-than-the-sun smile! And I keep telling her, not yet, but soon. It is such an honour to know you all. I am so grateful to be working with you."

Tears are flowing freely now, Barbara and Nurse Clare's mascara wreaking havoc as usual. Royce clears his throat; he too has a story to tell.

"I will keep my story short. As you know, Luther's father Frederick and I met as final year students at Queenville University. We stayed in touch. I was at this young man's baptism. His second name is Royce. I arrived a week after Sapphira's birth, celebrated Ellie's first birthday with them and visited again before Benedict was born – and other in-between times. He is a son to me.

When I was commissioned by Save the Children to tell a story about the lost children in the forest, I had *no* idea the story would be about finding Luther.

I went in with the retrieval team, with Nurse Winnie, on a long, dark bumpy road into the forest. There I found Luther, lying on the floor of Johnston and his wife Josephina's hut, seemingly lifeless; a very long thin stick of a young man. I did not realise it was Luther, my best friend's son. I did not recognise him at all, even though I had seen him some months before. It is thanks to finding the family photo I had given each of them that I realised it was Luther.

I didn't think he would make the journey. Yet Nurse Winnie never even thought about *not taking* him. As soon as she arrived she put a nasogastric tube down his nose and fed him, even throughout the night. That's when I began to see the sheer dedication of everybody. I remain humbled by such dedication, such caring.

And goodness, is Luther a tough one! The road, as I've said before, was bumpy. It had rained in the morning and we became stuck in the mud rather frequently. And still Luther just lay there, absorbing the oral rehydration solution, the bumps in the road, the many delays.

Then I broke my leg and lay next to him on the drive back to Adair. And when I woke up once or twice, thanks to some very strong plant painkillers, there was George, Luther and I, intertwined. It felt *so* good.

I felt so good being able to do something for my best friend's family. So, I am particularly happy and grateful to be present on this auspicious day. The story I wrote during my convalescence really awoke the love in the British nation's hearts, and Save tells me the support and financial contributions have soared like a comet. Thank you."

Everybody is looking at me now, waiting for my response. Hands over my heart and tears rolling down my eyes, I have such a huge lump in my throat, all I can do is simply nod my thanks to everyone, my heart in my eyes.

∞

At last we are ready to move towards Room Two. Barbara smiles at Royce. "Royce, could you please carry Luther? Firstly, because you are the tallest person here, which means his feet won't drag on the floor. Secondly, because he is the son of your best friend and thirdly, as he is to be borne away like a king, it is more appropriate that it is done from a great height!"

The whole procession now moves the ten steps towards Room Two. They sing Ma's song '*You raise me up*', which brings back that strong memory of Ma raising her hand less than an inch in the rain in the field of UXOs.

They clap their hands; do little dances, extending the ten steps to a quarter mile. I feel snug in Royce's arms. I feel his heart pulsating strongly, manly, against my chest. He looks down at me, smiles, plants a kiss on my forehead.

The whole event begins to feel a bit surreal, yet the emotions are so strong. They are so happy for me, for the efforts they put in that have paid off, that life is good. Nurse Clare, all professionalism gone after the speeches, is hugging everybody, laughing and crying.

One little toddler from Room Three wanders in, sees Barbara's face streaked with runny black mascara, points his little finger at her and starts to laugh and laugh. This defuses the surging emotion of the event, making it slightly more contained.

∞

I am exhausted by the ceremony. I close my eyes and rest on my bed that faces the door. I open my eyes when I feel a gentle caress on my arm. George. Great big black eyes looking at me. I wink at him. After a long moment, he winks back. I smile. He smiles. Climbs onto my bed. We snuggle together.

Chapter Thirty Six

"Hello, big fellow! Very nice to see Luther Royce Wiggins with a smile on his face again!"

Gives me a bear hug, like Papa used to. Don't want to think about that yet. Royce and I talk about this and that. He talks, I nod, say a few words now and again.

"Nurse Clare has forbidden me to ask about your time in the forest! She says you are still too frail. Shall I tell you a little about my journey and how I found you?"

I nod.

"Right, we'll see how it goes. I'll stop as soon as I see it is distressing you, or tiring you. Deal?"

I nod.

"Well, you know, I have been covering conflicts since I met your father. Well, I arrived the day after that massive conflict at Camp Alpha took place. I saw your father's body amongst the many in the church. I buried him. Very sad moment. Then I wrote a story about your father in the Sunday Times. Our friendship. His dreams. His family. His work. I was given an award for it. I would rather have my friend alive and be chatting to him. Yet another part of me was so grateful that I could do his life and character justice with my tribute to him. I'll give you a copy of the article. I have been searching for your mother, you and Sapphira ever since.

Then I wanted to write about children lost in the forest. Their story, their family, how their time in the forest touched other lives en route. Save The Children, who run this Children's Centre, commissioned me. Little did I know that I would then meet *you*, the son of the man that had brought me here, whom I wrote about.

So, I travelled with Nurse Winnie and Solomon, laughed with them, shared their water and biscuits, pushed the truck out of quagmires. I saw Johnston and his wife caring for you and George and others in the forest. I slept in the same room as you and George. I wondered about George. Then Johnston mentioned that your girlfriend Cecilia had passed through there a few days ago. She told him all about the little boy there, called George, who does not speak.

My story is essentially Johnston's story. He opened up like a rose in spring. He said he *never* speaks so much.

When I first saw you, I didn't think you would be able to make the three-hour journey to the Centre. Nurse Winnie merely looked at me and said: '*Of course* he'll be fine. Whatever is, is.' And here you are.

Nurse Winnie is the nurse who collects the children who have been found in the forest by Johnston. She and Solomon, the driver, visit Johnston and his wife Josephine every week to take supplies for them deep in the forest____"

"How's Lindi?" I interrupt quickly. I can feel myself getting panicky as Royce continues about the forest – I feel panic rising. Feelings rising I can't deal with at the moment. *Phew*!

"Lindi? She's fine, thanks. During the return trip with you, I fractured my leg and returned to England___"

"Why did you call her Lindiwe?" More diversionary tactics.

"I was in South Africa covering the inauguration of Nelson Mandela, just talking to the folks who had waited so long for that day of freedom to arrive. Dulcie was pregnant at the time so couldn't accompany me to Johannesburg. In one of the homes, there was this little beauty. About five years old and an only child. I asked her name. It was Lindiwe. Asked what it meant. The mother said it meant 'the awaited'. I thought this was the perfect name for my child as well."

A long pause. Royce looks at me before continuing.

"I was really lucky. It was her holidays, so we had a really good two weeks together before she left for her boarding school again___"

"She loves boarding school? Being away from home?"

"Absolutely loves it. Her best friend is with her. And she has made even more friends. As an only child, having all these friends around her more than compensates for the lack of siblings. I organise myself so that I am at home for her holidays. Otherwise she stays with my parents for a while, short spaces with her mother."

No topic is safe. This talk makes me remember my own family and it hurts, really, *really* hurts. I close my eyes. Shut out the world. I want Royce to stay but I don't want him picking at my raw wounds.

"Shall I go?"

With eyes closed, I shake my head, tears threatening. Take a few breaths. Oh God! This is too painful! He brings his chair nearer, gently rubs my shoulder, his cheek against mine whispering nothings into my ear. Keeps rubbing until I am calm again. Until I have put all my pain in a little cupboard again, until the right time, whenever that is. If ever.

∞

I'm in Room Two. Just sitting. Utterly black mood. In an abyss. Wanting to go back to Room One when all I did was survive. Too weak and sick to feel. To think. Here all the reality of life is coming up to meet me. They say I'm depressed. Severely depressed. Depressed! Of course I am! Who wouldn't be!

All I want is my family, and all I get is lack of family. That's the depressing bit. I feel sooo angry with God and the universe. What more can I do? I've prayed and asked and searched and searched. Taken action.

Well, have I not fine-combed the forest looking for Sapphira? Have I not sent Red Cross messages to Ellie every week? Have I not *always* kept an eagle eye on Benedict? Where has that got me? I'm alone! And I'm supposed to be this *man*, now! All I want to do is curl up and die. But, if I do that, then I don't get to be with Ellie, or see Sapphira, or even Ma. And now I'm sooo weak. But not too weak to have thoughts. Sad thoughts. Bad thoughts. Feeding tube in my nose. Can't even walk more than three steps. Life stinks! Disgusting. Shitty. Worse than a sewer. Hell. Damn rotten!

"Hello Luther"

"*Kelsho,* Nurse Clare."

I turn my face away from her. Let her get on with the feed, then leave me alone.

"I see this young man in front of me; handsome, highly intelligent, a future leader, having a setback, like we all do. He needs to break through it, though. At the moment, he's too overwhelmed and weak to do so by himself."

Yeah, yeah, yeah.

"Name me a few world shattering world leaders."

Oh hell! Just leave me be.

"Luther"

"Can't think of any."

"Just one."

Silence.

"Please?"

"Jesus!"

"Yes, him. Anyone else?"

"Mohammed, Buddha, Mandela."

"Yes, anyone else?"

"Oh God!"

"Yes, God as well ___"

"Well, *where* is He now? What's He doing right now for me, eh? Killing off all my family! Some *leader*, that!"

"Well, how do you see God? As a bearded old man, with endless super powers to destroy whomever he feels like?"

I don't even bother to answer.

"Well, I remember the many discussions we had with your mother in Save's tents in the camp. So, what if you took your parents' perception and saw God as Grace or Divine Being or Infinite Intelligence, or like energy, for instance?"

Still no answer.

"You know, if you move your hand here, you can feel the movement elsewhere, can't you? It's basic science. So if you move your hand angrily here, you feel that angry movement over there as well, don't you?"

"What has this got to do with me? With God?"

"Change your negative energy into positive energy. All the top leaders you mentioned, all of them said that unconditional love heals. I once read of a woman who opened her heart, just let her love fill the room, and the dying flowers revived. Imagine if you can break through this barrier of darkness, of hell, to that kind of love? Remember what you taught me, us, at the camp? *Kiff*. Have you stopped practising it?"

I turn to look at her.

"Nurse Clare, thank you, but I'm not in the mood for miracles."

"Just have a go at a little one. What have you got to lose? "

No response. This feed is taking *far* too long today.

"Give me one little example of what your parents did that kept their love going?"

"Sex?"

"Luther! OK, what else?"

"Can't think."

"Just a small gesture. Something one did for the other. Go on."

Long silence.

A smile flickers around my mouth at the memory.

"What?"

"My parents, especially my father, used to sing to each other, and to us. Instead of saying something, they would sing an appropriate reply. What I really liked was that they would wake to a special song, programmed the night before. Papa would select a song and we would all wake up to it. My parents said it set the good mood for the day."

I reminisce over some of the songs – and the look Papa and Ma shared at the breakfast table. Makes me tingle all over again.

"Once it was '*Have you ever loved a woman*' or Jennifer somebody '*I am your woman, and you are my man*' or '*Simply the best*'. All very romantic. Papa would have it on repeat mode. We would be singing it at the breakfast table. Ellie loves singing. And when Benedict woke up, he and Ellie would be singing the song until we left for school."

Nurse Clare leaves with a wink. *Kiff*. Job done.

∞

Royce visits every evening when he is in Jamari. Every evening a little more connection with the past, until I decide it is enough. When it is too stressful.

"When I was with Johnston, there was a girl called Veronica. Said she was in the same class as you. Do you remember her?"

I nod.

"Want to know about her?"

I nod. She wasn't interested in me, so I wasn't in her. I had my fan base and she wasn't part of it. Quiet girl; intense, angry with life. Probably reminded me too much of the way Sapphira behaved, so I steered clear of her. Still, I'm interested to know about her.

"Well, she was in tears most of the time. She had fled to the forest and eventually found shelter with a farmer's family there. Married the son and was expecting a baby. According to the law, she was under age and had to return with Nurse Winnie to the Centre and afterwards to Juxon, like all the other children. She was very, *very* angry. Had refused to leave with Nurse Winnie twice before. Her young husband couldn't leave the farm or return with her to Juxon. This time Nurse Winnie brought two Red Cross Letters with her. They were from her mother, living in a camp just north of Adair. After much heartbreak, she decided to go to her family. How do you feel about that?"

I shrug. "I probably would have done the same. My greatest wish is to see my family all together again."

"This brings me to the intention of that story. That was a mere precursor to what follows. Ready?"

That old burning heat in my stomach smashes into my thumping heart. I nod. Royce holds my hand. Smiles.

"I have a Red Cross Message for you from Cecilia. The staff gave it to me to give to you. Here you are. Would you like me to stay?"

I shake my head. Say goodbye to him.

∞

I fiddle around with the letter, turning it over and over. Scared. Terrified. I can't open the letter. I can't bear bad news at present. I put it under my pillow. It had waited this long. It can wait a little longer.

∞

Today is black again. I am *so* downhearted because I still feel very weak, because I can't deal with all these emotions bombarding me. All these emotions that have been hibernating are now demanding attention - all at once. I don't know where to start. All are so intense, too raw.

I don't feel I have accomplished anything since arriving here at the Centre. If there is progress at all, it is sooo slow I think it has stopped. What is going to happen to me? What is happening to Ellie and Grandma Meertel? Where is Sapphira? Is Ma alive? Why can't I even open a letter from Cecilia? Where is my courage, my manhood? Why do I feel *so miserable*?

"Luther!"

I shake myself out of my black reverie, pay attention to Nurse Clare. Hadn't even realised she was here, pouring feed down my tube.

"I was asking whether you know the story about the man who was shipwrecked many years ago?"

"Robinson Crusoe? Tom Hanks?"

"No, neither of them. A story that has been going around for years, that is told over and over again."

"No." I really don't feel like one of Nurse Clare's stories, inspirational or otherwise. I just want to stay in this deep black hole. Just pour the feed down me in silence this morning, please.

"Well, some time ago now …" My request is ignored; I have to listen now.

"So anyway, he eventually drifts towards this nearby beach. Tired and exhausted, he lies there for a while, grateful to be alive. It is very quiet. He becomes fearful – where are the people of this island? Who is going to help him return to civilisation again? Will the inhabitants be friendly – what if they are not?

The sun is growing hotter and hotter and he moves towards a shady palm. Still no people. He feels he *has* to investigate. Caution in every step, he walks around the small island. Not another soul; it is small and completely uninhabited. He becomes panicky – how is he going to survive? Who is going to come and rescue him? How will they find him? As far as he can see there are no other islands, no ships passing by.

On his way back towards the beach he finds a small stream of water and drinks thirstily. By now the sun is blistering.

So, rather than just lie around feeling sorry for himself, he decides to gather all the driftwood and make some kind of shelter. Once the shelter is built, he lies down to sleep. He had not realised how exhausting the swim to this beach has been. That evening, before sunset, he returns to the stream to slake his thirst.

The weather turns cold and overcast; thick clouds hang threateningly overhead. He is glad he has made a shelter. Before going to sleep, he spends ages sitting on the beach watching out for a passing ship. Nothing.

The next day the clouds continue to be as heavy and black as his mood. He is in *such* despair. He walks around the island again to make sure he has seen no food or people. While he is searching for food and company, thunder rumbles ever so loudly and lightening snakes the sky. He returns to his shelter. On the way, he sees great clouds of smoke billowing skywards. His shelter has been hit by lightening! The blaze is huge and fierce. He cannot rescue *one* piece of wood. Of all the places in the world to pick, it had to choose his shelter!

He is so upset, disillusioned and angry. He shouts: "God! Now you have taken away my shelter as well. What more? What more? I have nothing left except my life. Take that too because I don't know what else to do. Take it now! At least let me not suffer! At least be kind…"

Cuddled up in his misery and despair, it is only when the sailor calls him repeatedly that he turns in wonderment. He sees two men rowing a dinghy towards him. He is astounded! A miracle. His prayer answered.

"Thank you so much! How did you find me?"

"Oh, that was easy. We saw your smoke signal and came to have a look."

Nurse Clare is looking at me, waiting for a response. I don't have one. I haven't a clue what she is expecting from me.

"Luther, can you see how your despair may be a smoke signal for others to come to your aid? We are all here, eager to help you break through this."

I nod. I am truly impressed. How does Nurse Clare do it? The right story at the right moment. She must be like Sapphira; devouring every book she can lay her hands on. So! My black cloud is only a moment of despair. Bloody long moment, I have to say. Pray, who is *my* saviour?

∞

"What are you feeling right now?"

Face in pillow, head turned away from Nurse Clare giving my midday feed.

"Fed up. Fed up that nothing right is happening."

"Uh huh. And how is this fed up making you feel, really?"

"Anger, red hot anger." I can actually feel my heart thumping, threatening to explode!

I take short breaths. Open my mouth to speak. Can only groan. Thump the pillow.

"So, what's behind this anger?"

I'm still feeling this rage that is *possessing* me.

Eventually "Despair, fear, not knowing, wanting the comfort of my past, my family. Like it used to be! I don't want to talk anymore, PLEASE."

"Well, I'll leave you alone if you could just tell me what's at the heart of that despair, Luther?"

I humour her and comply with her request, allow the despair wash over me, through me. I don't know what else to do. I just lie there.

After a while, a kind of peace fills me. Like when I was a child and really cried and cried. That feeling of cleansing, energising liberation. I sigh a deep sigh. Turn on my back. Eyes closed. Fall asleep.

∞

That was three days ago. Royce is visiting this morning.

After two weeks in Room Two I am now in Room Three and walking slowly around the room twice a day. I am really not in the mood for visitors today, even Royce; even though he is leaving soon.

Barbara had added some of her songs to my MP3 player. Today Royce is carrying with him a magazine, filled with glossy advertisements. The MP3 player is still on the bed.

After the usual greeting Royce asks me what songs I am listening to.

"Norah Jones."

After a long pause I tell him it was Ma's favourite song. Royce just looks at me, exactly like Papa would have done. Says nothing. Sits next to me, flicking through the magazine.

My eyes are not taking in much. I reply to Royce's questions monosyllabically. When it is time to go, I really don't want him to go, but I am too miserable to know what I want or to tell him so.

"Luther, can I help?"

A nod.

"Luther, look at me."

Eyes meet. Immense longing. Unadulterated sorrow. Tears threatening, brimming, spilling.

Royce touches his forehead to mine. Stays thus a while.

"Is it an easy thing for me to do?"

Another nod.

"Can I do it now?"

Another nod.

"Tell me what you want me to do, Tiger."

A long pause. A sob.

"A hug."

The dam bursts, at last.

∞

In the afternoon Royce returns, smiles at me whilst sipping from his water bottle. "Want to share the good news?"

I wave Cecilia's letter at him. "My first love. I met her in the camp in Jamari. Shortly afterwards she disappeared, never to be seen again. Then, after many days or weeks in the forest searching for Sapphira, we met again. She had two little children with her. They both died. She was pregnant. She and her sister had been raped one night in their tent. I proclaimed the baby, and all the others she would have, mine."

"Goodness! Frederick to a T. In looks and ways. Your parents would be so proud of you. Johnston told me Cecilia was with you and was very reluctant to leave you. He said he was already carrying two young children and couldn't carry you as well. When he returned for you, you and George had strayed off the path and it another full day to find you again.

Like Veronica, Cecilia also refused to leave Johnston's place, but eventually Nurse Winnie persuaded her to go. She said you could keep in touch with Red Cross Messages. Apparently some eminent Save people from England were visiting a few health posts they were sponsoring, and there were two spare seats in the plane, one for her and another for a rather ill little girl."

I pass the letter to him. He looks at me, smiles, then reads the three sentences out loud.

I'm staying at the library turned maternity home in Keating Road. Run by marties. Cecilia.

"Hmm. Seems she needs a little reassurance that you'll be there for her, eh?"

"But I told her and *told* her that I would be there for her."

"Well, everything is still a bit topsy turvy. An encouraging reply might help her. What do you think?"

"Hmm. Of course I'll send her a reply."

∞

"Luther! We are going to run out of paper soon! How many drafts do you need? You've already used ten pieces of paper. Let me help you. Not write it, just prepare for it. OK?"

I nod. Everything I have written so far seems so trite, either over-confident or not confident enough, a lie. I don't want to make promises I cannot keep.

"OK. This is how I used to write to my husband-to-be when he was studying accountancy down in the south. From nineteen to twenty-two years old. It worked for me. So. Take a few deep breaths. Now close your eyes. More deep breaths. Now, open your heart as wide as the universe. Allow everything to be bathed by this love in your heart. Take your time. I usually imagine it to be a light that shines brightly on everything. Now focus that light on Cecilia. Fill her with love. See the two of you together. Let that light - that love - grow even more brightly. Take a deep breath. Open your eyes and write. Write everything that comes. Let your pen flow."

A song comes to mind. So I write the chorus of Lonestar's words to Cecilia.

I'm already there. Take a look around. I'm the sunshine in your hair. I'm the shadow on the ground. I'm your imaginary friend and I know I'm in your prayers. I'm already there. Luther xx.

That should do it! Unoriginal, but hey! Totally appropriate! Why struggle to innovate when I can copy so perfectly!

∞

"Good evening Royce!" I open my arms for a bear hug. Smile at him. Chat about the day. Little things. No big things.

"You know you said you buried my father? Did you see my mother? Hear anything about my mother?"

"Unfortunately not. I asked around, looked in at the various clinics and hospital, but could not see your mother there at all. Got no leads on her or your and Sapphira's whereabouts."

"You see, I haven't told anybody this yet. But I keep thinking about it. When I was in the forest, waiting for Johnston and losing my way, I collapsed. Don't know anything after that. But I had this vision. A very strong light. Made me feel *so* happy. Really, *really* happy. Can't quite put that feeling into words. I was drawn towards this bright light. It felt sooo good, I wanted it to stay.

Then my father and Benedict appeared. Benedict was running in and out of Papa's legs, like he always did. I could hear his giggles. Papa had his hands out to me, urging me to come. Benedict too was chanting, "Come Luther, come" I felt myself moving towards them. Irresistible. Uncontrollable. Then I saw Ma. She was standing a distance from them, nearer to Sapphira and Ellie. The three of them just standing there, bathed in light. Not calling me. Just smiling. I saw Papa and Benedict fading with the light as Ma and my sisters still remained, bathed in this light. Then that too faded. The next thing I remember is Nurse Clare here at the Centre."

"Wow! Amazing. I've heard of people having near death experiences, but I've never ever met anybody who did. What do you think is the message there?"

"That my mother is still alive? If she too were dead, would she not be standing with Benedict and Papa?"

"I can't honestly tell. Seems an excellent deduction, though. What does Nurse Clare say?"

"Haven't told her yet. Will do so now that I have told you."

"Interesting. Speak with Nurse Clare; it's quite intriguing. Here, I've brought another Red Cross Message for you. From Ellie, I presume? I was thinking, probably the same as you, and especially after what you've just told me, how about writing a letter to you mother? It will find her, eventually, won't it?"

"Yes. It's that 'eventually' that frustrates me. It takes sooo long! This letter has taken weeks to arrive here. Nurse Clare sent my letter at least a month ago."

"Well, you know, they're doing their best. So best to start now and decrease that 'eventual' time, don't you think? Read Ellie's letter while I fetch some Red Cross Messages for you to write and I'll take it to the Red Cross office.

Dear Luther. I have no letters from anybody, except you. I miss you. UNICEF is preparing the school here in Carton, so I shall be going to school very soon. Grandma Meertel says its time for you to return to Carton. Please find the others and come home soon. I really miss you. Hugs and Kisses, Ellie.

Chapter Thirty Seven

It's been thirteen weeks since I arrived here at the Children's Centre. I have been moved to the adolescent boys' tent. The long tent is half full. I don't know any of the nine other boys here. I don't talk much. Merely listen. Our stories are similar, more or less. From somewhere in Juxon to Hamilton, to somewhere in Belling, usually Jamari, to the forest, to Jamari and now waiting to go to Juxon again. Full circle. Alone for the moment. Going to who knows what. Not quite a conversation piece, we agree. No schooling here. Way behind with our education. What next?

There is talk of all of us transferring to Juxon in the next few days. A bus leaves for Juxon every Friday. Every cell in my body is apprehensive. I *can't* leave Sapphira here. We came together, we *go together*!

∞

And what about the offer Royce made me before he left?

He said my parents and he made a pact many years ago. He and his wife Dulcie attended my parents' wedding three months after theirs in England. They promised each other they would care for each other's family should anything happen to either one. Even when Royce and his wife divorced, the pact remained.

"Luther, I take that promise seriously. I will always care for all of Frederick's family. His children are my children. His son, my son. His tigers, my tigers."

After a long while of fidgeting he continues.

"Can I make a suggestion? If, and I sincerely hope not, but if, if it is only you and Ellie left, and no stone was left unturned to find Sapphira and your mother, would you consider living with me in England?"

I stare at him, still fidgeting. Stunned silence. Wow!

"Sometimes we have to let go of things. Accept that loved ones will never return. No! No, no, *no*! I'm not saying give up *now*. I'm saying when *everything possible* has been done. There are many miles to go yet. All we know now is that Ellie is in Carton. So, I will start providing for you from the moment you leave here. Schooling, home, help, whatever it takes. Visits. Regular visits. Close contact until all of you are adults and after."

"What if we find Sapphira?"

"Included in the package!"

"George?"

"Of course. If we can't find relatives."

"Cecilia and her baby?"

"Included."

"You mean, we can all stay with you in England?"

"If you so wish. If all of you decide thus. Or you can stay here with your grandmother and I'll provide for all of you."

Another long silence. I remain shocked and confused by this sudden offer.

"What if my mother is still alive? What if we find her?"

"Your mother is an utterly resourceful person. She will provide for you. And if she needs support to set up her life again without your father, I'll be there."

After a long while I ask tentatively: "Like marry her?"

"Whoa! Some bridges may take a while to cross. This was not quite what I intended!"

"But would you? Even with one leg?"

"Listen, your mother, *even* with one leg, would still retain that 'certain' something that made us all envious of your father. Your mother is *some* woman. I don't think I could fill your father's shoes. Nice thought, though..."

"And Lindi?"

"Lindi, like me, has always wanted a truckload of kids in our home..."

"Yes, but would she want to live in Juxon?"

"Why not? She could attend Montgomery's, like you. Anyway, we are way ahead of this discussion. I just want you to know that you have more choices than you think you do. It might make you feel less despair than if you have to carry your family's burdens all by yourself. I want you to know that I will always be here for you and the entire Wiggins household. George included. Cecilia and baby as well. OK?"

I nod.

∞

More options, more confusion. Going to England would be wonderful. Would Cecilia and her baby wish to come with me? Would Sapphira want to practise British law? Does she still have her burning desire to set the legal world on fire? What if Ma marries Royce? What if she doesn't want to?

What if she wants to marry someone else? What if, what if, what if….

∞

I go to a small knoll upon which I sit and view the world. We all seem to have our 'alone' spaces. Close but never touching. Inches away from each other, yet in a different world. Our space. Away from the noise of the smaller children, the games, the temporariness of this place. There are rumours that it will shut when all the children are returned to Juxon. It will be closing soon, they say. So, just sitting.

Next stage.

Today is Monday and the next stage is seeing who will be arriving here today.

A bus brings children from the forest every Monday. A handful. There are rumours that this too might stop soon. My heart froze when I heard that. What if Sapphira is about to reach Johnston's place? He cannot read or write! Will he and his wife bring the children to Adair, like they did the first time? I flip through the manuscript Royce left me. His notes on his trip to the forest. Read a few pages again, where Johnston is telling his story.

"We left a few older children here, to hunt and to look after the sick ones and help Josephina and the other women who had come to help us. We walked slowly,

carrying the weaker children, eating whatever we could pick. Of course, the older ones made sure the youngsters in their groups ate as well. We drank where there was water.

To keep our spirits high we sang.

We let the children rest in the afternoon so that we could gather more food. Walter, the healer's son, was with us; he knew what to pick and eat and helped the children to choose the right berries and roots.

We left some of the sick children there as well. Those who just couldn't make it through the three hours it would take to get to the Children's Centre."

After pausing for a while, Johnston picks up the story again.

"We reached Adair the next evening, after two days of walking. The people there told us that the marties don't stay there; they return to Jamari every evening.

Everyone was extremely upset on hearing this. The children were really hungry and weak now. We had no more food.

Everyone in Adair - the displaced and the very poor - all put their hands in their supplies to give us some food for the next part of the journey.

Again we had to leave those children who were becoming too weak to travel. We promised the people there the marties would collect them soon.

On we moved to Jamari, now with about sixty children.

Just before sundown on day six of our contact with the Red Cross, we reached Jamari. Many of us were carrying a child.

We asked the whereabouts of the Save the Children office - but it was a Saturday evening and they had all gone home by then. So we walked to their house! At first the guard would not even call the marties. Then he looked and saw all the children in the street.

Johnston laughed out loud. "You should have seen his face! All eyes. He ran to the house and a huge foreign woman came. She had the reddest lips I have ever seen! She introduced herself as Barbara. She was the nurse.

She took one look and just opened the gate to allow all of us into the compound, all the while shouting towards the house. It was as if we had disturbed a bees' nest, but these were organised bees! Very organised.

Those who were being shouted at, shouted at others and so on until the last person started to move. Everyone came running. One tall, thin man was on the radio all the time and then on the phone.

I had never seen these things before. The children told me what they were and how they worked. They had seen the marties and their helpers talking on them in the camps. Save has a big compound and we were all led to sit in one section.

More people arrived. The marty nurse Barbara came over to me and introduced herself to me. She told me they would be feeding all of us in their compound because the Children's Centre, where the children would be going to in the morning, would not have the supplies nor the staff to prepare a meal for us.

Now people began rushing around like bees from a smoking nest. Cars with many emblems and writings on them, coming and going! Marties and town people coming and going. Everybody talking on these radios.

There were cars coming into the compound, people filling the two trucks with all kinds of things. People were writing on pieces of paper, shaking hands, moving out of the compound and others immediately filling their space. The busiest market place I've ever seen.

They must be very, very rich to just give like that. I wanted to watch all this, but I was called by the tall marty. His name was Curtis. He wanted me to talk with him about how all the children came to be at my place.

Yes! Johnston would do that. He knows where to go now, what to do, whom to contact. Sapphira would be fine with Johnston. Maybe I can leave now. Go to Ellie. Wait at home.

∞

It's after lunch. I'm sitting in my space. Looking out towards the huge gate. I bring my knees up to my chin. Put my arms around them to stop their shaking. Pick at scars until I draw blood.

It's time for the bus to arrive. Even the smaller children quieten. The small hill that overlooks the entrance and the walk to the admission room is filled with children. Sitting close, never touching. All eyes focused at the spot where we can see the bus approaching. Quiet. A sob escapes me. Today, maybe today, God, Sapphira will be on that bus! Please, please, *please*. My mantra continues in my head, my heart, deep in my cells.

Children are lining the twenty yards or so that the newly arrived will walk towards the admission room. Staff members keep them separate behind a thick rope. Why? I don't know, I cannot fathom and I haven't asked.

A dust ball heralds the arrival of the bus. Frozen and rooted to the spot, I'm not breathing. Feel my heart thumping away. The gate is opened; the bus stops at the parking lot. The gate is closed.

Nurse Clare and a few staff members from the Feeding Centre are beside the bus. The bus door is opened. All of us wait with bated breath. Nurse Clare and a staff member enter the bus. They carry two young children to the Feeding Centre. I don't look. Not interested. Neither of them is Sapphira.

My eyes are riveted to the bus door. My mantra continues – please, please, *please*. I quickly check each child as they appear - too small; boys; too old. The bus door closes. The gate is opened. The bus leaves. The gate is closed. I put my head on my knees. Tears fall into my heart - and onto my knees.

George comes to me. Takes my hand and holds it to his heart. We snuggle. I cry and cry and cry.

My shadow keeps holding my hand. Thank God for shadows.

∞

Days later, and a few of us are in the admission room having a meeting with two staff members. George and I are with about twenty others. I didn't know it doubles as the discharge room as well. We are told that we will all be leaving tomorrow. We are returning to Juxon.

Many are going to stay in local Save the Children Centres until someone from their village or town comes to claim them. Phew! That must be horrible. Going from nowhere to goodness knows where. Not knowing if someone is there who knows you. At least George and I will be going to Ellie and Grandma Meertel. George will stay with us until someone claims him as brother, son, grandson or family friend.

In my heart of hearts, I would prefer him to be my brother. How can I let him go when we have been through hell together? Healing together? We are *bound* together. Still, I might have to accept what my heart does not want. What I know George does not want. Would be *sooo* good to find Ma and then we can adopt him. Or Royce can adopt all of us.

I am still fluctuating between going to Ellie and waiting for Sapphira. I mean, what was the point in going around in circles in the forest if I leave now? I don't seem to have an option here. Even Nurse Clare says it is best I go to where I know Ellie is waiting. And should Sapphira pass this way, all her information will be processed that much quicker because they know where I am.

Hmmm. True. But….

∞

Friday morning, seven o'clock. After an extremely restless night tossing and turning on my narrow camp bed, I wake up, drenched in sweat. Weak. Shivering. Stomach ache. Vomiting. Diarrhoea. The works. I'm stretchered to the small clinic, George trotting next to me. Barbara arrives. I am too sick to respond to her. Given oral re-hydration fluid. The bus leaves without George and me. I am too sick to care.

By one o'clock I'm feeling better. No more shivers, diarrhoea or vomiting. Still weak though. I eat some soup and then manage the evening meal.

Sunday, I'm able to eat my lunch and am back on my space on the knoll on Monday afternoon.

And so it continues for a further two weeks. Recovering from sickness by Sunday afternoon, recovering from disappointment and lack of appearance of Sapphira by Thursday morning. Drains me. My weight is dropping. Nurse Clare comes to visit me on a Thursday morning.

After the usual greetings she tells me one of her famous stories.

"Not too long ago, we had a girl here. Called Priscilla. You may have heard others talking about her? She was fourteen years old, funny and bright – very bright. She was quite a clown, always first on the stage when we were celebrating events. She was happy to be here. She'd lost all her family – or so she thought. She used to help the staff entertain the little ones; she was very helpful and considerate. She was the eldest girl in a family of six children. One day, whilst dancing and singing in the toddler room, we heard this little scrap of a child scream out: *Silly, silly,* ***Silly****!* We laughed.

Priscilla stood stock still, and then turned to look at this little scrap. Screamed and screamed as she ran to the child. It was her three year old sister Malia, calling her 'Scilly'. To cut a long story short, Priscilla refused to return to Juxon after this. She reasoned that if one sister could miraculously appear, then others would come to the Centre as well.

Every Thursday evening, she would come and say 'thank you' and 'goodbye' to everyone, pack her belongings and go to bed. Every Friday morning she would have a raging fever, so weak so could not get out of bed. By Friday afternoon, she was recovering and by Friday evening she was the 'belle of the ball' again.

So, what I'm suggesting is, we forget this Friday morning bus to Juxon. We do not send you across the border until you are ready to leave. Whatever it is that needs to be achieved first. Is that OK with you?

Yes? Good! All I ask is that you come and speak with me, tell me how you are doing. Remember, *you* come to *me*. You've had your *Onashi* ceremony. To me you are a young man and I expect you to behave as such. Remember the story about the man shipwrecked on the island? Yes? So, send me smoke signals and I will come running. You know that, don't you?"

I nod. Give her hand a squeeze. A hug. I sit for ages afterwards, connecting the events as she had done. Hmmm. I did not connect all these things at all. Marvellous woman; marvellous me, marvellous body for expressing what I *really* wanted to do.

Practise, practise, practise listening to my 'inner voice' as Nurse Clare suggests. Actually, Papa used to say this as well. Now I'm claiming it too.

∞

I just can't do this alone. This waiting. This 'what if'. I remain fearful, almost panicky. Have I made the right decision? Should I have gone to Ellie, an absolute known? Or should I continue to wait here, for a needle in a haystack? The place is closing soon, so I can't stay here forever. Have to come to some kind of decision soon.

I seek out Nurse Clare. Talk to her about my dilemma.

"Luther, can you remember a time when you felt you had courage?"

"No."

"What about the time you were in the forest? When you and George were roaming around? Nobody else around in this big scary place, and you, a city boy with no inkling what to eat, save the berries you know and the roots someone told you were okay? Didn't you feel it was courage that got you through that?"

"No."

"What was it then?"

"A feeling of someone looking after us. Maybe my father. Maybe God. Most times I didn't think – it hurt too much."

"Like a feeling of being protected?"

I nod.

"Was this feeling there all the time?"

I shake my head.

"What was there then, before or between this feeling of being protected?"

"Terror."

"I bet it was; I would have been terrified if it had been me. What made it so terrifying?"

I hesitate. I can feel the still fresh scabs around my heart stretching, breaking free; feel the raw pain inside again, filling my chest, my whole being. It hurts. It still hurts so much. A huge burning pain. A long silence.

"I had just seen my father shot. I saw him and my mother just lying there. I froze. Stayed frozen since then because it hurt less."

Another silence.

"What made you run?"

"My father's eyes. He was begging me to run to safety." George has sidled up to me; climbs on my lap.

"So, what did you do?"

"I greeted him. I put my hands over my heart, said *Kelsho,* then I ran. I don't know if he saw the greeting. What if he didn't? Then I never said 'goodbye' to him? It makes me so sad that I never said 'goodbye' to my father."

"Here, wipe your tears. We can say 'goodbye' to him now, what do you think?"

"How?"

"OK, all of us. We close our eyes and breathe in and out until we are calm and peaceful. Let us start. Are you calmer yet? Now, imagine him sitting here in this room, right now. Can you see him? Good. What would you like to say to him?"

"I would like to say thank you to him and ..."

"Luther, speak to him as if he is here right now."

I take a deep breath. There is a huge golf ball in my throat now, threatening to cut off my air supply.

"Take a few more breaths Luther. Good."

"Papa, I miss you *sooo* much. I wish you were here by me now and always. I am so sad without you."

"And if he could reply, what might he say?"

"Everything is as it is, Tiger. I am always with you. You know that, don't you? I am with you always, remember that. He is singing the Lonestar song."

"Which part?"

"The second chorus."

"Sing it to me"

"I'm already there. Don't make a sound. I'm in the beating of your heart. I'm the moonlight shining down. I'm the whisper in the wind and I'll be there till the end. Can't you feel the love that we share? Oh! I'm already there."

"What a beautiful voice......"

"Thank you, but I want you here *now*, with me, helping me now. I am so weak, so alone, so sad."

"What is he saying to that?"

"He says what Royce says, that I have many fathers, they are all here to help me through this time. He says young men are allowed to show all their emotions, including crying."

"So?"

I sit there, just feeling. I am still so *sad*, and yet there is a feeling of relief washing over me. A long pause.

"I don't really need to say 'goodbye', do I? Since Papa is always here?"

"So what do you want to say now?"

I am overcome with tears. I have never spoken like this before.

"Thank you for being around. Thank you for everything."

"Good. Now that you know that, does it feel better?"

"Yes and no."

"Hmmm. I know what you mean."

Then another voice whispers, "Papa and Mama and Shamara are always with me?"

A whisper. A little whispered question.

Nurse Clare responds as though this was quite normal. "Yes George, all of them. Looking after you. Allowing Luther to be your big brother, your father, your mother, and your friend. And guess what? After we've finished talking here, I'm going to organise a big celebration for you, to celebrate your talking to us again. Congratulations. Well done!"

∞

We sit in companionable silence. Nurse Clare speaks again.

"How did this young man come to be with you? Your little shadow."

"He was in my way, in my path of escape, just sitting there, frozen like I had been. Without thinking I picked him up, carried him with me."

"Isn't that courageous?"

"No, I feel that was pure instinct."

"And in the forest, how did you feel when you and others were in the forest?"

"Confused; very confused, like all the others. Afraid and confused – all I wanted was to find Sapphira. I was angry with her as well, for not waiting, for not stopping at the edge of the forest to see if any of us in the family were following."

My chest is heaving. I can feel my heart throbbing like mad at the memory of that anger, confusion, shock. Nurse Clare is sitting close to me, not touching, looking at something or nothing in the distance. Treating me respectfully, like a man. I take a deep breath, and then another and another until I have composed myself. I touch my Tiger's eye.

"What if she felt so afraid as well, *so confused* and *so angry* that *you* were not waiting for *her*?"

"Sapphira is *never* confused! Afraid yes, angry most probably, but definitely *not confused*. She would have been formulating her plan whilst running. That's her."

"Well, what if she was confused about what to do because the family plans that had been formulated were becoming null and void?"

"She would probably ask everyone if they had seen me, maybe our parents as well. When we used to play games, Sapphira never *ever* looked back; she always keeps her eyes on the end, on the goal."

"Always?"

"I can't honestly think of a time when she has ever stopped, turned around to check on those lagging behind, and waited. Never."

"What happens when she is with your younger brother and sister?"

"Oh, they would have to shout and shout before she stops."

"So, she does look back, when she is called to do so?"

"Yes, called very loudly indeed."

Another pause. Each with their own thoughts.

"When do you do that?"

"Do what?"

"Have your eyes so fixed on your goal, you don't see or hear anything?"

Long pause. Hmmm.

"When I was in the forest, looking for her."

"How did you do that?"

"Keep focused? I suppose I didn't join any groups until much later, when Cecilia came along. I prayed every morning for the right direction to take. I talked to George, telling him about Sapphira – good things. Actually, I am finding it incredible to think that I found so many positive and good things to say about her! I asked every group that we met whether they had seen her."

"How did you describe her so that they would have been absolutely sure they would know her?"

"I showed them the photograph. I told them she is exceptionally tall for a thirteen year old. And her brown eyes are exactly like mine and that she has a very direct and probing look. They would know when she looks at them! Oh! She also has a wide gap between her top two front teeth."

"So there you were, initially very afraid, in shock, confused and angry. How did you manage to become so courageous?"

I stay still for a while. I really don't know. Just then, George wanders back into the room, a huge smile on his face. I hadn't even noticed him leaving. Wiggling his way between Nurse Clare's legs, he comes to me, takes my hand, looks at me.

"I know! George likes to hold my hand. Look! He is doing so now. When he first did so, I remembered holding Ellie and Benedict's hands when crossing the road. I felt their trust in me to get them across the road safely. It made me feel good and confident and *strong*. So, every time George put his hand in mine, it gave me courage to continue, didn't it, George?"

He nods and smiles, leans back against me.

"So you see! Courage. I knew you had it – everybody does. You could not have survived your ordeal without courage."

"Well, uh, I felt my other hand was holding my father's, or perhaps God's. That restored my confidence that we will find each other again, each family member. Except now and again I become unsure. I doubt and I despair."

"Welcome to the human race! We *all* do that. Well, how about if today we only concentrate on courage? Think only of courage. Of courageous deeds you read about or remember; other people's courage, your courage. Remember other times, however small, when you were courageous. And every time you do so, every time you feel that feeling of courage again, give a small smile. How about that?"

I nod, smiling.

"So, Luther, George, I hope to see many smiles today, yes?"

We smile as we leave the room.

"Yes. Thanks for everything else, Nurse Clare."

"It is my absolute pleasure, Luther. Bye for now."

George goes up to her, gives her a huge hug – and whispers 'thank you'. I see her wiping away tears as George and I leave.

Kiff. Add a smile; my repertoire is increasing, synergising.

∞

Waiting on the knoll is less nerve-racking now, although still fraught with expectations, and tensions continue to ride high. Such a feeling of utter loss, aloneness, loneliness.

Non-stop-chattering hoarse-voiced George comes to sit with me most times now. I know I have someone and, thanks to Nurse Clare, I know there is always another Monday. My weight increases and I am feeling stronger again; strong enough to help with the younger children. Being my mother's son, domesticity is burdensome to me and I offer to help with paperwork instead, or teach younger children at their morning school.

Having had to entertain Benedict with books and games is benefiting me now and I enjoy playing games with and teaching these four-to-six year olds. Maybe there's a teacher in me as well!

Barbara comes to me during a morning session, wearing a floral tent of a dress. The little children run around her, using her voluminous skirt as a headscarf, playing hide and seek in and around her dress.

"*Kelsho,* Luther! How are you this morning? We had an email from Royce last night. He is arriving here in a week's time. The Sunday Times is sending him here. They want him to do a follow up on you. Oh, to be so famous! Hey?"

∞

It's Monday afternoon again. I'm sitting on my knoll as usual. Since Nurse Clare had told me that I will return to Juxon when I feel it's the right moment, we've had more long talks.

"Remember when we had the ceremony leaving Room One? In your speech, you said how all the staff had held hands and held a vision of me walking tall and strong to the bus at the gate? Yes?

Well, how do I do this *every day* for Sapphira? See her getting out of the bus? How do I start?"

"Good! Excellent idea. Well, what is the first thing you'd like to do when you see her?"

"Shake her senseless for not waiting for us, for me to see where to run to!"

"Oh! Oooh.... Let's make it a bit more *positive* shall we? Remember *Kiff*? What if it is Ellie alighting from the bus?"

"Oooh! I'd run to her, sweep her off her feet! Dance around with her."

"So, how about moderating that for your big sister, who will be *so* famous one day as Juxon's - if not the world's - leading lawyer. *Kiff*. Imagine, in ten years' time, she is on television, telling her story of your reunion, and all she can say is how angry you still were!

It's in the *past*. She is alone as well, you know. Goodness knows what she has been through. Show some compassion! Forgive her peculiarities. Both of you have experienced things you never dreamed of. Both of you have grown older, wiser. Do you want to react to her the same way you did all those months ago? Have you learned nothing?! Come on now, improve your vision! Close your eyes and let's do some practice runs."

I close my eyes, take a few deep breaths and ..... Wow! It's there!

"I'm sitting here with George. I see her getting out of the bus. She's taller. Well dressed. She looks straight ahead of her, as if she is not expecting anyone. There's this surge of energy, also lots of joy and gratitude that fills my whole body. George and I walk down to the admissions room. We arrive there just as she is about to enter the admissions room. I say "Sapphira, *Kelsho*." She turns to me and greets me."

"What does her eyes look like?"

"Shining. Bright. Huge smile on her face. We stand looking at each other, silly grins on our faces. Then I hug her."

"Well done Luther. Now keep practising. And relax! Nothing happens when you are all so tense."

I practise. It feels good.

The bus arrives.

No Sapphira.

Not this Monday.

Next week.

∞

I sit on my spot practising. It's easier, probably because it is not a Monday. In between I re-read more of Royce's writings.

Solomon informs me, "Round the next corner is Jacob's place. The healer. We stop there for some lunch and to get more water for the truck." The truck has been heating up and losing water.

Just before the next corner, a wild pig and his family suddenly appear and run across the track. The little family scatter in all directions. Solomon swerves suddenly and ends up in a small ditch.

"Easy one, Royce." Solomon laughs. "Two minutes and we are at Jacob's place. I can smell the lunch." We put a log lying nearby under the front wheels and Solomon eases the truck out of the ditch. "Easy, see!" Solomon laughs as he slowly moves over the log. I am still in my fun mode, my 'I am having a wonderful adventure' mode, and find myself laughing.

Suddenly, I slip down the muddy slope and fall just in front of the rear wheels. Solomon brakes, but not before the wheel rolls over my lower right leg. Before the pain could register, Solomon jumps out of the truck and hauls me up the slope out of the way of the truck. He jumps back in the truck to clear it completely out of the ditch. Calls to Nurse Winnie.

Everything is happening lightning fast. I am still in a kind of daze, probably in shock. I hardly feel Nurse Winnie remove my boot. She pulls up my trouser leg. She is working quickly before the shock subsides and the pain comes.

"You are so lucky, my brother. It's broken inside, and not much. No bones sticking out, maybe just a crack or two, and we are near Jacob's place. He is a bonesetter

as well. Are you blessed! Solomon will fetch him. He will set your bones and we can eat something and be on our way."

Her matter of fact voice and explanation subdue the rising panic in me. Her whole attitude and the way she is talking, suggests that it happens all the time. I am merely another statistic. Don't think anything about it; don't make a mountain out of this molehill.

Suddenly the pain kicks in. "Do you have anything for the pain?" I ask.

Nurse Winnie shouts something to Solomon as he and the girls set off for Jacob's place. Then she laughs her outrageous laugh. "Jacob has the best and strongest pain killer you can imagine. You will feel as if you are floating on a cloud. Just wait."

"How long do I have to wait?" I ask after about five minutes. I look down at my leg. Nurse Winnie has cleaned off all the mud. It still looks straight, although there's a swelling, a huge bruise and pain – lots of pain.

"If he is at home, he will come soon. Bring the pain killer and his materials."

I had met Jacob and his wife Maria briefly on our way to Johnston's place. A quiet man. I had noticed that Solomon was very respectful to him and I ask Nurse Winnie why.

"Because he is a healer, not only of people, but of animals as well. Has a great knowledge of local herbs and plants, as his father did, and his father before him.

They're a family of healers; the gift is passed on. He is training his son, Walter. Walter's young son is showing great interest in going around with the two of them. You will see. Your leg will be healed in no time, even better than before."

About fifteen minutes later, Jacob and Walter arrive. Jacob has an old glass bottle in one hand and some long reeds in another. I begin to become slightly annoyed. How on earth is he going to set my leg with a bottle and reeds? We greet. Jacob hands the bottle to me, motioning me to drink. It's some kind of strong tasting, probably lethal, home brew with a heavy mixture of herbs, honey and other ingredients I can't identify.

"Drink!" Nurse Winnie encourages me with a laugh. I take a few more swigs of this not unpleasant tasting spirit. It hits my empty stomach like a huge ball of fire. Spreads quickly throughout my body as if someone has turned the central heating up to maximum.

"Wow, I love this stuff" I say to Nurse Winnie as she arranges a pillow of moss and leaves under my head.

Some time later, in my semi-oblivious state, I am aware of Walter supporting my thigh and knee while Jacob straightens my fractured shin. I am also aware of young George holding my left hand. I look at him. He has left Luther! He winks at me, biscuit in hand, then returns to the back of the truck. To Luther.

My leg is not painful at all. Ever the journalist, I say to Nurse Winnie that I want to see what Jacob is doing.

"I'll tell you, then you can just rest. It is best that you lie completely straight and horizontal. First Jacob and

Walter looked to see what kind of fracture you have, which bones are damaged, how long your leg is. Then they went into the forest to get leaves and plants. That took just over fifteen minutes, because this is their local area and so they know where to find all their ingredients. Then they boiled all the ingredients together. Then Jacob washed your leg with this solution. Then he made a poultice and covered your leg with it. Thank goodness your trouser leg is wide, so that we could just pull it up to your groin."

She continues. "Then Walter held your leg while Jacob gently straightened it. Somewhere in between, Walter made a soft mat with the reeds and string. I gave them some cotton-wool pads to cover your leg. So now Jacob is holding your leg straight while Walter is putting the thin reed mat around the cotton wool padding. Jacob will tie the mat firmly around your leg, keeping the true alignment. And that's it. You stay in this incarceration for a month. After that, you are fine. Happens all the time."

"Please tell Jacob and Walter that I am very grateful." I say to Nurse Winnie. I ask her how I can repay them.

"Jacob says that you must be patient and wait for a month before beginning to walk. You will have a perfect leg like this."

"Does the family need anything? Can I get them something from town? I would really like to show my appreciation."

"He says, thank you; they are provided with everything they need here.

I am hoisted up to the back of the truck, next to Luther. The lad is as tall as me. Nurse Winnie has just given him another feed and turned him. He is facing me. George is squashed between Luther and the vehicle's side. Veronica and Nurse Winnie move to the cab to give me more space. Everyone had shared a meal with Jacob's family. They brought George's and my food to us. The three little girls sit quietly on my other side. I had taken some more of Jacob's potent painkiller to ensure a pain-free journey. I like the stuff – it works instantly and potently.

Lying on the soft mattress I remain semi-oblivious to the journey. I feel the warmth of the little girls using the left side of my body as a pillow. My left arm is around two of them, a third little girl is holding my hand. George is across all of us. Luther's thin, cold hand is in my right one. How this happened, I cannot fathom; I just accept. I give his hand a little squeeze. Luther's fingers move ever so slightly. In the darkness, with the truck bumping along, and in this semi-conscious state, my eyes fill with tears of gratitude. How wonderful to be lying here with five children. Sisters and brothers for Lindi.

The truck is still bumping along. And I am still free from pain. I put off thinking about what will happen when we get into town. I will probably have to fly home. Using the medical evacuation insurance policy for the first time ever. I decide to simply savour these moments for now. To me, this feeling is utter contentment.

I re-read that part again and again.

Luther's thin cold hand is in my right one. How this happened, I cannot fathom; I just accept. I give his hand a little squeeze. Luther's fingers move ever so slightly. In the darkness, with the truck bumping along, and in this semi-conscious state, my eyes fill with tears of gratitude. How wonderful to be lying here with five children. Sisters and brothers for Lindi.

∞

It is the third Monday after I started my visualisation. My *Kiff*. I've added to the vision. Seeing myself, George and Sapphira alighting in Carton and seeing Ellie jumping up and down with Grandma Meertel. Feels good. Today is the day! Of this I am sure. It feels different.

Twenty six minutes past three. No bus yet. More than an hour late. Most unusual.

Fourteen minutes after four. No bus yet. George wanders off to play.

At a quarter to five, we see a dust cloud edging towards the gate. Tension fragments into brittle icicles. I'm fine! I know, like I *know* Sapphira is on this bus!

Relax. Relax. Deep breaths. Slow deep breaths. Sapphira's on the bus, so why be anxious?

The medical staff enter the bus, carry out three small children, support a bigger boy towards the clinic.

Slow deep breaths. Stay relaxed.

Younger children step off first, walk along the line of children searching for someone familiar. Even from this distance I can see the majority of the older children look exhausted, crushed, walking stones, drained of any emotion they ever had.

I don't think it has registered with them that we on this side of the rope have been in the same situation as them. They probably see us as a blur as they move to the next stage in their lives, somewhere where they were told they would be fed and watered and have a bed for the night.

Why am I sitting here when I know Sapphira is on the bus? Come on! *Trust*. Believe!

I edge towards the admission room. Stand there. Breathe slowly. Say thank you for Sapphira getting off that bus any second now.

There she is! Taller. Smartly dressed in a brightly flowered dress. Long hair hanging loose. Does not look around. A huge sob escapes me. Thank you, thank you, *thank you*. It worked! This stuff works! She looks straight ahead. The procession moves slowly as some children look into the crowd, some shouting names of loved ones while all the time being shooed along by Nurse

Winnie. Sapphira looks straight ahead. Nears the admission room.

"Sapphira. *Kelsho*."

Hears me. Gasps. Sobs. Her hands come up to her heart immediately. The sun is in her eyes. She squints. Still can't see. I move.

"*Kelsho,* Luther. You waited. You *waited*. Oh Luther, Lu, *Lu*"

Bear hug. *Big* bear hug. My heart is bursting.

∞

"I know it's in the past, and I'm not angry about it, but I'm still curious to know why you didn't wait to see where I was heading."

"It was exactly the same for me. Why has my family deserted me! Why couldn't they wait for me?! I thought you were at my side. Then a mass of people pushed past and I didn't see any of you again. I shouted and shouted. Two different people said you had *definitely* gone left. So that's where I headed. I didn't know about Papa and Ma. I thought you were all safe and *looking for me*! I rushed ahead to get to you. Then, when I eventually reached St. Giles, the big sea port in the south, there were no Red Cross Messages. I *knew* you would have left one there. I sent you two from there.

∞

After the first hour or so, we do not talk much. It is OK to just be together.

George comes to us. Holds my hand, looking at Sapphira.

"Who is he?"

"George, meet your sister Sapphira."

"Sister?"

"Uh huh. I picked him up as I was running away from the carnage. Pure instinct. Been with me ever since. My shadow. Everyone says its OK for him to stay with me. With us. Until such time, you know. If ever."

Sapphira continues to stare at George.

After a long while she says: "You know who he is, don't you?"

"Who?"

"He looks just like that little boy who played with Benedict at Kavari Quay on our way to Hamilton?"

I look, but I don't remember.

Sapphira keeps looking.

"I'm *sure* he is that little boy. Red car. Volvo. His father was a teacher from Chessletown. His mother was pregnant. Oh! What was his name? Certainly not George. Hang on! Wasn't that his father's name?"

I look at him. Is he?

"Is George your father's name?"

He shakes his head. Points to himself. "I'm George!" Runs away to play.

Will we ever know? Trust Sapphira for remembering.

∞

Tuesday evening. Sapphira and I are sitting on my space on the knoll. Watching the sun slowly dipping behind the hill beyond. Just sitting. Enjoying the sheer joy of being together, of having found each other, of having waited. Sharing the bottomless sadness of a father gone forever. Not knowing where our mother is; if she has gone as well. We are leaving for Juxon on Friday. Next up, Ellie! At least a certainty there. Sapphira tells me of her stay with a Belling judge and his family until the UN started repatriating the Juxonese refugees by boat to Kavari Quay. The bus was late because the driver had to divert to a pick-up point in Jamari town to pick her and other children up from the ferries. I tell Sapphira about Cecilia who is waiting for me in Parrish.

"I hope Grandma Meertel will be able to feed another two mouths."

"Of course she will. She'll love doing so. We *will* be looking for Ma right away, won't we? Luther?"

"Of course. First priority."

We watch Royce coming through the gate, getting out of the car, being instantly surrounded by a bunch of children, George included, with arms outstretched. He lifts George on his shoulders, looks towards the knoll, gives a wave. Comes towards us.

Recognises Sapphira. Puts George down to return to his friends. Crosses his hands on his heart. His smile as wide as his face. "*Kelsho,* Sapphira!"

Grabs hold of the tall crying girl. Big bear hug. Sapphira does not let go. He sits down with her. Puts his free arm around my shoulders. The sun eventually hides behind the hill, leaving a beautiful golden glow.

"I was visiting the Save compound last night and Barbara didn't say a word! Spent the whole day with Barbara and Tom Yon, still no word of warning! What a lovely surprise though. Welcome back from wherever you were, Sapphira. You are safe now. You two look so much like your father. It's quite uncanny."

"Hmmm, Ma used to say she was merely the incubator for the two of us. She said when Ellie was born she finally realised she had a hand in it."

"I suppose you three are leaving for Juxon on Friday?"

We nod. Still recovering.

Royce continues to talk. Everyday things that have happened while he had been back in London. I become calmer.

"Oh yes! How could I forget! It's seeing Sapphira again, I suppose. Another Red Cross Message!"

I take it. Open it. Recognise the handwriting.

"Who?"

Shocked into silence, I allow Sapphira to take it from my nerveless hands.

"Ma! Ma! Oh God! Ma! *Oooooooh*!"

She shouts, she screams, she jumps around. Uncontainable.

Royce holds on to me. Grabs hold of Sapphira. Just holds us. I feel my heart bouncing off his.

We sit down. I read the message. Over and over and over again.

Dear Luther. Thank God you are alive. I am with Grandma Meertel and Ellie now. Please come home. **We** *can search for Sapphira. I love you. Ma x.* ∞

I look at Royce.

After a long while I ask: "We *will* we be seeing you in Carton, won't we?"

"Luther, try stopping me!"

"On this visit of yours?"

"Absolutely! You are my Sunday Times article!"

I look up at the sky. So blue, so clear, as infinite as the symbol of my mother's love for me. As mine for her. More than infinite.

Lightning Source UK Ltd.
Milton Keynes UK
06 February 2010

149649UK00001B/3/P